Library of Congress Number: 2021910093

ISBN: 978-0-578-90423-8 (Paperback)

Edited by Deborah Chiel

Cover and image configuration by Alison Lew Bloomer

This is a work of fiction. All the names, characters, businesses, places, events, attribution of beliefs and political views, and other references and descriptions in this book are either entirely the product of the author's imagination or have possible historical parallels but are used purely in a fictitious manner. All quoted material other than quotations from the Bible (or other sources for which citations are given or evident) were written by the author and do not constitute or purport to reflect any actual statements, actions, attitudesor characteristics of any person, religion, group or country.

Alo'el's Dissent

Dedication

For my wife and soulmate Robin Phillips. And for Halley, Nick, Katie and my wondrous grandchildren, Luna and E.J. And to the memory of my beloved son, Emmet, and my parents, Abraham I. Katsh and Estelle Wachtell Katsh.

Epigraph

"*For the urging of man's heart is evil from his youth.*"
  Genesis 8:25

"For the love of money is the root of all evil: which while some coveted after, they have erred from the faith, and pierced themselves through with many sorrows."
  First Epistle of Paul to Timothy (1 Timothy 6:10)

"God gives us the capacity for choice. We can choose to alleviate suffering. We can choose to work together for peace. We can make these changes – and we must."
  Jimmy Carter
  Nobel Prize Lecture (2002)

"My biggest dream and hope for future generations is to live in a world where there is no war."
  David Dushman, who on Jan. 27, 1945, was the first Allied soldier (Russian) to enter and bear witness to Auschwitz.

Contents

Prologue

The group of divine beings stood before a solid gold table on which were stacked thousands of thin stone tablets. When inscribed, the tablets would define the physical, spiritual and other characteristics of the "human beings" the group was creating for a new world.

Alo'el was the sole dissenter. Although the group had made the decision to proceed, she again moved for inclusion of eighteen tablets she made which, if included in the official designs, would diminish the forces of greed and envy that she felt would otherwise dominate human civilization.

"We are programming them," she said, "to adopt ten commandments as the bedrock for a just and humane society." This is of course all well and good. But there is a basic design problem. The first nine commandments prohibit or require certain behaviors. You shall not murder or steal or lie. You shall honor your parents; you shall not give false testimony. The beings we are designing can obey such injunctions. It's the tenth and what I believe is the most important commandment that I question. It is the commandment that directs these beings how to feel—or not feel. 'Thou shall not covet.' My objection is that the tablets for this world will produce entities programmed to do just that—to be covetous, envious.

"You believe that by giving these beings free will and the ability to reason, they will be able to overcome their inclination toward greed, toward evil. I think you are clearly wrong, and it troubles me that I am the only one who sees this. Free will and reason alone will be insufficient. If we do not change the design—if we do not include these eighteen tablets—we will create a world doomed to unimaginable suffering."

Q'aphael, the leader, rose to respond to Alo'el. He was dressed in a white gown and wore a breastplate containing twelve shimmering gemstones. He replied, "It is true." Their inclination toward greed will sorely vex these beings. Their envious natures will incentivize them to pursue evil. We respect your views, but we believe that by giving humans free will and the ability to reason, they will be able to comply with the tenth commandment, no less than the commandment against murder. Virtue means nothing if it is for free, if it is not consciously chosen as an alternative to greed and evil. I believe that these humans will reason their way to a better form of society than killing and starvation.

"Anyway, we all understand it is an experiment. If it fails, we will return and incorporate your eighteen tablets."

Q'aphael held up his hands, palms facing outward, thumbs touching, the middle fingers of each hand split apart.

The twelve stones of his breastplate sparkled and focused an intense beam of light on the thousands of tablets, engraving millions of symbols.

Q'aphael brought his arms down.

"It is done. Our brother *Yhahveh* will stay to observe, assist, and report."

Fathers and Son

Miriam and Michael Ornstein had two children, Leah and Nathan. Their friends said they were wonderful parents. They had always planned to have a third child, but now they'd run into a medical roadblock. Diagnosed with prostate cancer three months earlier, Michael had undergone successful radiation treatment and was now cancer free. But the radiation had all but destroyed Miriam's chances of getting pregnant. Their fertility specialist, Dr. Daniel Standish, advised them that their chances of conceiving were less than 10 percent.

They kept trying, however. A 10 percent chance was not zero. But the process became a never-ending nightmare. Both Miriam and Michael, especially Miriam, fell into a depression each time the pregnancy test came back negative. After six months of hormone injections for Miriam, and "sperm washing" to increase the potency of Michael's sperm, Michael announced that he'd had enough. Dr. Standish nodded understandingly and suggested they consider using a sperm donor. "We've had excellent results."

Miriam liked the idea, but Michael refused to consider it for the same reason he wouldn't consider adoption. The child would not be biologically related.

Dr. Standish wasn't surprised. Many of his male patients had the same reaction. Some couples worked out their doubts through therapy. But Dr. Standish suspected that nothing could persuade Michael to change his mind.

Miriam was keenly disappointed; nothing she said could change Michael's mind. Michael also felt a deep sadness, but his reaction was tinged with a sense of relief. They'd lived with the burden of failure—his failure—for too long. It was time to move forward with their lives, to appreciate what they had, not what they wished they could have.

But Miriam wasn't ready to let go of her dream. She had reveled in her previous pregnancies, and both times, she'd had quick, relatively pain-free deliveries. Miriam adored Michael and hated the idea of deceiving him. But, ultimately, she decided to proceed. She didn't tell anyone—not her sister or her best friend, Bonnie, or Dr. Standish about her plan.

She did her homework. After many days of research, she found NuBorn, one of the most highly regarded sperm donor clinics, with offices throughout the United States, Europe, and Israel. According to their brochure, which Miriam hid at the back of her underwear drawer: "We screen our donors as carefully as if they were going to father our own children. And above all, we promise absolute discretion."

NuBorn's Manhattan offices were next door to the NYU Medical Center on Thirty-First Street and First Avenue. They decorated the offices in warm, sunny colors with cozy chairs and couches. Many of the men, all of whom had been carefully screened, were multiple donors who knew the routine: check in on the third floor; go to a "collection room;" choose from one of the many plastic-wrapped pornographic magazines; ejaculate into a labeled specimen bottle; and hand the bottle to the attending nurse. They received two hundred dollars for each "emission." The would-be mothers met none of the donors, although they spent a great deal of time studying information about them, thanks to the binders overflowing with information provided by NuBorn. Miriam's most important requirement was that both the donor's parents be of Jewish ancestry. Other criteria included above-average intelligence, an unblemished medical history, and no red-haired ancestors. She couldn't imagine what Michael would think if she gave birth to a redhead. As to the actual identity of the donor, Miriam would know nothing, which was her preference.

Miriam identified a donor who fulfilled all her requirements. Nonetheless, one subject the comprehensive donor questionnaire did not ask about was the location or shape of birthmarks. Miriam couldn't possibly have known that the donor she selected manifested two tiny birthmarks, one on each shoulder blade, each displaying a hand, palm facing out, with thumb extended and the middle fingers split apart.

The insemination procedure took less than ten minutes. Five weeks later, Miriam and Michael Ornstein celebrated her pregnancy as a miracle. Dr. Standish felt otherwise. He had not yet reported to Miriam and Michael the results from testing the last semen specimen Michael had submitted. There had been no improvement; in fact, there had been a further deterioration of his sperm's motility and morphology. There was no realistic chance the baby could be his biological offspring. Standish concluded that Miriam had undergone donor insemination without her husband's knowledge. This presented the doctor with a moral dilemma. Both Miriam and Michael were his patients. If he gave them the results of Michael's latest test, he might destroy the couple's marriage. If he didn't, he would cover up Miriam's deception. He knew that his ethical duty was to give his patients—both of them—the report. Then again, a doctor's oath was to "do no harm." One could interpret the statement as encompassing psychological as well as physical harm. Dr. Standish considered himself a healer, not a bureaucrat. Miriam would give birth, no matter what he did. There was no good answer. As he dropped the report in his shredder, he decided he had made a morally dubious decision for a legitimate reason. When Miriam told Michael that she was pregnant with a boy, he insisted on naming their son Daniel, after the doctor who he thought had helped them achieve a miracle.

Two weeks after Opening Day at Yankee Stadium, Avi Cohen, finishing his second year at NYU's medical school, had splurged on two expensive field-level tickets right behind home plate. The Yankees were playing their archrivals, the Boston Red Sox, and Avi was excited about going to the game with Natalie, his fiancée. He exited NuBorn's office, where he had just made a "donation." He was able to earn about $400–$600 a month from its sperm donor program. Avi welcomed the extra income, and he liked the idea of helping families who had fertility problems.

He was in a great mood. The sun was shining after days of rain. Avi began walking to Natalie's apartment building on Second Avenue. First Avenue was empty. As a native New Yorker, Avi considered it his civic right to ignore traffic lights if there was no oncoming traffic. When Avi saw no traffic coming up First Avenue, he began to cross the street. As he did so, the First Avenue bus, which had stopped to pick and drop off passengers a block away, pulled away from the curb to continue up the avenue. Avi heard the chime from his iPhone. It was a new text message from Natalie, filled with emojis of love and smiles. It was the last message he would ever see.

The funeral was a somber affair. Avi's siblings, Elenna and Steven, both gave moving eulogies. At the morgue, it surprised the assistant medical examiner when he realized that what he had initially thought were tattoos on Avi's shoulders were actually birthmarks. He took a close-up picture of the birthmarks for the morgue file and archived it with the rest of the information about Avi Cohen's death.

Daniel,
"Blessed of Yhahveh"

I n Leviticus, the third book of the Bible, it is written, *"On the tenth day of this seventh month ye shall afflict your souls. . . . And ye shall do no manner of work in that same day; for it is a day of atonement, to make atonement for you before the Lord your God."*
Known as Yom Kippur, the Day of Atonement, it is the holiest day in Judaism. According to Jewish law, everyone aged thirteen and older is required to fast from sundown to sunset. The rabbis had held that the prohibition on any "manner of work" forbade any activity performed on a normal workday, including driving, cooking, or using electricity.

It was the eve of Yom Kippur. Daniel Ornstein was ten years old. Two months earlier, his grandfather had died after a long illness. Miriam Ornstein had begged her mother, affectionately called Gusma, to come live with her in Brooklyn, where they had a house with plenty of room. Gusma said she would consider moving, but for the time being, she wanted to stay in her own apartment on Walton Avenue in the Bronx, and she especially wanted to spend Yom Kippur at home. It was a day when mourners said the Kaddish prayer for family members who had died. Gusma wanted to say the prayer for her husband in the small Orthodox synagogue two blocks away that the couple had attended for many years.

Given the circumstances, Miriam decided that the family should spend this Yom Kippur in the Bronx with her mother. Because they could not drive or take public transportation, they made arrangements for sleeping at or near Gusma's apartment. Daniel would sleep on the sofa in the foyer of Gusma's one-bedroom apartment. Miriam and Daniel's older sister Leah would stay with friends of Gusma, who lived nearby. Unfortunately, Michael Ornstein could not join them. He was in China, the lead defense counsel on one of the biggest antitrust cases ever brought, which involved dozens of lengthy depositions of Chinese nationals. He would take part in Yom Kippur services at the Kehillat Beijing Synagogue.

Daniel ordinarily loved visiting his grandparents' apartment, which was located a few blocks from Yankee Stadium. During home games, the roar of the crowd echoed through the streets. It was a family-friendly neighborhood, with many playgrounds where the younger children skipped rope and played hide-and-seek, while the teenagers spent hours at the baseball diamonds and basketball courts. On a hot summer afternoon, Daniel liked nothing better than getting an ice cream soda at Addie Vallens on 161st Street between Gerard and Walton Avenues. And, on special occasions, his grandfather would take the family to Roxy's, which had the best corned beef sandwiches Daniel had ever tasted. But on this somber visit, Daniel could only dream of corned beef and ice cream sodas.

In Gusma's traditional Orthodox synagogue, the men sat downstairs; the women sat in an upstairs balcony. If Daniel's father had been present, Daniel would have sat downstairs with him. But because he was not yet thirteen, the age of bar mitzvah, he joined his mother, grandmother, and sister in the women's section.

The cantor led the congregants in chanting the solemn Kol Nidre prayer. At the Jewish day school he attended, Daniel had learned about the Kol Nidre prayer, composed in the sixteenth century, which literally meant "all vows." In the late fifteenth century, Spain and Portugal had issued edicts expelling all Jews from their countries. Many Spanish and Portuguese Jews, facing death if they did not convert to Catholicism, swore their acceptance of Christianity, but continued to practice Judaism in secret. Kol Nidre was the prayer that these "conversos" or "Marranos" recited, asking God to pardon these vows.

Daniel noticed that his mother was shaking and weeping, tears flowing down her face. Gusma was hugging her, brushing her hair back from her forehead like she did when Miriam was a child, whispering words of calm. But Miriam was inconsolable. "Forgive me, God," Daniel heard his mother mumble as the cantor sang the Kol Nidre. "Forgive me for my sin. It is more than I can bear."

What sin? Daniel wondered. Surely his mother, who had not been home, had nothing to do with the tragedy.

The tragedy. It was how they referred to the event that had occurred seven months earlier. Daniel's parents had gone to hear the New York Philharmonic at Lincoln Center in Manhattan. His twelve-year-old sister, Leah, had a sleepover at a friend's house. His brother Nathan, who was fifteen, was babysitting for Daniel when a fire broke out. Daniel escaped, but Nathan was found dead of smoke inhalation next to the garage door.

Investigators from the fire department repeatedly questioned Daniel about what had happened; how and where had the fire started; whether he and Nathan had been in the same room when the fire broke out; why hadn't they escaped the fire together? But Daniel couldn't remember anything from the moment his parents had left for the concert until he found himself outside the house, wrapped in a blanket provided by a fireman. His doctor had suggested he see a therapist who was an expert in trauma and PTSD. When the therapist gently suggested that maybe he didn't want to remember, Daniel wondered whether she could be right. But no, he wanted to know what had happened. He missed his brother so much it hurt. Nathan's death might have been his fault filled him with terror, magnified by his mother's insistence that her responsible fifteen-year-old son would never have played with fire or allowed his younger brother to do so. Deep down, Daniel sensed he had done nothing wrong. But even though his mother didn't say it aloud, her attitude convinced Daniel that she blamed him.

Before the tragedy, Daniel had felt special in his mother's eyes. For years, at bedtime, she would read him stories about the history of the Jewish people and the ancient cultures of Egypt and Mesopotamia. His favorites included *How the Spider Saved King David*; *Moses and the Burning Bush*; *The Boy Who Found the Star of David*; and *The Magic Handkerchief*, a story about a beautiful cloth handkerchief which had the symbols of Daniel's birthmarks and had magical powers. After the tragedy, his mother had become bitter and distant. There were no more bedtime stories. Daniel put himself to sleep by telling himself these and other stories that he knew by heart.

On that Erev Yom Kippur, Gusma kissed Daniel goodnight and left a dim light burning in case he needed to get up during the night. He would go to synagogue with her midmorning the next day, and they'd meet up with his mother and Leah.

Sometime around one in the morning, Daniel opened his eyes. The apartment was dead quiet. Nightmares had plagued him almost every night since the tragedy. But tonight, he had awakened not because of a dream but because he was soaking in sweat. And he realized that the hair on his arms and head were standing on end. It was a phenomenon he'd heard about but had never experienced or even believed was possible. Daniel was also experiencing a twinging sensation on his right and left shoulder blades where he had two tiny birthmarks. Each mark was in the shape of a hand, palm facing forward, with an outstretched thumb and the middle fingers split apart.

Daniel hated the marks. They made him feel like a freak, even though Leonard Nimoy, Mr. Spock on *Star Trek*, had made the hand configuration famous. Mr. Spock would hold up his hand, palm forward with the middle fingers split apart, and say, "Live long and prosper." Nimoy had not made up the hand symbol. Thousands of years earlier, in the Jewish temples in Jerusalem, the Kohanim, the priestly caste of Levites, would join their hands together, palms out, thumbs touching, middle fingers split apart, to give the blessing prescribed in the Book of Numbers (6:24-26): *May the Lord bless you and keep you; may the Lord make his face shine upon you and be gracious to you; may the Lord turn his face toward you and give you peace.*"

In modern times, Orthodox synagogues such as the one Leonard Nimoy had attended, Jews who traced their ancestry to the Kohanim came forward on major holidays to stand on the dais in front of the congregation. They raised their prayer shawls over their heads, holding them aloft with their hands arrayed in the iconic Kohanic configuration as they chanted the blessing.

Neither Michael nor Miriam could trace their lineage to the Kohanim, and Daniel didn't associate his birthmarks with the Kohanim or the priestly blessing. His mother and various therapists had used Mr. Spock's habitual greeting to convince Daniel that his birthmarks, although "very unusual," were far from freakish. Now, he sat up and wiped the sweat from his face, rubbed his shoulders. Suddenly, a musical melody of indescribable beauty began to play in his mind and resound throughout his body. And now standing before him was Nathan's image, hologram-like. He was dressed in the robes of the Jewish high priest. As described in the Book of Exodus, the vestments included a breastplate made of a thick fabric embroidered in gold, scarlet, and royal blue. Embedded in the fabric were twelve gold settings, three settings in four consecutive rows. Each setting contained a sparkling gemstone. Attached at the corners were golden rings to guide blue linen straps around the high priest's waist and over his shoulders. Nathan also wore a miter, a headpiece, with a solid gold plate etched with Hebrew letters.

Nathan looked at peace, his expression understanding and loving. His outstretched arms held a set of eighteen smooth, square, and very thin stone tablets. As Daniel watched, the tablets rose from Nathan's arms and a laser-like beam emanated from the stones and etched four symbols onto every inch of the surfaces of all of the tablets.

The tablets settled back into Nathan's arms; the laser-like beam shut down. Nathan placed his open hand on Daniel's face in exactly the same loving gesture his mother had used before Nathan's death. "You are blessed of *Yhahveh* and have been chosen to unlock these Tablets of Destiny," Daniel thought he heard Nathan say.

And then, as Nathan withdrew his hand, everything—the image of his brother, the breastplate, the stones, the music, the tablets—faded and vanished. So did the pain he had felt at the sites of his birthmarks. Daniel found himself alone in the dimly lit foyer of his grandmother's apartment. His heart was pounding as he hoped that Nathan and the images would reappear. Nothing happened. But the moment imprinted itself in his mind forever.

He went to the kitchen, drank deeply from the faucet, and went over in his mind every detail of the experience. Needing to do something to dispel his anxiety, he took a notebook out of his school bag. Trance-like, without conscious thought, he began drawing but soon closed his eyes and fell into a deep sleep.

When he awoke, he could not believe what he saw in his notebook. He had drawn not only a picture of the breastplate, but above and below the picture, he drew images of his birthmarks. And on the bottom left, there appeared five characters, ⟨ᴚᵧᴚᴚ⟩. They were different from the characters on the tablets Nathan had held but were similar enough to suggest that they came from the same alphabet or writing system. But what did any of it mean? Daniel had no idea.

Daniel suddenly felt the energy of the experience drain out of him. He was now more exhausted than terrified. As he had done when he was a toddler, he crept into Gusma's room and got into her bed. Enveloped by her warmth, he immediately fell asleep.

The next morning, after sitting through two hours of prayers in the synagogue, he didn't feel well. He went back to his grandmother's apartment and slept for most of the day. Shortly before sundown, he returned to the synagogue for the *Ne'ilah* service, signaling the end of Yom Kippur. One of the congregants blew the shofar, made from a ram's horn, and the congregation recited seven times in Hebrew, *"The Lord is the one who is God."*

The family then returned to Gusma's apartment for the traditional "break-fast": bagels, lox, blintzes, and other assorted dairy dishes. Daniel was starving. He suddenly realized he had fasted the entire day.

It was after midnight by the time the family returned to their home in Brooklyn. Daniel covered himself with blankets and pillows and rocked himself to sleep. When his father returned from China, he would talk to him about his vision of Nathan and the drawing. Michael Ornstein had been home from China only twice since the tragedy of Nathan's death.

Daniel slept for about an hour before he awoke from a vivid dream. Wanting to capture what he had dreamt, he again took out his notebook, this time drawing a picture of a cave on an island by a broad river, of a beautiful woman, with her face obscured, and of Nathan, dressed in the regalia of the Jewish high priest, standing next to her. He was holding what appeared to be the same set of thin stone tablets, as in the vision he witnessed the night before.

Daniel had always shown great artistic talent and he produced a remarkably precise drawing of the vision in his dream. When he finished, it occurred to him to write a narrative of what he had experienced at Gusma's apartment and back home in Brooklyn. However, the next thing he knew, his mother was shaking him awake. He had fallen asleep at his desk and slept all night with his head on his notebook.

As a child, Miriam had learned to read Hebrew from her father, Rabbi Dr. Reuven Leon Wachtell, who had been Professor of Hebrew and Bible Studies at City College in Manhattan. Miriam had enjoyed sitting with her father as he researched and wrote articles and books that were well-received by the rarified community of scholars specializing in these subjects. One book was about the Paleo-Hebrew alphabet, a Phoenician- derived writing system used by the Jews in ancient Palestine.

Daniel's school was closed on the day after Yom Kippur. When Miriam entered Daniel's room that morning, she shook him awake. He wordlessly got up from his desk and fell headlong onto his bed. Miriam was about to leave the room and let Daniel sleep when she noticed the notebook on his desk. She opened it and was stunned to see page after page of Paleo-Hebrew script. Miriam couldn't believe that Daniel had written in the ancient alphabet, especially since the writing appeared to be that of an expert scribe. She decided to examine the notebook more closely when Daniel was out of the house.

Daniel behaved normally when he came into the kitchen an hour later. He had toast and orange juice and told his mother that he was going to join his friends in Prospect Park's basketball courts. He would be gone for most of the day. As soon as he left, Miriam went back into his room, retrieved the notebook from Daniel's desk, and went into Michael's home office. Examining the notebook, Miriam saw that on the last pages of the notebook, Daniel had drawn two pictures. The first was of the breastplate worn by Nathan in his vision, and the second, of an island on a river, with Nathan standing next to a beautiful woman and holding a set of thin stone tablets.

On Michael's office computer, Miriam accessed an equivalency chart to translate the Paleo-Hebrew words into ordinary Hebrew. She wrote her Hebrew translations in Daniel's notebook, each word on top of its Paleo-Hebrew equivalent. Miriam spent three hours translating letter by letter what Daniel had written. When she was finished, she was dumbfounded. Daniel had composed an elaborate mythical legend: an adventure story about a meteor; a shepherd named Ivri; a chamber in a temple with moving walls; a sacred breastplate as in his drawing; birthmarks such as Daniel had; and a set of eighteen stone tablets etched with strange symbols.

Miriam was terrified. Not of the drawings. And not of the fact that her son had vivid and imaginative dreams. But it was surely impossible for him to have written an entire narrative in an alphabet he couldn't possibly know.

As soon as Daniel returned, Miriam confronted him about his writings. Daniel was bewildered. Yes, he told her; he drew two pictures on the back pages of his notebook. "But then I fell asleep," he said, about to burst into tears. "I didn't write any words. Mommy, please, I don't know what you're talking about."

For a moment, Daniel considered telling his mother about his visions of Nathan at Gusma's apartment. But before he could do so, his mother abruptly turned away and marched into Daniel's room. The notebook was on the desk where she had replaced it. Other than the last two pages, which depicted Daniel's drawings, all she found were dozens of blank sheets.

This is bullshit. Daniel is playing me. Miriam screamed in frustration, threw the notebook on the floor, and stormed out of the house.

Daniel was terrified. Already, at the age of ten, he suffered from PTSD symptoms which the doctors attributed to Nathan's death. After the tragedy, Daniel had trouble dealing with his mother's varying moods and depression. He missed his father. He couldn't wait to tell him everything when he returned from China. Daniel picked up the notebook from the floor. There were no markings in Paleo-Hebrew on any of the pages.

Praying for his father's early return, he sat on his bed, put his head in his hands, and cried.

Daniel would never have the chance to discuss his vision, dreams, writings, or drawings with his father. Michael Ornstein was one of 287 persons on Asian Air Flight 68, lost over the Pacific Ocean on a direct flight from Beijing to JFK International Airport in New York.

3

Ivri's Journey

I vri rejected his wife's suggestion that he postpone taking out the flocks until the next day. Had he agreed to her suggestion, he, too, would have been killed. Ivri's community lived in Eradu, one of the semipermanent Bedouin encampments in the valley of the Tigris and Euphrates rivers. These great rivers ran north to south through Mesopotamia, forming its fertile plains. Caravans of traders carrying spices, metals and other goods moved north and south along the rivers.

Ivri was a shepherd, twenty-five years old. Blessed with sharp vision and cursed with decaying teeth, he was a thin, muscular man with a salt-and-pepper head of hair and matching beard. He had two extremely unusual birthmarks, one on each shoulder.

He was on the fourth day of a seven-day excursion with his flocks of sheep and goats. It was a beautiful spring day. A breeze tempered the afternoon heat. Water was abundant. It was a day when a man could celebrate life. Ivri sat on a rocky crag with a view of his flocks; he had placed his blanket and pack beneath a nearby overhang. As the moonless night approached, he posted torches on the periphery of his flock. He worked hard, as always, to protect his flocks from predators. Especially on moonless nights, however, no precautions could defy the prowling lions. They also had to eat.

Ivri sat and watched the sun begin its journey back to its lord, the god Shamash, who would preserve it for the next day. As his flocks of sheep and goats grazed on the rich grasslands which the gods had bequeathed to mankind, he played his wooden flute and daydreamed of his wife and children. Ivri had his favorites among the flock. In one game he played to amuse himself, he imagined that one of his rams, whom he had named Naphtali, was an intellectual outlier and philosophical provocateur. In often heated exchanges, they would debate various questions of existence, such as what sacrifices were best designed to convince the gods to grant male offspring and to bestow life after death in the Great Garden.

Ivri hoped that the goddess Ereshkigal, who presided over such matters, would grant him and his family eternal pleasures in the Garden. His chances were uncertain. His people believed that the gods reserved the gift for royalty and the highest tiers of society.

Ivri prepared his dinner of lentils, barley cakes, pistachios, and beer. Naftali was close by, expecting some treats. Giving voice to his philosophical curiosity, Ivri said to him, "I don't see why the gods reserved eternal life in the Garden for the king, the court, and the chieftains. What is the point of living this painful existence if there is no reward for those who lead honest lives, and no punishment for the officials who lead lives of immorality and greed? Why should I not sell some of these sheep, keep the money, and tell Lord Kish that lions attacked?"

Ivri's lively imagination imputed a dismissive response from Naftali. "There are no answers to your question. All we can do is trust in the gods."

"Ah, Naftali, it's easy to understand your reluctance to confront the great existential questions. Your kind has been blessed with purpose: feeding the hungry and providing wool for clothing."

Naftali, sensing there were no treats in the offing, grunted and sauntered away, while Ivri took pride in what he considered an incisive retort.

Ivri was about seven miles from his home in Eradu, a settlement favorably situated on the western bank of the Euphrates. He visualized the tents spread out in a large circle, defining the community's boundaries, and serving as a defensive perimeter. He imagined the cooking and other daily activities taking place around the enormous statue of the moon god, Nanna, and the smaller idols of other gods. At fixed times during the day, the high priest would offer sacrifices on a large bronze altar. The organs and most of the meat would be distributed to the families.

It was then, as Ivri was imagining his beloved settlement, and enjoying his meal and the magnificent panorama, that he saw a blinding light from the east. A fiery object lit up the night sky. Traveling at an impossible speed, it suddenly exploded into a blazing shower of boulders and rocks. The earth beneath him trembled. Seconds passed, and then a blast of wind and earth hurled him to the ground. Flaming dust clouds rained down glowing hot pebbles. The ferocious winds swept away Ivri's flocks of sheep and goats, including his beloved Naphtali, as if they were nothing more than leaves scattered by a breeze.

Curled up under the overhang, Ivri felt pounded by the fiery wind. He suffered a bloody gash on his leg. As he bent over to care for the wound, he was blown against the wall behind him. He felt a searing pain as his head hit the rock. Then he saw darkness and felt nothing.

When Ivri awoke hours later, his head and legs throbbed with pain, and he felt a desperate thirst. The blasts of wind had ripped apart his water phaltu, which was now empty. Naphtali was nowhere in sight. Several thousand carcasses—his entire flock—lay scattered over what had formerly been prime grazing land; it was now a landscape of ash-covered death.

The blast had created a cloud of earth and debris that had blotted out the sun. The temperature had plummeted. Ivri was not dressed for cold weather, and his fire-making kit was nowhere to be found. He stood up and squinted, hoping to find some sign of life, despite knowing that nothing could have survived the devastation. The orange glow of the explosion, which had created a huge mushroom cloud, covered the entire horizon; his tribe, his wife and children, and all his relatives and friends were surely dead.

Eradu traders had left weeks ago on their annual marketing trip to Midian under the leadership of Sengrel, Eradu's high priest. They were not due back for several weeks. Midian was a month's journey to the southwest. Sengrel and his traders had most likely survived. They soon would learn of Eradu's fate. Ivri hoped the Midianites would let them stay.

Dazed in physical and emotional anguish, he wanted to scream his pain and anger at the gods. He did not want to live in a world bereft of everything he held dear. Why had this happened? Why were the gods so cruel and arbitrary that they would destroy so many lives in an instant? Why had he been spared?

A stillness enveloped the land, as pervasive as the roar of devastation only hours earlier. The cyclone of wind and debris had spent its deadly strength, leaving a barren land. What to do? Where to go? Ivri lay on the hard ground, intermittently dozing off, feeling guilty because he didn't want to wake up. But suicide was *hassoor*, taboo. Ivri felt compelled to ignore the unwelcome urge.

Many hours passed before Ivri's innate survival instincts fought free of his sense of despair and helplessness. He was used to walking great distances and to living with various physical ailments. His leg wound was painful, but the leg was not broken. He had recurring spates of dizziness, but he could walk. As the horizon came back into view, Ivri could see a fiery orange light in the distance. He stood up and began limping in its direction.

His provisions were gone. He had no water and nothing with which to make a fire. He doubted he could go much further when he came upon a dying ibex. Using a sharp stone, he hastened its death and consumed its blood and a portion of the tenderloin. While it was normally *hassoor* to eat an animal's meat before a priest offered a sacrifice of the innards, the law allowed such consumption if it was necessary to save a life. He rested, and when he felt his strength returning, he produced a fire by rubbing two ibex bones together on a bed of dried moss. He roasted as much ibex meat as he could carry. He still needed to find water; he would not survive much longer with the few drops he had been able to squeeze out of the roots of dead plants.

It took five days for Ivri to reach the center of the smoldering blast crater. When he arrived at its perimeter, he saw water spouting from the crater's center. He navigated his way to a spot from which he could recover enough to drink and fill a new *phaltu* he had fashioned from ibex hide. It did not look altogether clean, but Ivri's years of shepherding told him it was safe.

After drinking his fill, Ivri emerged from his feelings of hopelessness. He would test his destiny and do what he could to survive for as long as possible. It was chilly, as the sun had still not reappeared. Using some coals from the crater, Ivri made a fire, lay down in its warmth and fell into a deep sleep.

When he woke up, he explored the extraordinary crater. He had no frame of reference to help him understand the cataclysmic events he had witnessed the sudden eradication of his family, his tribe, and everyone else in the area. Ivri shuddered at the power of the gods. He could not fathom what purpose or reason accounted for the destruction they had unleashed.

Looking about, he noticed that the far side of the crater was emitting an array of colors. He walked around the perimeter and saw twelve glimmering stones among the smoking coals. He descended as far as he could without burning his feet, then fashioned a pole with which he dragged the stones out of the coals. They were all of the same size.

The stones glimmered majestically. As he touched them, he felt bathed in musical tones of exquisite elegance. The birthmarks on his shoulders twinged. Ivri knew nothing of magic, nothing of matters known only by the priests. He could think of no reason for these phenomena. He made another pouch of ibex hide and placed the stones inside.

The more urgent matter was to find a clan or tribe that would accept him, where he could mourn his losses. Perhaps there would be a priest who could explain the mystery of the glowing stones and how they affected him. But he would have to be careful. A new clan might well consider the stones as evidence of witchcraft. They might condemn and kill him and offer him as a sacrifice to the demonic god, Ooshlah. He thought about burying the stones but felt a connection to the stones that restrained him.

Ivri knew of no nearby settlement that could have survived the fireball. Believing there were sizable settlements to the south, he began walking in that direction.

Ivri struggled to survive for close to three weeks in a landscape that was barren of life. He suffered from constant aches, but he drank little, knowing he needed to preserve water. He didn't know when he'd next come upon another source. As he walked, he experienced feverish hallucinations his sleep was fitful, regularly disrupted by dreams of robed priests making the sign of his birthmarks with their hands, and of a set of smooth stone tablets around and above which the stones danced in glimmering colors. He dreamt that his uncle, Sengrel, the leader of the Eradu trade caravan to Midian, appeared to him and said, "You are blessed of *Yhahveh*. You bear the instruments of humanity's salvation."

On the twentieth day of his journey, he came to the city of Ur. The city was much larger than Eradu. Both communities worshipped the moon god Nanna. Ur boasted an enormous tower, a ziggurat, twenty meters high, which served as a temple to the god.

The explosion and the clouds of ash which they'd seen in the far distance had terrified the people of Ur. When Ivri told them he was the sole survivor from Eradu, the elders welcomed him as a guest and refugee from the disaster. They gave him food and fresh water the healers treated his wounds. He slept in the healing tent for nearly a full day.

The city waited expectantly to hear from the stranger who survived the cataclysm. After two days of experiencing the special hospitality with which Bedouins treat important guests, Ivri felt rejuvenated and looked forward to social contact. A large segment of the population gathered around him in the city square at the temple to Nanna. Ivri took his time giving the populace a thorough report of his epic experience and journey. His survival and his firsthand report had a calming effect on the community. The people knew that large and small rocks would occasionally come from the sky and hit the earth. But the scope and power of this blast were unprecedented.

Having explored the site of the impact and traveled for days in the blast area, Ivri was in a unique position to explain, as best he could, what had happened, and to reassure the city's population that he had seen no evidence of any more boulders falling from the sky. His survival and his first-hand report of his journey had a calming effect on the community. The people knew that large and small rocks occasionally fell from the sky and hit the earth. But the scope and power of this blast was unprecedented.

The king ordered that the city treat Ivri as an honored guest; he charged the high priest Meshech with his care. Ivri continued to mourn his losses, but the warm reception he received from this gracious community muted the feelings of terror that had been his constant companion for so many days. Meshech took him on walks around the city. Ivri responded to the requests, by young and old alike, for stories of life in Eradu, and he willingly responded to the many requests to retell the ordeal he had survived.

He was rewarded for his evident goodness and lack of guile by the community's growing acceptance. They made several sacrifices to Nanna to commemorate and mourn the destruction of Eradu.

One story Ivri decided not to share immediately was his discovery of the glowing stones and how he seemed mystically connected to them. The connection terrified him, and he tried not to think about it.

Ivri's one unfulfilled need was for a place to mourn in private, as was the custom in Eradu after the funeral services.

Several days had passed since Ivri arrived in Ur when he awoke from a dream stranger than any he'd ever had before. A voice, gentle yet firm, that he didn't recognize, commanded him to collect various yarns and fibers, as well as weaving and smelting tools, and seek a place of solitude outside the city. After assembling the materials, Ivri told Meshech that he wished to find a secluded setting where he could mourn his family and his community.

"Of course, my friend. Take your time. It is also a custom among us when a tragedy strikes a family. I hope you will return and ask to live with us permanently," Meshech replied.

"I am in a great debt to you. Your community is righteous and caring. I desire nothing more than to return and make a new home here."

He passed through Ur's cultivated fields of wheat and barley and, no more than five miles from the city, encountered an endless stretch of barren rocky desert. It was the same kind of terrain through which he had passed in traveling from the crater. He felt as if he was being urged to go south and headed in that direction. He thanked whatever instinct had persuaded him to pack ample provisions for a long trip. The sack with the twelve stones sat securely on his belt.

Day after day, Ivri walked and gave full vent to his grief his wife and children, his family and tribe, all gone. He was periodically overcome by the need to sit, cry, and wail, thinking of his two young boys and his beautiful baby girl. Oh, how he yearned to sit surrounded by his kin, warmed by the hearth fire, discussing how better to defend themselves against hostile raids. He dreamed of making love to his wife, of waking up with her beside him, of the happy noises of a joyful household.

On the sixth day, Ivri passed an acacia tree, known for its dense wood, resistance to decay, and its exceptional beauty when polished. Ivri somehow understood that he was to cut off a thick branch, chop it into pieces, and add the wood to the other items in the large sack he had brought from Ur.

Three days later, not sure why he had decided to go back and crisscross the area where he had found the acacia tree, Ivri saw a small hill not twenty feet from where the tree stood. At the bottom of the hill, he discovered the entrance to a cave. He was at a loss to understand how he had not noticed the hill days earlier when he had come across the tree. He cleared away rocks and dirt to enlarge the opening and lowered himself inside. He was surprised to find the cave was mostly underground, extending about twenty yards deep, and high enough for him to stand up inside. Shafts of sunlight shone through cracks in the roof, illuminating the wet, stone walls with shimmering streaks of bright light.

Ivri walked to the back of the cave and found himself in an oval area with shelf-like rocky outcroppings. A vein of what appeared to be pure gold protruded from the back wall.

Ivri used one of the tools he had brought to remove a chunk of the gleaming metal and set it on a shelf. He jumped back as a fire suddenly ignited around the gold and transformed the block into twelve identical gold settings. He marveled that the settings were perfectly sized for the stones. As he stared at the settings, he felt a powerful force take hold of him and place him in a trancelike state. As if he were an outside observer, he watched his hands weave the threads and yarn he had taken with him into various priestly vestments an ephod and a girdle a miter with a gold plate a white robe with pomegranate-shaped balls hanging from its bottom and a thick woven breastplate. The front of the breastplate had twelve slots, three in each of four rows. Ivri placed one gold setting in each of the slots.

Finally, as if he were an expert carpenter, Ivri observed his hands moving on their own to fashion a lustrously polished chest from the acacia wood. It would be suitable for holding the breastplate and other vestments.

He was exhausted and desperately wanted to sleep, but the gods were not yet finished with him. On a shelf of the wall that contained the vein of gold were eighteen thin, perfectly square, smooth stone tablets. Stuck to the edges of the tablets were flakes of the gold that Ivri had worked. Ivri then saw the twelve sparkling stones rise into the air and shine intense beams of light on the surface of the tablets. They etched the eighteen of the tablets with four symbols repeated thousands of times.

Like most of his tribe at Eradu, Ivri knew how to read and write common household and commercial terms, anything more sophisticated was beyond his ken. He knew what cuneiform writing looked like, but these characters bore no resemblance to any markings he had ever seen. On the bottom right corner of each tablet was a tiny drawing of two hands, palms forward, thumbs touching, and middle fingers split apart.

The stones came to rest next to the breastplate. Ivri picked it up and inserted the stones into the twelve settings. To his surprise, he discovered that even though the settings were of the same size, and the stones were also identical in size, each stone appeared to have an assigned place. And once inserted into a specific setting, he could not remove the stone.

Physically drained and hoping his ordeal was over, Ivri huddled on the floor under the small blanket he had brought. He slept for most of a day. When he woke up, he shuddered at the memory of how his arms and hands had been manipulated—how the glowing stones had risen into the air and etched the eighteen tablets. When he entered the cave, he couldn't name a single one of the gemstones, nor had he seen examples of most of the stones. Now, he was familiar with each and somehow knew them all by name: carnelian; topaz; smaragdite; carbuncle; sapphire; emerald; jacinth; agate; amethyst; beryl; onyx; and jasper.

Ivri pondered what he should tell Meshech when he returned to Ur. He had little choice about whether to go back. There was nowhere else to go. The people of Ur appeared to be generous and hospitable. But in the circumstances, if he made full disclosure, no doubt the Ur Council of Elders would accuse him of devil worship. The chest, breastplate, and shimmering gemstones would be difficult enough for the people of Ur to accept. It was best, he thought, that he should not attempt to explain anything about the tablets. He would leave them in the cave. He could come back later, if he survived, to retrieve them.

The townspeople of Ur greeted Ivri with great excitement and many questions about where he had gone, what he had seen, what dangers he had faced. They quickly organized a feast at the center of the village where Nanna's temple, the great ziggurat, stood. All the families gathered around their fires. The priests burned their sacred incense. Each family set up tables on which they laid out a variety of breads, cakes, and other baked foods, along with jugs of sweet wine and beer. They offered portions of roasted goats and lambs in sacrifice other portions were consumed. Instead of the typical gossip about the other families, villagers indulged in endless discussions about the still-vivid memory of the huge fiery blast.

As his safe return had occasioned the feast, Ivri was expected to tell the story of his journey. Ivri did not disappoint. He had always been one of his clan's best storytellers, and he very much desired to be accepted into the Ur community. Not wishing to dissemble with those he wanted soon to call brother and sister, he decided that he would tell the entire story, leaving out only a description of the tablets he had left in the cave. With theatrical embellishment, he described the first moment he saw the fire from the sky. He had the rapt attention of his audience and could sense their keen interest and empathy. But as soon as he disclosed his discovery of the sparkling stones, the audience became noticeably uneasy. They became more agitated when he told of his work in the cave and then displayed the breastplate. The group's unease then turned into a paroxysm of shouting and growing hostility.

Meshech rose and raised his arms. The assembly quickly grew silent.

"What kind of magic is this?" he demanded of Ivri. "You think you are Marduk's prophet? That you can play games with our most sacred beliefs and traditions?"

Utterly perplexed, Ivri bowed his head and said, "I mean no disrespect. I am beyond grateful that you have welcomed me after the destruction of my home and village. I am a stranger here, and I do not know your traditions. I swear that what I have told you is the absolute truth about what I saw and experienced."

In the communities of the Tigris-Euphrates valley, an oath was sacred, never lightly to be ignored. Meshech declared the meeting over and directed everyone to their homes. He placed Ivri under detention in the turoasta, the "tent with the cage." There would be no more work or other activities that day. Meshech issued an order barring any discussion of Ivri's story until the Council of Elders examined the mystery.

Meshech was first among equals on the council. He could trace his family back to the earliest settlers of Ur. On countless occasions, he and other members of the council had sung their foundational legends to the adults and children. On this day, having dismissed the congregation and placed Ivri under detention, Meshech sat at the altar in the lower portico of Nanna's temple. How could Ivri have known about, let alone fashioned, the legendary breastplate? Had he truly found Marduk's stones in the meteor's crater? Had he really found a vein of gold in a cave that suddenly had materialized in the desert? Acacia trees were not local to the area. Where and how had Ivri gotten the wood? The chest Ivri displayed was a magnificent work of art. How had this simple shepherd been able to craft it?

Meshech considered himself an excellent judge of people. He was cautious and conservative; the well-being of the community was his only concern. For his clan's peace of mind, Meshech would not hesitate to condemn Ivri as a false prophet, cut out his entrails, and lop off his head. But he concluded that he should not disregard Ivri's story as a hoax just because it appeared inconceivable. The problem was not that Ivri had told of a direct intervention by the gods in human affairs. The people of Ur expected and experienced such occurrences each time the sun rose and set, or the moon went through her cycles, or the flowers bloomed or died. Rather, it was the story's precise relationship to the clan's own legends that had caused the congregation's hostile reaction, and that persuaded Meshech not to discount Ivri as a madman or charlatan.

Meshech summoned Ivri before the council. They gathered around a table deep inside the ziggurat, lit by torches. They posted armed guards at the entrance. Ivri was told to relate his experience. "You must leave nothing out. We need to hear every detail."

After listening to Ivri's tale and his candid responses to the many questions he was asked, Meshech concluded that Ivri was telling the truth, fantastic as it sounded. Of course, Ivri could have been a victim of hallucinations. His experience could have been a grand trick played by a mischievous god. But Meshech did not think so. He nodded toward Atmench, the oldest and most conservative member of the council. Atmench stood up and related the tribe's foundational legend.

"They tell the story of a time before the beginning. The primordial gods of the universe—Apsua, Nanna, and Anu, representing the Upper, Middle, and Lower Ways—decided they would create a new world. They employed for this purpose twelve magical stones. They harnessed their powers using a breastplate worn by Apsua, an exquisite woven fabric of blue, scarlet, and gold threads. The stones lay in settings of the purest gold, the gold of the gods, three stones in each of four rows.

"To assist in the project, Anu secured the help of various lesser gods. However, the primordial god Tiamet undermined their plans. She corrupted several of the lesser gods, and with their help, she murdered Apsua and stole the breastplate. Incensed, Anu ordered loyal gods to kill Tiamet and her evil cohorts and to retrieve the breastplate. But each of these gods failed in the face of Tiamet's great powers.

"Finally, the warrior god Marduk agreed to take on Tiamet and her allies, but only on the condition that, if he succeeded, he would become the supreme god. They would give him the breastplate. He would control the creation of the new world. Anu and Nanna, and the other gods seeking to end Tiamet's reign of terror, all agreed.

"Armed with powers over the four winds and having fashioned a three-pronged spear blessed by the great god Enki, Marduk defeated Tiamet. He cut her in half, and with her upper body, he created the heavens and the earth. With her lower half, he made the mountains, and with Tiamet's tear-laden eyes he created the seas and the two great rivers, the Tigris and Euphrates."

Pointing to the wall, Atmench said, "Here is an engraving of the battle."

"You can see Marduk on the right and Tiamet on the left."

Atmench took a hefty swig of the potent beverage from one of the jugs that sat on the table. He continued, "Upon defeating Tiamet, the gods kept their word". They acknowledged Marduk as the supreme deity. They gave him fifty names to celebrate his status as the ultimate power in the universe. Marduk took possession of the breastplate and its twelve magic stones.

It took Marduk many days to fashion the designs he deemed desirable for his new creations. He recorded these designs on thousands of stone tablets. He called them the Tablets of Destiny. In encrypted symbols, they set forth the physical, mental, and spiritual qualities of the race of beings he had created.

Once he finished the tablets, Marduk donned the breastplate and the various other magisterial vestments of a high priest. The breastplate's twelve magic stones scanned the tablets with intense rays of pulsing, colored light and generated the specified physical materials required to fashion his new race of human beings. Marduk then founded large communities such as Uruk and Ur, and he built towering ziggurats—towers devoted to his glory and to the glory of his chosen gods. One example is the ziggurat tower dedicated to Nanna, here in Ur.

When Marduk concluded his many acts of creation, he carved a chamber in this temple, devoted to his beloved Nanna. In the chamber, he placed the eighteen tablets. He placed the magisterial robes and miter he wore during his work of creation in a beautifully crafted chest. He removed the stones from the breastplate and cast them to heaven. Then he swallowed the woven breastplate.

This is what our legends say. Interestingly, in one account, Nanna does not agree with an aspect of Marduk's design for mankind. She tried to convince Marduk that humanity's nature should be free of envy and greed. Otherwise, she argued, they would be doomed to lives of evil, slaughtering each other in horrible wars and genocides, incapable of enjoying the wonders of existence.

"Marduk rejected her proposal. He took the position that the gifts of free will and reason would enable humankind to resist the seductive forces of greed and envy."

Atmench sat down. Meshech nodded to him in thanks and recognition of his erudition and wisdom.

Ivri sat speechless, filled with anxiety. Were the tablets in the cave the same tablets Meshech had described? It sounded as if they were the same. But Meshech said Marduk had locked the tablets in a chamber in this temple. How and why did this new set of tablets appear in the cave?

"I think you can understand our predicament," said Meshech. "You claim to have found these glowing stones in a meteor crater. Then you find a block of the purest gold in a cave that suddenly appears in the desert. And then you tell us that the gods manipulated your hands to fashion the precise fabrics, vestments, breastplate with gold settings, three in each of four rows, and a wooden chest, exactly as described in our legends."

The tension and uncertainty among the council members were palpable. And now, after having lost his family and tribe, Ivri's life hung in the balance before the Ur Council of Elders deep in the depths of a massive ziggurat, the largest artificial structure he had ever seen. He took a deep breath and said, "I understand your doubts and your need to protect the community from false prophets and charlatans. But I would ask you to consider the circumstances. You saw the giant explosion. I know nothing about your legends. I am as baffled as any of you by the experiences I have related. We know the gods control our every second of life. If the gods can eclipse the sun and moon, create devastating floods, and do all the other things they do, what I told you could be the truth."

"Perhaps *Lamashtu* bewitched you," Atmench gruffed. "Why is that not a more believable explanation? She always hated Marduk. This could be a spell she cast. This breastplate may look like what our legends describe. But the objects you fashioned may be cursed. If we accept you and your magical objects into our city, we could doom the entire community."

The Council of Elders respected Meshech. They invariably accepted his recommendations, which reflected a balance between risk and reward, between the status quo and the potential for new ideas to improve the community's quality of life. Meshech did not believe that worst-case scenarios should drive important decisions. It was easy to fixate on the risk of devastating outcomes and do nothing. But the easiest course of action also led to stagnation. Taking a prudent risk could promote a better future. But how to decide whether a risk was prudent? One could not know in advance, hence the awful doubt and conflict that bedeviled good leaders.

Here, Meshech did not think it was a close question. He said to his brethren, "Anything is possible. But we aren't dealing with someone who just claims a vision. While the gods could make us believe anything, in this case we must question whether we are being duped by the machinations of gods bent on harming humanity. We have in our hands a real breastplate and stones. If we believe in our traditions, as we daily profess to do, we must assume this is real. But we have yet to apply the final and most important test."

Then Meshech turned to Ivri and said,

"There is a critical facet of our legends that is known only to council members. It is this: When Marduk created the chamber deep within this ziggurat, he marked the entrance with a seal, an engraving that depicted a particular hand configuration. According to our legend, access to the chamber is impossible except for a person born with birthmarks in the configuration of these hands. There are stories about ambitious men who have attempted to enter the chamber. All died instantly. Our tradition says it was because none of them had the birthmarks."

Ivri was dumbstruck. He silently removed his tunic and allowed each council member to examine his birthmarks. They took turns looking at what they believed to be the handiwork of the gods. Mumbling prayers, they looked to Meshech for guidance. Meshech, who was just as bewildered, picked up the chest Ivri had brought and motioned for Ivri and the council members to follow him. They ventured about fifty meters along a corridor that led deeper within the temple, to an area few of them had ever visited. There, on the wall to their left, they could see an engraving of two hands with palms facing out, thumbs touching, and middle fingers spread apart. Meshech and the other council members stood in a semicircle as Ivri placed his hands upon the etching and wiggled his palms and fingers to fill the engraved design. Ivri felt the wall vibrate, then split apart at the junction where his thumbs met. The group gasped in amazement. Two sections of the wall separated and rotated on their axes, creating a corridor into a dimly lit chamber.

A wooden chest, made of acacia wood, with the exact dimensions of the chest Ivri had crafted, sat on a stone table. Unlike his, this chest was covered with symbols, which seemed to Ivri to be similar to the symbols that the stones had etched on the tablets. The chest also displayed the hand configuration. Ivri placed his hands in the grooves. The chest clicked open, but it was empty. Ivri opened the chest he had made, took out the breastplate and other vestments, and placed them in the empty chest. The chest he had made, now empty, glowed briefly and disappeared.

Resting against a nearby wall were eighteen thin stone tablets which displayed etchings of the same four symbols Ivri had observed on the tablets in the cave. They also displayed a tiny etching of Ivri's birthmarks on the bottom right corner. Next to them was another tablet with five etched lines, like sentences, which included additional symbols. As in the cave, there were many gold flakes sticking to the tablets' surfaces. But these couldn't possibly be the tablets from the cave.

Ivri was soon thankful that he hadn't told the council about the tablets in the cave. Later, when he went back to look for the cave and the tablets, all he could see in every direction was the flat desert. The mystery intensified when Ivri returned to the chamber in the temple. The chest with the breastplate was there, its twelve stones twinkling. The vestments were there, but the eighteen inscribed tablets had vanished.

Even Atmench, the council's most conservative member, agreed with Meshech's assessment that Ivri was a holy man. Meshech recommended that they train Ivri in the rituals of the Ur priesthood and elevate him in due course to the position of high priest. The council agreed unanimously, and the king gave his approval. Ivri became a revered eminence within the community. He had no difficulty finding a wife. She gave birth to five children, three of whom were boys. The older two boys bore the same birthmarks as their father.

Ivri and the council discovered that on occasion, the breastplate served as an oracle. But Ivri's assessment was that the breastplate responded to entreaties only in the most pressing situations. Once, with the Akkadian army poised to break through the walls of Ur, Ivri begged for help. The stones flickered a message that Ivri interpreted as positive. Hours later, the Akkadian army was gone. Ivri's experiences with the stones and the tablets convinced him that the breastplate had a deeper purpose than serving as an oracle or weapon. Ivri knew his successors would lack his personal exposure to, and experiences with, the tablets. He etched in cuneiform on dozens of clay tablets the story of his journey from Eradu, recounting his magical experiences in the cave, and later in Nanna's temple. The clay tablets were eventually lost, but the stories became known as the Ivri Legends and were told and retold for centuries.

4

Counterfeit Truths

It was a beautiful day. A group of children sat next to the statue of Nanna in the central square of the great city of Ur. Terah finished telling portions of the Ivri Legends, which they never tired of hearing.

Terah smiled. "That's some of the story. You'll hear more of the Legends when you're older."

The Legends were now more than a thousand years old. They had been handed down orally by storytellers at festivals and around family hearths. No record existed of anyone having had the birthmarks that were so central to the legends. But historical truth was not the essential function of a legend. Its primary purpose was to marry the community's past, present, and future to a set of beliefs, to form an enduring culture.

The city of Ur had realized unprecedented wealth from its position at the juncture of the Persian Gulf and the Tigris and Euphrates rivers. Ur's citizens included farmers, traders, teachers, and priests. Ur's new king, Ur-Nammu, had recently handed down the earliest known written law code. Ur was becoming a center of progressive thought and policies. The city's streets circled the Great Ziggurat of Ur, the temple to Nanna, visible for miles. An architectural marvel, it was a rectangular pyramidal structure, made of baked bricks laid with tar. No one knew how long ago it had been built. On the two annual feast days, the high priest would emerge from the temple wearing the priestly robes and breastplate. He was flanked by the two *selebs*, the only priests, aside from the high priest, who were allowed to enter the temple and be privy to its secrets. Each *seleb* held a bronze figurine in the shape of a ram with its horns stuck in a thicket. The high priest would present himself to the king, his court, and the assembled citizens of Ur. He answered the king's questions about the city's prospects for survival and prosperity, making a show of consulting the sequences of blinking stones on the breastplate.

Terah, the high priest of Ur for the past ten years, was forty-five years old: an imposing figure with a salt-and-pepper beard, a prominent nose, and intense black eyes. An inventor of novel processes for working with clays, pigments, wood, metals, and stones, he had become wealthy from his business of crafting and selling stone and wooden idols. He had three sons and two daughters, all of whom lived within Terah's villa. Avraham, his youngest son, was sixteen. His brothers, Nachor and Haran, had each married into important families. Alas, Haran's wife had died giving birth to Baasha. After Terah became high priest, Haran and Baasha took over his business. Nachor was in charge of the family's herds of sheep and goats. Avraham worked in developing the family's relatively new agricultural enterprise. The land was ideal for cultivating species of wheat that had previously grown wild.

Terah's wife, Ichtar, came from one of the oldest families in Ur. Legend had it that her family enjoyed direct ancestry from Ivri. At Avraham's birth, it terrified Ichtar to see that Avraham had the two birthmarks of the Ivri Legends, one on each shoulder blade. She worried that the king might perceive a threat to his royal station. Also, Avraham could be judged an evil spirit and killed as a sacrifice to the demonic Ooshlah. Ichtar grabbed a blade from among the birth instruments. As Avraham cried piteously, she scraped off the birthmarks. She explained to Terah that the baby had been born with abscesses she had to remove. Neither of Ichtar's other sons, Nachor and Haran, had exhibited any strange birthmarks. By the time Baasha was born, Ichtar was too old to serve as a midwife. Baasha's birth took many hours, requiring extraction from his mother's womb feet first. The two midwives who delivered Baasha were unsuccessful in their Herculean efforts to save his mother's life. As they were not familiar with the Ivri Legends, Baasha's tiny birthmarks went unnoticed.

When Avraham was four years old, he and his brother Nachor sneaked off to ride a donkey who was not trained well enough to carry two mischievous boys. The boys kicked the donkey's sides, urging him to go faster. But the stubborn animal got spooked and stopped short, throwing Avraham to the ground. He landed hard on his head, his eyes rolled back, and he entered a sloot, a coma; he could not speak, move his body, or open his eyes. Death seemed certain. They placed him in his father's bed and prayed that because he was lying in the high priest's bed, Nanna would notice the boy's predicament and grant a cure.

Ichtar and Haran kept constant watch. They dripped water in his mouth and helped him swallow. Terah offered many sacrifices and crafted beautiful new idols in Nanna's image. He visited Avraham as often as his public duties allowed. Even the king came to offer support. The ordeal gripped the citizens of Ur, who held Terah's family in great respect and loved the lively and precocious Avraham.

Sara, Nachor's daughter, was also four years old and Avraham's best friend. She displayed incredible devotion; she insisted on staying by Avraham's bed and on taking her meals by his side.

Referring to him by his nickname, Sara asked, "Will Avi die?"

Ichtar hugged her tightly.

"We don't know," she said. "We are praying Nanna and Nintinugga will use their healing powers."

"What will happen to Avi if he dies?"

"Do not be sad. If he dies, he will join our great ancestor Ivri in the afterworld, in the Great Garden."

On the fifth day, they shooed Sara away. Terah, Ichtar, and Haran gathered around Avraham's bed. Every breath seemed labored. His eyelids fluttered. No one knew if this was a sign of life or approaching death. As the sun struck midday on the sundial, Haran saw a slight stirring of Avraham's right hand. "Look," Ichtar said, as Avraham opened his eyes. His breathing became smoother, and in an almost inaudible voice, he asked for something to drink.

Over the next several weeks, Avraham grew stronger and eventually recovered. But the accident had serious and lasting repercussions. As he grew older, it became clear Avraham had become a savant, an *eled pela*. After a single reading (and, some thought, at times without having seen the writings), he knew by heart thousands of the cuneiform clay tablets stored in the king's library. Avraham seemed able to sense emotions and moods. And he was prone to trances, during which he used his reed stylus to pen clay tablets in a language neither he nor anyone else understood. These attributes were not the only reasons people regarded Avraham as an oddity. He was a good five inches taller than most of the men in the clan and, even more exceptionally, had a head of thick, bright red hair such as no one had seen before.

But none of Avraham's peculiarities diminished the community's respect for his intelligence and eloquence on subjects both common and arcane. The city greatly appreciated and honored him for his new irrigation and farming techniques, as well as his treatments for a variety of physical ailments. The king gave Avraham the accolade, "Blessed of Nanna."

Sara grew up to be a beautiful woman. She turned the heads of many men who tried to draw her away from Avraham. But Sara's profound love and respect for Avraham never wavered.

Terah dreaded the biannual feast days for Nanna. Those were the days when, dressed in the high priest's ornate robes, he was obligated to perpetrate the ultimate fraud upon Ur's population of devout Nanna worshippers. For centuries, the priests of Ur—Ivri's direct descendants—had borne the birthmarks of the splayed hands, one on each shoulder. The population of Ur regarded the marks with equanimity, as a normal and expected physical characteristic of the priestly class.

The significance of the marks only became clear centuries before Terah, when a plague almost wiped out all of Ur's population. The epidemic swept through the entire Tigris/Euphrates valley. Ur's survivors intermarried with the population of Kishon, a neighboring city to the east. Its population moved to Ur, a much larger city. Kishon had always worshipped Nanna as its chief god. But the priests and citizens did not know the Ivri Legends. Its priests used a breastplate different from Ur's. None of Kishon's population displayed Ivri's birthmarks.

The first two generations of high priests in the mixed population of Ur had the birthmarks. Neither child was the product of a mixed marriage. Priestly affairs proceeded much as before. The problem arose when Areshet, who was not a pureblood Urite and possessed only one birthmark, was chosen as the new high priest. When he attempted to open the chamber by placing his hands on the etchings, he fell unconscious to the floor. Two days later, he regained consciousness, mumbled something in a strange language, and died. The two senior priests, the *selebs*, chose another priest to take Areshet's place. The second priest lacked birthmarks on either shoulder. As soon as he tried to open the chamber, he too, died.

Citing omens attributed to Nanna, the priests canceled the annual feast scheduled for the next day. The priests promised an especially elaborate feast in three months' time. Although disappointed, the citizens of Ur accepted the explanations.

The *selebs* faced an unprecedented crisis. Contrary to their age-old customs, they shared the secrets of the temple—most importantly, the existence of the chamber and its contents—with several other priests. The *selebs* and their new acolytes sacrificed dozens of bulls and rams. They cloistered themselves and fasted for days, praying, and consulting sacred texts, but to no avail, two more priests died trying to open the chamber.

Finally, the *selebs* came to understand that, in ascribing magical powers to the birthmarks, the Ivri Legends reflected historical truth. They faced an existential crisis. The breastplate ceremonies were central to the Nanna feast days, and the feasts were fundamental to the community's way of life. But the chamber was now inaccessible. No priest nor any other member of the community exhibited both marks. The breastplate and festivals were also the source of the tithes that accounted for the power and wealth of the priests. Power is not something that those who have it are keen to surrender. For all these reasons, conceding the loss of the breastplate was not an option.

And so, they devised a plan that was strictly followed from that era forward. By the time of Terah, the priests had used the stratagem for hundreds of years. They lost to myth and legend the magic of the chamber and of the original breastplate.

The ruse involved the use of a counterfeit breastplate, with the same kinds of gemstones in settings of gold. They were painted with a phosphorescent chemical so that they glimmered, somewhat like the authentic stones. During the Nanna festivals, the high priest and *selebs* removed four of the stones from the breastplate. They painted the chosen stones with a special chemical composition. In exactly one measure of their timekeeping, approximately fifteen minutes, the stones lit up. With the four stones sparkling on his breastplate, the high priest supplied commonsense answers to the king's questions.

Apart from the high priest and the two *selebs*, no one knew of the deception. They felt deeply relieved that Nanna never seemed upset by their duplicity.

Prior to becoming high priest, Terah did not know that his job entailed misrepresenting the breastplate to the citizens of Ur. The high priest and the *selebs* entered the temple only for the biannual Nanna festivals. The work of the ordinary priests lay outside of the temple: slaughtering the animals for sacrifice, performing the daily rituals and chants, tending to the poor and sick. As an ordinary priest, Terah had never even entered the temple. He had never seen the breastplate, save on the high priest's chest during the festivals.

On the first of the great festivals over which Terah was to preside, the *selebs* dressed him in the vestments, breastplate, and miter. He presented himself before the king and the people. The king approached, bowed his head, and asked the questions he deemed critical for the well-being of the city. Terah sang a traditional story of the Ur tribe. The conclusion of his chant was timed to coincide with the illumination of the four chemically treated stones on the breastplate. As always, the congregation gasped and fell to their knees. Terah then explained the message conveyed by Nanna through the particular configuration of the illuminated stones. The message was never explicit, it was a blend of favorable projections mixed with warnings and risks, positive enough for the great celebration to proceed with a sense of optimism and gusto. The women served the roasts and stews of lamb and goat and many types of breads and cakes. The citizens of Ur imbibed huge quantities of wine and ale and danced for hours.

Terah always fasted for two days prior to a festival. After he completed his tasks as high priest, he would retreat to his house. He locked himself away with a mutton chop and a cure of potent brandy. As always, at these times, he pondered on the fraud he had once again perpetrated, not just against the citizens of Ur but also against the king himself, and he constantly worried: Would Nanna forever accept the deception?

5

A Finely-Balanced Transaction

For as long as he could remember, Avraham had felt a compulsion to enter the holy temple of Nanna and explore the powers of the breastplate. He was mysteriously immune from the inhibitions that dissuaded the rest of the citizenry from even considering such blasphemy. He shared his fantasy with no one but Sara. The inseparable childhood friends had married several years earlier. But as much as Avraham loved Sara, he felt compelled to proceed.

Avraham proceeded on a warm night; he was all but invisible in the blackness of the new moon that commenced the summer month named for the god Tammuz. The temple entrance stood open and unguarded. The stories of horrific suffering and death for those who attempted unauthorized entry were more than sufficient as a deterrent. Avraham had hidden in his cloak a phosphorescent stone that he had pilfered from the family's idol workshop. He had placed it by the fire for a full hour; he knew from experience that this would give him at least ten minutes of light in the total blackness of the temple. Once he was inside, he could light the pine knot torch he had also hidden under his cloak.

Entering the great temple, Avraham proceeded along a narrow corridor of slick, black-ridged stone walls. At a fork in the corridor, he decided to go to the right and suddenly felt a sharp pain as his leg hit what felt like stone. He shone his light upon what he saw was a stone table, in the center of which sat an ornate wooden chest.

Torn between curiosity and terror—would he be the next one to die?—Avraham slowly opened the chest. Expecting wonders, he experienced disappointment. The breastplate, miter, robes, and ephod were all there. The twelve gemstones were in plain view. Two bronze figurines, each depicting a ram stuck in a bramble thicket, flanked the chest. But something was not right. Nothing about the breastplate suggested the sacred, magical vestment whose embedded stones were alive with flashing sequences of light on the feast days. The two figurines seemed real enough, but they were historical icons. Unlike the breastplate, they were not objects of enchantment.

Avraham's disappointment lessened his apprehension about having trespassed onto sacred territory. He put his phosphorescent stone away, lit the pine knot torch, and peered along the corridor leading further into the temple. He suddenly felt a tingling sensation on each shoulder. He thought back to his tenth birthday, when his mother had told him that just after she gave birth to him, she'd scraped away from each of his shoulders birthmarks that were shaped like hands, with fingers split apart, just as they were described in the Ivri Legends. She had made Avraham promise not to tell anyone else, and he had all but forgotten Ichtar's story until this moment. His heart pounding, carrying his torch with an outstretched arm, he pressed on into the pitch-black corridor.

He progressed approximately thirty yards further before he abruptly stopped. The scars on his shoulders were stinging. His mind was suffused with a melody of exquisite beauty. Suddenly, he experienced a phenomenon he had heard about but never believed was possible. On his arms and the back of his head, the hairs were standing up, exposing his sweaty skin and scalp to the chilly air.

Avraham stared closely at the wall in front of him. Something looked different from the surrounding rock. He saw an engraving of two hands, thumbs touching, and the four fingers of each hand split apart between the middle fingers. Avraham felt lightheaded and unsteady as he placed his hands on the indentations. A moment passed, then another, and then he felt an almost imperceptible vibration, followed by a grating sound as the wall split in two. Quickly removing his hands and stepping back, he watched as the walls rotated on their axes to form a path into a room that was illuminated by a dim amber light. On a table in the middle of the room stood a wooden chest. It was identical in form to the chest he had examined earlier. But this one was brilliantly polished and had etchings of the hand configuration.

Avraham placed his hands on the etching. The cover clicked, and the lid sprang open. Within the chest were a breastplate, robes, a miter, and ephod, all identical to the contents of the first chest. But there was one extraordinary difference: The stones embedded in this breastplate sparkled with an unnatural radiance. The exquisite melody reached a loud crescendo in Avraham's mind and sent chills throughout his body. A still, small voice whispered what sounded like both a blessing and a prediction, as well as an unmistakable command: "I am *Yhahveh*. You have been chosen. You and your descendants will devote your lives to the fulfillment of humankind's potential, its intended destiny."

Avraham reached into the chest to remove the breastplate but was distracted by a noise from behind him. He turned around and saw Haran, standing behind him, his mouth agape. Avraham lost his balance and fell to the ground, his head slamming against the stone floor. And then he heard and saw nothing but black.

Haran carried his brother out of the temple, gently placed him under a grove of trees behind Terah's house and lay down beside him. After some time, Avraham regained consciousness. The brothers lay silently side by side, each waiting for the other to speak. Avraham wondered how much Haran had seen. And Haran wanted answers to his many questions. Haran moved to break the silence, but Avraham held up his hand to signal that he was not ready to discuss whatever Haran had witnessed.

"Tomorrow," he said, and disappeared into the house.

The next day, Avraham and Haran took a walk among the trees and shared their experiences.

"Brother, I have to go back to the temple," Avraham said. "The voice I told you about commanded me. This is my destiny and my burden. It may be fatal for anyone else; for all I know, whatever is there, maybe Nanna herself, will envelop me or extinguish my human life."

"Does Sara know?"

Avraham shook his head. "I've talked about the idea with her, but she warned me not to go. She has no idea I've visited the temple. And though you are a witness, you must forget what you saw. If I am caught, I will be disemboweled, my head hung on a pole at the entrance to the temple."

Haran, who had a conservative disposition, knew that returning to the temple was an insane idea. It was *hassoor*. But the experience had deeply affected him. He had always considered himself inferior to his older brother, Nachor, and his savant brother, Avraham. Now he could be a participant in a mystical experience. His normal inhibitions melted away. "I'm going in with you. Please, it's my choice."

Avraham considered abandoning the mission, although he felt as if he couldn't ignore what he was convinced was a divine calling. Avraham thought of ways he could proceed without Haran's knowledge, but Haran kept a close eye on his brother. After a few awkward days, Avraham finally relented. Haran had the right to choose his own path. The brothers would go together.

They waited for the next new moon. With only faint light from the torches at the city's perimeter, they proceeded into the temple. Avraham used his phosphorescent light until they were far enough inside to light a torch. They proceeded past the table with the counterfeit chest and cautiously made their way to the wall, where Avraham showed Haran the etching in the shape of two hands joined at the thumb, with the middle fingers split apart. Impulsively, Haran went and placed his hands to fit into the indented shape. Nothing happened.

"Do exactly what you did last time," Haran said.

Avraham placed his hands over the marks. Once again, the wall split apart and folded inward, revealing the dimly lit chamber, the table, the chest. Entering the chamber, he carefully wrapped the chest in the linen cloth on which it sat. He felt a strong urge to retreat. He glanced at Haran and saw that his brother was trembling, his eyes unfocused. He was wobbling, extending his right arm, reaching out to Avraham for support. But before Avraham could grab hold of him, he fell to the floor and stopped moving. Avraham knelt beside him. He put his ear to his brother's chest and listened in vain for a beating heart. His brother was dead.

Baasha, Haran's son, was a handsome lad with bright blue eyes, a trait not seen in Ur since Ugat, his great-great-grandfather. His good looks, however, did not translate into a pleasing disposition. Perhaps it was because he had emerged from his mother's womb at an abnormal angle, permanently deforming his left leg, and he walked with a pronounced limp. Whatever the reasons, Baasha grew up angry and bitter. His soul was engulfed with envy. What others possessed, he coveted. And equal to that, what he wanted was for them not to have it. At a young age, he already had considerable charisma, and was the leader of a growing number of young men who were dissatisfied with their lives.

Baasha adored his father, who had showered him with unconditional love. From the time he was a small boy, Baasha had followed Haran whenever and wherever possible. On the moonless night when Avraham and Haran proceeded with their plan to re-enter the temple, Baasha awoke to the sound of Haran leaving the room they shared. Where, he wondered, was his father going in the pitch-black dark of the night?

As Baasha silently followed his father, he was stunned to see him heading toward the temple. Why was he violating one of Ur's most basic prohibitions? Baasha was relieved to see that Haran was following his revered Uncle Avraham. He assumed that the brothers were acting on Terah's orders. They must be engaged in some urgent temple business. Baasha could think of no other explanation. He positioned himself behind an outcropping of the wall surrounding the temple and forced himself to stay awake as he waited for his father and Avraham to reappear.

The walls to the chamber had closed; the torch would die out in minutes. Avraham sat next to his brother for a long time. The chest containing the breastplate sat on the ground next to him. What should he do with Haran's body? What should he do with the chest? How was he to get himself and the chest out of the temple without leaving incriminating signs? Should he reopen the chamber and return it? He felt torn, but he possessed a profound secret: This was the true breastplate, and these were the actual stones. He had no idea how or why he had been led to discover the truth. But he now knew that the priests had devised a way to have ordinary gemstones light up in sequence at the festivals. Avraham was certain that no one in Ur, not even the king or Terah, suspected the truth.

Avraham rekindled the torch's flame. He picked up the chest, left the temple, and hiked to an orchard a mile from the city. After burying the chest in the soft earth, he returned to Ur. He would come back to the orchard after he figured out a better hiding place. Then he sneaked back into the temple. He dragged Haran from the chamber area back to the table where the chest with the counterfeit breastplate sat. Returning to the area of the secret chamber, he walked backwards to that table, erasing any traces of footprints, as well as the impression Haran's body had made when Avraham had dragged it from the chamber area. Then he wiped away the footprints he had left in entering and moving about within the temple. All that was left were the footprints Haran had made in walking from the entrance to the table with the counterfeit chest. If Avraham's plan worked, someone would notice his sandal prints leading from the house to the interior of the temple. Terah would be summoned to enter the temple, and he would find his son where Avraham had left him. There could be but one conclusion: Haran had died at the hand of Nanna. He had committed an inexplicable act of sacrilege. No other footprints or other signs would be apparent. Nothing would suggest that someone had gone deeper into the temple. No one would know that the real chest had been hidden away in a long-forgotten chamber and was now in Avraham's possession.

No one would know—no one except Baasha—that Avraham, too, had been in the temple that night. Baasha followed his uncle when he left the city's perimeter. He assumed that Haran was still in the temple, occupied with the tasks he imagined Terah had assigned. About a mile outside of the city, Baasha saw Avraham enter a fruit orchard and then exit twenty minutes later. Trailing Avraham back to the city, Baasha saw him enter Terah's house and returned moments later holding a brush and a cloth. Avraham then hurried back inside the temple.

Confused, Baasha sat down on the ground to wait for his father. About thirty minutes later, he saw Avraham coming out of the temple, holding the brush and a dirty cloth.

Baasha waited for four long hours. He felt more and more convinced that his father was dead. But why would his beloved uncle have killed his own brother?

It was now almost first light. In the distance, Baasha saw that Terah had gone out to the settlement's latrine area. Baasha knew his grandfather's routine; Terah would now pad his way back into the house and make his morning draught of mead.

Baasha ran to intercept his grandfather. "I woke up in the middle of the night and saw *Abba* getting dressed to go out. I think he went into the temple."

"Did you actually see him go in?" asked Terah.

Baasha feigned confusion.

"I think so. But I waited; he never came out."

Terah immediately left the house and went into the temple. It seemed to Baasha, waiting at the entrance, that Terah was inside for an eternity. When he emerged, he was carrying Haran's body and howling with grief. His wails drew the rest of the household. Word of Haran's death spread quickly through Ur. The townspeople wept and joined Terah's family in a cacophony of mourning. Baasha was inconsolable. A deep hatred for his uncle welled up within him.

Terah placed his son's body at the foot of Nanna's statute in the public square. He went to King Ur-Nammu to notify him of Haran's blasphemy and death.

The king and Terah had never gotten along very well. The king was envious of Terah's lucrative idol-making business. He decided to use the circumstance of Haran's blasphemy to expel Terah and his entire family. He would then appoint Peleg, his eldest son, as "trustee" of the business. If Terah did not return within a year, the business would devolve to his son. Terah expected the king's action. He had already had discussions with close relations in the city of Charan to the north. He would move his family and resettle there.

That night, as the family sat together to discuss the tragedy and the order of exile, Baasha stealthily went to the orchard where Avraham had disappeared. He found the site where Avraham had buried the object he had removed from the temple. Baasha dug it up. Removing the linen in which Avraham had wrapped it, he stared in disbelief at the beautifully crafted and polished wood chest.

Baasha suddenly felt his birthmarks stinging. It was a new sensation, joined by another remarkable event: a melody of profound beauty pervaded his being. Feeling both fearful and excited about what he might find, Baasha tried to open the chest by lifting its lid. It would not open. Then he then saw the engraving of two hands with thumbs touching and two middle fingers split apart. Baasha placed his hands so they fit into the shapes. The lid clicked open. Baasha opened the chest and removed the breastplate and other vestments. He felt a presence, and perceived a still, small voice that identified itself as *Yhahveh*. Baasha shuddered and heard the voice speak to him. "You will be the father of a great nation; you must trust in Avraham and his descendants, for by them you and your lineage will also be blessed. You must never worship any other god but me." Baasha sat still in the desert's cold night air, sweat pouring down his body and evaporating at the same time. He felt deathly chilled. He didn't know what to do. He was the only one who knew of Avraham's involvement in Haran's death and of his theft of the city's holiest treasure. And he could not fathom what to make of the message he had just received from an entity calling itself *Yhahveh*.

At length, Baasha decided to return the stolen chest to the temple. He assumed that Avraham had killed his father because Haran had tried to prevent Avraham from stealing it.

Baasha stole back into the city. He entered the temple and followed a path that looked as if somebody had recently used it. At the end of the path was a stone table, to his utter amazement, upon the table lay a chest of identical size and appearance to the one he was carrying. Various symbols had been carved upon it, but none of the symbols or engravings showed the hand configuration. He easily opened the chest and saw a breastplate that appeared identical to the one in the chest Avraham had buried and that he was now carrying. A chest he was attempting to return. How was this possible?

Baasha saw the imprint of his father's body on the ground. Fearful of suffering the same fate, he closed the chest on the table, returned to the orchard, and replaced the chest where he had found it. As soon as he returned home, he took a number of clay tablets and drew images of the chest, its markings, the breastplate, and the stones.

He hid the drawings, then slipped into his sleeping space. He spent the rest of the night wide awake, his mind inundated with feelings of hateful envy. And terror, as he finally allowed himself to focus on the message from *Yhahveh*, who had proclaimed that he was the only god and that Baasha should trust in Avraham. The dissonance between Baasha's thirst for revenge and the deity's admonition was too painful to bear.

Terah's world had collapsed within one day. Why had Haran entered the temple? He was a good son, a solid citizen, if somewhat dull of wit. He was a follower who would never do anything so blasphemous. Something did not make sense. Although he had no reason to blame Avraham, his mind itched with suspicion.

His formal demotion as high priest, and the appointment of his successor, would occur in a ceremony the next day. The king's chief minister, a friend of Terah's, would give him ample time to arrange matters for the migration to Charan.

That night, while he was still the highest-ranking priest, Terah went back into the temple. Holding a bright torch, he examined the chest sitting on the table. Nothing seemed amiss. He walked further back into corridors he had visited only once before, when he became high priest ten years earlier. He looked at the floor and the wall with the hand etchings. Had the surface of the floor been disturbed? It seemed so. Terah was now firmly convinced that Avraham was the central actor in this fatal and ruinous tragedy. Haran lacked the curiosity and confidence to enter the temple and violate a principal *hassoor* of the city. Avraham had curiosity and confidence in abundance. Terah knew in his heart that Avraham did not kill Haran, at least not intentionally. But he held Avraham responsible. *Not guilty but responsible.* He wondered: *Is there a distinction?*

Avraham lay next to Sara on a grassy knoll they had frequented since childhood.

"He just fell and was dead."

He had told her everything that happened. Sara, never a big fan of Haran, was nonetheless horrified to hear how he had died. She comforted Avraham and encouraged him to cry, something he would never do in front of anyone else. Avraham's description of the hidden chamber and how he had opened it fascinated her, as did the magical breastplate and stones, the melody, the voice. Her soul soared. There was a divinity after all. Would she have a role in her husband's destiny? Might this god bless her with a child?

Avraham told her that, as soon as he could escape the city unnoticed, he would clothe himself in the vestments and the breastplate. He was sure there was more to the message from the divinity who called himself *Yhahveh*. He would have heard it if Haran had not appeared.

Several days before they were scheduled to leave Ur, Avraham volunteered to take a flock of his brother Nachor's sheep out to pasture. He left at first light. Once beyond the city gates, he directed his junior shepherd to take the sheep over the ridge. It was not far from the orchard. Avraham had to have answers. Was the voice in the chamber the voice of a god? Was it speaking from the chest? From the stones? *What exactly were he and his descendants supposed to do*? Retrieving the chest, Avraham placed his hands on the etching of the two hands with thumbs touching and middle fingers spread apart. The chest clicked open. He dressed himself in the robe, ephod, and miter. When he donned the breastplate, his mind became suffused with the beautiful melody he had heard in the hidden chamber in the temple.

That moment would define Avraham's future. He stood at the break of dawn among the orchard's grape vines and peach trees. The still, small voice returned. He sensed his soul being touched by an entity that once again identified itself as *Yhahveh* and instructed him to undertake a journey west from Charan, to the land of Canaan. He was to be *Yhahveh's* prophet, speaking truth to a world of people so frightened by the hardships of life and the mysteries of death that they sought solace worshiping inanimate objects, sacrificing animals, and even making offerings of their own children. Avraham understood that his destiny was to stand up against superstition. He would help eradicate the widespread practice of child sacrifice. He would preach the need for mankind to resist and replace envy and greed with gratitude and goodwill.

In return, the land of Canaan would forever belong to Avraham and his progeny. *"[U]nto thee, and unto thy seed, I will give all of these lands, and by thy seed shall all the nations of the earth be blessed themselves."*

It was a finely-balanced transaction: Avraham and his progeny would receive a bountiful land in exchange for their embracing a way of life that embodied and demonstrated *Yhahveh's* message to all of humanity.

Avraham walked with Sara to the outskirts of the city. He hesitated to tell her about *Yhahveh's* message. How could they have descendants when he and Sara were childless? They had tried everything, conferred with the best healers, even consulted a shaman from a neighboring tribe. Nothing had worked. But she was his partner in all things. And so he told her everything—the message from *Yhahveh*, the responsibility the god had placed upon him, and the reward if he undertook that responsibility.

Sara had mixed reactions to the message; the sudden appearance of a deity that spoke to humans was difficult to accept. But when she realized two months later that she was pregnant, she no longer wondered about Avraham's faith in *Yhahveh*. When she told Avraham, his elation shook the core of his being. He hugged Sara and reveled in her joy. If they were fortunate enough to have a boy, they would name him Isaac—meaning it was something laughably wondrous.

After Avraham moved the hiding spot for the chest to a nearby cave, he sat at the entrance to think about the new future that awaited him. Then he heard a commotion. A caravan was passing by, close enough for Avraham to see a man whipping two young girls. Avraham was well-acquainted with the practice of slavery; it was ubiquitous and legal. But in Ur, at least, strict rules governed the treatment of persons who for whatever reasons had lost their personal liberty.

Avraham approached the caravan and moved to restrain the taskmaster from continuing to whip the girls. It was Silash. Avraham knew the man. He was a no-nonsense businessman, known for his interest in only one thing: profit.

Silash drew his sword. Avraham, unarmed, raised his hands and smiled. "*Ealotway*! I mean no harm."

There were ten slaves in all. Eight children were standing outside a cage. The two young women were on the ground, writhing in pain. Apart from their current anguish, they looked healthy; their clothes were filthy but of apparent good quality.

"How much do you want for these poor wretches?" Avraham asked. Silash had obtained the slaves a week earlier, when the Acaru clan invaded and destroyed their home in Kish. As the owner of the well-cared for, healthy children of the now-deceased king, Silash stood to make a handsome profit.

Silash recognized Avraham and put on a welcoming smile.

"Peace unto you, Avraham. I did not recognize you. Why would someone like you be interested in buying slaves?"

"I am a distant relation of the king," Avraham lied. "It is my obligation to care for his kin."

"You realize these are royalty. They will get me an excellent price in Damesek. But seeing as they are your family, and I have not spent too much on upkeep, I can part with them for three hundred shekels. It's a very good price, special for you."

Avraham replied, hoping Silash had not heard the news of Terah's demotion. "Your view on 'upkeeping' these children is foreign to me. My father, just to remind you, is the high priest in Ur. It would not take more than a word to have the king send a legion of troops to catch up to you and bring you back for trial. We are standing on territory claimed by Ur. And we don't condone the whipping of slaves."

Silash raised his hands in mock surrender.

"My friend, let us not argue. First, you must allow me to wash your feet and serve you dinner."

As dictated by custom, he proceeded to treat Avraham as one must treat a guest. After a splendid dinner, Silash offered Avraham a beautiful female slave. Avraham politely declined. He then told Silash of his mission for *Yhahveh*. Silash listened thoughtfully. He apologized for whipping the young girls; they had infuriated him by refusing to do any work, citing their "royal status."

"When you're defeated and captive, you can't just sit back and demand free food, protection and other royal treatments. These people are my property now. Am I wrong?"

Avraham chose his words carefully: "My God tells me that a person owns his own labor. It is his property to use however he sees fit. He can contract to sell his labor for a short time or for years if he likes. But the sweat of his brow cannot be stolen. Nor may a servant be treated inhumanely. That too is a crime against God. Those who would treat other people as inferior invite others to treat them in the same way."

Silash sat silently; it was unclear whether he was listening politely but ignoring Avraham's sermon or was actually weighing his words. But it was clear that Silash wanted the visit to end. The next day, Avraham returned, paid Silash the newly agreed-upon price of twenty-five shekels, brought the ex-slaves back to Ur, and integrated them into Terah's extended family. The leader of the group, Eliezer, became Avraham's devoted servant for the rest of his life.

Avraham was surprised when Silash showed up three days later at the gates of the city and asked to speak to him. Avraham wondered whether he was reneging on their deal.

Silash approached Avraham and bowed his head.

"I have had discussions with my family," he said, gesturing to the group of men, women and children standing at a distance.

"We would like to join your community. We know various crafts. My two sons are hard-working and responsible. Selling slaves is a very lucrative business, but the role of taskmaster is distasteful to me. And, as you put it, 'stealing the sweat of another man's brow' is inhuman. You are correct, and we wish to seek a different path. Your vision, your mission for *Yhahveh*, touched our souls. We would like to make our home with you. May the gods bless you with many children."

6

Smashing Idols

Baasha would be the only member of Terah's family to join Avraham in his journey to Canaan, a land far to the west near the Great Sea. Baasha had heard about *Yhahveh* from Avraham. Before leaving Ur, Baasha went back into Nanna's temple. He was determined to solve the mystery of the duplicate chests. His fears had overcome him the last time he entered. This time, he would solve the puzzle.

Baasha approached the chest sitting on the table, flanked by the two figurines showing a ram with its horns stuck in a bramble thicket. He opened the chest and took hold of the breastplate. The stones were not glimmering. His birthmarks were not stinging, and he heard no melody. It was not the same chest he had dug up in the orchard.

He went back to the orchard and discovered the chest was missing. Avraham undoubtedly had moved it. In the distance, he saw an old man, sitting at the foot of a small hill, wearing tribal clothing Baasha did not recognize.

The old man had cooked a stew of lamb and lentils and invited Baasha to sit and share his meal. Baasha accepted the invitation.

"Where are you from?" Baasha asked. "What brings you to this land?"

"My name is Sengrel," the man replied. "I am a priest of Midian, a domain hundreds of leagues to the southeast, almost to the lands of the pharaohs. My family's distant ancestors were refugees from a city, Eradu, which was destroyed countless ages ago by a meteor that caused unspeakable destruction."

He drank water from his *phaltu*, then passed it to Baasha.

"You are here to find and explore the chest Avraham buried in the orchard, is that not true?"

"How can you know that?"

"Show me your shoulders," Sengrel said.

Baasha always kept them covered. But something in the old man's voice told him this Midianite might hold the answer to his mysterious birthmarks.

Sengrel inspected the marks, nodded, and partially removed his cloak to show Baasha he, too, bore the marks. "Tell me what you know of the Ivri Legends," he said.

Baasha shared with Sengrel what he had learned, mostly from Ishtar, about Ivri, the meteor, and the glowing stones."

"There is more," Sengrel said.

He closed his eyes and recited his story.

"Ivri's progeny displayed these birthmarks. Serving as the high priests, they had access to the chamber to display the breastplate on the biannual feast days. In the wake of a plague, Ivri's tribe of priests intermarried with a neighboring tribe which did not have the birthmarks. As a result, only a few of the offspring exhibited the birthmarks. Eventually none did. The priests lost access to the chamber. Those who attempted entry by placing their hands on the engraving fell dead. Desperate, the priests crafted a counterfeit breastplate with the same precious stones."

"Where did they get the stones?"

Sengrel opened his eyes. He handed Baasha a parchment scroll.

"These are the instructions for creating a breastplate, and the recipes for the coatings needed to make selected stones light up after a set time elapses. The real breastplate has unimaginable powers. It can display events before they occur. It can destroy armies. But its true purpose is more profound. Together with the Tablets of Destiny, should they ever reappear, the nature of humanity could be altered."

Baasha had never heard about such tablets. He was about to ask about them when Sengrel stood up to leave. "I have said what I came to say."

But Baasha had more questions. "Wait, is the chamber still there?"

"It is."

"Can you tell me what happened to my father?"

"As I said, the legends predict that anyone who attempts to open the chamber but lacks the birthmarks will die." He held up his hand. "No more questions." Then he walked away southward. In a manner of minutes, he was out of sight.

Baasha finally understood the puzzle of his father's death: Avraham had not killed Haran. He had entered the chamber and taken the original breastplate, leaving the counterfeit chest intact on the table near the temple's entrance. As the chamber was inaccessible and never visited, and the counterfeit chest was in its normal spot, nothing would seem amiss to Terah or the *selebs* when they went into the temple to retrieve the chest on feast days.

It was a brilliant plan. Avraham obviously had not counted on his risk-averse brother, Haran, showing up.

Avraham was not guilty of murdering his father, but he was clearly responsible. He had instigated a blasphemous misadventure and had allowed Haran to take all the blame. It was Haran and his family who would be identified with this crime. It was Haran's name they would curse. All this, while his ignoble uncle would go down in history as an exalted prophet.

Baasha could think of nothing but wreaking vengeance, even if it took generations. The breastplate belonged to Haran's family. They would somehow, someday, take it back. Then, it would be Avraham's descendants who would be dependent for salvation on the nation that Baasha and his descendants would establish.

Baasha did not attempt to discover how Avraham was planning to conceal the chest during the migration. He was in no rush, he was methodically mustering his own faction of followers, young men who were eager for adventure in a new land. Baasha would wait to claim the breastplate until after they settled in Canaan. There, he and his followers would split off into a new tribe and go their own way.

The trip to Charan took one month. Avraham impressed the population in that city as he had the community in Ur. He spent many days sitting at the central plaza, fielding questions and helping people come to understand and accept their trepidation of the unknown. Life was a series of terrifying events and uncertainties. When listeners confessed they were afraid—of sickness, hunger, death—Avraham reassured them with words that sounded strange but proved consistently effective.

"Fear is natural, it is important. We're supposed to be afraid of many things. Admit the truth, and it will lose its power to terrify you."

The priests and authorities of Charan left Avraham alone; he never challenged the supremacy of Nanna or the reality of other gods. They saw his popularity and knew he would not be staying long. Best not to give cause for discord.

Baasha, too, was active in Charan. Despite his youth, he gained additional followers, mostly poor shepherds who were eager to pursue adventure and riches in a foreign land.

The trip from Charan to Canaan took three months. For the settlement of his tribe, Avraham chose a southern area midway between the Jordan River, to the east, and the Mediterranean, the Great Sea, to the west. The name of the city, Hevron, meant community or group.

Searching for an appropriate place to hide the chest, Avraham found a complex of caves near the city which he bought from the Hittite tribe for four hundred shekels. It was called the *Ma'arat Hamachpelah*, the "double cave." At the entrance was a corridor that led to a T-shaped intersection, with a cave on each end. Avraham placed the chest at the far wall of the cave to the right.

Avraham's wisdom impressed the local tribes. He provided solutions for problems that had long plagued the local populations. He shared healing methods and taught them new irrigation procedures; storage techniques for meat and vegetables; and new strategies for fertilizing fig, date, and other fruit trees. In helping the local populace in these ways, Avraham did the opposite of foreign tribes that had invaded, conquered, looted, and supplanted indigenous populations. Avraham had enough followers and adherents to form a strong militia. But though he was careful to organize his tribe for defense, he had no appetite for military contests. Neither did he want to force his views on anyone.

Avraham no longer curbed his radical ideas about religion. His many followers, now his own tribe, shouted their dedication to the one and only god, the incorporeal *Yhahveh*. Avraham poked fun at the idea of a god responding to someone rubbing a lion's tooth. What kind of god would stoop to such a demeaning form of worship? At Avraham's rallies, one could see many people in attendance furtively removing their hands from their pockets. When they went home, they would put these *terafim* in the bottom basket. But for many, discarding them, regarding them as mere trash was a bridge too far. Most could not bear having them tossed aside with assorted junk. They restored them to their former status after a few days. But some burnt them with the rest of their garbage. Avraham delighted at every sign of progress.

Avraham's new religion was unique, and not only because *Yhahveh* had no form. Unlike all other belief systems, his did not promise an afterlife, a paradise for those who worshipped *Yhahveh* or did good deeds. Avraham taught that paradise was living an ethical and enjoyable life here on Earth. What came later was beyond humanity's understanding. To speculate about the afterlife was to provoke superstition, which Avraham called the "bane of humanity."

Yhahveh advised Avraham that it would take many generations to achieve a spiritual revolution. The agricultural revolution had occasioned a profound remodeling of society in the Near East. Great urban centers had been established, providing safety and circumstances favoring cultural development. The revolution was accompanied by an explosion in complex and horrific pagan practices, which the people thought necessary to assuage and thank the gods. The most abhorrent of the practices was child sacrifice. Avraham would serve as *Yhahveh's* instrument to demonstrate that such practices were not required to secure divine favor.

Moloch. The gruesome god to whom the Canaanites had for centuries sacrificed their children.

The Phoenicians, a Canaanite sect, spread their cultic practice as they conquered Carthage and other areas in North Africa. They ruled as far west as Sicily. A contemporary historian described the gruesome nature of the practice. *"There stands in their midst a bronze statue of Moloch, its hands extended over a bronze brazier, the flames of which engulf the child. When the flames fall upon the body, the limbs contract and the open mouth seems almost to be laughing until the contracted body slips quietly into the brazier. Thus it is, that a certain 'grin' is known as 'sardonic laughter,' since they appear to die laughing."*

Child sacrifice was no longer practiced in Ur. Avraham recalled a discussion he'd had with his father when he was nine years old. Terah was in his workshop, fashioning an idol for a midlevel official who had two daughters and wanted a male heir.

"Father," Abraham said, "we learned in school today about the bronze figurines that the *selebs* bring out of the temple on the feast days. They depict a ram with its horns stuck in a bramble thicket. But the explanation did not convince me that the figurines represent our gratitude for our livestock."

"That it did not convince you doesn't surprise me," Terah said. "I will share the truth with you, but as with other matters I've taught you, this is for you alone to know."

The sacrifices, Terah explained, originated at a time when there was constant fear of starvation. "People thought, 'Surely the gods will sustain our family if we give them what is most precious to us.'" The priests promoted the practice. They received huge donations from families seeking to ensure that their children would infrequently be chosen as "honorees," the euphemism used to describe the victims. The priests forced parents to dance, drink, and celebrate—in some cities, to engage in fertility rites and orgies—while their children were burned alive in Moloch's stove.

"No society would embrace such a practice unless it delivered results essential to the community's survival. The logic of child sacrifice became circular. If such a horrific practice weren't necessary, the community wouldn't agree to do it."

"Why is child sacrifice no longer practiced here in Ur?" Avraham asked.

"In a conversation I once had with the king, he suggested the gods wanted more grown-ups to serve them, to build towers and temples and so forth. But I don't think it is so simple, although I never argued with his explanations. I think it had something to do with the Great Flood. As you know, many legends describe the rains that continued for several weeks and flooded the valleys. Other legends attribute the flooding to the melting of huge ice floes from the north. Whatever the cause, thousands of people died. There was much suffering for many generations. The floods had a permanent effect on the areas' water supply, and. . ."

Avraham interrupted Terah. "Do you think the child sacrifices stopped because they had to replace the many who drowned, because they needed shepherds and farmers?"

Terah stroked Avraham's head, delighted by his son's intelligence and intuitive thinking.

"Yes, my son. But it was not just shepherds and farmers. The population in general had been artificially reduced. At the same time, the flood had created many more pastures and arable lands, opportunities for expanded farming, and increased herds of cattle, sheep, goats, and other animals. These developments led to more settlements, more agriculture. It was a convenient time for the high priest to divine that the gods wanted the practice stopped. They fashioned the figurines to commemorate the event."

Terah's explanation of the figurines fascinated Avraham. As usual, he sensed the truth of his father's words.

Now, Avraham divined *Yhahveh's* unmistakable command that he confront the Canaanites with their cruel ritual. He invited the tribal chieftains and priests from the neighboring tribes and clans to a great feast, to celebrate the summer equinox at the summit of the Moriah Mountains. He would offer a sacrifice there, on the huge rock that legend called the Foundation Stone, the center of the world. Avraham led twelve-year-old Isaac, his nephew Baasha, and an entourage of followers on the two-day journey to the mountain.

As they made their final approach, Isaac said to Avraham, "Father, I see the fire and the wood, but where is the lamb for the burnt offering?"

Avraham was consumed with anguish. The deity whom he worshipped and could not disobey had commanded him to sacrifice his beloved son, which he could not imagine doing. He placed his arm around Isaac's shoulder. Avraham and his servants had brought cedar wood, a type of wood known to burn quickly and to be extremely hot. Now, he arranged the wood on the stone surface and doused it with flammable sap. He placed a lit torch within easy reach.

From the sacred chest he had brought with him, Avraham took out the vestments of the high priest. Isaac helped him put them on. The twelve stones on the breastplate shone brightly in varying sequences. The assembled people stood all around, watching in awe. Baasha was the exception. His eyes were blazing with envy.

Avraham motioned for Isaac to approach the altar. He placed a blindfold on Isaac's head, lifted him onto the wood, and soaked his robes and the cloth with more sap.

Not a word passed between father and son. Avraham lovingly placed his hand on Isaac's cheek. It had a soporific, hypnotic effect. Isaac felt peaceful. His trust in his father and the god he proclaimed was of an absolute, perfect quality. He closed his eyes and waited for *Yhahveh's* embrace.

Suddenly, as Avraham raised his arm to strike his son with the knife, he fell into a trance. He dropped the knife as the stones in the breastplate enveloped him in a cloud of colored light.

When the cloud dissipated, he awoke and fell to the ground. Looking up, he saw Isaac standing before him, alive and beaming with pride. Tears flowed down Avraham's face as he slowly raised himself from the ground. The audience of tribal chiefs and priests were on their knees, heads bowed. Avraham said to Isaac, "Son, repeat to me exactly what just took place."

Isaac described a scene that future generations would retell and glorify.

"Father, you were in some kind of trance. You took me off the altar. A ram suddenly appeared behind you, stuck in the thicket. You slaughtered it. After placing it on the altar, you reached down for the torch. But as you picked it up, the wood spontaneously ignited. In just a moment's time, the ram and wood were consumed entirely."

'Oh Lord, *Yhahveh*,' you said, 'I would have gladly given to you my son, my only son, my beloved Isaac.'

"Seven lights on your breastplate then lit up and flashed in a sequence." Then you said,

"The Lord *Yhahveh* speaks to me now." He tells me,

"I do not want you to kill Isaac. I have chosen this day to tell the world that human life may not be used to barter with God for riches, long life, or anything of value. These are not your children; they are mine. I have given mankind the ability to discern right from wrong, and the free will to follow what is right and reject what is wrong. You and your descendants will show the way for all the nations of the world."

"All twelve stones on the breastplate flashed in a succession of sequences. And then the breastplate went dim, and you awoke from the trance."

A great celebration and feast concluded the unique assembly. The next morning, Avraham and Isaac began their walk home.

"I was terrified," Isaac said, "Would you have killed me?"

Avraham had expected the question, just as he expected that his precocious son would find the answer he had prepared deficient.

"Only *Yhahveh* knows," Avraham offered, placing his arm around Isaac's shoulders. "These are divine events beyond my understanding. I am deeply sorry, my son."

7

One People,
Two Temples

Six months after these events, Sara passed away. Avraham was inconsolable. His true love, his partner for life, the only person he could fully confide in, was gone.

Avraham buried her in the second cave of the *Ma'arat Hamachpelah*, the cave to the left of the fork at the end of the corridor. He constructed a casket made from an oak tree. In an elaborate ceremony, attended by hundreds of people from neighboring clans, Avraham placed the coffin at the terminus of the cave. Avraham, Isaac, and his growing camp of followers mourned Sara for thirty days.

Several weeks after the burial, Avraham entered the cave to ensure security for the sacred chest. The chest had its own lock—the etched hand configuration on its cover. But someone could still carry the chest away. Avraham entered the corridor leading to the two caves and went into the chamber to the right. He found a large opening on a stone shelf near the rear wall; he also found a slab of smooth stone to place over it. He etched the configuration of the two hands on the stone slab. When he tried to remove the stone without placing his hands on the etched grooves, he could not remove it. When he placed his hands on the etching, he could remove the slab.

One night, when Avraham was away doing business with Midianite traders, Baasha stole inside the caves. He was certain Avraham had hidden the chest in one of the two chambers. Entering the chamber to the right of the fork, Baasha noticed a stone slab in the corner that appeared to cover an opening at the bottom of the wall. The slab had an etching of the unusual birthmarks on Baasha's shoulders. Baasha grabbed the edges of the stone covering and tried to move it, to no avail. But when he placed his hands on the etching, he found he could easily move the stone slab. Removing the covering, Baasha saw and removed the chest. It also had a drawing of the hand configuration and would not open unless Baasha fit his hands onto the image.

Baasha was overjoyed finally to see the real breastplate and its glowing stones, as well as the high priest's other vestments: the ephod, robes and miter. His shoulders began to sting, and he perceived the mystical, exquisite melody Avraham had heard. He picked up the chest to carry it away but was amazed that he could not exit the cave carrying it.

Baasha wondered whether this was why Sengrel had given him the knowledge to create a duplicate breastplate.

Baasha quickly resolved that he would use Sengrel's instructions to create a new breastplate. He would use it to legitimize himself as high priest and undisputed leader of the growing number of people who disliked Avraham's condescending moralizing. On the command of Baasha, they embraced *Yhahveh* as the one and only God and became as fanatical in that belief as Avraham's tribe. Baasha would leave for later the puzzle of getting the real breastplate out of the cave.

Baasha advised Avraham of his wish to go his own way. He thanked him for his generosity, his support, and his loving kindness during a difficult time. Baasha also advised Avraham that he would go back to Charan to take a wife from among the women of their family. He had already chosen Malka, Nachor's granddaughter.

Avraham was proud of his nephew. He thought the plan was a good one. He was pleased that he had helped secure a good future for his brother's often tormented son. He organized a banquet in Baasha's honor.

The lands Baasha had selected lay at the foothills of Mount Gerizim, about thirty miles north of Jerusalem and east of the Jordan River. He called his city Shechem, meaning "to rise up." The entire area, from the Jordan River to the Great Sea to the west, came to be known as Samaria. Baasha's tribe would be known as the Samaritans.

Nachor gave Baasha and Malka a gala wedding. They stayed in Charan for two weeks and then returned to lead his tribe to Shechem. On the summit of Mount Gerizim, he built a temple. Using the drawings he had made long ago in Ur, and with the help of the instructions and stones he had received from Sengrel, he fashioned vestments and a breastplate that duplicated the originals. The most time-consuming aspect of the project was getting the same kinds of stones as the original twelve; only a few were native to the area. He sent out two trusted aides, one to Egypt and one to Tyre in Phoenicia. They brought back the smaragdite, carbuncle, carnelian, beryl, onyx, and jasper. Each one of the twelve stones had to be cut to the same size.

When they completed the project, Baasha summoned his tribe of Samaritans to the temple. He had treated selected stones in the breastplate with the chemicals Sengrel had specified. In front of the assembly, Baasha lifted the breastplate, mumbled an incantation, and watched the expressions of awe and fear as the stones lit up in a seemingly random sequence. They prayed for *Yhahveh's* blessing in their new land.

Enjoying his power and not wishing to call his breastplate's magic into question, Baasha did not prioritize his goal of securing the real breastplate from the cave in Hevron. It would be a task for future generations. He fathered over two dozen children with Malka and his other wives and maidens from different families, including two of Avraham's daughters. But none of them was born with the strange symbols. Baasha knew the birthmarks had skipped generations; he was confident they would eventually appear in his lineage.

Baasha disclosed the importance of the birthmarks to no one but the two priests he ordained to help him administer the temple. He called the threesome the Trio; it operated much like the *selebs* in Ur. On a parchment scroll that was known as Baasha's

Commentary, Baasha laid out the history of his birth in Ur; the death of his father, Haran; Avraham's dishonesty; the critical significance of the hand configuration for opening the real chest; and the Samaritans' holy obligation to get the authentic breastplate. As to *Yhahveh's* statement to him in the orchard, Baasha stated *Yhahveh* had told him the Samaritan nation would show the benefits of ethical monotheism to the world, that *Yhahveh* had designated Mount Gerizim as the only "place that the Lord your God has chosen to put his name and make his habitation there."

Baasha ordered the Trio to cut off and mummify his hands upon his death. They were to preserve them in the event that they acquired the authentic breastplate and there were still no Samaritans who had inherited the birthmarks. Baasha doubted the idea was workable, in which case, the community's only recourse would be to kidnap a non-Samaritan who had the marks.

Revered by a swelling number of disciplines who embraced his philosophic and religious views, Avraham turned his attention to how he would complete the training of Isaac in the secrets of *Yhahveh* and the breastplate.

It was dark by the time Avraham and Isaac arrived at *Ma'arat Hamachpelah*. They stopped in the cave to the left to say a prayer at Sara's burial chamber. Avraham knew that the time was not far off when they would bury him next to Sara. He was satisfied with his life's long journey, pleased to have served *Yhahveh* and to have given others the opportunity to understand His way.

Avraham showed Isaac the chest's location in an opening at the wall of the second chamber. He pointed out the engraving of the hand configuration on the chest and on the opening's stone cover. Explaining to Isaac how Haran died, Avraham emphasized that only someone who had the birthmarks could open the lid. Isaac had long ago asked his father what the birthmarks on his shoulders meant, but until now, Avraham had never given him a satisfactory answer. Father and son sat down, and Avraham told him everything that had transpired at the temple in Ur and thereafter and everything he knew about the magic of the breastplate.

Isaac was astounded at the enormity of the mission *Yhahveh* had chosen for his family.

"*Yhahveh*, the one and only God, speaks to me in a silent voice," Avraham said. "He will commune with you as well. The essence of what I learned is that it's human arrogance to think we can understand the divine. We end up inventing God in our own image. I do not pretend to know what *Yhahveh* is; I just know what He is not."

Isaac understood the essence of what Avraham was saying. Controlling his fear and following his father's directions, Isaac placed his hands and removed the lid to the opening, and then he removed and opened the chest. Avraham helped him put on the vestments and breastplate.

As he did so, Isaac's mind was touched by the still, small voice his father had described. He sensed the same message. *"Sojourn in this land, and I will be with thee and will bless thee; for unto thee, and unto thy seed, I will give all these lands; and by thy seed shall all the nations of the earth bless themselves. My servant Avraham has taken the first steps. You will take another. You and your descendants will show the way. We want you to succeed."*

The majesty of the message stunned Isaac. And *Yhahveh's* use of the word "we" was disconcerting. Were there other divinities beside *Yhahveh*, the "one and only God"?

In retelling *Yhahveh's* message to his father, Isaac did not mention Yhahveh's use of the word "we." As to the rest of the message, Avraham nodded. He and his progeny were being tasked with a mission for "all the nations," in return for which *Yhahveh* would award them this land.

Twenty years later, Isaac and his son, Jacob, laid Avraham to rest in the chamber to the left of the double cave, next to his wife, Sara.

Isaac said to Jacob, "You will bury me here as well, and it shall also be your place of eternal rest."

When Jacob turned twelve, Isaac took the youth into the double caves and revealed the opening in the wall. He told Jacob everything that Avraham had told him. He showed Jacob how to access the chest by placing his hands on the etchings. He helped Jacob put on the vestments. Jacob then felt his birthmarks twinge, experienced a melody of intense splendor, and heard the still, small voice that had spoken to his father and grandfather. The message was the same: *"I am Yhahveh, the God of Avraham, and the God of Isaac, thy father. The land whereon thou liest, to thee will I give it, and to thy seed. . . . And in thee and in thy seed shall all the families of the earth be blessed."*

Jacob carried out Isaac's instructions. He buried his father in *Ma'arat Hamachpelah* next to the sarcophaguses of Avraham and Sara and Isaac's wife, Rebecca. When Jacob died, they buried him next to his forebears.

Jacob's twelve sons became the Israelites, the Twelve Tribes of Israel. Only the tribe of Levi displayed the birthmarks.

The Israelites spread out and occupied portions of northern and southern Canaan. The northern tribes joined with the Samaritans. They formed the Kingdom of Samaria. Shechem was its political capital, the temple on Mount Gerizim, its spiritual center.

The Israelites settling in the south of Canaan—the tribes of Levi, Judah, and Benjamin—formed the Kingdom of Judea, with its capital initially in Hevron and then in Jerusalem. The Levites insisted that they alone were authorized to offer sacrifices to *Yhahveh* and that sacrifices could only be performed in Jerusalem, "the place which *Yhahveh* your God has chosen out of all your tribes to put His name there." The two kingdoms argued incessantly about whether *Yhahveh* wanted His temple at Jerusalem or at Mount Gerizim.

To meet the challenge posed by the invading Philistines, the "Sea Peoples," the two kingdoms merged. Jerusalem became the capital for the so-called United Kingdom.

King David was the architect of this new polity. In 940 BCE, his son, King Solomon, built the iconic temple to *Yhahveh* in Jerusalem. David and Solomon understood that the temple and the continuing practice of animal sacrifices were intended by *Yhahveh* to help the Israelites in their ongoing transformation from polytheistic Bedouin tribes to monotheists living within cosmopolitan cities and occupying land with defined borders. Known for his wisdom, King Solomon openly raised a question humanity has forever struggled with: What is God? *"But will God indeed dwell on the earth? Even heaven and the highest heaven cannot contain you, much less this house that I have built!"*

When King Solomon died, there was a fight for succession. The Philistines' threat was diminished. Within a few years of Solomon's death, the United Kingdom divided back into the Kingdoms of Samaria and Judea. They were still one extended family, united in their worship of *Yhahveh*. They used almost the identical Torah, the sacred book of *Yhahveh's* laws and commandments. But politically, they were separate, sovereign countries. The Samaritans rededicated their temple on Mount Gerizim, restoring it to great splendor.

Some two hundred years later, in 721 BCE, the Assyrians from Mesopotamia invaded Canaan. They destroyed the Kingdom of Samaria. Many were exiled to Assyrian-controlled lands far to the east.

The Levite priests in Judea urged their surviving northern cousins to give up their temple and worship *Yhahveh* in Jerusalem. The Trio on Mount Gerizim declined the invitations, dismissing with contempt the Levites' obsessive insistence that Jerusalem be recognized as the sole venue for *Yhahveh's* temple.

The critical break in relations between the two groups of Avraham's descendants occurred when the Samaritan high priest, whose wife was an Assyrian convert to Judaism, married their daughter to the son of a Judean prince. The Levites at the Jerusalem temple refused to recognize the marriage's validity; they banned the couple from the Judean Kingdom and repudiated the Samaritans' standing as legitimate disciples of *Yhahveh*. The split between the descendants of Baasha and those of Abraham became permanent.

8

Back to Egypt

King Zedekiah reigned in Judea over five hundred years after King David, and one hundred and fifty years after the destruction of the Kingdom of Samaria. Jerusalem had become a bustling cosmopolitan city. It supported a large economy based on pilgrims who brought animals to be sacrificed at the temple on the three annual festivals: Passover, to celebrate the exodus from Egypt; Shavuot, seventy days later, to celebrate the wheat harvest; and Succoth, the fruit and wine festival in the fall. During the festivals, thousands of Levites and their assistants serviced the needs of the people, who set up temporary housing within and outside the city. Musicians played flutes and lyres. The Levites sang Psalms as hundreds of thousands of worshippers flowed in and out of the temple's precincts.

But even as Jerusalem flourished, the Judeans worshipped pagan deities. Some continued to practice child sacrifice. The Judeans had all but repudiated the transaction *Yhahveh* had concluded with the Patriarchs: that in return for the bountiful life their descendants would enjoy in their own land, they would adopt the Torah's commandments as a way of life; accept Yhahveh's incorporeality; abandon idol worship; renounce greed and envy; and become a moral and ethical model, a "light unto the nations." For decades, the Jewish prophets had inveighed against the Judeans' failure to heed the nature of the religion they had promised to follow. Cried the prophet Isaiah, *"I am sick of your sacrifices. I don't want your fat rams. Who wants your sacrifices when you have no sorrow for your sins?"* The prophet Micah pointedly reminded the Jews that their mission was to exemplify the Torah's emphasis on social justice. *"Will Yhahveh be pleased with thousands of rams, with ten thousand rivers of oil? It hath been told thee, 'O man, what is good, and what Yhahveh doth require of thee: only to do justly, and to love mercy, and to walk humbly with thy God.'"*

Zedekiah would be the last direct descendant of King David to sit on the throne of Judea. In 586 BCE, the Babylonian king, Nebuchadnezzar II, laid siege to Jerusalem and would soon destroy the city and its magnificent temple. The priests and King Zedekiah's political and military advisers argued about how to resolve Nebuchadnezzar's demands for surrender. Some were in favor of paying the exorbitant tribute he demanded; others insisted *Yhahveh* would rescue His holy city. A large faction of the Jewish army, the "zealots," opposed capitulation and threatened to revolt if the king accepted terms of tribute. The breastplate yielded no clear guidance, igniting the king's wrath against the high priest, Zadok.

The Babylonians had destroyed the other fortified cities of Judea. There was no reason to believe they would spare Jerusalem. From his years of experience with the breastplate, Zadok understood it did not offer guidance simply because the high priest invoked a crisis. The true purpose of the breastplate remained a mystery.

Zadok walked out of his office at the temple and descended to the pool of Siloam, outside the temple's walls. Zadok sat and meditated upon the current crisis and his people's history. Several years after the destruction of the kingdom of Samaria in 721 BCE, the Assyrians under King Sennacherib returned to Canaan. They destroyed Judean cities and laid siege to Jerusalem. The Judean king, Hezekiah, joined in the supplications of the high priest Zachariah, promising to put an end to the worship of Baal and other false gods. To their great relief, five of the twelve stones on the breastplate began to glow. Zachariah reported hearing the still, small voice. It assured him the Assyrian threat would be eliminated, which it was, that very night. As reported in the Book of Kings: *"And it came to pass that night, the angel of Yhahveh went forth, and smote in the camp of the Assyrians a hundred fourscore and five thousand; and when men arose early in the morning, behold, they were all dead corpses."*

King Hezekiah was good to his word. He launched a campaign to eliminate pagan worship in the land. He rededicated the Judeans to the sacred covenant their ancestors had sworn to honor. But no sooner did he die than the pagan practices reemerged and expanded throughout the land.

Zadok's worst fears were realized the next day when the Babylonian army smashed through the outer walls of Jerusalem. Zadok walked into the Holy of Holies, an area that only the high priest was allowed to enter. The Ark of the Covenant, containing the two stone tablets on which *Yhahveh* had etched the Ten Commandments at Mount Sinai, had always been secured in the temple's Holy of Holies. Two days earlier, Zadok had sent off the ark with one of his most trusted lieutenants, a monk-like figure who would bury the ark and himself with it. No one, including Zadok, would ever know its location. Scribes had recorded the commandments on hundreds of clay tablets and papyrus scrolls. To allow the ark to exist outside the confines of the temple would transform it into a shrine, enticing pagan worship and all manner of superstitious practices, negating the central core of Judaism.

Zadok was more worried about the breastplate and the embedded, shimmering stones. He was a witness to their inexplicable attributes. And he believed their purpose was not yet fulfilled. The ancient chest holding the breastplate and other vestments of the high priest was the only other item kept within the Holy of Holies. Two weeks earlier, Zadok had removed the chest from the Holy of Holies. He had clothed himself in the vestments and breastplate and, for the first time, experienced a direct communication with *Yhahveh*. Zadok was astonished at the complexity of the assignment he was being given.

Zadok then picked up the chest and wrapped it in a linen cloth. He gave it to his faithful servant, Hilkiah, and instructed him on the first act of a divine drama that would take two and a half millennia to unfold.

Although they were not members of the tribe of Levi and did not exhibit the birthmarks, members of the Yokani clan of the tribe of Judah routinely performed various duties within the temple. Jeda was a respected Yokani clan member who had been working in the temple for ten years. But Jeda was a Samaritan spy. He was a staunch believer in Baasha's legacy, holding that *Yhahveh* had chosen the Samaritans, not the Levites, to possess the breastplate and to implement its divine purpose at the appointed time. Now, under instructions from the Samaritan high priest, BabRama, he settled behind one of the temple's great pillars to watch the movements of Zadok and Hilkiah.

That night, Jeda saw Zadok give the chest to Hilkiah, who briefly disappeared into the priests' cloaking room. He emerged holding the exquisitely carved chest that, to Jeda's knowledge, had never been taken from the Holy of Holies. BabRama had foreseen that Zadok would likely remove the chest for safekeeping. Jeda was exhilarated at the chance he now had to secure the sacred object for the Samaritans.

Hilkiah fastened the chest on his wagon and drove to the *Ma'arat Hamachpelah* in Hevron, twenty miles to the south, where Avraham had once hidden the chest. Keeping a safe distance, Jeda followed on his mule. Hevron had long ceased to be of any strategic significance to the Kingdom of Judea. It had gone untouched by the Babylonians.

Arriving at the site before dawn, Hilkiah descended the staircase. A respected engraver, Hilkiah complied with Zadok's surprising request. Over the next three hours, he chiseled a drawing of the breastplate on the limestone wall at the staircase's fifth step. At the top and bottom center of the drawing, he etched representations of the strange birthmarks the Levites had on their shoulders. At the bottom left, he etched the word for *Yhahveh* in Paleo-Hebrew (⅂ℽ⅂⅂ꟼ).

After completing his drawing, Hilkiah followed the corridor to the cave to the right and found the opening in which he was to place the chest. He did so and then reached over to move the stone slab to cover the opening. But before he could move it, a tremendous weight crashed down upon his head.

Jeda watched Hilkiah's dead body fall to the floor. He also dropped to the floor, feeling violently ill, just as BabRama had warned him.

"You are a soldier, and we are at war. Hilkiah's demise is legal and required. To feel guilt and remorse in such a situation is natural and will be accounted to your credit."

Recovering his emotional balance, Jeda dragged Hilkiah's body to the side of the cave, picked up the chest, and ascended the staircase. Once out of the caves, he felt a sense of relief. He had fulfilled his people's centuries-old dream: to take possession of the sacred breastplate.

Jeda rode all night on bumpy sideroads unfamiliar to the Babylonian invaders until he reached Shechem. He ascended to the temple on Mount Gerizim where he met BabRama and proudly presented him with the chest. The two priests congratulated each other. They immediately went to the temple and offered a sacrifice of thanks to *Yhahveh*.

BabRama had known Jeda all his life. He also knew that Zadok was an extremely clever individual. He had to be sure Zadok hadn't somehow fooled his young acolyte. And so, with great reluctance, he told Jeda what he must do next.

Devout and obedient, Jeda unhesitatingly placed his hands upon the etchings on the chest's cover. BabRama was both saddened and relieved when Jeda fell to the ground, dead.

BabRama would have killed Jeda anyway. He had to achieve complete secrecy. Now he also had the proof he needed.

He wrapped up Jeda's body and carted it away, just beyond the border of Samaria. He felt great sadness as he buried the body and recited the prayers for the dead. Then he returned to the temple at Mount Gerizim. Sleep was out of the question. He spent the rest of the night reflecting upon his people's blessed new reality.

BabRama did not have the birthmarks and was, of course, reluctant to place his hands on the etchings. He took a metal tool and tried to pry open the chest. As he'd expected, he did not succeed. He then dug out Baasha's mummified hands and tried them on the chest. He was not surprised when, once again, he didn't succeed.

Given that none of the Samaritan priests, including BabRama, carried the birthmarks, acquiring the chest was but the first step. He reluctantly concluded that they would have to bring into the Samaritan fold one or more Levites who had the birthmarks. Thus far, despite the specter of Jerusalem's imminent destruction, none of the stubbornly devoted Levites had agreed to join the Samaritans' cause. The sticking point was always the Samaritans' insistence that the temple on Mount Gerizim was *Yhahveh's* sole, chosen abode.

BabRama was in no rush. They had waited many generations to reclaim the breastplate. Their population was exploding with new converts, refugees from Judea. As a practical matter, the counterfeit breastplate worked well. BabRama wrote a scroll that recounted how they had obtained the authentic chest and placed it among other legal and historical records the Samaritans kept in the remote Wadi Dalia cave, next to the lands of the *Ta'âmireh* Bedouins.

BabRama had never killed another human being. He rarely drank alcohol. With time now to mourn the loss of faithful Jeda and reflect upon the acquisition of the real breastplate, he fetched out of storage a bottle of liquor, a gift of visitors from Nineveh. After saying the required blessing, he drank until he could no longer distinguish between his remorse and elation.

Zadok's plan was proceeding apace. Like most Levites, Hilkiah had the birthmarks on both shoulders. Zadok and Hilkiah had long known about Jeda's allegiance to the Samaritans. When Hilkiah had taken the chest from Zadok, he stopped in the cloakroom and opened the chest. He removed the breastplate and other vestments and placed them in a chest which he and Zadok had carefully carved over several days. It had the etchings of the hand configuration and was identical in all other respects to the authentic ancient chest. Into the old chest which Avraham had crafted centuries earlier, Hilkiah placed a piece of iron wrapped in a thick cloth, giving the chest equal weight. Zadok assumed BabRama, on receiving the ancient chest, would order one of his priests to open it. The priest's death would prove the chest's authenticity. That it contained nothing of value would remain unknown.

Zadok was certain BabRama would have ordered Jeda to kill Hilkiah. In fact, he was fairly sure Jeda, too, would shortly be reported missing.

Zadok retrieved the chest with the authentic breastplate from the cloakroom, where Hilkiah had made the switch. He wrapped the chest in linen and left his beloved temple for the last time. He told Hilkiah's wife the sad news about her husband dying on a secret mission, assuring her that her family would be well provided for. It was a cataclysmic time; thousands were dying every day from battle and starvation. Hilkiah's wife took no solace in the misery of others. She cried and wailed and cursed the day Zadok was born.

Zadok assembled a diverse group of approximately three thousand men, women, and children who wanted to go into exile with him in Egypt. According to various treaties between Egypt and Judea, dating back several generations, a sizable contingent of Jewish soldiers, together with their families, were stationed on Elephantine Island. The island was located on the Nile, hundreds of miles south of the Giza plateau and Luxor, where the pharaohs had built great pyramids, temples, and tombs.

King Zedekiah was weak. His sycophantic inner circle of false prophets told him only what he wanted to hear: *Yhahveh* would save Jerusalem again, just as He had in the time of his great-great-grandfather, Hezekiah. They also naively assured him that Egypt, also a target of the Babylonians, would lend them assistance. That, too, did not transpire. Within three days, the Babylonians burned Jerusalem to the ground and reduced to rubble the temple that had been a wonder of the ancient world. They massacred tens of thousands of people; some streets were said to have literally flowed with blood. Tens of thousands of Jews were placed into captivity and exiled to Babylonia.

When Jerusalem was in peril during the Assyrian siege, King Hezekiah had built a tunnel to bring water into the city from the Spring of Gihon outside the city walls. Zadok and his followers now used this tunnel as their escape route. They waded through the water as it flowed against them.

Camels were waiting as they exited through a hidden opening. In addition to the chest, Zadok brought plans for the construction of a new temple to *Yhahveh*. Hundreds of years after the Exodus of their ancestors from Egypt, the Jews were headed back.

9

Hidden Cylinders

Elephantine Island lay to the west of the city of Aswan on the Nile's east coast, a natural location for defensive fortifications. According to the polytheistic Egyptian religion, Elephantine Island was the dwelling place of Khnum, the ram-headed god of the so-called Nile Cataracts, accumulations of enormous boulders that broke the flow of the Nile. The First Cataract was due south of the island. It was a natural impediment to foreign navies seeking to invade Egypt, the breadbasket of the ancient world.

The long-established Jewish community in Elephantine welcomed Zadok and his entourage. They were especially pleased with the plans for a replica of Solomon's Temple in Jerusalem. Zadok hired an Egyptian mathematician, Imhotep, to scale down the designs of the Jerusalem sanctuary. They finished construction in two years. Despite its small scale, its elegant design drew praise from both Jews and non-Jews.

Zadok next turned his attention to the remaining and even more complex tasks *Yhahveh* had assigned him. First, Zadok needed to find a cave that matched the image he had received from *Yhahveh*. The chest had probably been placed there many years ago, perhaps even centuries.

As high priest, Zadok did not have to explain his comings and goings. Disguising himself as a merchant, he rented a room behind a merchant's stall in the town of Aswan, across the Nile to the east, and bought the necessary materials. He spent two weeks in Aswan, contracting with a gemstones merchant and with various artisans for specialized weaving and smelting services. Two weeks later, he returned to Elephantine Island with a duplicate of the chest and the high priest's vestments, including the breastplate with its gold settings and twelve stones. He had secured the right chemicals to infuse a faint glow in the stones and a further treatment for selected stones to shine brightly on holidays, and as otherwise needed. After Zadok had substituted the duplicates for the originals, he covered the authentic chest with a linen cloth and carried it out of the settlement. On the southwest slope of the island, he found a funnel-shaped cave that matched the description *Yhahveh* had given him.

Using a torch to light his way, Zadok walked at least one hundred and fifty feet to the back of the cave. He was stunned to find a large boulder with an embedded, glimmering gemstone, a jasper, one of the twelve stones in the breastplate. His birthmarks twinged as he touched the stone. He assumed the stone must have some significance in *Yhahveh's* plan, but he had no idea what it might be. Walking back to the cave's entrance, he noticed a narrow opening in the wall to his right. Squeezing through it, Zadok saw there was a depression in the floor that was large enough to place the chest. He carefully inserted the chest and covered the opening with a nearby rock that fit perfectly. No one who was not looking for something hidden would have reason to guess there was a sacred artifact hidden in the floor. Zadok was certain that he had found the hiding place *Yhahveh* intended for the chest.

Zadok rested, ate a meagre portion of dried venison, and drank some water. Then, as *Yhahveh* had instructed him, he took precise measurements of the distance to the cave from various locations. Finally, he drew a picture of the boulder at the terminus of the cave that contained the jasper gemstone.

Before leaving Jerusalem, Zadok had taken books, records, and other items from the office of the high priest. Among the items he had selected were two pieces of the finest leather, as well as two small cylinder-shaped ornaments made of bronze. Now, sitting in the sunlight at the entrance to the cave, he wrote identical messages on each piece of leather. On one side, he drew the coordinates of the map. On the other side, in a fine Paleo-Hebrew script, he wrote that the map led to the chest that held the sacred breastplate and vestments of the high priest. He added a warning: It was forbidden for anyone without the Levite birthmarks to open the chest. The punishment was certain and instant death. When he was finished, Zadok shaped his hands in the special configuration and placed them on the pieces of leather. The words, symbols, and lines on both sides were immediately encrypted. Only someone with the birthmarks would be able to decipher the message and the map.

Zadok tightly rolled up each leather manuscript. He inserted them into the bronze cylinders and, using special tools he had obtained in Aswan, soldered the caps onto the cylinders. He etched the word "breastplate," unencrypted, on the outside of each cylinder, as well as a tiny image of the hand configuration.

Zadok gave one of the cylinders to his Levite colleague, Izak; he instructed him to deliver it to Yechezkael, the head of the Jewish community in Hevron, one of the Judean towns to which Jews had fled upon the destruction of Jerusalem. Although it was no longer a politically important city, it was still the location of the *Ma'arat Hamachpelah*, the Cave of the Patriarchs, the holiest site in Judea, save for the ruins of the temple in Jerusalem.

Arriving in Hevron, Izak told Yechezkael that he had an urgent message from Zadok. Yechezkael was pleased that Zadok, the former high priest, had escaped the Babylonian carnage, but he wanted no part in any conspiracy to resist the conquerors. The Judeans would have to await *Yhahveh*'s deliverance, even if millennia might pass.

"Relax, my friend. I am not here to foment a revolt," Izak assured Yechezkael. "I seek your help in making sure that future generations can rebuild our land when *Yhahveh* decides it is time."

Following the script that he had rehearsed with Zadok, Izak recounted how they had saved the magical breastplate used in the temple.

"This cylinder, which Zadok has sent you, contains directions to where he has hidden the breastplate. Zadok says it could be many generations before *Yhahveh* will choose someone to read the message and allow the breastplate to be found. For now, Zadok has asked that we conceal this cylinder in the Cave of the Patriarchs."

Yechezkael agreed to Zadok's request. He led Izak to the grotto and down a corridor. Then he hid the cylinder in a crevice above the opening where Avraham had stored the chest over a thousand years earlier. He was surprised when Izak began chanting a prayer for the dead and dying. A moment later, he saw that Izak was holding a sharp knife. Before he could ask why, Izak took a quick step closer, then plunged the knife deep between Yechezkael's ribs and into his heart. Yechezkael died instantly. Izak then drank the poison in the capsule Zadok had given him and fell to the ground. The two men lay dead, side by side. No one aside from Zadok would ever know where and why they had disappeared.

Zadok placed the second cylinder inside the new temple, inside the Holy of Holies, within the replica of the Ark of the Covenant. Zadok had now completed the complex set of tasks that *Yhahveh* had commanded him to execute. He had no idea what the end result of his efforts would be. All he could imagine was that at the right time, the right person would appear to find and decipher the scrolls in one or both of the cylinders. That person would follow the map, retrieve the breastplate, and carry on as *Yhahveh* directed.

Egypt fell to the Persians in 525 BCE. The Jews had been allies of the Persians. One hundred eleven years later, when the Egyptians revolted and briefly regained control, they persecuted Jewish communities, including the community on Elephantine Island. They destroyed the Jewish temple Zadok had built, but the metal cylinder survived in the ruins. Four hundred years later, the cylinder found its way to a shelf of uncatalogued items in the Jewish section of the Great Library of Alexandria.

A unique repository of some forty thousand ancient documents and artifacts, the library deteriorated over several centuries from fires, theft, and lack of funding. Many of the scrolls and books in the Jewish section, including the mysterious cylinder, were saved by the family of Joseph Marxus, a Greco-Jewish scholar in Alexandria. In the year 120 CE, Demetri Marxus, a great-grandson and Greco-Jewish scholar in Alexandria, transferred a large number of the texts and artifacts, including the cylinder, to the chief rabbi of the Ben Ezra Synagogue in Fustat, a town to the south of present-day Cairo, where a new Jewish community had been established.

All that the Marxus family knew about the cylinder was that it was very old and, at some point, had found its way to the Great Library. Judging from the one word, "breastplate," etched on the cylinder, they thought it might have something to do with the breastplate of the high priest in Solomon's Temple. They knew that such cylinders had been used in Judea hundreds of years earlier to secure important scrolls. But not being Levites, they felt prohibited by the etched word, and by the hand configuration, from breaking open the cylinder.

The cylinder rested in the Ben Ezra Synagogue for some seventeen hundred years until it was discovered in 1896 by Rabbi Solomon Schechter, a lecturer in Talmudic and Rabbinic studies at Cambridge University. Friends had given him a page in Hebrew, which they said came from the synagogue's storage room. He recognized the manuscript as a page from the Wisdom of Ben Sira, written between 200 and 150 BCE. It was a major find for biblical scholars. For nearly one thousand years, the only known versions were in Greek, and Greek translations of ancient Hebrew texts were notoriously imperfect.

Schechter raised the necessary funds to travel to Fustat and spent most of 1896 working in the confines of a ten-by-fourteen-foot room filled with layers of dust and all manner of documents, including old Torah scrolls and religious artifacts. What Schechter identified in his "sacred trash bin" were some three hundred thousand Jewish manuscript fragments, the largest and most diverse collection of medieval manuscripts in the world. The room and its contents became known as the Cairo Genizah, the word *genizah* in Hebrew meaning "hidden." Buried under a pile of manuscripts, Schechter found the ancient cylinder created by Zadok.

Schechter transferred the bulk of the Genizah materials, including the cylinder, to Cambridge University. On returning home, he arranged for an expert to remove the soldered cap, revealing there was a scroll tucked inside. He extracted the scroll. The leather was still soft and flexible. He had examined other leather samples from ancient Judea that matched the one in the cylinder. He dated the leather approximately to the time when the First Temple was destroyed in 586 BCE. The Paleo-Hebrew letters making up the etched word breastplate on the cylinder also matched the lettering used in contemporaneous writings.

The leather had been very carefully cured, subjected to a so-called fatliquoring process whereby oils were reapplied to leather to achieve exceptional suppleness and durability. Shechter had the leather placed between two glass plates, which were expertly taped together. But despite his repeated efforts, he was unable to decipher the writings or symbols on the scroll. He allowed the best scholars that he knew to examine the scroll. They also failed.

Schechter died in 1915, but in his will, he requested that certain of the Genizah objects, including the cylinder, be donated to the new university being planned for Jerusalem by the World Zionist Organization. Cambridge complied with the request and transferred the materials to the Hebrew University when it opened in 1925. In 1965, the Hebrew University gave the cylinder and the glass-enclosed scroll to the newly established Israel Museum.

10

Young Man Goes West

Daniel was tormented by his experiences in high school. It was not just that he insisted on wearing Duoderm patches to cover his birthmarks. Miriam told him that his friends would accept that he had strange birthmarks, but Daniel knew better than his mother how boys his age behaved. He would rather suffer ridicule for the patches than be labeled a freak. Fortunately, the birthmarks were so small that they were almost impossible to see from more than a couple of inches away. The patches eventually became an accepted fact of who he was, like the hearing aid his classmate Joel wore.

Far more troubling were his nightmares about Nathan's death. Perhaps his dreams depicted what had actually happened? But the images vanished as soon as he woke up, gasping for breath. When Miriam mentioned the "tragedy"—the phrase she still used—his stomach would seize up with agonizing pain.

Daniel's insular, self-protective nature kept him from developing normal social relationships. Daniel's sister, Leah, was busy with her active social life. She cared for Daniel and even had her friends set him up with their younger sisters. None of the dates ever worked out.

Daniel's distress was reflected in bouts of depression and panic. Both Miriam and Daniel's teachers were increasingly concerned about his mood swings. He began meeting with a therapist, who referred him to a psychiatrist. He was diagnosed as likely suffering from PTSD due to his experiences when Nathan died. The psychiatrist prescribed Imipramine and Prozac for depression and Klonopin for anxiety. The medications helped, but what also enabled him to survive his painful high school years was his obsession to "find answers."

Daniel surprised his mother when he asked for his grandfather's library of five thousand books. They covered everything from history and religion to science and math, and any other subjects that had piqued his grandfather's eclectic interests. Miriam reluctantly agreed to store the books on shelves in the basement of their house. Daniel set up a comfortable space for himself and spent many hours reading and contemplating the kinds of existential questions that he could not ask—or expect to be answered—at the Jewish high school he attended.

Dr. Fern Kreinen, the librarian at his school, became an invaluable mentor. She was a widow with grown children who had great empathy for Daniel. She saw his sadness and loneliness but also recognized his promise. To some extent, she gave him the mothering that Miriam had withheld from him ever since Nathan's death. Daniel trusted her. Apart from his therapists, she was the only one in whom he fully confided. When Daniel finally showed her his birthmarks, Kreinen, an ultra-Orthodox Jew, saw the marks as a sign that God had chosen Daniel for a divine destiny.

Based on his research of the medical literature and discussions with physicians, Daniel understood that the chances of someone being born with his birthmarks—the same birthmark on both shoulders—were so remote as to be impossible. There was yet a further mystery. None of the hundreds of pictures of the high priest's breastplate in books and on websites included the Paleo-Hebrew letters for *Yhahveh*, ᕦᕒᕦᕒ, that Daniel had included in his drawing without even realizing that he had written in the ancient Hebrew alphabet. Neither did any of them portray the hand configuration on the top and bottom of the picture. By the end of his senior year, his search had yielded a great deal of fascinating information, but no answers. As to Dr. Kreinen's optimism that Daniel had been chosen by God for a sacred mission, Daniel could not find solace in a theory that presumed the existence of an Old Testament–like divinity. He read the New Testament and the Koran and various books on Christianity and Islam. He thought Christianity's Trinity, a concept not found in the Gospels, was too close for comfort to polytheism, and he saw little theological difference between Allah and *Yhahveh*.

Daniel received perfect SAT scores and achieved the highest GPA of his classmates. Expecting him to apply to the top universities, Daniel's mother, college counselor, and teachers were shocked when he refused to even fill out any applications. Miriam was furious and embarrassed by his decision; but she couldn't change his mind. *Poor woman,* the college counselor thought. *Losing first her son and then her husband. And then all of Daniel's difficulties. It's hard to imagine her pain.*

His counselor needn't have worried that Daniel would become an aimless dropout. Daniel had long fantasized about what he would do after high school. Before he continued his search for answers, he needed to get away from the cloistered atmosphere of the yeshiva, the Jewish day school he had attended from first grade through high school. Thanks to his father's will, money was not a problem.

And so, the day after graduation, barely eighteen years old, Daniel threw out his anxiety medication and took off on a brand-new BMW motorcycle. He rode cross-country to meet up with a member of Sum-Et, a mountaineering fraternity centered around Mount Hood and Mount Rainier in the Cascade Mountains in Washington State.

Daniel leased a room near Paradise Lodge at the foot of Mount Rainier and embraced the climbing culture. He trained for two years to be a mountaineering guide. When he wasn't busy learning and practicing his climbing skills and scaling Rainier and adjacent mountains, Daniel studied orienteering and became an expert with a topographical map and compass. He also became an accomplished archer and bowhunter. He went off the grid for many days, camping and hunting at remote mountain locations. He could hit a rabbit at twenty-five yards with his bow. He learned how to field dress, skin, and butcher the deer and other game he killed. He shot nothing he or his friends would not eat. The all-consuming physical and mental demands of these activities overcame his panic attacks far better than any of his medications. Daniel finally found peace of mind. He found friends from all walks of life who accepted him.

Before he left, he had packed up several hundred of his grandfather's books and had them shipped ahead to Paradise Lodge, where they were waiting when he arrived. They were a bridge to a Jewish identity he still cherished and a means of continuing his effort to understand the mystery of his birthmarks and the other seemingly unnatural events that had confronted him. He knew his time in the Pacific Northwest was just a pause in his search for answers. He was in no rush. As his grandmother Gusma had often said, "When it's time, you'll know."

Daniel was a shade over six feet tall, slim, and fit at one hundred eighty pounds. His left hand was constantly pushing back a lock of hair that fell over his hazel-colored eyes. His deep baritone voice was a great asset in conversation. Many women discerned Daniel's special qualities. But sooner or later, his relationships fizzled. The women all had the same complaint. "He wasn't present enough; there was a lack of commitment." As one woman wrote to him, "You're a treasure, but it's locked in a safe, and you won't—or can't—share the key."

11

Men and The Mountain, Brothers Again

The genesis of the name Disappointment Cleaver was shrouded in mystery. It referred to the spot on Mount Rainier, 12,300 feet above sea level, at the edge of the Nisqually and Ingraham Glaciers in Washington State. Climbers might not have known the origin of the name, but they had no difficulty understanding the location's significance. Many exhausted climbers, disappointed because they couldn't push on to the summit at 14,400 feet, descended from that spot to Camp Muir at 10,000 feet and then to base camp at Paradise, at 4,500 feet.

It was June, the first of the three months during which climbers most often tried to summit Rainier. Daniel had been in the Pacific Northwest for five years and had been working for the last four years as a guide for RMI Adventures. On this day, he was leading a group of seven climbers on a rope team. They had hiked up a day earlier to Camp Muir. The weather service had predicted a sunny day. It was 1:00 a.m., a good time to begin the summit climb, because the snow would be solid. They would reach the summit in five to six hours. Once the sun was up, some areas would turn slushy, creating potentially dangerous climbing conditions.

The climbers on this day ranged in age from seventeen to sixty-five. The slope was steep at the massive rock marking Disappointment Cleaver. Guides had hammered pitons into the rock so that climbers could rope in and rest securely. Anything—or anyone—not properly secured risked sliding thousands of feet down the sixty-degree slope.

Daniel never tired of observing the scene.

The sun was peeking its head over the horizon. By a trick of vision, a crescent moon seemed close enough to reach out and touch. Lit up by the rising sun, moon, stars, and the headlamps worn on the foreheads of the team members, the glacier presented an otherworldly environment.

At this height, Daniel experienced physical and spiritual bliss. It was what drove serious climbers to endure the pain, exhaustion, and danger of climbing to treacherous peaks.

He chewed on a Baby Ruth bar and drank water. Dehydration at high altitudes was a killer. Even experienced climbers could become disoriented and take dangerous risks. Two days earlier, the team had participated in a five-hour training drill. On a moderately steep slope, they had formed a rope team and practiced the "self-arrest." Each team member took a turn falling and beginning a rapidly accelerating slide on the slick snow. They were taught how to twist their bodies around and, facing the slope, strike the pick of their ice ax deep into the snow, raise their knees, and dig in their crampons. Then they practiced how to react upon hearing the panicked call, "Falling!" Each team member would immediately fall to the ground and dig in. The entire team would be the anchor for the person falling, whether or not he or she successfully self-arrested.

Daniel secured each member to the rope line by a two-foot length of nylon webbing known as a sling, which he tied to the climber's harness with a locking carabiner. Whenever he led a team, Daniel told the story of Marty Hoey, a world-class climber who had led over one hundred ascents of Rainier. Attempting to be the first American woman to summit Everest, she succumbed to altitude disorientation and, after a rest stop, failed to properly re-secure her harness. The harness came loose, and she fell six thousand feet to her death.

It was an ending that Daniel's team member Raymond Pierce, a billionaire movie mogul, was precipitously close to re-enacting. He had unhooked the carabiner that attached his harness to the rope line. Daniel had seen it happen before. Disoriented climbers who needed to relieve themselves found it hard to maneuver while they were tied to a rope line. Some of them panicked. Most climbers bought modern climbing apparel, which had front and rear sections they could easily unzip. If you had to go, you went. Some climbers wore diapers. But there was one overriding rule on this kind of climb: You never took yourself off the rope. Daniel had repeatedly lectured the team to talk to him about problems or concerns that could affect the climb. Pierce, however, who had the money to buy an entire brand of sophisticated climbing equipment, wore a style of woolen pants that could have been advertised in a nineteenth-century Sears Roebuck catalogue. He was out of breath, gasping for air as he struggled in humiliation.

Daniel watched in horror as Pierce lost his balance and began a fatal slide. Daniel yelled "Falling!" As the entire team fell to anchor themselves, Daniel dove down the slope, reaching for Pierce's flailing hand or the loop on his pack. He prayed his team was properly executing the arrest maneuver. If not, his weight, combined with Pierce's if he could grab hold of him, would drag the entire team down the mountain. He suddenly realized that Pierce seemed clearly beyond his reach. It was then that Daniel saw his arm begin to glow and extend its length, allowing Daniel to grab the webbed loop at the top of Pierce's backpack. He gripped it tightly. He looked at his arm and saw nothing unusual.

He had no time now to think about the strange event that had allowed him to hook onto Pierce. The rope team was now straining to hold two people, who together weighed over four hundred pounds. But the line held.

Daniel screamed at Pierce, "Don't move! Not an inch!"

He reached down with his free arm, grabbed one of the carabiners he carried on his belt and slapped it onto the loop of Pierce's pack. Then he slammed his own ice pick into the snow to add further strength to the team's effort. It took several long minutes for Daniel, screaming instructions nonstop, to help Pierce and himself crawl their way back to the security of the anchored team and the rock.

The team reassembled and rested against the huge outcropping. Daniel was breathing hard, soaked with sweat, and trembling at the dangers he and his team had faced—the risks he had exposed them to. He could have dragged the entire team into a death slide. *Did I do the right thing?* In such situations, there was no time to think. Guides had to trust their training and react instantly in extreme situations.

Furious, Daniel said loudly, "Stupid freakin' idiot."

Pierce heard nothing. His body was wobbling and shaking, and he was gasping for breath. Daniel, his professionalism taking over, pulled out a canister of oxygen, set the flow, and gave Pierce the mouthpiece. Then he put his arm around the billionaire. As if speaking to a child, he said as calmly as he could, "Raymond, we're all here with you. You're safe now. You understand? You're safe. Just relax, you'll be fine."

Pierce, sucking on the oxygen, began to come around. He nodded that he had heard Daniel. Daniel kept his arm around Pierce and sat with him. Checking for signs of serious shock and injury, he asked a series of questions to which Pierce was able to respond. He was basically all right. His eyes were focused. His dangerously rapid breathing and heart rate were beginning to slow. To the team's great relief, Daniel announced that Pierce should be fine.

Daniel hurried to bundle Pierce up in two sleeping bags and used locking carabiners to secure him to two of the fixed pitons anchored deeply in the rock. Along with some food bars and two large canteens of water, he stuffed a bunch of hand warmers into Pierce's pants and inside his soaking, layered sweaters.

Pierce was in no immediate danger. It was not uncommon to wrap up and secure an exhausted or sick team member in this way. Using his satellite phone, Daniel called headquarters. They would pick up Pierce by rescue helicopter in less than one hour and medevac him to Seattle's Swedish First Hill Hospital for a thorough examination and any treatment he might need.

Some weeks after he returned home, Pierce wrote personal notes to Daniel and each team member. When Daniel got Pierce's letter, he hoped the mogul wasn't sending money. He was pleased to find only a very gracious, handwritten thank-you note, including a quote from the Talmud.

"Whosoever saves a life, it is ascribed to him as if he hath saved an entire world."

Daniel had personally interviewed and approved every member of his climbing teams. After reading Pierce's humble note and knowing how hard Pierce had trained for the climb, Daniel stopped second-guessing his decision to accept him as a team member.

At the time, after securing Pierce, Daniel could only guess at the emotions gripping his team. He had an obligation to them to continue to the summit. Some of them had used precious savings to make the trip. They had all trained for months and knew the risks, including the possibility of being wrapped up and left for a helicopter pickup. And they were aware of how they could be dragged down the mountain if someone lost his or her footing. They were a good team; they had bonded well over the past three days. Pierce had been a strong member until he had apparently become disoriented by the high altitude.

It was an experience none of them would ever forget. But they'd been at Disappointment Cleaver for almost an hour. Daniel would have to push them now, given the shortened time to sunrise.

Despite temperatures below zero, the climbing had created so much body heat and sweat that the climbers carried their heavy parkas in their backpacks and wore them only at rest stops. Too much body heat got trapped when a climber wore a heavy parka while climbing, quickly leading to exhaustion and, in extreme cases, hypothermia. But taking one's parka off when it was time to resume the climb exposed accumulated sweat to the exceptionally dry air at high altitude. The sweat quickly evaporated, chilling the body.

Daniel had already discussed this issue with the group, but he felt now was a good time to remind them of what they faced if they chose to continue.

"As I've told you a number of times, your body temperatures are now way below what they were when we stopped. As soon as you remove your parkas and we start to climb, you will feel so cold you will want to beg me to go back. That's just the way it is. Now, does anyone want to wait for the helicopter with Pierce?"

No one raised a hand.

"Okay, for the next ten minutes, while we climb and warm up, we need to be disciplined and strong in our commitment to ourselves and one another. You're a great team. I have no doubt we will make the summit."

Anika Taloosah, a tall, striking, extremely fit forty-five-year-old woman from Ghana, shouted, "*Bari mu tafi!*" She had called out the phrase, which meant "Let's go!" on several occasions during training and the climb. Now, the entire team raised their ice axes like soldiers raising their rifles upon the battle cry and shouted along with her.

Climbers, like skiers, used a method known as the duck walk: Both feet pointed outward, splayed at an angle, so that the entire foot was placed on the ice. Climbers also practiced the "rest step" along with "pressure breathing." After each step upward, the climber rested for a second, sucked in a breath, and forcefully blew it out. For many, climbing in this way became a meditative experience.

They were climbing straight up a slope at vertical angles ranging from forty to sixty degrees. Even when climbers used the rest step and pressure breathing techniques, their need for oxygen at these altitudes outpaced its supply. Every step was agony.

Daniel was in top physical condition. He steeled himself against the freeze he would feel upon storing his parka. Pleased to see the team's determination and enthusiasm, he took his first step. He shouted the prearranged signal for resuming the duck walk: "Quack!"

But as he took that first step, time froze. It seemed to Daniel as if the members of the rope team stood as motionless as statues. Astounded, he saw before him a holographic image of Nathan, dressed in the regalia worn by the high priests in the ancient Jewish temple in Jerusalem. Nathan reached out his hand and touched Daniel's forehead, flooding Daniel's mind with a vision of Pierce falling. In the vision, Daniel's arm was not long enough to grab hold of Pierce, and Daniel watched helplessly as Pierce fell thousands of feet to his death. *It's true*, Daniel thought. *I knew that my arm was nowhere near long enough to reach Pierce. But then my arm glowed, and I was able to grab hold of his pack. Nathan elongated my arm!*

The vision then morphed into the image presented in Daniel's long-ago Yom Kippur dream: Nathan, standing in front of a cave on an island by a broad river, next to a tall woman, her face obscured. He was dressed in the regalia of the Jewish high priest and held a set of eighteen stone tablets. The apparitions grew dim and faded away. Daniel was back on the mountain, ready to recommence the climb with his team. During the rest of the way to the summit and back to Paradise, Daniel pondered what these visions meant. But he had an inkling. Nathan was sending him a message: *You need to move on.*

Daniel knew it was true. His visions were proof that he was either mad or had been born for a special purpose. He didn't think he was crazy. He understood, however, that he was different from other people. He had the physical marks to prove it. He could no longer hide behind breathless vistas and life-threatening experiences. He recalled one of Nathan's favorite Bible stories–the one about Jonah, the insubordinate Jewish prophet who sought to avoid God's summons to travel to Nineveh. He had been ordered to warn the city of its impending destruction if it did not change its wicked ways. Rather than travel to Nineveh, Jonah boarded a ship going in the opposite direction. God called forth a great storm. When Jonah's shipmates discovered he was running away from his god, they were sure that he was the cause of their perilous condition, and they threw him overboard. The sea immediately calmed. A whale swallowed Jonah and transported him to the shores of Nineveh, where the humbled prophet delivered God's message.

Maybe Nathan put the memory of the story in his head. Regardless, on the descent that day on Mount Rainier, Daniel understood it was time for him to move on, to resume his quest for answers.

When the team finally reached Paradise Lodge, Daniel took them to the "summit room" for a celebratory toast. He told them Pierce had been taken to a local hospital for observation. So far, he seemed to be fine.

Daniel, glass raised, said what everyone was thinking.

"You are all champion climbers. You all know that only a tiny percentage of the population would ever attempt to summit this mountain. You all know that many have died trying. What you might not know is that only half of those who try succeed. I saved that statistic for you until the end. And at this moment, your bodies are telling you why."

"You will remember today for many reasons. But far more important than your physical accomplishment is that all of us, together, saved a team member from a terrible fate. And so, my friends, to your health and to a blessed life. As they say in Hebrew, *L'chaim*! To life!"

He raised his glass, as did everyone else.

As the gathering was breaking up, Anika, the beautiful woman from Ghana, came over to Daniel. She lightly touched and then gently gripped his arm and whispered, in a conspiratorial tone, "Are you Jewish?"

"Yes, imagine that, a Jewish jock," Daniel said, smiling.

Anika's grip tightened suggestively. Smiling broadly, she whispered in Daniel's ear, "I think I've only met Israelis, who I've assumed are Jewish. But they never helped me save someone's life and climb a mountain of ice."

"Well," said Daniel, acutely aware of Anika's intimate gestures, "that whole scene was a first for me too. You never know what can happen up there."

The champagne had enhanced the natural high Daniel was still experiencing from the climb. Anika began to gently caress his arm and Daniel felt enveloped by her intoxicating aroma, a mix of sweat and a hint of a cologne Daniel did not recognize. Anika then put her arms around Daniel's neck and kissed him lightly on the mouth. If Daniel were to observe the prohibition on intimate fraternalization with clients during the typically two-day climb, he would have to break off now. But, with the climb itself over, Daniel felt free and happy to put his arm around Anika's waist and guide her to the private room to which he was entitled as an RMI guide. In the morning, she was gone. She left a warm note and a business card. Daniel was both surprised and impressed that he had spent a passionate night with the deputy foreign minister of the Republic of Ghana.

12

Recollections Recorded, Memories Revived

Standing at Disappointment Cleaver, with the promise of dawn on the horizon, forty-year-old Lloyd McBride was having the best day of his life. He couldn't imagine ever again experiencing such exhilaration. He was fatigued but confident in his ability to carry on to the summit. He lived in Yakima, just ninety miles southeast of Mount Rainier. On a clear day, he could see the massive mountain through his windows. He'd dreamed of summiting the mountain from the time he and his wife had moved to the area. This past year, he'd finally had the time to train.

He pressed the camera icon on his iPhone and hit the video button. He slowly turned around in a circle, wanting to get the full panorama. He touched the button for "2x" to get a close-up of the members of his climbing team. He focused for a moment on their leader, the impressive Daniel Ornstein, then swung the camera lens around, recording images of each of his team members. When he focused the camera on Raymond Pierce, he recorded a video of Pierce breaking his link to the rope line. McBride would have captured more of the moment but for Daniel's yelling "Falling!"

McBride had attached his iPhone to his parka by a safety cord. He let it go as soon as he heard Daniel yell. Along with the other members of the team, he dropped to the ground, slammed the pick of his ice ax into the snow, brought his knees to his chest and pressed his crampons into the snow as hard as he could. He felt an enormous pull as Daniel grabbed Pierce. The team had executed a flawless arrest maneuver.

Lloyd McBride was a mild-mannered individual, a pharmacist by trade. The experience he had just witnessed, in which he had been an active participant, felt like a punch to his stomach. Before he could get back on his feet, he was violently ill. He wasn't the only one. It was traumatic to experience up close the border that so casually separated life and death. McBride picked up his wet phone and put it into his soaking wet pocket. He said little for the rest of the climb and declined to join the team for the traditional champagne toast at Paradise's Summit Room. He thanked Daniel and took an RMI-embossed card with Daniel's cell number. Then he got into his pickup and drove home to Yakima.

When he stepped out of the truck, he realized how exhausted and achy he was.

Leaving all his equipment in the truck, he went into the kitchen, grabbed an ice-cold Olympic beer, and then plopped down on his favorite chair in the living room. A second Oly quickly followed the first. He knew drinking alcohol in his condition would completely wipe him out, but he didn't care. He stripped off his clothing, took a long, steaming hot shower, and fell into bed. He immediately dropped into a deep sleep. He didn't hear his wife, Elizabeth, when she came home and called his name. When she got no response, she went upstairs to their bedroom, where he was fast asleep. She covered him with a warm blanket and gave him a loving kiss on his forehead.

The next morning, over a leisurely breakfast, McBride told Elizabeth about the events he had experienced. Then he went to clean up his equipment. His iPhone was still attached to his parka. He tried turning it on, but it was dead and remained so even after he charged it for two hours. Eager to view his pictures from the climb, he took the phone to a nearby Apple store.

"Water damage," said one of the staff.

"But you can fix it, can't you?" McBride asked. "Or at least retrieve the video?"

"Sorry, that phone is history."

McBride had no alternative but to buy a new iPhone. When he returned home, he tossed his dead phone into a drawer in his study, which contained an assortment of outmoded or dead computers, disk drives, phones, and other devices.

Two years after his Rainier summit climb, on a bright Sunday morning, Lloyd McBride was watching CNN when Wolf Blitzer announced that "billionaire movie maker Raymond Pierce was found dead today in his Hollywood Hills mansion. Sources tell us that Pierce apparently committed suicide by deliberately overdosing on a combination of sleeping pills and painkillers."

McBride was shocked by the announcement. How ironic that he and his fellow climbers had risked their lives for a person who would ultimately kill himself. He vividly recalled filming his team members and then dropping his iPhone to obey the command to fall and self-arrest after Pierce had unhooked himself.

His iPhone. Elizabeth knew a woman, Nanda Ronin, who had been one of Bill Gates's earliest hires at Microsoft. She'd retired at forty-five, invested her stock options wisely, and moved to Yakima to start a craft brewery. She loved beer and ale, and Yakima was known for the quality of its hops. Although Microsoft was a software company, Nanda was a supergeek and had become an expert on the intricate circuitry and microchips within computers.

Lloyd dug out the old iPhone from the drawer in his study. Elizabeth called Ronin, who graciously volunteered to come over and see what she could do. She showed up two hours later, carrying a toolkit.

The screws securing the iPhone's cover were incredibly small. Ronin had the correct size screwdriver and quickly took the phone apart. It was as she expected. The culprit was a metal connector that had shorted out when the phone got drenched by the snow and then spent hours in McBride's soaking-wet pocket. She took out a dead phone she had brought along and extracted a perfectly serviceable connector. Ronin didn't have any means to solder the part to McBride's old phone; instead, she used some mechanic's glue to hold the wires in place so she could determine whether the phone could be turned on. She could not reattach the phone cover, but that wasn't necessary to see whether the phone would work.

Ronin gently arranged the pieces and was immensely pleased when the phone flashed its startup screen.

"Lloyd, get over here. The phone is working."

"You have the magic touch," Lloyd said, surprised and impressed. "Now, we need to access the last video on the phone camera and email it to me. That way we'll have a copy even if the phone dies again."

Ronin knew exactly how to do what McBride wanted. McBride told her his email address, and within fifteen seconds, a copy of the video appeared in McBride's mailbox on his MacBook Pro.

The Pierce incident had received quite a bit of publicity, and Ronin was as eager to watch the video as Lloyd and Elizabeth McBride, but she'd have to wait. Her own phone rang with an urgent call from her brewery manager. A new worker had carbonated hundreds of newly capped beer bottles, and they were exploding at a catastrophic rate.

Settling down together on the couch, Lloyd and Elizabeth opened the video. It first showed an eerie panorama of moonlit snow. Then it slowly panned to various members of the rope team, each with a glowing headlamp. The video then focused on Raymond Pierce who had just worked himself free from the rope line and lost his balance. He seemed to be diving off the cliff. Daniel's voice, screaming "falling, falling!" could be heard in the background, followed by a jumble of scenes as Lloyd's phone fell to the ground. Fortuitously, the camera was still directed toward Pierce. The film showed Daniel hurling himself down after Pierce and stretching out his arm. But Daniel's arm was at least a foot short. And then, suddenly, Daniel's arm began to glow. The space between them disappeared. His hand latched onto the loop on Pierce's backpack.

"What the hell?" Elizabeth exclaimed. "That guy's arm just started to glow and got longer."

Lloyd McBride's astonishment took the form of stunned silence. He searched his mind to recall the scene his iPhone had recorded. But when the video was being recorded, he was in the process of self-arresting. He had not seen what the video had recorded. And now he could not believe what he saw.

They watched the video several more times.

"Can you get in touch with the guide?" asked Elizabeth.

Lloyd had saved Daniel's card in his desk drawer. He punched in his number.

Daniel sounded surprised to hear from McBride. "Are you calling about Raymond Pierce? I heard about it on the news."

"A tragedy," said Lloyd. "But that's not why I'm calling."

He explained how he'd recovered the footage from his cell phone and described what he and Elizabeth had just seen.

Daniel had never doubted his visions on Mount Rainier, but here was physical proof. Having no intention of sharing his history of visions, Daniel pretended to be mystified. He asked McBride to email him a copy of the tape and promised to call back.

Daniel watched the video several times over. Then he called McBride. "It's nothing, Lloyd. What you saw—what your phone recorded—is known as a light flash, a kind of visual phenomenon known to occur on the mountain at that time of day."

Lloyd was relieved to hear what sounded like a perfectly plausible explanation. But Elizabeth was not persuaded.

"Lloyd, there is nothing normal about the video," she said. "That man is lying."

McBride often teased Elizabeth about being a conspiracy nut. But after watching the video again, he was persuaded that Daniel's story couldn't be squared with what the video clearly showed: Ornstein's arm had glowed and grown longer. Elizabeth was right. Daniel Ornstein was lying.

"You know what I'm thinking, right?" Elizabeth asked.

McBride nodded.

Elizabeth's brother, Maxwell Binqus, was an eccentric billionaire who spent fortunes researching paranormal events. Binqus's Institute for the Study of the Unknown was world famous. Elizabeth felt certain her brother could come up with a more credible explanation than the guide, who was obviously hiding something.

She dialed her brother's private number. They hadn't spoken in some time, so they spent a few minutes chatting about their families. They agreed it had been too long since their last get-together.

"If only you didn't live so far away," Elizabeth said, as always.

"So true," her brother replied, not bothering to remind her that she was the one who had moved away from their native Massachusetts to live on the West Coast.

Elizabeth told her brother that the person falling down the mountain was Raymond Pierce, the media mogul billionaire who had just committed suicide, and that the RMI guide saving him was named Daniel Ornstein.

Binqus was happy to humor his sister's request. He sent the video to Pamela Jaffe, a senior science investigator at the Institute. When Binqus received her report two days later, he called Elizabeth and Lloyd. He did not like lying to his sister, but he confirmed Daniel's explanation that it was a visual distortion, typical for that time of day and elevation.

13

~~Billions, Only to Die?~~

T he "Reverend" Maxwell Binqus was not an ordained priest or minister. But he
didn't disavow the honorific title bestowed upon him by his loyal followers.
In just ten years after graduating with a PhD in history from the University of
Massachusetts, he had amassed billions of dollars as a nontraditional TV preacher. He
made no apologies for taking advantage of the wealth-generating opportunities that
capitalism offered. He had a talent for conveying the strength and relevance of the Bible's
prescriptions for a world defined by social justice.

Binqus grew up on a farm on the outskirts of Otis, Massachusetts. From the age when
he could first shovel manure and pull up roots, he was assigned precisely such jobs for
many long hours. He was sexually molested by his cousin and beaten without mercy by
his alcoholic father. His mother, a gentle, kind woman who provided him with a love
comparable in goodness to the evil dished out by his father, died when he was ten years
old. The one saving grace of his early childhood was his sister, Elizabeth, who was three
years older. When he was twelve and Elizabeth was fifteen, she ran away from home. She
lived with relatives, worked at various odd jobs, and eventually paid her way through the
University of California at Davis. She married a young pharmacist, Lloyd McBride, who
persuaded her to move to Washington State, where he could satisfy his fascination with
the outdoors, especially mountain climbing.

Growing up, Binqus spent hundreds of hours alone in a room high above the horse
stables. He loved history. There, in his little cubicle of solitude, he studied books he was
able to obtain thanks to the charity of his Methodist church and of local bookstores
making room on their shelves for the latest best sellers and VHS movies. He memorized
the Sermon on the Mount by the time he was five. Within the space of the next seven
years, he was able to recite by heart most of the Old and New Testaments, as well as
the U.S. Constitution, Declaration of Independence, and the "Four Freedoms Speech"
by FDR.

He started at Farmington River Middle School when he was twelve, skipped two
grades, lost his virginity to Gail Kasdan at the age of thirteen, went to high school in
the nearby town of Lee, graduated at sixteen, and, at seventeen years of age, married his
high school sweetheart, Josanne, also seventeen. They took over an empty cabin on the
outskirts of the farm. Josanne gave birth to the first of their four children seven months
later. When his father died, he sold half of the farmland he inherited and earned a

BA degree from nearby Amherst College in Springfield. He continued at the University of Massachusetts to obtain a PhD in biblical philosophy, writing his dissertation on the question of who was created in whose image—man in God's or God in man's.

Binqus was not a farmer. On the property, in addition to an experienced manager and overseer, he housed a large group of workers who planted and harvested the crops, milked the cows, and did everything else needed to make the farm profitable. Binqus made the farm into a showplace of modern farming methods. Of his many accomplishments, the farm was the only one that Binqus thought would have impressed his almost illiterate father, had he lived long enough to see it. Binqus often thought of the irony of his earning a fortune beyond what his father could have imagined. Then again, many great men and women had suffered through atrocious childhoods. Throughout his life, he would criticize himself for a failure of empathy for his father, whose cruelty was undoubtedly the result of a childhood filled with its own traumas.

The farm expenses barely dented Binqus's fortune. He poured his wealth into the Binqus Institute for the Study of the Unknown. It had a staff of fifty full-time, well-paid, dedicated researchers who pursued varied disciplines, including archaeology, linguistics, Egyptology, physics, genetics, and Old and New Testament studies. The Institute's mission was to investigate allegedly paranormal events, as well as possible truths and unrecognized phenomena embedded within mythologies, and to provide a forum for scholarly discussion and research. Binqus invited physicists, biologists. sociologists, psychologists, writers and poets, shamans, Buddhists, and scholars in other disciplines. The Institute was housed in a modern building on five acres near the farm. It had a circular court with stone tables and comfortable wicker chairs, surrounded by replicas of antique and modern statues and sculptures. On all sides were flower gardens and fruit orchards, creating an environment Binqus hoped would be conducive to contemplation and dialogue in the pursuit of wisdom. Consistent with his belief in *mens sana in corpore sano*—a healthy mind in a healthy body—guests and staff could swim in a glass-enclosed Olympic-sized swimming pool and work out in a fully equipped gym, which gave the feeling of being outdoors, even when the outside temperatures dipped into the single digits, as they often did in winter.

Binqus began paving his path to extreme wealth when he registered various .com and .org sites such as DivinityForU.com and HolyAssembly.org. His businesses expanded to include mass assemblies, first in person and then on television. He did not hide the fact that he was not ordained and had not even attended a seminary. Because of his huge, enthusiastic audiences, some mistook him for another television evangelical. He was nothing of the sort. Though he extolled the ethical teachings of the Old and New Testaments, he argued that organized religions were based upon superstitious beliefs and practices that had caused incalculable harm to humankind over many millennia.

The evangelical establishment anathematized him. But he did not back down. He explained and emphasized his views by discussing the evangelists' avowed objective of transforming the secular American republic into a Christian enterprise.

"I find it disheartening," Binqus said to a packed audience at a guest lecture he gave at the University of Massachusetts at Amherst, "to listen to various high-level officials talk about how they pray to Jesus Christ for policy guidance. What's wrong with that, you might ask? Well, my friends, it seems that these days God is talking to everyone—Catholics, Protestants, Jews, and Muslims. But the recipients of God's wisdom expound very different messages, which just so happen to agree with whatever their political agenda may be.

"My friends, if the old cliché were in fact true, I can guarantee you that the Founding Fathers have all turned over many times in their graves."

The principal architects of the American republic were deists; they embraced a philosophy that rejected the notion of a divinity who exercised power in the affairs of humankind. Thomas Jefferson went so far as to fashion his own version of the New Testament, using a razor and glue to eliminate all mentions of miracles. Jefferson explained that his Bible retained only, and I quote, the *'words coming from Jesus, which are as easily distinguishable as diamonds in a dunghill.'* And let's be clear. By 'dunghill,' Jefferson was referring to the stories of the resurrection, virgin birth, walking on water, raising people from the dead, and all the other miraculous events. Benjamin Franklin, Washington, Adams, and Madison all expressed similar views. Indeed, the Jefferson Bible was printed by the Government Printing House and distributed to every new member of Congress from 1904 to 1954.

"In his Second Inaugural Address, Abraham Lincoln said, 'Both the North and South read the same Bible, and pray to the same God; and each invokes His aid against the other.' It seems clear that for Lincoln, the belief that the same God could take sides in a human conflict was so absurd that he saw fit to mock the notion in arguably the most important speech of his life."

It was a deliberately provocative lecture. Some of those present were deeply offended. A large group stayed behind to voice their opinions, ask questions, and demand clarification. After Binqus's lecture was published in the *American Journal of Religious Traditions*, titled "Is God on Our Side?" evangelicals stopped donating to libraries that subscribed to the journal.

For Binqus, his successes and fame were bittersweet. It was one thing to preach what he believed was common sense and to remind people of the secular nature of the American Republic. It was an altogether different matter for him to reach some form of inner peace. Some part of him wished he could embrace the traditional view of God held by the major religions. The view, as the poet John Dunne, a fervent Catholic, wrote in 1609—that we "Die not. . . . One short sleep past, we wake eternally. And Death shall be no more; Death, thou shalt die." This was the view that sustained much of humanity for millennia—a belief in an afterlife. As Paul said in 1 Corinthians (15:32), "If the dead are not raised, let us eat and drink, for tomorrow we die."

But in Binqus's opinion, with science having confirmed the superstitious character of many beliefs concerning paradise, hell, resurrection, angels, and many other articles of religious faith, the belief in an afterlife was increasingly losing its power to elicit positive behavior during life. In the two thousand years since the writings of Paul, humanity has only increased its propensity to engage in murderous wars. World War II killed seventy million persons. How, Binqus would wonder, do you get people to believe in an afterlife of peace and joy in the face of human nature that shows no sign of changing. Especially when the ticket to heaven is not tied to good deeds but simply faith.

On the other hand, if Binqus lacked faith in a traditional deity that was active in the affairs of men and offered a joyous afterlife for believers in Jesus, he was infused with the most intense curiosity about what he called "mysteries in plain sight." How could it be that, by dividing the circumference of a circle by the length of its diameter—two numbers that are finite and knowable—you end up with an infinite, "irrational," number, *pi*, 3.141592653 . . . ? The same number, without end—without the possibility of an end. And then there were the mathematically and empirically proven facts—proven to the extent humans were able to prove anything—of quantum mechanics, of alternative universes, and "particular entanglement." These were not mythic stories of burning bushes or human resurrection. These were phenomena in plain sight, but beyond the capacity of the human mind to understand. *Were these the places where God was to be found?*

It was to the search for answers to these mysteries—and, more basically, to the question that men and women have been asking themselves for tens of thousands of years, *Why am I here, only to die?*—that Binqus devoted his life and fortune.

14

"You're Supposed to Be"

S hortly after what became known in climbing lore as the "Pierce incident," an elite group of climbers invited Daniel to join an expedition to climb Mount Aconcagua in Peru. At 22,837 feet, it was the highest peak in South America. Daniel declined the invitation. As much as he loved to climb, he'd been persuaded by the events on Mount Rainier involving Raymond Pierce that it was time to refocus his energies on the mysteries that continuously haunted him. For years, the mysteries revolved around the visions he'd had on Yom Kippur when he was ten years old. Now, with the visions on Mount Rainier and the message he discerned from Nathan to "go home," he knew it was time to re-engage in the quest he had put on hold when he graduated from high school.

Now twenty-three years old, Daniel decided that he would return to New York to attend New York University. It had excellent departments in physics and biblical studies. Given his stellar SAT scores, perfect high school GPA, compelling gap year experiences, and his excellent recommendations, his application for admission was granted right away. His oldest friend, Amos Rivlin, with whom he had stayed in touch, was now finishing his junior year at NYU. He had also chosen to chase a dream after high school, spending two years at an ashram in Santi Niketan, India.

Amos was delighted that Daniel would be returning and found him an apartment on Sullivan Street in Greenwich Village, where the NYU undergraduate campus was located. Daniel told Amos that he would be returning to New York at the end of July. The lease would start on August 1. Amos would be a senior during Daniel's freshman year. After graduation, Amos and Tamara, his Israeli fiancée, would get married. Amos would then make *aliyah* to Israel.

Ever since he'd joined RMI as a guide, Daniel had intended to invite Amos to come out to Rainier for a summit climb. Now would be the perfect time.

"Climb Mount Rainier?" Amos said. "I've done some rock climbing in the Gunks, but I've never done alpine climbing. I'd love to come out and see what you've been up to all this time. I have two weeks free in June. Would that work?"

"That would be perfect. It will be the experience of a lifetime. I'll take care of the gear and pick you up at the Seattle airport. In the meantime, you need to train your ass off. I know you work out, but this will test your limits."

"I'm in great shape, man," Amos said.

"Not for this, you're not. Trust me. I'll send you a training program. Make sure you follow it. It's your aerobic capacity, not just strength, that will be critical."

"Don't you worry, my friend. I won't let you down," Amos said.

After Amos got settled at Daniel's small cabin near Paradise Lodge on Mount Rainier, Daniel put him through the same two-day practice course he gave his clients. Watching Amos, he assessed that he would reach the summit, but not without serious discomfort. Daniel was comfortable that Amos had the physical strength to make it. The question was whether he could push beyond the profound urge to quit that so many exhausted climbers experienced during the grueling last two thousand feet of the climb. It was for all climbers, and would be for Amos, one of the most severe tests of willpower and courage they would ever confront. For a climber on a rope team, quitting in front of his fellow climbers would be a humiliating experience, and the fear of such humiliation was in such cases a critical impediment to quitting. Daniel hoped that this psychological factor would operate as powerfully in a situation where the climber stood to lose face only with his close friend. Or maybe it would operate more powerfully. Daniel hoped so, but his experience told him no.

When they reached Disappointment Cleaver, they put on their heavy parkas. Daniel showed Amos what had happened during the Pierce Incident. Amos was not so much engrossed by the vivid demonstration as he was by the difficulty he was having breathing. As always, Daniel carried bottled oxygen. But he had no intention of giving any to Amos to make the climb easier. In Daniel's view, the problem for fit but novice climbers on a mountain like Rainier was almost entirely mental. Climbing a steep, icy, alien-looking landscape was terrifying. Daniel thought Frank Herbert had it exactly right in *Dune*: "Fear is the mind-killer."

Whatever Amos had understood intellectually from Daniel's briefings, he was now absorbed by his extreme physical discomfort. *I should have trained harder, and I should have come out here earlier to adjust to the altitude*, he thought. *I'll try my best not to disappoint Daniel.*

He imagined Daniel, a Star Wars enthusiast, quoting Yoda's admonition to Luke Skywalker: "Try not. Do or do not; there is no try." But Amos also knew that it was not Daniel's probable disappointment that he was most concerned about. It was his own.

Once again, Amos felt the piercing cold when he put away his parka to resume climbing. Waiting for his muscles to warm him up was torture. Amos's moment of crisis came when they reached a final rest stop at 13,200 feet. They were 1,200 feet from the summit at a seventy-degree vertical angle, hard climbing at any altitude. Amos felt he could go no farther. His muscles were screaming with pain. There was no air to breathe. He was freezing, his willpower weakening with every step of the duck walk. And the steep slope at this height terrified him. He felt an emotion he'd never before experienced: the dread of imminent death.

His confidence was gone. He was nauseous with fear. *I just can't do it. Is there really shame in that?* Unwilling openly to admit that he was desperate to quit, he made exaggerated sounds of labored breathing, hoping Daniel would notice and take pity on him.

Daniel sat stone-faced, seemingly oblivious to his friend's sounds of anguish. He had seen dozens of climbers in Amos's exhausted condition. He understood the message

Amos was sending him with his moans. He'd expected this time might well come. He thought, *Now is Amos's critical moment.* And just as he'd also expected, Amos finally confessed his predicament.

"Daniel, I've reached my limit. I'm totally exhausted and terrified. I'm sorry, but I need to go down."

Daniel, his manner devoid of sympathy, stopped gnawing on a chunk of frozen Reese's Pieces. He put his thickly gloved hand on Amos's shoulder, looked him in the eye, and said the same words that his guide had used five years earlier, when he was on his first Rainier summit climb and had felt the same urge to quit.

"Of course you're exhausted and terrified. You're supposed to be."

Daniel handed Amos a water bottle and rose to his feet. Adjusting his harness and checking on the rope, he indicated that he was anxious to resume kicking steps in the snow, the unenviable job of the leader on a rope team.

Amos realized that Daniel had no intention of turning back. By his movements, Daniel was saying, "No way," and Amos could not bring himself to beg. Not yet, anyway. He was not bleeding through the nose or ears, like the climbers Daniel had told him about. And even those climbers had not quit just because they were exhausted. They had pushed on until the leader of the rope team assessed potentially fatal distress.

As Amos drank the water, the import of Daniel's message sank in: *I'm at 13,200 feet. Of course I'm exhausted. Of course I want to turn back. That's what I'm supposed to feel. It's normal. I will trust Daniel. There is no try.* Amos hauled himself to his feet.

They climbed slowly and silently for another hour. The only sounds were their loud breaths and the crunch of their crampons on the snow. The sun had risen and was providing blessed warmth. The methodical steps they were taking alleviated Amos's panic. Nothing and everything filled his mind as the alien environment, the excitement, the growing anticipation of reaching the summit at any moment, fueled a second wind.

Finally, the steepness of the mountain's pitch faded. Daniel proclaimed the words that Amos had tortured his body and mind to hear.

"Congratulations, my friend, you have summited the mountain. It's an accomplishment you will always remember and be proud of. And I'm truly proud of you."

Amos emerged from his climbing stupor. He looked up and saw the panorama of an enormous crater whose ridgeline was outlined in snow and ice. Below them were the rocky peaks they had surmounted. He was standing at the fifth highest spot in the continental United States. He turned to Daniel, who never tired of the sights and feelings one experienced at the summit. They hugged and rejoiced in the triumph of athletic success and the special love of comrades who had to trust each other with their lives through a perilous adventure.

They drank water and ate chocolate that was melted from being carried in the inside pockets of their steaming jackets. Amos snapped photos of climbers he could see below, antlike figures duck-walking their way up the glaciers.

Daniel had warned Amos, "The climb is only half over at the summit."

Amos soon understood Daniel's warning. The sun had warmed the snow, creating areas of slush. He had to bend forward and keep his weight over his boots. Four hours later, when they reached base camp at the Paradise Inn, Amos's knees were screaming with pain.

Daniel had helped hundreds of climbers who had experiences similar to those of Amos. He was proud of his friend. Amos thanked Daniel for a "mesmerizing" experience. They waited to celebrate fully until after they reached Seattle, a three-hour drive to sea level, where, after checking into their hotel, they enjoyed massages at the spa and twenty-four ounce "summit steaks" at the Metropolitan Grill. The next day, Daniel drove his utterly exhausted friend to the airport and then returned to Paradise.

15

Pathways Home

After finishing his senior year at NYU, Amos got married, and he and Tamara bought an apartment outside Tel Aviv and moved permanently to Israel. When Amos's father became terminally ill with cancer, Amos received a compassionate leave from his two-year mandatory service in the Israeli army. Amos and Tamara returned to New York and were at his father's bedside when he passed.

They spent time with Daniel, talking about their experiences in Israel, what it was like for Amos to go from being an American civilian to a member of the Israeli military, and how Daniel, was making out as a sophomore at NYU.

"It's hard not to enjoy the thousands of tourists, students, and the mix of shops in the Village," Daniel said. "But the truth is, I'm feeling isolated. I had a real close group of friends at Rainier. Although I grew up in New York, I have no interest in finding classmates from my days at the yeshiva. Going bowhunting takes time, which I don't have. And the climbing clubs in the city are amateurish, not to mention that the highest mountain within driving distance is Mount Washington in Maine, and it's thousands of feet smaller than Rainier and the other mountains in the Cascades."

"I understand," Amos said gently. "For years, you've been doing stuff that most New Yorkers don't do—climbing mountains, going to motorcycle rallies, hunting. But I have a piece of advice. As I was climbing that mountain with you—barely able to breathe, scared and exhausted—you told me, 'You're supposed to be.' And I would say that at this point in your life, with all you've been through, 'You're supposed to be'—confused, uncertain. You need some time to figure out what you want to do. You'll work it out. You'll reach your summit, whatever or wherever it may be. I have total confidence in you."

Amos described the joy he felt every time he landed at Ben-Gurion Airport in Tel Aviv. "You get off the plane, you smell the eucalyptus, everyone's speaking Hebrew. . . . If you have a Jewish consciousness, you know you're home. As a new Israeli citizen, I'm required to do army service for two years. It is incredibly hard for someone like me to get used to, but after a while, you feel even more connected, more a part of the society there. A crazy and dysfunctional society to be sure, but it's home."

Tamara joined Amos in encouraging Daniel to take advantage of NYU's Junior Year Abroad Program at the Hebrew University in Jerusalem.

"The two of you are very persuasive," Daniel said. "I'll definitely consider the idea."

Even during the five years he'd spent in the Pacific Northwest, Daniel continued to nourish his fascination with ancient mythology and Jewish history. He remained hopeful that some book, some footnote in one of the journals, some allusion, would trigger an understanding of his birthmarks and visions. After he had settled at his cabin near Mount Rainier, he arranged for the shipment of a few dozen books from the library he had inherited from his grandfather and was in storage in Brooklyn. He read and reread many of the volumes.

Daniel didn't find the Bible curriculum at NYU very challenging. He already knew much of what he was studying, except for the course about the Samaritans, in which he was given an assignment to write a paper about the Samaria Papyri. These were fragments of papyri dating from 350 BCE, found in a cave in the Wadi Dalia about ten miles north of Jericho in the West Bank, near Mount Gerizim where the Samaritans lived.

Daniel had been to Israel with his parents when he was seven years old. He had studied Hebrew in school and had gone on a four-week trip with his tenth grade class when he was fifteen. But those were parent and tourist visits when he was much younger. And he could not honestly say that he invariably enjoyed the time he was there. Nevertheless, Daniel was tempted to go. Sometimes, Dr. Kreinen had once told Daniel, "One has to wait for that special feeling in the gut that says you've made a profoundly good decision." Daniel was beginning to sense that feeling. His inexplicable birthmarks were signets of Kohanic royalty tracing back to the Jerusalem temples.

That spring, Daniel spent several days by himself, camping and bowhunting for turkeys in the Adirondack Mountains in northern New York. He thought best when he was alone in a wilderness setting. It didn't matter whether he had a successful hunt or even if he saw a target. Sitting up in a tree in his portable hunter's chair, he found the quiet—disturbed only the sounds of nature—meditative, often hypnotic. Time passed unnoticed. He didn't need to focus his thoughts. He would eventually fix upon a topic he wanted to consider. By the time he returned to Manhattan, he had decided to take Amos's advice.

Daniel resolved that the first thing he would do when he got to Israel would be to explore the Dalia caves himself. It would not be an easy trek. The caves were accessible only by traversing extremely rocky terrain.

He saw the expedition as a last fling before he hung up his harnesses, ice ax, and other climbing gear. When he discussed the idea with Amos on Facetime, his friend looked terrified. "Daniel, what you're talking about is insane and impossible. It's suicide. The area is deep in the West Bank, which, as you know, is controlled by the Palestinian Authority. It's protected by its well-armed, professional militia. They would welcome the chance to torture, maim, and kill a nice Jewish boy from New York who was found wandering in the Samarian hills. Or you'll be tortured, maimed, and killed by the Bedouins who've lived there since before the Israelites came three thousand years ago."

Daniel reluctantly concluded that Amos was right. To make such a trip on his own would be foolish. He would need official permission. "Okay, Amos, relax. I'm just gathering information."

Daniel thought about whether he knew someone who might have the clout to arrange safe passage for him. Over his years of guiding, he had collected hundreds of business cards and personal notes. He was looking through them when he came across the note and card given to him by Anika Taloosah, Ghana's deputy foreign minister. He smiled as he remembered the passionate night they had shared and that she'd urged him to visit her.

Daniel didn't know what to expect. But when Anika heard from Daniel that he'd like to arrange a video call, she immediately agreed. And when the call connected and they saw each other, they felt the same affection and passion they had shared on that special day at Mount Rainier. But Anika was disappointed when she realized that Daniel wasn't calling to plan a visit. When Daniel explained his plan, she burst out laughing,

"Daniel, you are really insane. But *me do wo*; it means, 'It's what I love about you. This will take quite an effort. But I'll do it—on one condition. If you survive your attempt, you must promise to come here for a visit. I will take excellent care of you."

"Anika, that's a promise I'm happy to make and fulfill."

"Let me see what I can do," Anika said. "And if you go, please don't risk your life again for some idiot like Pierce."

Days passed, and Daniel heard nothing from Anika. He abandoned his idea of trekking to the Wadi Dalia. He was making final preparations for his move to Israel when an envelope arrived at his apartment by messenger from the Office of the Consulate General of Ghana. It included a Ghanaian passport and relevant visas, all of which signified the agreement of Jordan and the Palestinian Authority to allow one Daniel Ornstein a four-day pass to travel to the Wadi Dalia. The documents required Daniel to sign several waivers, and Anika had included a playful love note which, as undoubtedly intended, made Daniel eager to see her.

He wasted no time. He canceled his flight to Israel and bought a round-trip ticket to Amman, Jordan, on his new Ghanaian passport and Jordanian visa. When he landed in Amman, he rented a jeep and drove to the location from which hikers and climbers approached the wadi.

Daniel was back in his Greenwich Village apartment ten days later. He wrote many pages in his high school notebook, detailing his trip. He then changed his travel plans again and flew to Ghana for two weeks of romance with the nation's deputy foreign minister. They stayed at the luxurious Royal Senchi Resort Hotel. Daniel was reluctant to leave. He had never before experienced such luxury and so much intense lovemaking. And if not for the experience he had at the Dalia cave, if not for meeting with the mysterious Bedouin named Sengrel, if not for the drawing Sengrel had left for him to find, he might have stayed longer. But now he knew he was on a track that might well provide what he called his "answers." He also knew it would not be fair to Anika. She was in love with him, but, as much as he adored her, he did not share the depth of her feelings.

At Ghana's Kotoka International Airport, they hugged each other tightly.

Daniel kissed her and said, "God bless you."

Anika responded, "And to you as well. *Awurade nhyira wo Nyame nhyira wo Onyankopɔn nhyira wo Yehowa nhyira wo.*" Daniel responded in Arabic, "*Inshallah,*" meaning "God willing." They parted, sharing the special smile reserved for joyful new lovers.

"Why in hell are you coming here from Ghana?" an incredulous Amos demanded to know when he picked up Daniel at Ben-Gurion Airport in Tel Aviv.

Daniel embraced his friend, smiled wickedly, and said, "Amos, let's go to that famous Tel Aviv bar you once told me about. This is a story you won't believe. To tell it properly, I need some tequila, which I doubt you have at home. And I want to know all about your experiences driving a tank in the Israeli army."

"Okay," Amos said. "Tamara is visiting her parents in Haifa. She'll be back tomorrow. You'll stay with us this weekend. I'll drive you to your dorm in Jerusalem. It's not far from where my unit is stationed."

They went to the Imperial Cocktail Bar on HaYarkon Street. Daniel ordered a double of Patrón Silver. Since Daniel insisted on paying, Amos ordered a double of Macallan's eighteen-year-old single malt whiskey.

"Now would you please tell me what you've been up to?"

While Daniel described his adventure, omitting the most personal details, Amos ordered another Macallan's, followed by a couple of Goldstar, Israel's most popular beer.

Daniel had never shared with Amos any of the mysterious events that he had experienced. He had never confided in Amos about his birthmarks. Now he refrained from telling Amos about his meeting and discussion with a man named Sengrel and the drawing Sengrel had left on the ground. Even so, it was quite a story. He told Amos about Anika, their night after the Pierce climb on Rainier, and how she had gotten him safe passage to the Wadi Dalia in exchange for Daniel's agreement to a man's wildest dream.

"You were right about the Bedouins. I don't think they would have been impressed by the documentation Anika gave me. I had to run and hide from a bunch of armed Arab herdsmen. I don't know what would have happened had this woman, Rayut, not shown up. She was part of the nearby Samaritan community. The Bedouins knew her and immediately retreated. In fact, Rayut had to decline their invitation for her and me to join them for dinner."

"Daniel, you seem to hit it off best with strange, alien women," Amos said, laughing. "What happened with Rayut?"

"It was nothing like that. She took me up to the temple at Mount Gerizim and introduced me to the Samaritan high priest, a man named Sanballat. He invited me to dinner and explained the history of the Samaritans, starting with Avraham's nephew Baasha, and their claim to be the authentic inheritors of the Mosaic religion. He said that the break with Judaism took place two thousand years ago, because the Samaritans would not abandon their claim that God had chosen Mount Gerizim rather than Jerusalem for His temple. Today, the sect has fewer than one thousand members and is facing extinction. He and Rayut were members of the governing Trio, the other being Yehoshaphat Aharoni, a doctor who works at the Hadassah Hospital in Jerusalem."

Daniel became reflective and said, "The community is in turmoil; you can feel their dread of disappearing, of sharing the fate of so many other long-extinct Jewish sects.

But they are not without hope. I attended their afternoon prayers. The Samaritans end their service with a prayer composed by the fourth-century Rabbi Baba ben Nathaniel. The prayer's doleful nature is tempered by its final optimistic refrain, repeated seven times: *'In His great wisdom and mercy, Yhahveh will gather us to this sacred mountain so that we may fulfill our holy mission.'*

"I am determined to learn more of the Samaritans and their struggle against extinction. I know very little about them. They're interesting, and their story is disheartening. The Jews and Samaritans, two ancient and blood-related peoples, should be united."

"Good luck with that; it would take a miracle," Amos said.

Although he couldn't believe that Daniel had knowingly violated dozens of domestic and international laws, Amos loved every word of the fantastic tale.

"Unreal! I can't wait for Tamara to hear this. Coming from anyone but you, I wouldn't believe one word myself."

Daniel thought back to when he found the location of the cave where the Samaria Papyri had been discovered. He was stunned to see an old man sitting in front of a fire at the entrance to the cave. Dressed in traditional Arab robes, the man had just finished cooking a meal. He'd filled a large wooden bowl with boiled rice that appeared to be saturated in some kind of oil or butter. A generous amount of boiled mutton was piled up on top of the rice.

The man picked up a jug of water and washed his hands. Then he offered the jug to Daniel and said, "My name is Sengrel. And you are Daniel, blessed of *Yhahveh*. Please eat with me. I knew you were coming and made enough for both of us. Our custom is to use only our right hand to take the food."

Without waiting, he dug his right hand into the food and rolled the rice into balls, in which he included a piece of mutton. Fascinated by Sengrel's comments and invitation, Daniel washed his hands and joined in the meal.

"I'm not used to eating with my hands," he said, "certainly not in the way you're doing. But I'll try."

Using only his right hand, Daniel scooped out some rice and ate it as best he could. Picking up pieces of mutton was easier.

"Who are you, and why did you call me blessed of *Yhahveh*?" he asked.

Sengrel did not answer immediately. He continued to roll the rice balls and eat the meat. Daniel ate enough to calm his hunger pangs and waited for this strange man to speak. When Sengrel was finished, he picked up another jug, took a long drink, and then offered it to Daniel. It was the most delicious milk Daniel had ever tasted and reminded him that Muslims didn't drink alcohol.

"My forebears came from ancient Midian. Before that, from Eradu, a city that was destroyed by an enormous rock, a meteor, in which the gods had embedded the holy stones and returned them to earth, into the hands of Ivri, your ancient ancestor. As he was, you are blessed of Yhahveh; and it is your destiny to provide humanity with a means to subdue its inclination to evil. You will also be the instrument by which the Samaritans will be saved."

Daniel was dumbfounded, as much by Sengrel's mystifying predictions as by the confidence with which he delivered the incredible prophecies. Daniel was about to speak when Sengrel held up his hand to signify "no questions." He then said, "You came to see the cave." Handing a torch to Daniel, he slightly bowed his head and said, "Go."

Daniel took the torch and went inside. The cave was very large, which made sense, because the Samaria Papyri suggested that, at times, many people had taken refuge in the cave. Daniel walked through most of the cave but found nothing. It obviously had been emptied of whatever artifacts or old papyri had been stored there.

Daniel was eager to resume his conversation with Sengrel. Who was Ivri? Where was Eradu? How can the Samaritans be saved? What possible role could he have in these mysteries?

But when he emerged from the cave, the old man was gone. The fire was out; the bowl, the jugs, were gone. There was nothing to reveal that a man had sat and spent time making a meal and eating and then purporting to deliver prophetic messages.

But there was one item on the ground that had not been there before—a fine piece of leather with a drawing on it. It was an exact duplicate of the drawing Daniel had made from his dream when he was ten years old, on the night they returned to Brooklyn after spending Yom Kippur with his grandmother. A drawing of a cave on an island by a broad river, a woman with her face obscured, and Nathan, standing next to her, dressed in the regalia of the Jewish high priest and holding a set of thin stone tablets. Daniel rolled the leather carefully and placed it in his pack. Later that day, when he reached in to examine the drawing, it was gone. Daniel was astounded and frightened that he had been made witness to yet another inexplicable event revolving around this drawing. On the other hand, he thought, *I'm clearly in the right corner of the world.*

Daniel knew that most people in Israel traveled by bus, both within and between the cities. But he was too independent and impatient to rely on buses as his primary means of transportation. Soon after settling into his dorm room on Mount Scopus, where the main campus of Hebrew University was located, he took the bus into the Muslim Quarter of the Old City, where he had been told the best bike shops were located. He bought a Vespa, an Italian scooter that was much smaller and far less powerful than the BMW K12100 he'd owned in the Pacific Northwest. In Jerusalem, with its crowded streets and narrow, hilly lanes, the Vespa made more sense.

Daniel had experienced his share of biking mishaps. There was the time he had totaled out on a Suzuki motorcycle on a winding road through the Cascades. Georgette, a member of his climbing group, had graciously volunteered her chalet while he recovered. She made him very comfortable and lovingly attended to his injuries—even after they had mostly healed.

Driving a scooter was different from driving a motorcycle, a lesson Daniel learned two weeks after he arrived in Jerusalem. The scooter's wheels were much smaller than those of a motorcycle. On his BMW, Daniel used the front brake ninety percent of the time to keep the center of gravity forward and prevent the front wheel from losing traction. On a scooter, the rider's weight needed to be somewhat more centered; the rear brake needed to be used slightly more often.

Jerusalem streets were slick in the evening, as the intense sun gave way to chilly desert nights. When Daniel took an especially awkward curve leading out from the university dormitories, he applied too much front brake. His back wheel skidded and threw him into a tree on the edge of a beautifully landscaped garden.

When he woke up, he found himself lying on a bed, an IV inserted into his left arm. He had a bad headache, his throat felt dry, and his back hurt. He slowly turned his head and discovered his first cousin, Varda Artzi, sitting next to his bed.

"Varda! Where am I?"

"Welcome to Hadassah Hospital," Varda said. "It's always good to see you, although you could have found a better way to let me know you'd arrived in Israel."

Varda was twenty-eight years old, married with two children, and a member of a religious kibbutz south of Tel Aviv. She'd grown up in Passaic, New Jersey, within easy driving distance of Brooklyn, and their families had frequently gotten together. Daniel and Varda had become close friends and regularly corresponded while Daniel was working at RMI.

"I was planning to call you, but I only got here ten days ago, and I've been busy settling into the dorm."

"And," interrupted Varda, "buying a Vespa instead of taking buses like everyone else?" She tried to sound stern, but the gentle hand she placed on Daniel's arm told him how delighted she was to see him.

Daniel suddenly realized that he was on his stomach, and his hospital gown was pulled down to his waist. As always, he felt extremely self-conscious about someone seeing his birthmarks, which he kept covered with round Duoderm patches. Lots of people used such patches to cover sores, small wounds, or ugly pimples and blemishes.

"Good thing you had my name and phone number in your wallet," said Varda.

A doctor in a white gown with a stethoscope hanging around his neck walked over to Daniel's bed. "I'm glad to see you're finally awake," the doctor said, speaking in English with an Israeli accent. "You had quite a fall. You're lucky not to have killed yourself."

The doctor was holding an iPhone. Daniel immediately became concerned that the doctor had taken pictures of his birthmarks.

"You have some bruises on your back and a Grade 3 concussion. You'll probably have a headache, and you might feel confused for a few days. I'll give you a prescription for extra-strength Acamol for your back. It's the equivalent of Tylenol, and it should relieve the pain. If it doesn't, you can page me at the number they'll include on your discharge papers. But stay off your feet, relax, and get someone to teach you how to ride a Vespa."

The doctor laughed, but Daniel wasn't amused. "We'll keep you overnight for observation. I'm sure you can be discharged tomorrow."

As soon as the doctor left, Daniel reached behind to his shoulders and checked that the Duoderm patches were in place. They were. It reassured Daniel. His injuries were concentrated in his lower back. The doctor did not see the marks. Daniel was too groggy and distracted to notice the name on the doctor's gown: Dr. Yehoshaphat Aharoni.

Daniel was discharged the next day and cabbed it back to his dorm. The doctor had been right about the pain in his back. Daniel took two Acamol and stuck the rest of the pills in his drawer. He'd had concussions before and knew that a lot of sleep and plenty of water were the best cure. Two days later, he felt well enough to retrieve his scooter. He was pleased to discover it hadn't suffered any mechanical damage. The crushed front fairing could be easily replaced.

16

Strange Bedfellows

lizabeth McBride didn't know her brother's office email address. She had sent the video to Binqus as an attachment to the Gmail address he said was for personal mail. She would have been shocked to learn of the precautions Binqus had taken to ensure that emails to his work address, and other communications to his office, were protected from interception by the most advanced encryption protocols available. They were at least equal to those used by the National Security Agency (NSA), the United States' famed electronic spy bureau. In fact, as a technological challenge to improve its own capabilities, the NSA was constantly attempting to crack the elaborate security of the Binqus Institute. They had easily hacked into Binqus's Gmail address but had thus far failed to unlock his office account. As Binqus was on the agency's watch list of potentially disruptive American "influencers" (a domestic surveillance activity of almost certain illegality), they monitored Binqus's Gmail and hoped people sent the same message to both addresses.

Elizabeth's email was intercepted by Tony Powers, an NSA agent with a long history in "black ops" and "wet work," the euphemisms used for off-the-books assassinations. He didn't care about politics. As far as he was concerned, all politicians were the same. Powers' focus was narrow but intense. He was a devout soldier of the evangelical movement known as Christian Zionism. He knew that many people thought he was crazy, but he didn't care. His truth was valid; theirs was not. They were destined to languish forever in the fires of hell.

Powers and his fellow evangelical Zionists insisted that the period of Rapture and Christ's Second Coming—when they would literally "meet the Lord in the air" on their way to heaven—depended on Jewish sovereignty over "Greater Israel." By this designation, they meant every inch of the area described as the Promised Land in the Old Testament: all the land occupied by the Palestinians on the West Bank, plus a fair amount of Jordanian territory east of the Jordan River.

Many people had commented on the strong support the evangelicals gave to the Haredi Jews. Ebenezer Albright, the famed professor of religious studies at Oxford, succinctly explained the curious alliance:

"The Haredi group of ultra-Orthodox Jews, together with extreme right-wing Zionists, have achieved political supremacy in Israel. Their number one goal is to achieve a Greater

Israel—to 'in-gather' all the Jews from the Diaspora, build a new temple, and restore a Jewish theocracy. They don't subscribe to the Second Coming of Jesus. But in the short term, these Jews are thrilled to get the help of the evangelicals in obtaining U.S. military and other assistance. The evangelicals seek the same short-term objective—the re-establishment of Greater Israel. And they are just as thrilled to have the Jews lay the needed groundwork for Jesus's return. When Jesus does come, the Jews who haven't accepted Jesus will go to Hell with the rest of the heretics, including every 'satanic' Catholic, Muslin, Hindu, atheist and agnostic. You may never find a stranger set of bedfellows."

The evangelical movement had worked for years to place its disciples in various positions of importance in agencies and departments of the U.S. government. Powers was a perfect example, as was his boss at the NSA, K J. Quinn, a former four-star admiral and its current deputy director.

All in all, several thousand evangelical Christian Zionists occupied positions of influence in the military and civilian agencies of the government. Through blogs, symposia, and conventions, these and other evangelical zealots were on the lookout for paranormal events that might herald the new era. Powers, sitting at a computer consul in the basement of NSA headquarters at Fort Meade, Maryland, was occupying himself with such searches while recovering from wounds he'd received during his most recent assignment in the field. The NSA's complex algorithms, which were partially based on work done by the Binqus Institute, allowed him to search millions of emails sent and received by governments, corporations, and individuals around the world. They flagged emails or attachments using words or terminology, or containing video frames, that matched the search parameters specified by the inquiring information officer.

Powers was about to light a cigarette, a violation of numerous agency and building ordinances, when his computer beeped and zoomed in on Elizabeth's message, instantly opening the video and displaying the picture of Daniel Ornstein's gleaming elongated arm. Powers was an operations man; although a true believer, he wasn't knowledgeable in the scholarly aspects of the evangelical theology. Quinn, he knew, had an encyclopedic knowledge of evangelical doctrine. He dutifully copied the video for Quinn, who would know whether the information was significant. Powers lit and sucked on his cigarette, wondering how many more painfully boring days he would have to suffer through before being allowed back in the field.

When Binqus received Debra Jaffe's report on Lloyd McBride's video, he sat back in his desk chair and thought about a book he'd once read, *The Celestine Prophecy*, which explored the significance of coincidences. Just that morning, he had received the same video from Admiral K.J. Quinn of the NSA, whom Binqus had worked with two years earlier on the NSA's encryption project.

"You are the most brilliant guy I know in the area of paranormal phenomena," Quinn said to Binqus. "And I know that you've handpicked your staff and put together a magnificent organization. So, notwithstanding your outrageous fees, I want to hire you to analyze this video and tell me what in the world we are looking at."

"Well, K. J., I love you, too. Always nice to hear from such a fan. Let me take a quick look."

Binqus opened the file and saw the exact same images he saw in the attachment to Elizabeth's email—images of a person's arm glowing and extended by a good foot, allowing for an improbable rescue of a man literally falling down a steep mountain.

"That's quite a video," Binqus said, playing innocent. "Are you sure it's authentic?"

"Yes, I'm certain. My people will tell me when and where this image was created. What I need you to tell me is how such a phenomenon is possible, if it is, in fact, a paranormal occurrence."

"I've studied hundreds of flashy-light phenomena," said Binqus. "This looks like a trick of nature, but we'll get you an answer. How fast do you need it?"

"Don't go overtime on me, Maxwell. I can wait. It's not the kind of inexplicable event I'm especially interested in. But who knows where it might lead?"

Indeed, thought Binqus, *where might it lead?*

Binqus had examined hundreds of UFO sightings and other videos and pictures of what he called "flashy lights." And so, upon seeing the video attached to his sister's email, assuming the video had not been faked, Binqus had no doubt he was witnessing a true paranormal phenomenon. Binqus told his staff to get him everything they could find out about Daniel Ornstein. They examined hundreds of databases to which they had access, scanning pictures with facial recognition software. When they got a hit from the Hadassah Hospital in Jerusalem, they immediately forwarded it to Binqus. Included in the file were the pictures of Daniel's back and shoulders that the nurses had taken while he was still unconscious after his scooter accident.

Binqus summoned one of his resident medical experts, the eccentric Dr. Wade Herring III, a lanky, red-haired geneticist.

"What are these? Are they tattoos?"

"No, Maxwell, these are birthmarks. How in the world . . . ?"

"I know, incredible, aren't they? Tell me, Wade. Is it possible for someone to have birthmarks on both shoulders in the exact shape of a hand, especially a hand with such a specific configuration?"

"Maxwell, you're asking me a rhetorical question. Anything is possible, except some things are too unlikely to be possible. And this is one of them. Could it be a fluke of nature? In this particular context, I can't bring myself to say that. I'd say the chances would be one in a Googleplex."

"A Googleplex?"

"Yes. It is a mathematical term. A one with a hundred zeros following it. I thought every geek knew that."

Binqus laughed. "Go on."

"Well, you're talking about today, right? At some point, we'll have technology that will allow us genetically to program human attributes—substantive attributes such as strength and cosmetic traits such as the shape of birthmarks. We'll even be able to program personality traits. I'm glad I won't be here for that debate. But you're talking about what will probably be centuries in the future. And this photograph is how old?"

"It was taken recently."

Herring left, shaking his head. Binqus felt an adrenaline rush. The pictures of Ornstein were not only inexplicable, but they eliminated any doubts Binqus may have entertained about the authenticity of the video. He needed to tamp down his excitement and wild imaginings. But still. Who was Daniel Ornstein?

Binqus instructed his staff to find out whether the Hadassah Hospital had any DNA samples of Ornstein. He was excited when the answer came back in the affirmative, along with images of the DNA sequences. Binqus didn't understand what any of it meant, but he was sure his staff would.

Binqus turned the investigation over to Dr. Laura Victor, director of the Institute. A former chancellor of the University of Massachusetts, she had a piercing intelligence and insatiable curiosity about what she called "credible mysteries." She had written her dissertation on King Solomon's Temple and immediately recognized the hand configuration as that used by the Kohanim when they blessed the congregation. As a *Star Trek* enthusiast, she also recognized the configuration as that used by Mr. Spock when he raised his hand and intoned, "Live long and prosper."

Victor was staring in disbelief at the pictures of Ornstein's birthmarks. Binqus smiled and said, "Laura, you're not the only person to be stunned by what you're seeing."

She did not break her silent stare for a full minute. Then, she said, "Okay, you've got yourself a true candidate for the aliens or alien objects we've been looking for. And now you want me to find out what we're missing."

"Precisely," Binqus said. "I don't like suddenly shifting around our research programs. But humor me. Spend whatever you have to spend but find me answers."

"I love spending your money, Maxwell. I'll make you proud on that score. Seriously, I can't wait to see where this will lead. We'll send the photograph to all the research committees. And all the scholars we are wholly or partially funding around the world. That's dozens of brilliant people, many of them PhDs. Maybe we'll get lucky. Give me a couple of weeks."

17

Yael

aniel loved the idea and the reality of the Hebrew University. It was a testament to the "People of the Book," the catchy phrase Muhammad used to describe the Jews in the Koran. For Daniel, the mystique was enhanced by the location of the university's campus on Mount Scopus. To the east, the Judean Desert fell precipitously to Jericho and the Jordan River, and then farther down to the Dead Sea, the lowest point on Earth. To the west was the walled Old City, which encompassed the Temple Mount where the two Jewish temples once stood. It was now the site of the Mosque of Omar, or Dome of the Rock, and the al-Aqsa Mosque. The Old City stood in contrast to West Jerusalem, which developed in the nineteenth and twentieth centuries into a modern cosmopolitan city. Surrounding communities lined the picturesque hills, which led to Tel Aviv's beautiful sandy beaches on the Mediterranean Sea.

On this unusually warm November afternoon, Daniel was attending his class on the book of Genesis, taught by Professor Nechama Lenowitz, a highly respected biblical scholar. The subject was the sacrifice of Isaac. The story described God's commandment to Avraham to sacrifice *"thy son, thine only son, whom thou lovest, even Isaac."* Lenowitz focused on the duplicative clauses as being intended to emphasize what an incredible demand God was making of Avraham. The text related that Avraham journeyed with Isaac to Mount Moriah, as God had commanded. But as he took up his knife to perform the sacrifice, an angel of God reached out to stop him. *"Do not harm the boy and do not do anything at all to him, for now I do know you are faithful to God because you have not withheld your son, your only one, from me."* The angel then showed Avraham a ram stuck by its horns in a thicket and told Avraham to substitute the ram for Isaac.

Although Daniel was familiar with the story, he had not thought about it for some time. In a course he had taken at NYU on the history of Mesopotamia, he learned about Leonard Wiley's excavations of the ancient city of Ur in 1924. In the ruins of the city's temple to the moon god, Nanna, Wiley found two identical bronze figurines depicting a ram stuck in a thicket of branches. Daniel felt a rush of adrenaline. He raised his hand. When Lenowitz called on him, he asked about Wiley's discoveries.

"Yes," Lenowitz said, in her Polish-accented Hebrew, "Wiley's figurines do, indeed, raise provocative questions. Many scholars have dismissed the idea that the Ur figurines are related to the Biblical story. But I don't think it's possible to argue that it's mere coincidence."

Sitting on the other side of the classroom, Yael Gileadi, a twenty-six-year-old kibbutznik and former army captain, listened to the discussion. Although not religious, like many secular Israelis, she had studied the Bible as the story of her nation's birth and early history. She had understood the story as a dramatic demonstration of the depths of Avraham's faith in God. But the story had never sat easy with her. Was Avraham truly ready to kill his son? And what did it say about God? What kind of divinity would pretend to want such a sacrifice? What, in fact, was the point of the story?

Yael stared across the room at Daniel. She had seen him in class and around campus and had registered his good looks. His question revealed an intellectually curious mind. Many Israelis her age had little respect for the American students, especially those who came to the university for just one year and spent more time playing tourist than student. The Israeli students had already fulfilled their mandatory stints in the army after high school. They were older and more mature. Many, like Yael, had seen combat; too many had been wounded or had lost friends in the ongoing strife between the Israelis and the Palestinians. Yael generally shared her friends' perspective. But she had to admit, if only to herself, that she was surprisingly curious about Daniel Ornstein.

Daniel had also noticed Yael. Actually, he had more than just noticed her. He was very attracted to her. She was tall and long-legged, with hazel eyes and long black hair that was always pulled back in a ponytail. She wore no makeup, as far as he could tell. She usually wore a pair of khaki shorts, a white blouse, and sandals. Daniel thought she was the most beautiful woman on campus.

At the end of the class, Daniel noticed her walking in his direction. He glanced over his shoulder to see who was waiting for her and then was taken aback when she stopped in front of him. Daniel was not a novice when it came to women. He had just spent two weeks with a gorgeous woman in Ghana who said she was in love with him. But now, for some reason he could not fathom, he felt as if he were fourteen years old and trying to figure out how to ask a girl for a date.

"You asked an interesting question about the figurines," she said abruptly, not bothering to say "Shalom" or introduce herself. "Are you a student of Babylonian mythology?"

His heart pounding, Daniel said, "I'm interested in the relationship of the Bible to the myths of other people who lived in the area." Sweat was trickling down his underarms. He felt incredibly stupid. She must think he was a real nerd. *Is this the best I could do?*

Yael turned to leave but then stopped and said, "If you're interested in this stuff, you ought to take Professor Stein's class. He is brilliant. I haven't been able to fit his class into my schedule, but I will."

Determined to continue their unexpected interaction, and even though it was late in the afternoon, Daniel said, "Would you like to get some lunch?"

Yael had lots of experience with pickup lines. This one rated a failing grade. Although she was curious about Daniel, she decided playfully to adopt the outmoded stereotype of the detached-yet-friendly-yet-somewhat-bitchy Israeli woman. She gave Daniel a condescending half-smile, and replied in Hebrew, "No, thank you." Then, in a confusing gesture of possible interest, she added a brief wave as she walked away without looking back.

Daniel cursed himself for his ineptitude. He experienced the all-too-familiar ache of depression. Deciding to blow off his next class, he headed back to his dorm room.

Despite his numerous successes in various areas of athletics and his brilliance as a student, melancholia and anxiety had remained his constant companions for as long as he could remember. From years of experience, he knew that, for him at least, his emotional pain was best handled by sleep. So, in midafternoon on a beautiful fall day in Jerusalem, he lay down on his bed, put the extra pillow over his head, and closed his eyes. Recalling word for word his conversation with Yael, he fell asleep, fantasizing about how he could make a better impression in future encounters.

18

Logic, Experience, and Matchmaking

Daniel's cousin, Varda, was well-known in Israel for her articles and television appearances. She was currently writing a book on Jewish practices on secular kibbutzim. She had been traveling around the country, interviewing current and former kibbutzniks.

Varda was in Jerusalem for three days, staying with her sister-in-law Kinneret. Today, she would visit with Daniel to catch up and see how he was faring after two months in Israel. Daniel saw her waiting for him in the lobby of the Mount Scopus student center. He paused to appreciate her smiling eyes and a face that radiated warmth and brightness. During his time in the Pacific Northwest, he had looked forward to her letters. They were written in the smallest script imaginable and communicated real feelings along with interesting experiences. Daniel had seen her briefly at the hospital after his scooter accident. Daniel was grateful that she was there when he awoke, but she did not stay long after the doctor reported that Daniel would be fine.

Now, they walked around the campus and talked about family and everything else for over two hours. They eventually got around to reprising their years-long debate about the Israel-Palestine question.

Varda came to her Zionism as an Orthodox Jew. She believed that God had promised the land of Israel to the Jewish patriarchs and their descendants. Daniel was a secular Zionist, as the founders of the modern Jewish state had been. In his view, Judaism, the religion, was but one aspect of Jewish nationality: a people having a distinct history and culture, inextricably connected to a specific geographic homeland.

The Palestinians had their own bona fide historic claims to the land. The United Nations recognized this in 1947, when they adopted the partition plan to create two separate states, one Jewish, the other Palestinian. The Jews accepted the plan, even though it gave them a small fraction of Palestine and lacked secure borders. On May 14, 1948, when Israel declared its statehood and independence, it was immediately invaded from the south, north, and east by the five bordering Arab countries. When Israel won the war, Jordan's King Abdullah aggressively moved to annex all of the land the United Nations had designated for the independent, sovereign State of Palestine. The Arab

League strongly opposed the move, with Iraq denouncing the plan as a clear violation of the Palestinians' right to self-determination. Nonetheless, at the Jericho Conference in 1948, Abdullah's "solution" to the Palestinian issue was adopted.

"The Palestinians could have had their state," Varda argued. "The Arab countries prevented a sovereign State of Palestine because they thought it would legitimize Israel. That was King Abdullah's main and ultimately prevailing argument for the Jordanian annexation. We've fought three wars against Arab nations that have openly embraced the goal of destroying Israel and inflicting another genocide on the Jewish people. Hamas still openly calls for the extermination of the Jews in Israel. We can't afford to be generous to people who wish Hitler had succeeded and teach their children to hate us. And why shouldn't we enjoy the benefits of our military victories any less than other countries that have secured territory by force? The concept of "manifest destiny" was invented to justify American massacres of native Americans, usurpation of their lands and violation of any number of treaties. We didn't have to make anything up. It's right there in the Torah, a land promised to us, the Jewish people."

Daniel agreed that in 1948, Jordan and the leaders of the other Arab states had destroyed the Palestinians' opportunity for statehood. "And I agree the wars launched by the Arab states in 1948, 1967, and 1973 were aggressive wars aimed at destroying Israel. But the argument you're making has two problems. First, it solves nothing. One of the greatest Supreme Court Justices, Oliver Wendell Holmes Jr., wrote that 'the life of the law is not logic, it is experience.' What he meant is that certain disputes will not yield to logical resolutions. Without a settlement based on compromise, your persuasive logic will achieve nothing."

"But the larger problem I have is that policies of apartheid, forced expulsion, and land usurpation are anathema to the fundamental values that define who we are as Jews. The first paragraph of Israel's Declaration of Independence identifies the significance of the Jewish people as having 'created cultural values of national and universal significance.' If we become no different from other nations, what's the point in having a Jewish state? In a world in which we abandon the Bible's call that we be a 'light unto the other nations,' what would be special about being Jewish? What would be special about Israel as a Jewish homeland? It's one thing to fail, as we all do, in meeting the lofty ethical precepts of the Bible and the Talmud. But the Jewish people have never abandoned these aspirational standards as the defining characteristic of the nation. Jews pray three times a day and thank God 'for not making us like the other nations.' For two thousand years, while in the Diaspora, we suffered all manner of massacres and persecution to keep faith with this paradigm."

Varda said nothing for a long minute. She then responded with not a little sarcasm and anger. "What you say is very nice and theoretically correct," Varda replied. "But you don't live here. The simple fact is that the Palestinians want to kill all the Jews in Israel. They support terrorists who stab women in the streets, blow up buses, cut the genitals off our killed soldiers, and run cars over children. When the Jordanians were in control of the Temple Mount from 1948 until 1967, they banned us from access to Judaism's holiest sites. And they took Jewish gravestones from the Mount of Olives and used them to pave streets and build latrines. Most people don't know these facts. But it's actions like these that have convinced many Israelis that the only thing preventing another holocaust is to have the strongest possible army and a sufficient number of nuclear weapons. And it's not just your stereotyped cutthroat Arabs that worry us. I needn't remind you, of course, that just eighty years ago, the oh-so-cultured Germans willfully and systematically slaughtered six million of our people, in European lands we had lived in for centuries, simply because we were 'different.' Survivors of two thousand years of pogroms and genocide cannot be expected to accept a Palestinian settlement that leaves us exposed to groups like Hamas and the Iranian imams who publicly and officially advocate the Nazi agenda of Jewish extermination. That is not logic, and it is not paranoia: that, my dear cousin, is what your supreme court justice called 'experience.' The Jewish value system does not include turning the other cheek to unbridled threats of yet another genocide."

Daniel took a deep breath. "What say we change the subject?" Daniel suggested. "Can we talk about your book?"

"You mean we should stop arguing?"

"Never," Daniel laughed.

"We can argue about something else," Varda said. "But I can't argue on an empty stomach. How about I take you to a great falafel place I know?"

Daniel nodded. "On that we agree!"

They stopped at Falafel Omisi, a popular lunch stop for students on Mount Scopus. While Varda loaded the falafel into a piece of warm pita, she considered the best way to introduce a subject that was of much more immediate interest to her than resolving the Israeli-Palestinian problem.

Varda loved matchmaking. She was keen on helping Daniel find a worthy woman, even if she was not Orthodox.

"Yesterday morning, I had a great meeting with Gidon Gileadi and his daughter, Yael, from Kibbutz Chalomim," she told Daniel. "He's on the faculty of the Hebrew University, and she was a captain in the Israeli army, the IDF. We spent an hour talking about life on the kibbutz. Then Gidon left, and Yael and I continued to talk. Daniel, she is perfect for you."

Daniel held up his hand. He did not want to be set up with an Israeli kibbutznik and combat veteran. He smiled and shook his head. "Varda, you're a compulsive matchmaker."

"That's what Yael said. Same words. And I stand guilty as charged. You can blame my mother, your Aunt Rivka."

Varda thought back to the discussion she'd had with Yael.

"So," she had asked, "do you have a family of your own, a husband, or a boyfriend?"

Yael shrugged. "No husband or family, and no serious relationship at the moment." Trying to end the discussion, she switched to Hebrew and said, "If you're some compulsive matchmaker, please don't."

But Varda was not easily put off. It was the hallmark of a good matchmaker to be deaf to anything inconsistent with the ultimate objective.

"Yael, listen, I have a cousin, Daniel, who's spending his junior year here at the University. Come to think of it, he may be in one of your classes. He's twenty-five, done a lot of interesting stuff, mountain climbing, archery. He has a warm heart, he's very smart, and he's a *chatich*, a real hunk."

Yael laughed. "A terrific guy, a superior brain, and a hunk. The perfect man. In my experience, they don't exist."

Ignoring the comment, Varda smiled impishly and said, "I don't know your type, but if you're up for meeting an imperfect but very interesting, unattached, good-looking, and exceptional individual, I could try and set something up."

Then, with a look that revealed her full-hearted feelings for her cousin, she added, "Daniel is different and very special. Whatever happens, you won't be wasting your time."

Yael listened to Varda, at first seriously annoyed that she was ignoring her explicit wish that Varda not try to set her up. But as Varda described Daniel, Yael realized he could well be the guy in her Lenowitz class. He had asked the incisive question about the figurines, followed by his clumsy attempt to ask her out. To be sure, he was handsome and quite obviously very bright, but Yael was drawn more by her instincts and sense that he did seem different, even special in some way, and not because of his entertaining clumsiness.

Yael smiled. "I think I may have already met your Daniel."

After lunch, Daniel and Varda walked through the Machaneh Yehudah souk, where fruit and vegetable vendors vied for the buyers' attention.

Daniel described the American and other foreign students he'd met.

"I love Jerusalem. But it's a little difficult on Scopus—socially, that is. I'm older and more focused on the schoolwork than most of the Americans here. And the Israelis have their own cliques. They don't seem all that interested in making friends with Americans. I've been thinking of renting an apartment downtown. I have a very good friend who said he'd help me find a place."

"That sounds like a good idea," Varda said. "The population is very international, even more so than the student body on Scopus. You might meet some interesting people. By the way, Professor Gileadi invited me to dinner at his home in Rehavia. I asked whether I could bring my American cousin, and, of course, he said yes. I think you'll feel very comfortable with them. They're not religious, although they keep kosher. They're a very interesting family. Professor Gileadi is very bright and engaging. Their son Mordecai is on active duty, and before she retired to write books, Ronit was a doctor in the medical corps. And maybe Yael will be there. So? Please say yes. I promise, you'll enjoy their company."

"Thank you," Daniel said. "I could use a good meal, and they sound like interesting people. But no matchmaking, okay?"

Varda avoided his question by glancing at her watch. "I have to meet someone in fifteen minutes, but I'll see you tonight." She gave him the Gileadis' address, a warm hug, and was off to her appointment.

Daniel returned to his dorm and googled Gidon Gileadi on Wikipedia. He had an impressive biography. Daniel was about to get up but paused and entered "Yael Gileadi" in the search bar. The page came up, and Daniel hit the link for "images." Yael was the woman from Professor Lenowitz's class. The picture was part of an article about a civil suit that a male officer had brought against Yael, because she had beaten him up when she found him molesting a female private. Staring at her picture on the screen, Daniel started to have a panic attack. Would Yael be at home for dinner with her parents? And if she were, would the occasion be a heaven-sent twist of fate or an agonizing blow to the possibility of any relationship? According to Google, she was twenty-seven, and she was single. But that didn't mean she wasn't in a relationship.

Daniel arrived exactly on time and was warmly greeted by Ronit and Gidon Gileadi. Varda was there, but Yael was not. Daniel was both relieved and disappointed. They gathered in the living room for typical Israeli hors d'oeuvres: eggplant salad; cucumbers and tomatoes; bourekas, a pastry filled with cheese; and freshly baked pita. Ronit urged him to help himself, but his stomach was in a knot. All he could think about was how he'd react if Yael walked through the door. He thought about his tryst with Anika in Ghana. He had developed strong feelings for her, but his attraction to Yael felt different. He couldn't understand it. Here he was, sitting with the parents of a girl he was totally smitten with, after having blown his one brief interaction with her.

His thoughts were interrupted when Gidon asked Varda when her book would be published.

"Well, I've finished most of my research."

"And your conclusion?" Ronit asked.

"The differences among these kibbutzim are very nuanced when it comes to Judaism. Some gather for holidays without traditional prayers; some say the prayers. Although not religious, a majority of the secular kibbutzim represent what I call an authentic Jewish experience."

"Much like Kibbutz Cholomim, as you described it. There's a spiritual regard for the land and our ancient connection to it."

Daniel asked Ronit about their children.

"Mordechai is in his final year of army service; he's planning to study medicine. Yael finished her army service—a decorated veteran—and she's now studying here at Hebrew University. I know I'm their mother and not objective, but they're both wonderful. We've been blessed."

Without mentioning his conversation with Yael, Daniel asked about Michael Stein, whose class Yael had recommended.

Daniel had looked up Stein on his computer. He had grown up on a kibbutz near Jerusalem. After his army service, he received his PhD in ancient religions and cognate studies from Princeton University. After several years of teaching at Stanford, he returned to his kibbutz and became the Tzi Harkavi Professor of Ancient Civilizations at Hebrew University. Stein had a well-earned reputation for incisive analysis in many areas of Bible scholarship.

Gidon Gileadi, like many Israelis of his generation, was an amateur student of Israeli archeology. He told Daniel, "Professor Stein is a very good friend. He and his girlfriend were just here for Shabbat dinner last Friday night. He's in charge of a dig at Megiddo. I should say 'another dig,' because I think there have been some ten excavations there in the last one hundred years. They've uncovered eight layers of civilization going back to 3000 BCE. He believes there was a community at Megiddo one to two thousand years earlier."

"I look forward to taking Professor Stein's course," said Daniel.

"You won't be disappointed. He's very popular. If you have trouble getting in, let me know."

Daniel had just finished a paper for his Archeology in Israel course, which covered the excavations in the Mount Carmel area, including some of the previous digs at Megiddo. "I was very impressed," he said. "A massive, five-thousand-year-old temple was found there. It ranks among the largest structures anywhere in the world from that time period. I'm looking forward to visiting it."

Daniel was about to describe other major discoveries in the Carmel Range excavations when he stopped short, worried that the conversation was too focused on him. "Sorry," he said, his face flushed with embarrassment. "I just finished the paper, and your mention of Professor Stein's dig got me going."

"Daniel's the smartest member of our family," Varda said. "I think he's starved for good companionship." Then, she added, intentionally keeping the spotlight on her cousin, "Daniel did some amazing stuff before he started college."

"Tell us," Ronit said.

Varda smiled. Even though Yael was absent, impressing the parents was always a prominent objective of a good matchmaker.

Daniel hated to be the focus of attention in this kind of setting, but he had no choice. "I decided to live out some of my boyhood dreams. I moved to the Pacific Northwest to study alpine climbing and to learn archery and hunting. I also joined a motorcycle club and rode the foothills of the Cascade Mountains. I'd been cooped up in a Jewish day school in Brooklyn for twelve years, and I was dying to try out a different life. It was a great experience, but eventually I decided it wasn't what I wanted to do forever. I'm especially interested in archeology and anthropology and in learning more about the Samaritans on Mount Gerizim." Daniel had no intention of discussing his illegal excursion to the Dalia cave. He smiled and said, "That's the most I've ever talked about myself, and I'm exhausted. Gidon, is your offer of a whiskey still standing?"

Daniel was rewarded with broad smiles as Gidon rose and fetched Daniel a scotch. Varda was beaming. She thought, *This was a home run. I forgot just how impressive and charming Daniel can be.*

Ronit said, "It's a shame Yael isn't here. I think she would enjoy our discussion. You both want to specialize in similar areas. She was planning to join us, but she got a last-minute call from her army unit. She's still a captain in the reserves. Now, no more bourekas, or none of you will have any appetite left."

Dinner was served: chicken, Israeli couscous, and fresh string beans from the kibbutz. The Gileadis' questions and expressions of respect made Daniel feel relaxed enough to ask Gidon what kinds of courses were offered in the linguistics department. Gidon recommended that if Daniel stayed on at the university for his senior year, which Daniel had said he was considering, he might want to enroll in Gidon's survey course.

After dinner, the group retreated to the Gileadis' living room. The conversation centered on Ronit's idea for a new children's book. Daniel was happy to sit back, relax, and listen.

When it was time to leave, Ronit gave Daniel a piece of paper. It said "Yael," with her phone number.

Gidon put his arm around Daniel's shoulder and said, "Daniel, If I can give you a piece of advice, when you ask a girl out for lunch, you might try to make the date for some time earlier than four in the afternoon. And it would be a good idea to introduce yourself."

Gidon momentarily maintained a deadpan expression. Then he, Ronit, and Varda burst out laughing.

"You have to get used to the fact that there are no secrets in Israel," said Varda. "It was actually an amazing coincidence that I interviewed Gidon and Yael after you talked to each other following your Lenowitz class."

Daniel was dumbfounded. All he could say was, "Thank you, I'll, um, follow your advice."

19

"Tell Me Daniel, Do You Believe in Paranormal Events?"

A mos helped Daniel find an apartment in an old but well-kept building off King David Street, close to Jaffa Gate, which led into the Old City. Exploring his new neighborhood, he immediately knew he'd made the right decision. As much as he loved the geography and physical beauty of Mount Scopus, downtown Jerusalem would offer more social engagement.

He had decided he would wait until their next Bible class to introduce himself to Yael. When he spotted her across the room, she acknowledged him with a brief wave. After class, Daniel took a deep breath and approached her.

"Hi, you must be Yael. I'm Daniel Ornstein. Your parents and my cousin think I should try again to ask you to lunch, but I should do it at lunchtime."

Yael smiled and reached out to shake his hand. Her hand was cool to the touch, her grip firm. "I'd like to have lunch, even at lunchtime, but I'm late for a class. If you're free, would you like to meet me at a lecture tonight here on Scopus? The speaker is Dr. Imat al-Baroody, the chair of Oxford's Center for Islamic Studies. He'll be talking about the Ottoman Empire and the effect of its demise on the Middle East. We can have a drink afterward."

While it was hardly a date, Daniel quickly agreed.

"So, I'll see you tonight."

Daniel arrived at the lecture hall ten minutes late. Yael was sitting in the third row with people seated on either side of her. Daniel found a seat in the back of the room. A faculty member introduced Dr. al-Baroody as having been educated in Saudi Arabia and Harvard University before he assumed his position at Oxford.

Al-Baroody explained how, for centuries, the Arabs in the Middle East lived in their own "bubble." They lived mainly in tribes, fighting over large and small territories. Although the Arabs were subject to Turkish rule, they had considerable autonomy, and all spoke the same language and practiced Islam. After almost a thousand years, in the early twentieth century, in the wake of World War I, vast territories came under the control of France (Algeria, Tunisia, Syria, Lebanon) and Britain (Egypt, Palestine, Iraq, Jordan).

"These areas," al-Baroody said, "had never been Western-style autonomous nation states. They comprised heterogeneous tribes, accustomed to Ottoman rule, Ottoman laws and customs, not those of Paris or London. When, in 1917, Britain recognized the right of the Jews to a 'homeland' in Palestine, it was predictable that the Muslim Arabs would vociferously object. Under Islamic law, Christians and Jews are allowed to live and practice their religions in Islamic territories. However, such land can never be subjected to a non-Islamic regime. Muslims are obligated to declare a jihad to liberate any such land and return it to Islamic sovereignty. For centuries, most Muslim rulers had been tolerant of their Jewish populations. Jewish communities flourished in Egypt and North Africa and in the areas of present-day Lebanon, Syria, and Iraq. But the asserted right to a homeland in Palestine, to be ruled by Jews, became a lightning rod for the boiling cauldron of anger caused by the decimation of the Arab world in the twentieth century."

Al-Baroody was rewarded for his lecture with a respectful round of applause. As the auditorium emptied, Daniel saw Yael chatting with other students moving toward the exit. When he waved for her attention, she separated from the group and came over to meet him.

They went to the Scopus Café, one of the popular hangouts for students near the campus. Yael ordered an Israeli beer, Daniel a Dewar's on the rocks. The lecture, which Daniel had found interesting, provided an easy topic for conversation. Then they talked a bit about their families. Daniel asked about her army service and professional plans after university. Yael asked Daniel about his gap years, his adventures as an RMI guide. It was a discussion much like the one that Daniel had with her parents at dinner.

"Have you signed up for Professor Stein's class?" Yael asked.

"I didn't know they'd posted the sign-up sheet. I'll do it tomorrow. I hear he listed Cross's book as the main text."

Frank Moore Cross had been a professor of Hebrew and other languages of the ancient Middle East at Harvard. Stein had received his doctorate under Cross and was considered an authority on the Dead Sea Scrolls. Stein had assigned Cross's iconic work, *Canaanite Myth and Hebrew Epic*.

"It's an expensive book," Yael said. "My father said you can use one of his copies."

"Yael, that would be great. Please, thank him for me."

"You can thank him in person. He told me to ask you to Shabbat dinner. You can meet my brother and my friend, Beni."

Placing her hand lightly on Daniel's forearm, she smiled. "We're a military family, and this is a command you cannot disobey. Friday, seven o'clock. Wear a white shirt."

"That would be great," said Daniel. "I look forward to it."

They talked for a few more minutes about classes they were taking, finished their drinks, said pleasant goodbyes, and went their separate ways. Daniel thought the date had been a disaster. He'd been dull, didn't have much to say. And Yael had a boyfriend. Beni!

Daniel took a deep breath, trying to absorb his disappointment. *Of course she has a boyfriend. She's smart and gorgeous. Why am I getting in deeper with this family? She's already accounted for. And yet, didn't the Gileadis specifically tell me to call her?*

He thought about phoning Varda to ask whether she knew what the story was with Beni but then decided not to. He didn't want anyone, not even Varda, to know how disappointed he was.

Two days later, Yael and her friend Shifra were jogging around the track next to the university's athletic annex. It was a popular location for runners and had facilities for many sports. Yael was telling Shifra about Daniel. She liked him but expressed caution. She had gone out with two New Yorkers and in both cases found them to be superficial.

"What does he look like?" Shifra asked.

Yael was about to describe him when she noticed Daniel in the distance. He was setting up to practice at the archery stand. It was a modern setup; the default distance to the target was twenty yards.

Yael saw Daniel move the target to the forty-yard mark. Yael had received a marksmanship award in the army for small arms. She knew how difficult it was to hit a target with a handgun at thirty yards. Not many could do it reliably. Few could hit a target at forty yards. Yael didn't know of anyone who could do it consistently at that distance. She was curious whether archery was more accurate at greater distances.

Yael and Shifra stood and watched Daniel.

He withdrew his bow from its case, nocked an arrow, and hooked his hand release into the d-loop attached to his bowstring. Letting out a breath, he pulled the bowstring to full draw. Holding the bow and hand release in a relaxed fashion, he fixed his aim at the center of the target. He allowed his thumb to gently pressure the release button. As he loosed the arrow, his hand remained high in a follow-through.

The arrow hit the target two inches outside the core of the bull's-eye. Daniel then made a minute adjustment to a screw on the bow, slightly shifted his stance and repeated the shot five more times. Each arrow went into the heart of the bull's-eye, forming a circle with a diameter of no more than an inch. People had stopped to watch and came over to meet Daniel.

Shifra put her arm around Yael's shoulders. "American or not, I wouldn't reject this one too fast."

Daniel wasn't looking forward to going to the Gileadis for Shabbat dinner with Yael's "friend," Beni. Had he deceived himself into thinking that she liked him? He wouldn't be the first guy to misinterpret the signals. Still, Daniel kept his hopes alive. Maybe she and Beni were just friends. On his ride home from his classes, he picked up a bottle of wine and stopped at a department store to buy a white shirt. He chose the better of his two pairs of chinos, showered and shaved, and hurried to arrive at the Gileadi home exactly at seven.

Mordechai was home for the weekend, a rare two-day furlough. He was bright, funny, and friendly, and he didn't fit the macho stereotype Daniel imagined for Israeli soldiers. Beni, who had arrived with Yael a few minutes before Daniel, seemed like a perfectly decent, if somewhat boring, fellow. He had been in Yael's army unit, and they had seen combat together. He seemed very much at home with the Gileadis. This was obviously not the first time he'd joined them for Shabbat dinner. And yet, while there was obvious affection between Yael and Beni, Daniel didn't get the impression they were romantically involved.

Ronit lit the Sabbath candles, and Gidon made the blessing over the wine and sang the Kiddush, the prayer sanctifying the Sabbath. Ronit recited another blessing, this one over the two braided breads, known as challah, that she had made that afternoon. It had been many years since Daniel had participated in any Sabbath rituals, and he experienced an unexpected melancholy, remembering what he'd once taken for granted and had then abandoned.

The conversation at the dinner table touched on politics, the latest border clashes, Israeli army maneuvers, and recent archeological excavations. They also discussed more mundane topics, such as where Daniel could get his scooter serviced, the lowest-priced outlets for petrol, and the best and safest times for Daniel to shop at the crowded Machaneh Yehudah outdoor market. After dessert, Mordechai, Yael, and Beni excused themselves and left. Hiding his dejected mood, Daniel rose to do the same.

"Daniel," Gidon said. "Can you stay a few more minutes?"

He led him into the living room and handed Daniel a glass of port wine.

The Shabbat candles gave a special glow to the apartment as they flickered down to their base. Daniel liked Gidon and Ronit Gileadi. Again, he felt a sadness, a longing. He had not experienced this kind of Sabbath warmth since he was a boy in Brooklyn. Before the tragedy that killed Nathan.

"Tell me about where you are living, and how you are getting on," Gidon asked.

"I like my apartment a lot more than the dorm on Scopus. Lots of activity, great places to eat," Daniel replied.

He was feeling anxious about Gidon wanting this private, unexpectedly personal chat. He began to stand up, hoping he could gracefully leave.

"Gidon, I really appreciate your hospitality," he said. "You have a wonderful family."

"I should thank you. We've enjoyed having you here."

Gidon hesitated for a moment and then held his hand up, signaling he had more to say.

Daniel sat back in his chair and tried to look attentive.

"You talked about your interest in ancient Middle Eastern civilizations," Gidon said. "As you know, my area is linguistics. I'm wondering whether you would like a part-time job as a research assistant on a project I'm involved with. I have been given a large grant to decipher the symbols on eighteen ancient stone tablets found by Leonard Wiley during his excavations at the ancient city of Ur in 1924. The tablets have tens of thousands of symbols or characters etched on both sides. There are only four characters, repeated in thousands of diverse sequences."

When Wiley died in 1929, he left the tablets to the University of Pennsylvania, which had funded his dig. He also left an affidavit setting forth very specific details about the cave where he found them, below a hill about a mile from the city. But the fact is that at the location he identified there is nothing but desert. There are no caves for hundreds of miles, and no maps or documents have been found that show there ever was a cave in that area. Regardless of where Wiley obtained them, the tablets have been dated to about 8000 BCE, ten thousand years ago. If true, it would be long before any known writing system. The symbols are etched in a beautiful, elegant script. It is not the work of schoolboys, as some have hypothesized. It's the work of a master scrivener.

"The tablets present a variety of other mysteries. On the bottom right corner of each tablet, there is a tiny representation of two hands, palms facing out, thumbs touching, and middle fingers split apart. It's the same hand configuration that the Kohanim use when they bless the congregation."

Daniel was no longer looking for a polite way to leave. He was astonished by what Gidon was saying. These could be the very tablets Nathan was holding in the first vision Daniel had had at Grandma Gusma's apartment, and the same as the tablets Nathan carried in his vision of the cave on Mount Rainier.

"You might know of the special practice performed in the synagogue on holidays," Gidon continued. "The Orthodox call it *duchanim*. It dates back to the temple period. The priests, the Kohanim, held their hands aloft in a particular configuration to give the priestly blessing."

"I'm aware of the practice and the blessing," Daniel muttered, almost inaudibly.

"Sorry, I forgot you went to yeshiva."

Daniel was trying not to show his excitement. *This is what I've been looking for.*

"For years, the best minds tried but failed to solve the riddles posed by these tablets. All efforts—and they have been exhaustive—failed. No one would fund any more research. Recently, however, an eccentric billionaire, Maxwell Binqus, got excited when he read reports about the tablets. Binqus is known for his interest in paranormal events. Wiley left the tablets to the University of Pennsylvania and the university has given precise replicas to the Israel Museum. Soon thereafter, Binqus gave a large grant to the museum to fund our project. So, my friend, would you be interested in participating?"

"Gidon, I'm very interested. But isn't Binqus some kind of television preacher?"

"Yes, but he's not what you'd expect. He's an odd character, for sure. But you can't call him crazy for thinking there's something weird about the tablets."

Gidon fell silent for a moment. Then he said, "Tell me, Daniel, do you believe in paranormal events?"

Do I believe in the paranormal? Daniel was very tempted to tell Gidon about his experiences. But having carefully guarded his secrets for his entire life, he shrugged and said, "I'm open to the idea. I've always been interested in physics. It's one of the subjects I've been focusing on in college. I still can't get my head around some of the new theories, such as alternative universes and quantum entanglement. The concepts are hopelessly counterintuitive. But I've read some of the published papers." He managed to force a laugh. "I hope a belief in aliens isn't a prerequisite for working on the project."

Gidon smiled. "Of course not. I was just curious. I'm old-fashioned. I can't get excited about aliens. But I have to say, these mysteries can get one thinking." Just recently, Haim Eshed, the former Israeli space security chief, claimed in a news interview that extraterrestrials exist. The Americans are no longer evading the issue as they have for decades. They have established an Unidentified Aerial Phenomena Task Force and have released a previously-classified report on videos taken by American war planes that document numerous UFO sightings.

"Anyway, although, as I said, the museum has good replicas, it has requested on my behalf that the university send us the originals. They should arrive any day."

Gidon told Daniel to stop by his office at Gi'vat Ram so that Yael could set him up with the relevant materials, introduce him to other members of the team, have him sign the confidentiality agreements, and explain further details.

"Yael is also working on this?"

"Didn't I mention that?"

On his drive back to his apartment, Daniel's birthmarks were mildly twitching, an occasional event Daniel could never explain. Tonight, however, he sensed it was because these tablets held the answers to the questions that had defined his life since he was ten years old. The tablets bore an unmistakable resemblance to the ones Nathan had been holding in Daniel's visions.

The next day, Daniel looked for Yael at the university's Gi'vat Ram campus, where Gidon had said he could sign up, but she wasn't there. After signing the required administrative forms, he was given, as a training exercise, about one hundred clay pictograph tablets found in the ruins of the grand library in the ancient Assyrian city of Nineveh. The Assyrian King Ashurbanipal had finished building this vast library complex in 660 BCE. He was not only a conqueror of most of the Levant; he had great intellectual curiosity. He ordered his lieutenants to collect all the literary materials they could locate throughout his realm—some thirty thousand clay tablets and a lesser number of papyrus scrolls.

To get a feel for what linguistics was all about, Daniel bought the classic book by George Yule, *The Study of Language*, and found a number of primary- and secondary-level video lectures by Gidon Gileadi. He watched several of them. Gidon's talent for simplifying complex material was evident from his introductory lecture in which he explained the transition from pictures to letters.

"Before we had alphabets," he explained, "the word for father, pronounced *AB*, was represented in writing by two pictures—the head of an ox, 𐤀, connoting a father's strength, and the symbol for a tent, ⌷, representing the father's domain." It's like using emojis. Here is a guy who likes fish. ☺ 🐟. You can see the meaning, but the symbols have no sounds. It is not a sound-based writing system.

"Alphabets, whose letters directly express sounds, such as English, Latin, Greek, Hebrew—have their roots in ancient Phoenicia. The commercial, seafaring Phoenicians needed a more efficient system of writing than thousands of pictures. They adopted an alphabet with twenty-two letters, each having a specific sound. The meaning of a word is communicated by the sounds of the letters in combination, not by pictures. In Hebrew, the word father would now be written as the combination of the first two letters of the alphabet, A[leph] and B[et]. Eventually, additional combinations of the same letters produced other words for father. For example, the word *Abba*, which is what my daughter calls me. We can now trace modern languages such as English directly to the ancient pictographs."

Daniel spent the first few days working at the Gi'vat Ram campus. On the fifth day, Daniel noticed Yael in the hallway. He waited a few moments and then walked out of the research room, ostensibly to get a cup of coffee. Yael spotted him and came over to say hello. They chatted for a few moments.

"I knew nothing about linguistics," Daniel admitted. "It's fascinating. I hope I can help on the Ur tablets."

"My father says you're a fast learner. The originals just arrived. We're all excited to see them. If you aren't too busy tomorrow, I'm going down to Hevron to see another member of our team, Yehudit Mizrachi; she's a retired professor of epigraphy at Tel Aviv University, a leading expert on ancient writing systems and a close family friend. My father wants her to look at the originals. She was wounded in a terrorist incident and uses a cane, so we didn't want to ask her to travel. My friend, Tzionah Avineri, has volunteered to drive me. She's an active duty colonel in the IDF."

Yael couldn't deny her developing feelings for Daniel. But she didn't want him to get the wrong impression from her invitation, so she said, "Tzionah's interesting, and she has a great sense of humor."

"That would be awesome," Daniel said. "Thank you."

"Ten o'clock tomorrow morning, at Kikar Zion."

Daniel saluted. Yael gave Daniel what he thought was an especially warm glance, turned to leave, and stopped. She turned back and placed her warm open hand on his right cheek for the briefest moment. Then she turned and was gone.

They both experienced a similar confused reaction.

Why in the world did I do that?

Why in the world did she do that?

Surrounded by cafés, a world-famous bookstore, and tourist shops selling all manner of goods, from cheap trinkets to army surplus and expensive robes and rugs, Kikar Zion—Zion Square—lay at the intersection of Jaffa Road and Ben Yehuda Street. Daniel met the two women promptly at 10:00 a.m. Daniel and Tzionah exchanged friendly get-to-know-you questions. She was a tall, attractive woman, dressed in an IDF military uniform, complete with a holster and gun. To his surprise, Yael was also in uniform and was carrying an identical sidearm.

"I have the original tablets here," Yael said, gesturing to a metal case she was carrying. "My father violated protocol by releasing them to us."

Yael was acting very businesslike. There was no hint of yesterday's intimate gesture. Before leaving, they stopped at Yael's favorite café on Jaffa Road for espresso and biscuits.

Hevron was located just inside the so-called Green Line. Over Israel's strenuous objection, the UN had included it within the "occupied territory" in the West Bank, administered by the Palestinian Authority. Daniel knew Jewish history fairly well, but he was vague on the specifics of Hevron's history after biblical times. Tzionah summarized some of the history.

King Herod built huge walls to surround the Cave of the Patriarchs. They still exist intact. It is the oldest continuously used prayer complex in the world. The area has changed hands many times between Christian and Arab rulers both before and after the Crusades. The Turks had control until 1918, when the British accepted the League of Nations' mandate to govern Palestine.

There's always been a small Jewish presence in Hevron, but there were few disturbances until Jewish immigration began in the nineteenth century as part of the Zionist movement. Then, in 1929, Arab mobs went on a rampage and killed sixty-seven Jewish men, women, and children. A British commission found that the riots, which weren't limited to Hevron, reflected Arab fears that the increasing Jewish population would displace the Arabs as 'overlords' in a Muslim land.

"In 1980, three Israelis, two Americans, and one Canadian—all students at a Hevron yeshiva—were killed, and another twenty Jews were injured, as they returned home from Shabbat prayer services. Not to be outdone, in 1994, Dr. Baruch Goldstein, an American physician, émigré to Israel, and fanatic Haredi Jew, entered the mosque. He used an army machine gun to mow down twenty-nine Muslims and wound another one hundred twenty-five, before he was tackled and killed by Muslim worshipers. Even today," Tzionah said, "the leader of one of the ultra-nationalist political parties in Israel brags that he has a framed picture of that mass murderer hanging in his home."

"Welcome to the Middle East."

Daniel saw the tears and deep sadness in Tzionah's eyes. Palestinians, he knew, had parallel depths of sadness, anger and mistrust. But there was nothing special about this modern conflict. From ancient times, millions had died in wars over control of this tiny strip of land on the eastern border of the Mediterranean. The Crusades were especially brutal. And yet each religion—Judaism, Christianity and Islam—preached that God was to be found within a person's soul, not in a parcel of land or on a particular mountain. Yael sensed her colleagues' emotions. Having experienced the same despondent feelings many times herself, she put her arms around Tzionah and Daniel and pulled them close. They sat that way for several moments, despairing that there might ever be peace in the land.

It was twenty-three miles to Hevron. The group squeezed into Tzionah's small Subaru, which had no air conditioning to quell the heat of the midday sun. The road passed Ramat Rachel, where Jacob's wife was said to have been buried, and through the center of Bethlehem. The terrain and many ruins along the road aroused a sense of antiquity, broken by numerous military checkpoints. Given Yael's and Tzionah's IDF credentials, the soldiers at the checkpoints cleared the car to pass.

Yehudit Mizrachi lived in Al-Dabbuya/Beit Hadassah, a settlement established in the 1880s by Jewish immigrants from eastern Europe. Her flat was on the second floor of an old apartment building in the center of the settlement, about half a mile from the Cave of the Patriarchs. Yehudit was a gray-haired woman in her mid-fifties. She welcomed Yael with a big hug and a softer one for Tzionah, whom she was meeting for the first time. Daniel received a firm handshake. Then she served tea in her living room, which was lined with bookshelves and microfiche containers and included a work area with powerful halogen lights.

Yehudit had studied pictures of the tablets. She had been unable to hazard an informed guess as to by whom and under what circumstances the tablets had been created. There was no parallel for the writings, no archeological find that provided any clues about how to unravel the images. She was eager to examine the actual tablets.

Yael opened her case and removed them. They were very thin, etched on both sides, and extremely lightweight. Everyone took a turn holding the tablets, feeling their texture, and marveling at the impeccable craftsmanship of the etchings.

Everyone except Daniel. He stood up and backed away from the table. His birthmarks were stinging. His mouth was dry, and his throat was hot. He felt flushed, as if he had a fever.

Daniel saw that Yehudit noticed his discomfort.

"If you have a couple of aspirins, and a place where I could lie down for a few minutes, I'll be fine," Daniel said.

Yehudit gave him aspirins and a large bottle of water and showed him into her spare room. "The bed is comfortable. Just relax. And drink the water."

Daniel's head was throbbing. "Thank you," he said, his eyes already closing.

Yehudit returned to the tablets. She examined the symbols carefully and at length under a powerful magnifying lens. The scientists had described the etchings as the oldest human writings ever discovered. The three women had a long, substantive discussion of various hypotheses as to the tablets' provenance. Yehudit finally stood up, hands on hips, obviously frustrated. But she still expressed confidence.

"It will take time, but we'll eventually figure this out. Whenever there's an intelligent writing system like this, there's a key that will unlock it. We must be patient. This may not be a language. Or these may be four letters of a larger alphabet. Or it could be a specialized language with only four letters."

They took a break to drink coffee and eat the food they had brought, including tabbouleh for Yehudit from her favorite noshery in Jerusalem.

Just as Yael was beginning to worry about Daniel, he reappeared. "How do you feel?" she asked.

"Much better," he said, although he wasn't being entirely truthful. He no longer felt feverish, and his birthmarks were no longer aching, but he still felt strange. "I have a bad headache and a sore throat. Pretty weird, since I never get sick. And to show frailty in the company of three beautiful women. Shame on me!"

"Don't worry, Israeli men are no different. They just pretend to be macho," said Yehudit.

"Did you make any progress?" he asked.

"Unfortunately, no," said Yael.

The tablets were on the table in front of him. He picked one up and ran his fingers over the ancient symbols. His birthmarks suddenly began to sting again, more painfully than he could ever recall. He felt feverish again. Something was very wrong.

He stood up abruptly and said, "I need to get some fresh air."

As he walked toward the door, Yael glanced at the tablets. The etchings on the tablet Daniel had touched were shimmering softly. Yael glanced over at Yehudit and Tzionah, but when she looked back at the tablets, the glow had disappeared. Had Daniel caused the tablet to shimmer?

She stood up to follow him and saw that he had stopped to look at a framed drawing on Yehudit's foyer wall.

Daniel was stunned, his gaze glued to the drawing. *This is an exact copy of the drawing I made at Guzma's on Yom Kippur. How is that possible?*

Yael gently touched his shoulder. "Daniel, what's going on? Did you see the tablet glowing? Did you somehow make that happen?"

Daniel stood transfixed, unresponsive. His skin was ghostly pale, he was sweating profusely, and his eyes looked blank, like someone in a trance.

"*Habbibi*, are you okay?" Yael asked. She gave him a slight shake to get his attention.

Daniel turned towards her, an incongruous half-smile on his face. And then he collapsed on the ground.

20

After All These Years?

Daniel's trip to Hadassah Hospital after his scooter accident was hardly a momentous event for him. Not so for Dr. Yehoshaphat Aharoni, the physician who had treated him. Aharoni had grown up in the city of Nablus, the ancient city of Shechem, about twenty miles north of Jerusalem. He was a Samaritan—indeed, a member of the Trio who had studied Baasha's Commentary from an early age. He lived four days a week in Jerusalem, close to the Hadassah Hospital in Ein Kerem. Pitching in for a friend on army reserve duty, he had taken a rare shift that evening in the emergency room, which was why he was on hand to treat Daniel. Little did he know that Daniel had visited the Samaritan temple on Mount Gerizim only a few days earlier during his trek to the Wadi Dalia.

When he'd noticed that Daniel had bruises on his back, Aharoni had a nurse turn Daniel onto his stomach. To ensure the doctor had access to every potentially affected area, the nurse removed the tiny, round Duoderm patches that covered two small areas on Daniel's shoulders. When Aharoni examined Daniel, who was still unconscious, he could not believe that lying in front of him was someone who bore the birthmarks of the Ivri Legends. He examined them closely to make sure they were not tattoos. They were not.

Following hospital protocol, the nurse took several pictures of Daniel's back injuries. The birthmarks appeared clearly. She also drew blood to test for infections or other anomalies. They would add the test results, including the now-standard DNA mapping, to the hospital database. When the nurse briefly stepped out, Aharoni took his own pictures on his iPhone. Then, violating the hospital's strict rules on patient privacy, Aharoni swabbed a saliva sample from Daniel's mouth and placed it in a glass vial. He would send the sample to an unaffiliated lab. When the nurse mentioned that the patient had worn Duoderm patches that covered the marks on his shoulders, Aharoni instructed the nurse to replace the patches. His hope was that Daniel would not realize anyone had seen the marks. Even if he suspected, he would doubtless conclude they were just being thorough.

He was putting his iPhone away when Daniel regained consciousness. After briefing Daniel on his injuries, he admonished him about the dangers of scooters; "motorcycles are safer" (a disputed assumption, as Daniel knew). He told Daniel that he was keeping him overnight for observation, wished him well, and left.

Under his own name, Aharoni sent the saliva swab out for mapping. He was excited at the prospect of briefing the Samaritan high priest, Sanballat, on the sudden appearance of one Daniel Ornstein and his miraculous birthmarks. He wanted to see whether he could establish a lineage that might lead to the discovery of others with the invaluable birthmarks. But he would wait until he had the map of Ornstein's DNA and could test those results on DNA databases.

Aharoni had an excellent relationship with Israel's minister of health. He requested his help in accessing otherwise inaccessible DNA databases. Aharoni explained that the Samaritans were looking for lost members of their diaspora community. The official was sympathetic to Aharoni's explanation and secured Aharoni access to major DNA databases, some government run, some private.

The DNA investigation yielded a promising hit from a hospital in Kathmandu, which shared digital files with a worldwide network of hospitals that included Hadassah. Elenna Cohen, who was very likely related to Daniel, had been a patient at the Kathmandu hospital after a hiking accident. Besides her DNA, they had pictures of her injuries. One picture showed scars on her shoulders in the exact locations where Daniel's birthmarks appeared.

In the two days since he'd treated Daniel Ornstein, Aharoni had amassed more than enough information to astonish Sanballat. Most members of the dwindling Samaritan community lived in Nablus, at the foot of Mount Gerizim. They occupied a semiautonomous region administered by the Palestinian Authority. Aharoni would have to stop and clear at least four checkpoints. The trip would take three hours. He had done it hundreds of times.

As he drove to Mount Gerizim in his vintage Triumph sports car, Aharoni contemplated the extraordinary information he had uncovered. According to the teachings of Baasha's Commentary, Daniel Ornstein should be safely able to open the chest that contained the sacred and magical breastplate. Crafted at *Yhahveh's* direction by the Samaritans' ancient ancestor Ivri, the chest and breastplate came to be controlled by the Samaritans' archenemies, the Levites of Judea. On the eve of the destruction of Solomon's Temple in Jerusalem, the Samaritans' high priest BabRama had been able to secure the chest, but the breastplate had remained inaccessible. Baasha had the birthmarks to open the chest, but his offspring did not. The chest remained in a hidden chamber of the temple on Mount Gerizim.

Aharoni was astonished that someone bearing the birthmarks had suddenly appeared and that, according to the investigation he had commissioned, Daniel's probable biological aunt, Elenna Cohen, had scars that suggested she, too, had been born with the marks. If Daniel Ornstein or Elenna Cohen could open the chest that held the breastplate, the consequences for the Samaritan community would be profound. Indeed, the whole world would share its good fortunes. Aharoni pressed the accelerator. The speedometer inched up to 146 kilometers per hour, just about the limit of the aging roadster.

Aharoni parked next to the south temple entrance. He walked slowly and deliberately, restraining his urge to run as he hurried up the steps to the high priest's offices on the second floor. When Aharoni entered Sanballat's office, the high priest looked up, smiled, and said, "Shalom aleichem, Yoshi! To what do we owe this pleasure?"

Aharoni said nothing as he placed the photo of Daniel's shoulders in front of Sanballat and waited for his reaction. But the high priest shook his head and said, "They are tattoos, so what?"

"That was my first reaction. But they are not tattoos. They are birthmarks."

"They cannot be."

"They are. That is a medical fact."

"I don't believe it."

Aharoni shrugged.

He gave Sanballat a copy of the file he had assembled. Sanballat took his time paging through it. Aharoni sat quietly, watching the high priest's expressions, accompanied by frequent verbal exclamations.

Sanballat rose from his chair and silently gestured to Aharoni. They proceeded through a hidden passageway and down a flight of stairs. Sanballat unlocked the door to a small, dimly lit, humidity-controlled room. He approached a table on which lay an artifact covered by a beautifully embroidered linen cloth. The high priest removed the cloth, exposing the holy chest believed to contain the sacred breastplate. It was an unquestioned article of faith that Jeda had been an eyewitness to Zadok's removing the chest from the Holy of Holies, and that Zadok's loyal assistant, Hilkiah, had then transported it directly to the Cave of the Patriarchs. Jeda had killed Hilkiah and brought the chest back to BabRama. Jeda had then given his life trying to open the chest, proving it was authentic.

Aharoni looked at Sanballat. "How do we proceed?"

Sanballat paused to think. It was hard to believe. But it seemed to be a true paranormal event, in accord with our legend. How long have we waited—and doubted? *Yhahveh,* forgive our uncertainties. *Yhahveh* be blessed. "You ask, what are we supposed to do? Do we kidnap Mr. Ornstein and force him to place his hands on the chest? You say he has been befriended by Gidon Gileadi. I know who Gileadi is. He is tied into the political establishment."

Aharoni nodded. "And that, my friend, is why I did the DNA analysis you saw in the file."

Aharoni took the file, turned to the page he wanted Sanballat to see, and pointed to various charts and explanatory information.

Sanballat squinted at the charts. "Okay, Yoshi, I skipped this page. I see large film negatives, like x-rays; they are labeled 'two-dimensional DNA gel electrophoresis.' I'm a little rusty on my biology. So, if you wouldn't mind, in English, please. What does all this mean?"

"After seeing the birthmarks on Ornstein, and while he was still unconscious, I took a swab of saliva and had a lab run a DNA map. The human genome consists of over three billion DNA molecules. But every human being has significant variations. Like fingerprints, the DNA genome for every individual serves as a unique signature. When the gene mapping of two people reveals certain correlations that normally we would not expect to see, we know that they are closely related. I checked more than a few public and private DNA databases, including one that's part of a worldwide consortium of hospitals, which includes Hadassah. I discovered a woman named Elenna Cohen, who is very possibly Ornstein's biological aunt. It's also possible they don't know about each other. I made further inquiries and found a picture of an Elenna Cohen in the hospital after she suffered injuries. The picture shows scars on each shoulder. I think Elenna Cohen was born with the birthmarks and subsequently had them removed. If she was born with the marks, then she should be able to open the chest. Ishtar's removal of Avraham's marks did not affect his abilities. I think we should approach her and ask whether she would be willing to cooperate with us."

"Yoshi," said Sanballat, "this is beyond fascinating. Obviously, I agree, we must follow up. Whatever you need. You've done a brilliant piece of research and analysis. *Alf Mabrouk*, a thousand congratulations!"

Sanballat was not known for expressing compliments. And Aharoni was not known for humility. So Aharoni's muted reaction to his praise surprised Sanballat.

"Yoshi, why the long face? This is cause for celebration, no? We may save our people from extinction and achieve our blessed destiny."

"Why do I seem less than ecstatic? Because Ornstein's birthmarks may truly be paranormal. It is hard to conceive of them being a fluke of nature. Especially given what we know of their prominence in our legends."

"So, what is the problem?"

Aharoni was hesitant to answer the question candidly. But he needed to.

"All these centuries, nothing. Now, suddenly, someone shows up with the birthmarks. I've always thought I believed in *Yhahveh* with my whole heart, unequivocally, without doubts. The problem is, I can't stop questioning why, after all this time, *Yhahveh* shows up and begins performing real miracles—not natural events that we attribute to Him, like making it rain, but truly unnatural, paranormal events. For over three millennia, He has not revealed Himself in such a way. Is this really *Yhahveh*? Maybe it was easier to 'believe' when he left us alone?"

Sanballat put his arm around Aharoni. "Those are interesting questions, aren't they? But a belief without doubt is not genuine. It is to your credit that you question, as I do, as do all who sincerely believe. Genuine faith comes from making a choice. It comes from the free will *Yhahveh* gave to humanity, perhaps His greatest gift."

Sanballat poured two potent drinks of Shechem ale, after which they drank several shots of another local favorite, one hundred–proof peach brandy. They sat watching the sun set and engaged in a ritual that was timeless and magical in its own way: they got drunk.

Sanballat slept poorly that night. The next morning, as soon as Aharoni appeared, he said, "Yoshi, one thing. When we approach Elenna, we must say nothing about her biological relationship to Daniel Ornstein. We know nothing about their involvement with each other, whether they're even acquainted. Perhaps he's the result of infidelity or artificial insemination. It's not information we need to share with her. We should just tell her that when we saw the picture you took of Ornstein at Hadassah Hospital, you decided to search various databases with face/body recognition software, to see whether you could find a picture of anyone else with the marks. And so, we found her. That's all she needs to know."

"I totally agree," said Aharoni.

21

Elenna

From an early age, Elenna Cohen had chosen her own path: independence and adventure over commitment, exciting experiences over finding the right man and settling down to raise a family. Thirty-seven years old, she was attractive, smart, and ambitious. She lived in Hastings-on-Hudson in Westchester County, just north of New York City. A world traveler and a runner with eight marathons to her credit, she owned a vintage clothing boutique on Columbus Avenue on the Upper West Side of Manhattan. Her life revolved around her friends, her family (her brother, Steven, his wife, and children), her store, her books, running, and a long string of lovers, not exclusively male. She loved to travel. Her last trip had been to a safari ranch in South Africa. Besides taking hundreds of photographs of the landscape and animal life, she had seduced her African guide, Oisin, with whom she'd shared many wonderful moments.

One of the few extravagant purchases she allowed herself was her La Marzocco espresso machine. On the day in question, she was making her morning latte when she heard the sound of the bell on her front door. The sound always made her happy. *I am a successful businesswoman*, she told herself whenever the first customer of the day walked in.

Elenna was mildly surprised to be greeted by a middle-aged gentleman who introduced himself as Dror Raskin, cultural attaché to the Israeli ambassador. They shook hands, and he gave Elenna his government identification card, embossed with a picture of the ancient temple's seven-branched menorah, the national symbol of the State of Israel. Then Mr. Raskin opened his briefcase and, with a bit of a flourish, presented her with a letter from Moshe Ayans, the Israeli ambassador to the United States. The letter looked authentic; it was an invitation to a meeting at the Israeli consulate in New York.

Elenna stared in disbelief at Dror Raskin. "What could the Israeli government possibly want with me?"

"Ms. Cohen, the ambassador is very eager to have you meet with a special guest, Dr. Yehoshaphat Aharoni, the associate high priest of the Samaritans from Mount Gerizim on the West Bank. Are you familiar with the Samaritans?"

"I've heard of them. Aren't they some sort of Jewish sect that performs animal sacrifices on Passover? That's about all I associate with them. I can't think of one reason why the Israeli ambassador would want me to meet Dr. Aharoni."

"The ambassador is good friends with the Samaritans. They are an important but rapidly shrinking community. They used to number in the hundreds of thousands, but there are now fewer than one thousand members. The high priest, whose name is Sanballat, asked whether you would do him the kindness of hearing what Dr. Aharoni has to say. The ambassador doesn't know why Sanballat wants this meeting, but he has agreed to sponsor it. It would take place in Israel's New York Consulate Office. After the ambassador introduces you, Dr. Aharoni would meet with you privately."

Raskin paused and then continued, "The relationship between this community and the State of Israel is important. We would be very grateful if you could do us this favor and meet with Dr. Aharoni. You can certainly decline the invitation, and you will never again hear from us. But I hope you will at least agree to the meeting. I have a limo waiting to take us downtown and bring you back."

Elenna excused herself and went to the back room of her shop. She called the Israeli Embassy, identified herself, and asked to speak to the ambassador. After several moments, the ambassador came on the line.

"Good morning, Ms. Cohen, this is Ambassador Ayans," he said, speaking with an Israeli accent.

"Good morning, sir. I'm calling because a man by the name of Dror Raskin is in my shop, claiming that. . . ."

"Forgive me for interrupting you, Ms. Cohen," the ambassador said. "Mr. Raskin is my personal representative, and strange as his request might sound, it's true that I sent him. Would you do me the kindness of coming to the consulate to meet with Dr. Aharoni and me? I realize this all sounds very mysterious, but I can personally vouch for your safety. If you're concerned about being kidnapped by a mad Samaritan. . . ."

"No, of course not." Elenna laughed. "But as you can imagine, I was surprised by the request. Give me a few minutes, Mr. Ambassador, and Mr. Raskin will have my answer."

Elenna's next call was to her brother, Steven. Neither of them could think of any reason why she shouldn't meet with Dr. Aharoni.

She walked out of her office and said to Raskin, "Okay, let's go."

They were silent from the moment they stepped into the limousine, which was waiting in front of the shop. When they arrived at the consulate, a man dressed in a brown military uniform stepped forward to open the door. Raskin led Elenna to a conference room that was tucked away behind the receptionist's desk. Moshe Ayans, the Israeli ambassador to the United States, was waiting in the room with Dr. Aharoni. Raskin introduced the two men and left the room.

An impeccably dressed steward of the Israeli Navy served cakes, juice, and hot drinks.

"Would you like some coffee?" the ambassador asked Elenna.

"Yes, please," she said, realizing she hadn't yet had her first cup of the day.

"Cream, sugar?"

"Just black, thank you."

He handed her a cup with a piece of cake on the side, and she settled into an oversized leather chair.

"Thank you for coming," the ambassador said. He then repeated the substance of what Raskin had told her at her store.

Despite her outward appearance of calm, Elenna was excited. It was not every day that she was invited to a foreign consulate to meet the representative of a strange religious sect.

Nevertheless, she concentrated on presenting herself as the professional New York businesswoman that she was.

"Gentlemen, I don't mean to be rude," she said. "But I have a store to run. Could you just tell me what's going on?"

"Ms. Cohen," Aharoni began.

"Please, call me Elenna."

"And please, call me Yoshi. Short for Yehoshaphat. It means 'God will give judgment.'"

Many years earlier, Elenna had taken several courses at the Jewish Theological Seminary. She decided to let them know they were not dealing with a Jewish ignoramus.

"Wasn't Yehoshaphat one of the kings of Judea, a descendant of David and Solomon?"

The ambassador, who had risen to leave the room, said to Aharoni. "Yoshi, I doubt one in ten Israelis know about King Yehoshaphat. You may have gotten more than you bargained for. Or exactly what you hoped to find. In any event, *b'hatzlacha*, good luck, to both of you."

After he'd left the room, Aharoni said, "Before I continue, I must ask you a personal question. You are under no obligation to answer. Were you born with strange birthmarks on your shoulders?"

Elenna was stunned. Had these people been investigating her?

"Ms. Cohen," Aharoni said. "You have my solemn oath, as a doctor and a Samaritan priest, that your response and any involvement in this matter is completely confidential."

Elenna was about to get up and demand to be driven back to her store. But then her curiosity got the better of her self-protective instincts. She put down her coffee and reached into her purse for the first of the three cigarettes she allowed herself each day. To her surprise, Aharoni took out a pack of cigarettes and lit hers and one for himself.

Elenna drew deeply on the cigarette and then said, "Yes, I was born with very strange birthmarks on my shoulders. They were in the shape of hands with fingers spread apart, like the hand configuration the Kohanim use to hold up their prayer shawls and bless the congregations on certain Jewish holidays. I'd be very interested in any explanation you can offer as to how I came to be born with them. I had them removed when I was fifteen, but perhaps you already know that. Tell me, Dr. Aharoni, what else do you know about me?"

Aharoni ignored Elenna's question. He was exhilarated by the possibility that sitting before him was someone who might have the power to save his people.

"What I am about to tell you may sound like fantasy," he said. "Maybe it is, although I would prefer to believe it is true. But we need your help to find out. The need for total secrecy is critical. Will you give us your word that you will disclose nothing about our meeting today?"

"No," Elena said. "I will not agree to anything until I hear what you have to say, and what you want of me."

Aharoni was silent for a moment and then nodded. "I understand. We will not ask for any commitment in advance. Once you understand what is at stake, I think you'll appreciate the reason we contacted you. And why I've asked you to keep what I tell you confidential."

"I know how to keep secrets. I am a highly educated and a successful businesswoman, which is more than I probably could say about the various imbedded double agents you people never seem to discover for decades."

She decided that an attack on Aharoni was uncalled for and she softened her demeanor.

"Sorry, Yoshi, I'm nervous. Can we get to the point? I want to know what I'm doing here."

Elena sat mesmerized as Aharoni told her about the chest and the role of the breastplate in saving the Samaritan community.

"But how did you find me?" Elena asked.

Aharoni told her everything short of her biological relationship with Daniel Ornstein. "Based on our conversation, if you're willing, you would travel to Israel to meet with our high priest, Sanballat. The Israeli government would chaperone you every step of the way."

Elenna's first concern was for her privacy. Facial recognition software! She replayed in her mind the information Aharoni had shared. *He's telling me only a person born with these birthmarks can open an ancient chest that's in the possession of the Samaritans—a chest created thousands of years ago by someone named Ivri, an ancestor of the patriarch Avraham. The chest contains a magical breastplate that allows a direct channel to God, who chose the Samaritans to save the world.*

Elenna dismissed the substance of the myth as obvious nonsense. But a free trip to Israel . . . to Mount Gerizim . . . to meet the head of this strange sect and participate in some magical ritual. For Elenna, no one could have scripted a more compelling adventure.

Sanballat was there to greet her when she and Aharoni arrived at Mount Gerizim. Elenna spent the next two days touring the Samaritan community, learning firsthand about its vanishing population. Sanballat saw *Yhahveh's* hand in Elenna's presence. Just as they were on the precipice of extinction, a savior had arrived. He brought her into the chamber room and showed her the sacred chest. He also told her the Samaritans' history, beginning with Avraham and Baasha. He showed her the 3,900-year-old leather scroll containing Baasha's Commentary, some of which he read and translated for her.

Elenna was a quick study. After just two days, she had concluded that Sanballat and his community fit the classic definition of a cult. They were insane—an insanity, to be sure, in the way of all messianic religions. Such sects could be dangerous if threatened. And this community was being threatened with extinction.

Sanballat had opened a Swiss bank account for her and her brother in the amount of five million dollars.

"One cannot put a value on a human life," Sanballat said, while they were hiking back from a point overlooking the entire Jordan Valley. "Nevertheless, we want to compensate you for our imposition on your time, and for possibly placing you at risk of your life."

"I would think this entire affair is ludicrous, and I wouldn't have come, except for one fact," Elenna said.

"What is that?" asked Sanballat.

"The impossibility of someone having been born with birthmarks in this configuration. The doctors told my parents the marks were unlike anything they had ever seen or found in the medical literature. But why are you so sure that only a person born with the birthmarks can open the chest? You told me about BabRama, and you said that his acolyte Jeda supposedly died trying to open the chest. But even if that's true, you're talking about something that happened twenty-five hundred years ago. Hasn't anyone tried since then?"

Sanballat had expected her question.

"Jeda is a person about whom we have a firsthand account, written by BabRama," Sanballat replied. "I realize someone might well disregard the Jeda story as an ancient fable. However, I will tell you what no one outside our community would know. There have been others, most recently ten years ago. A teenage boy from our community, who was studying Samaritan history, stole into the chamber and filmed himself placing his hands on the chest. We found his body and iPhone video the next day. We invented a scenario that forestalled a police investigation. Could he and the others have died from fright? That is a possibility. Aharoni is a medical doctor. He examined the boy and found nothing that would account for his sudden death. He also tested the chest holding the breastplate for lethal substances. All the tests came out negative."

Elenna said, "I had the marks removed. What makes you think their 'magic' still works?"

"Another important question. As I read to you in Baasha's Commentary, the answer is that according to our tradition, Avraham's mother removed his birthmarks upon his birth. Yet, that did not prevent Avraham from accessing the chamber in Nanna's temple in Ur or using the breastplate to condemn the practice of child sacrifice to Moloch."

At the break of dawn on the third day, two devout Samaritan women, dressed in white from head to toe, awakened Elenna. They washed her, purified her with virgin olive oil, and dressed her in a long-sleeved, white linen dress with red and gold trim. One of the women tied a scarf, dyed a deep blue, around Elenna's head. Another placed a generations-old necklace made of lapis lazuli and emeralds around her neck.

They escorted her into the Heichal, the altar room of the temple. Handwoven antique rugs covered the floors and hung on the walls, and the windows sparkled with intricately crafted stained glass. The benches, which could easily seat several hundred congregants, were made of polished oak. In the center stood a huge stone altar. The design of the room led the eye to a magnificent ark, which held the sacred Torah scrolls.

Aharoni was waiting for her inside. He was joined by Rayut, the third member of the current Trio. She bowed her head respectfully to Elenna. Sanballat then entered, dressed in the full regalia of the high priest: the ephod, the miter, a robe with golden pomegranates dangling from a blue trim, and a breastplate with gold settings holding the twelve gemstones, three stones in each of four rows. The vestments embodied the precise specifications dictated in the Book of Exodus for Aaron, Moses's brother and the first Jewish high priest. But it was not the original breastplate. The garment Sanballat wore had been fashioned by Baasha long ago, using instructions he received from Sengrel the Midianite, who traced his lineage to Ivri's home village of Eradu. Now, finally, they stood ready to retrieve the real breastplate, the actual stones.

The group stood in silence. Elenna thought she would experience panic. But she felt serene, uplifted, in a spiritual state.

Aharoni made a gesture, signaling that it was time. He took Elenna's hand and led her to stand in front of the ancient chest. She wondered, *What if I can't open the chest, and I don't die? Then what?*

Sanballat stood next to her, his lips moving in prayer. He fixed his gaze on the chest and nodded to Elenna. She placed her hands on the engraving of the hands, which were unusually warm to the touch.

She sensed a vibration. And then an inaudible click. As she gently pulled the lid up, the resistance of great age fell away. The lid creaked open. Inside the chest was a thick cloth, which was wrapped around an old, rusting piece of iron. There was nothing else. No intricately woven breastplate with gold settings, no miter with a gold plate engraved with the words *Kadosh L'Yhahveh*, Sanctified to *Yhahveh*. No stones. Nothing except a heavy rock.

Sanballat, Aharoni and Rayut felt abject loss and desperation. The future of the Samaritan people and culture had been forfeited. Its millennia-old dream of greatness, its destiny as Baasha had foretold, were not to be.

It had never occurred to Sanballat or any member of the Trio that the chest might not contain the breastplate. Even with her limited exposure to the Samaritans, Elenna could sense the devastating impact this would have on the community. Aharoni sat and cried. Sanballat stood before the Ark in which the Torah scrolls were kept and placed his prayer shawl, his tallit, over his head. His voice breaking with grief, he wailed a song of heartbreaking melancholy. Tragically, the third member of the Trio, Rayut, found no way to overcome the dissonance; she leaped to her death from an outcropping on the temple's dome.

The atmosphere of despair turned into an outright riot of pain when Auni, a young Samaritan, now convinced the entire Baasha legend was so much nonsense, ran into the Heichal, closed the chest and then placed his hands on the etching of the hand configuration. Convinced that he would demonstrate how the Trio had misled the community, he fell dead to the floor.

It was Thursday. Hoping there would be a joyful celebration after the chest was opened, Elenna had made plans to stay through the weekend. Whether or not the chest contained a magic breastplate or could be safely opened only by someone with the birthmarks, she had believed that the chest most likely contained something ancient, perhaps garments or other holy artifacts. Now, she saw that, twenty-five hundred years ago, BabRama had been the victim of a cruel stratagem conceived by his archenemy Zadok. Given Jeda's demise when he had attempted to open the chest, how could BabRama possibly have doubted that the actual breastplate was inside? That was the entire purpose of having Jeda sacrifice his life.

Auni's death caused still more anxiety because it clearly appeared that the chest itself had magical properties.

Sanballat called for a thirty-day period of mourning and meditation. He asked Elenna to stay for a week. Her unique ability to open the chest was proof that the Samaritans' beliefs had been well-founded. She was a blessed person; it would be comforting for the community to have her close by. Elenna did not mind. If she could in any way serve to alleviate the community's pain, she was ready to help.

22

Soulmates

aniel lay on the floor of Yehudit's foyer, drenched in sweat, his chest heaving, as if he were awakening from a horrifying nightmare. His body was jerking in a seizure. Knowing first aid from their military training, Tzionah and Yael loosened his collar, put a pillow under his head, and wrapped him in a warm blanket. The seizing stopped, but Daniel's breathing remained irregular. Yehudit had called the settlement's emergency medical services. The EMS team rushed Daniel by ambulance to Hadassah Hospital in Ein Kerem, the same hospital to which he'd been taken after his scooter accident. As they brought him in on a stretcher, Daniel suffered a severe seizure, creating a danger of aspiration pneumonia, which could be fatal. The ER team placed him on a ventilator under heavy sedation.

Yael and Tzionah insisted that Yehudit stay in Hevron. They promised to update her as soon as they knew anything. En route to the hospital, Yael called her father and asked him to call Varda.

Varda said she would leave immediately, and Gidon did likewise. As soon as he arrived, he found Yael and Tzionah in the waiting room just outside the ER. The three of them waited impatiently to hear what was wrong with Daniel and how he was doing. Two hours later, a doctor finally came to give them an update.

"Your friend is stable and no longer in danger," he said. "We put him on a ventilator and sedated him because of the severity of the seizure. Fortunately, his lungs are clear. We can discontinue the intubation later today. He hasn't had a heart attack or a stroke. I've seen similar situations with severe PTSD victims. On rare occasions, the most commonplace sights or sounds can trigger an extreme reaction, even years after the events. It's an area of brain science we are working to understand better, but for now, all we can do is have him rest. We've moved him to a room in the ICU and will do some neurological tests. He's American, yes? Are you his family?"

"We're close friends. His cousin is on her way," said Gidon. "Mr. Ornstein has a sister in Texas. Should we call her?"

The doctor said, "From a medical standpoint, I can't tell you his sister should fly over. In my opinion, he's no longer in danger. That's the best I can advise, but it's just from the medical perspective."

"Thank you," Gidon said.

Tzionah left two hours later, after Yael promised to keep in touch with her. Although Tzionah and Daniel had gotten along very well, there didn't appear to be any chemistry between them. Yael was relieved because she could no longer deny her feelings for Daniel.

The next morning, after the ventilator had been removed, and the sedation medication discontinued, Daniel regained consciousness. He was annoyed to have shown any weakness and to have inconvenienced Varda. "You shouldn't have come," he told her. "But I love you for it."

The neurological tests came back negative. But the doctor was concerned that Daniel was sometimes disoriented and was sweating through his sheets. He kept Daniel on an IV line with a saline solution to prevent dehydration. Daniel was having a recurring nightmare of the fire in which his brother Nathan had died. It was maddening. If the dream gave any details of what happened, Daniel could recall none of them. After two days in the ICU, he was transferred to a regular room, where he underwent a battery of psychiatric tests in an attempt to understand what might have set off the seizure. Daniel had had his fill of therapists and was politely uncooperative. He knew very well why he'd collapsed.

The discharge orders directed Daniel to rest for at least a week. Varda invited him to stay at her kibbutz, but Daniel declined the offer. He said that he didn't want to impose on her any further; in truth, having previously stayed at her kibbutz, he found its religious orthodoxy stifling.

Daniel wanted to get back to his own apartment and rest. As a mountaineer, he was used to taking care of himself in adverse circumstances. He would recover while eating takeout and watching movies on his computer.

"I'm concerned about leaving Daniel alone," Yael told her father. "When he collapsed and started seizing, I thought he would die right in front of us. What if we put him next door?"

The Gileadis had a long-term lease on the apartment next door to theirs. They usually rented it out, but it had been vacant for a month. Gidon had been thinking the same thing. The apartment was attached to their house by a door that opened onto their kitchen. When the apartment was being rented, they locked the door on both sides. Now, with Daniel recuperating, the door provided both privacy and accessibility suitable to the circumstances.

Both Gidon and Ronit were pleased that Yael was taking an interest in Daniel. Her last relationship had ended some months earlier. She was smart, engaging, and beautiful—and twenty-six years old. Her parents yearned for her to find the right match. Maybe Daniel would be the one. On the other hand, what if Daniel suffered from some fatal medical condition?

Daniel half-heartedly protested Gidon's offer. He hated to show vulnerability, especially to a military family. At the same time, he understood something truly frightening had occurred. It would be foolish to turn down the offer.

"It's more of an imposition for us to have to worry about you alone in your apartment than to know you're right next door," Ronit told him. "We won't disturb your privacy."

Before Varda left, she lectured Daniel in his hospital room,

"Now, *boychek*, listen to me," Varda said, using her New Jersey–accented matchmaker's voice and throwing in a Yiddish term of endearment. "Yael is one in a million. Why you should be so lucky, only God knows. But seriously, when the two of you are together, I see genuine affection. You both deserve happiness. Don't let this one get away."

Then, in a more serious tone, she asked, "Do you know what happened?"

"If I knew what happened, I would promise not to do it again. But I have no idea what the *it* is. Nothing like this has ever occurred to me. Maybe it was something in Yehudit's apartment. I don't know."

But Daniel did know. He very clearly remembered what had triggered his episode. But he had no intention of sharing it with anyone, not even with Varda. The framed drawing on Yehudit's wall was identical to the drawing he had made in his grandmother's apartment on Yom Kippur. How could that be possible?

Three days later, Daniel was feeling fully recovered. He was walking and speaking normally. He went to the hospital for a checkup and was cleared to resume all activities. While resting in the Gileadis' apartment, he had spent a good deal of time concentrating on the memories of his mystical experiences. His therapists had recommended that in the event of nightmares or panic attacks, he should recall and confront the details of the visions. The mental exercises had been helpful. But Daniel still shivered when he recalled the drawing on the wall of Yehudit's apartment. He was also mystified as to why his shoulders stung when he touched one of the tablets at Yehudit's apartment. *Is this never going to end? Will I never be free of these demons?*, he wondered.

At the same time, Daniel could not stop thinking about Yael. He was in love; in a way he had never thought possible.

Yael waited impatiently for Daniel to end his virtual isolation. She, too, was reflecting on the events at Yehudit's apartment and about her feelings for Daniel. There had been a number of men before she'd met Daniel. But she'd never felt for anyone else what she felt for Daniel. Varda was right. Daniel was different. And special. But what in the world was wrong with him?

When Daniel was ready to leave, he went next door to thank the Gileadis, who insisted that he join them for lunch. The conversation centered around Israeli politics. No one mentioned Daniel's seizure. After lunch, Yael stood up to clear the table. Her father waved her away.

"Yael, if Daniel's up to it, why don't you guys take a walk?"

Daniel was as desperate for exercise as he was to spend time alone with Yael. He said, "I was planning to go for a long walk as soon as I got back to my apartment. If you're free, I'd love to go with you now."

They strolled along Derech Ruppin, which eventually led to Mount Herzl, and the monument to Theodore Herzl, the founder of the Zionist movement in the late nineteenth century. They walked in an awkward silence loaded with sexual tension. When the road narrowed slightly and Daniel's arm grazed hers, Yael felt lightheaded. She yearned to wrap her arms around him and bring him close to her.

They began chatting about matters of no real importance. Without realizing how much time passed, they found themselves three kilometers from the Gileadis' home, at the Mount Herzl Cemetery. Daniel had never been to the site, and Yael hadn't visited it since her grade school days on a school trip.

They paused, but their thoughts dwelled far from issues bearing on the Jewish state. As they had been walking the last two kilometers to the cemetery, their swinging hands seemed to make contact more often. Daniel thought Yael must be able to hear the pounding of his heart. Yael was thinking the same about hers.

Trying to bridge the impasse, she said, "Are you going to tell me what happened at Yehudit's? I'm relieved that you seem much better. You really had us scared."

Without waiting for Daniel's response, and without consciously thinking about it, Yael slid her hand into Daniel's. They stood there, at the memorial for a man who had lived just forty years but had changed the world, experiencing the smoothness of each other's hands. They both sensed that their own lives were about to change forever. As if in a choreographed ballet, they turned toward each other, anticipating the magic of touching another's lips in a kiss for the first time. They kissed softly at first, then more passionately.

Daniel pulled away.

"Wait! Yael, how can you do this? I thought you're just about engaged to Beni!"

"Beni?"

Yael broke out laughing. She put her hand on Daniel's cheek, as she had, so impulsively, days earlier. This time, she let her hand linger. It was an extraordinary moment for Daniel. Not since before the tragedy, when he'd been the focus of his mother's unconditional adoration, had he experienced such open, unreserved love.

"Beni is gay, you big dolt! He saved my life in combat and is Mordechai's best friend. He's like a member of our family."

Yael put her arms around Daniel and hugged him tightly. Breathlessly, she backed away and said, "You obviously aren't fully recovered, but I promise, your cure is close at hand. Get us a cab. We're going to my place."

Daniel felt the intense tension that had been gripping his stomach melt away.

"Yes, ma'am," Daniel saluted, and hurried to hail a taxi.

Yael had a room in an apartment she shared with two friends from the army, both of them students at Hebrew University.

Her room was bare in the ways of college students who still regarded their parents' house as home. She had a bed, a desk, a table and computer, a dresser, and a small refrigerator. Her only personal item was a poster of Rona Kenan, an Israeli songwriter and singer with a soulful voice and an angelic face that radiated vulnerability and compassion.

Daniel didn't pay much attention to any of these details as he and Yael fell onto her bed. Their bodies fit together perfectly. They became one that afternoon—more than once. Detached from the outside world, they had no schedule apart from experiencing each other as they had dreamed about. They fell asleep in each other's arms. Yael woke up first. Daniel was still asleep, his rhythmic breathing gentle on her skin. The sheet was on the floor. She gazed at his athletic body, his muscular thighs and ripped stomach. She tenderly ran her fingers along the length of his arms, noticing a scar and wondering whether it was the result of a motorcycle accident or a souvenir from a mountain climbing expedition.

As she traced the muscles of his upper arms, she noticed a Duoderm patch that was falling off his right shoulder. She gently peeled it back and saw what looked like a tattoo. Taking a closer look, she realized it was a birthmark in the shape of a right hand with fingers parted. As a Jew and Israeli, she knew the shape; it was the Kohanic hand configuration. Then she noticed he had the same patch on his left shoulder. Gently removing it, she discovered the identical birthmark, except this one was of a left hand.

"Daniel, why in the world do you have these marks," she exclaimed, her voice raised. Swearing silently, he sat up. "Yael, let me explain. . . ."

"Daniel, these are not tattoos. They're birthmarks!"

Daniel reached out to embrace her, but Yael pulled away. Daniel cursed himself. He had made up his mind to share everything with Yael, starting with his birthmarks. But the joy and excitement of the moment had made him forget.

"Yael, please, calm down," he begged her. "I know they're weird; I was born with them. There wasn't, uh, time to tell you about them before.

"My whole life I have been resolved to figure out why I have them, and what they mean. Legends are told about Kohanim who have had these birthmarks. It could be a recessive gene. I've never heard that my family descends from the Kohanim, but maybe it's nothing stranger than that. I won't lie and say that I believe this explanation. Frankly, I strongly doubt it, but I guess it's possible. One day, I'll find the answer."

Daniel's words calmed Yael down. Searching her mind for a way to think of the marks as natural, she recalled her class on genetics. *There are all sorts of recessive genes. Obviously, that's what these birthmarks are.*

She got back into bed and put her head on his shoulder, now empathizing with how Daniel must have struggled with such freakish marks over the years, especially as a boy. "Does Varda know?"

"No. Aside from the shrinks I've seen and doctors I've consulted, only my mother and sister know. And my school librarian, who was a very good mentor and friend. And now you."

Yael regretted her outburst. She pulled Daniel into a hug and kissed him. "You're just full of mysteries, aren't you?" she said.

"Yael, you have no idea. There's a lot more I need to tell you. And I will, I promise. But first," Daniel said with an impish grin, "I think it's only fair for me to conduct a thorough inspection of your body, for any army listening devices disguised by your shrapnel scars."

Giggling like a teenager, Yael dived under the covers. Then she called out, "Okay, Mr. Ornstein, you may begin your *b'dichah*," using the Hebrew word for inspection.

Later that day, they held hands and walked around the Old City, taking their time to cover the three miles. They stopped at kiosks offering local delicacies: fattoush; Egyptian bread pudding; baklava; and knafeh, a kind of cheesecake. They contemplated the eight gates of the Old City. The Ottoman Turks had restored them in the sixteenth century. The Golden Gate, sealed shut in 1541 by Sultan Suleiman, faced the Mount of Olives. It was through there, some believed, that the Messiah would enter Jerusalem.

They sat on a giant ashlar stone, one of the thousands of finely cut stones that King Herod used to restore the Second Temple in 20 BCE. The ashlars were an engineering wonder: forty feet long, eight feet wide, and three and one-half feet tall, they each weighed approximately eighty tons.

Yael was feeling edgy. Daniel had said he was convinced the birthmarks were part of a greater mystery, connected to bizarre events that had occurred when he was a child, and once on Mount Rainier.

"Daniel, let's go to your place. I want to see your new digs. And I want to hear everything about these mysteries you keep hinting about," she said.

Daniel felt terrified; he was suddenly being called upon to disclose all the mystifying experiences he had kept secret. He was afraid he would lose her. As he had lectured so many climbers, he now instructed himself: *Of course I'm terrified. I'm supposed to be.*

As they began walking to his apartment, he told her about the death of his brother, the possibility that he was to blame, his never-ending guilt. And the most frustrating aspect of the situation was the fact that he could remember nothing of the incident.

Daniel told her more about the birthmarks. "No one can explain them. I've just had to live with them. My parents wanted them removed, but I refused. If I were religious, I would think they were a sign from God. I keep them covered, or try to, as you discovered."

When they were inside Daniel's apartment, Yael asked, "Can I see them again?"

"You want me to take off my shirt?"

"And more than that, yes, please," Yael said, as she began stripping off her clothes.

The new lovers fell on the bed and gave vent to their passion. Then they showered and lovingly washed each other's bodies, rekindling their desire. They made love again, this time very slowly. Joined together but not moving, they stared into each other's eyes, feeling their vulnerability, an intimate experience more powerful than any physical pleasure.

They ordered from Yael's favorite Chinese takeout restaurant and drank beer. Yael listened without interrupting as Daniel described his visions of Nathan on Yom Kippur and on Mount Rainier. He showed her the video of his elongated arm, stretched out to save Raymond Pierce. He told her about the pages of Paleo-Hebrew, which he had written, and which then had disappeared. And he recounted his father's tragic death and his estrangement from his mother and sister.

"My mother used to tell me stories from the Bible and legends from the Talmud. She also made up wonderful stories. The one I loved best was about a magic handkerchief with the hand configurations of my birthmarks. She said that if I covered my eyes with it, I could be transported to any place and time I wanted."

Daniel kept his old school notebook in the zipper pocket of his climbing pack. The pack was buried in a closet with other assorted mountaineering equipment. Now, Daniel retrieved the notebook and showed Yael a drawing he had made of how his hands looked on the handkerchief.

Daniel also showed her the drawings he had made on Yom Kippur, of the breastplate, and of the cave on a river where Nathan and an unidentifiable woman stood, with his brother holding a set of thin stone tablets.

Yael was captivated and moved by the stories Daniel told her. She hadn't imagined that Daniel was afflicted by so much psychic trauma. Still, she tried to resist seeing the events Daniel had described as paranormal. Very strange, yes; miraculous, no. She was inclined to believe that Daniel had fallen victim to the age-old process whereby people used "magical thinking" to explain bizarre occurrences. Daniel's birthmarks were indeed mysterious, but what else could they be but some freak of nature or recessive gene? As for the video from Mount Rainier, Daniel admitted that it could have been doctored, or it could have been a strange reflection of the rising sun. And his memory of writing Paleo-Hebrew, and his mother's reactions to the notebook, could have been just that—memories. He'd very likely converted another dream into memories of real events.

Yael gently tested her doubts. "Why couldn't the visions have been waking dreams, hallucinations? The appearance of Nathan seems to me a sign of your unconscious recognition that he doesn't blame you. He was in charge. You were ten years old."

Daniel picked up his notebook again and showed Yael his drawing of the breastplate. Yael recalled the moment when Daniel had collapsed as he stared at the framed drawing on Yehudit's wall.

And then it came to her. "You drew this same exact picture when you were ten?"

"Yes, the exact picture, down to every detail."

"But wait," said Yael. "So what? There is nothing miraculous about such a drawing. It represents the breastplate worn by the Jewish high priest in the temple. Drawings of the breastplate go back centuries. You probably saw one when you were a small boy. The Bible describes in exacting detail how the breastplate should be made and worn."

"This is different," Daniel said. "My drawing is not simply a copy of the breastplate described in the Bible. I've examined pictures in libraries, museums, and scholarly sources. They're all based on the description in Exodus. I agree that, theoretically, I could have seen a picture of the breastplate before that Yom Kippur. I don't think it's the case, but it's possible."

"But what is not possible is this," Daniel said, pointing to the top and bottom of his drawing, where he had drawn his birthmarks. Daniel also pointed to the bottom, where he had drawn he letters for *Yhahveh*, in Paleo-Hebrew (⟨ᴣʸᴣᴣ⟨), on the left.

"The symbols and words on the top and bottom of my drawing are exactly like those that appear on the framed drawing in Yehudit's apartment. No publicly available representation of any breastplate shows these markings. There is no rational way to understand how I made such marks on my drawing when I was ten years old. What I experienced was not a dream."

Daniel was committed to sharing everything with Yael. He reluctantly told her about Anika and his trek to the Dalia cave. He was about to describe the strange happenings at the cave when Yael bolted up from the bed and began yelling at him.

"Daniel, you're an impossible fool. I fought against Palestinian commandos in that area. It is beyond dangerous. I can't believe I've fallen in love with an irresponsible madman."

"Yael, I happen to agree with you. Ghanaian passport or not, I was stupid. My climbing days are behind me."

Daniel recounted his bizarre adventure with Sengrel: the drawing Sengrel had left was identical to the one Daniel had drawn in his notebook on the night his family had returned home to Brooklyn after Yom Kippur. And he told her of his encounter with the Samaritans who saved him from militant Bedouin.

Yael was emotionally exhausted. She lay down, closed her eyes, and spooned her body with Daniel's, who put his arms around her. The one thing she felt sure about was that her love for Daniel was real and unalterable. She had found her soulmate.

23

Spooky Action in All Directions

Daniel agreed with Yael's suggestion that they confide in her father. He was smart, highly educated and had an obvious interest in the subject matter. Most importantly, Daniel trusted him.

Gidon looked through the magnifying glass at Daniel's two birthmarks and shook his head. Then he excused himself and returned ten minutes later. "I just spoke with my friend, Aryeh Badash, in the genealogy department. I didn't tell him any details, but he confirmed that strangely shaped marks represent recessive genes. They can show up frequently, rarely, or never. Most often these types of genes get expressed once every few generations. But Aryeh has never heard of a person with marks that were in the precise shape of real-world objects."

"I don't know how to make any sense of this. I can't even guess at a rational explanation as to why Daniel has birthmarks in this hand configuration. I confess it's unsettling."

"Daniel," Yael said, "I want you to tell the story again, every detail: your vision of Nathan at your grandmother's apartment; Yehudit's drawing; and what happened at the Dalia cave. And show Abba the video from Mount Rainier of you saving Pierce."

Gidon was as shocked as Yael had been to hear of Daniel's solo excursion to the Dalia cave. Daniel explained what had happened at Disappointment Cleaver on Mount Rainier. He pulled out his phone and played the video McBride had sent him.

"Isn't Pierce the billionaire who committed suicide?"

"Yes. If he was trying to commit suicide that day on the mountain, he endangered the lives of my entire rope team. Fortunately, when he eventually succeeded, he did not take anyone with him."

Daniel took his time retelling all the events. He tried to give a flavor of how eerie and frightening it had been to see his drawing replicated on the wall in Yehudit's apartment.

"So, you can appreciate why I was taken aback by your question about whether I believe in the paranormal," he said.

"Yes, I recall the strange look on your face when I asked you. I was joking, of course. That was then. Right now, I feel as if we've entered the twilight zone."

"Now," Yael said, "I'll tell you something you don't know, but it fits into this story.

"A girl named Zahava Mizrachi created the drawing on Yehudit's wall. It was June 1967, right after the Six-Day War. She was the twelve-year-old daughter of the *aluf*, Brigadier General Moshe Mizrachi, who led the Israeli army into Hevron."

From the time of the Mameluke Arabs in the sixteenth century, the Jews were prohibited from entering the cave or the Herodian structure enclosing the cave. With the area back under full Jewish control for the first time since 70 CE, Mizrachi was determined to enter and determine the cave's condition.

After consulting various Arabic texts, Mizrachi identified a possible opening on the floor of the courtyard within the Herodian complex. The spot had been covered over with stones. Descriptions from medieval sources indicated that a staircase led down from the opening to the actual cave area. A corridor supposedly led from the bottom of the staircase to a fork, with a chamber on either side. On the left was the burial chamber; from the old documentary records Mizrachi examined, it was unclear what was in the right chamber.

Mizrachi chose a moonless night during the monthlong holiday of Ramadan, when Muslims fast from sunrise to sunset. To be doubly sure they would not be disturbed, Mizrachi ordered a curfew on the area. It was an order he had no authority to issue without approval from the prime minister's office, which he did not have.

Mizrachi and one of his lieutenants managed to pry an opening through the stones that was large enough for a small person to climb through. His 12-year old daughter Zahava was the obvious choice because she was small and extremely thin. He fastened a rope around her waist, both to lower her to the bottom of the cave floor and to keep her secure as she walked around. Mizrachi did not give her a camera, which in those days would have required an unwieldy flash connection and large bulbs. Zahava had a special artistic talent, and Mizrachi had given her a drawing pad and pencils.

Yehudit's last name is Mizrachi. She is Zahava's sister. Zahava died in an auto accident ten years ago. The drawing on Yehudit's wall is the original and only drawing Zahava made.

A silence settled on the room before Gidon clapped his hands for attention.

"I'll be damned if we don't make some sense of this," he said. "In a few hours, I'll make some calls. I'll give no details, obviously. The time differences are not yet right for me to call the people with whom I want to speak."

"What do you say about beer and shawarma? I'll order from Kol Hadvarim Tovim (All the Good Stuff). And, for the occasion, I'll get out my Blu-Ray copy of *E.T.*"

Yael groaned. "He loves the movie," she said. "Wait until he tells you how he met Steven Spielberg at a concert at which his niece was the featured singer." Holding up a finger in warning, Yael said, "Not now, Abba; you'll have to wait until I'm not around for you to tell it for the fiftieth time."

Everyone laughed and endorsed Gidon's plan for dinner and entertainment.

"I never thought I'd see the day when I could laugh about my little *pegamin*," said Daniel, using the Hebrew word for blemishes. For once, he was at peace with his mysteries.

The food arrived: delicious shawarma—spit-roasted lamb stuffed into a pita with cut up tomatoes, cucumber, and the spicy tahina and harif dressings. While they ate, the group took a break from the mind-numbing issues with which they were wrestling. They let the movie, which they had all seen multiple times, run on as they ate, watching and talking at the same time.

When it was time for the gathering to break up, Gidon looked at his daughter and Daniel and smiled.

"It's late. Why don't you both spend the night here? Yael, you can put Daniel wherever you want him to sleep. On the couch. In the apartment next door, the floor in any room but mine, or perhaps you'll figure out someplace more, uh, comfortable, okay?"

Daniel sat surrounded by pictures of Gidon, Yael, Ronit, and Mordechai, all decked out in military gear and medals. "I'm good with floors," he said. Gidon looked on with amusement as Yael, with an exasperated expression, took Daniel's hand and dragged him off to her old bedroom.

The group assembled at 7:00 a.m. the next day over coffee and toast. Gidon, who had been up all night making calls and doing research on the internet, gave a report about his conversation with one of the most renowned physicists in the world, Dr. Stuven Remyrksgaard, the Earnst Weilding Professor of Physics at the University of Stockholm. Remyrksgaard was currently on a four-year guest residency at Brookhaven National Laboratory in Long Island, New York.

Gidon rose as if he were giving a lecture to his class. Stuven had sent him an email summarizing the main points of what he'd told Gidon. He also emailed links to some articles he thought Gidon might find relevant.

"What Stuven said," Gidon began, "was about as unbelievable as your birthmarks. We made the right choice in watching *E.T.* last night."

"To protect our secrecy, I made up a story, somewhat analogous to ours. I told him a good friend, a Muslim, came to me with his ten-year-old son, who exhibited birthmarks with the exact color, shading, and dimensions of the so-called Black Stone. As you may know, this is a rock set into the eastern corner of the Kaaba, the ancient building in the center of the Grand Mosque in Mecca. Muslims revere it as an Islamic relic which, according to Muslim tradition, dates back to the time of Adam and Eve. I told Stuven the birthmarks—one on each calf—showed not only the stone but also part of the wall setting. And that they were precise, nuanced images."

Stuven is a highly regarded scientist who has conducted serious research on the paranormal events and phenomena such as telekinesis and clairvoyance. He began by observing that people, even very smart people, dismiss or simply ignore whatever they cannot readily understand. He sent me a quote from Einstein, who said, 'As a human being, one has been endowed with just enough intelligence to be able to see clearly how utterly inadequate that intelligence is when confronted with what exists.'

"Stuven sounded quite certain of his views on the birthmarks I described. He said the marks, if they were real birthmarks, were not possible except if one were to accept the idea of dimensional spheres, commonly called multiple universes. It's explained in some detail in one of the articles he sent me. You can read it at your leisure. The gist of what he said is that the concept of multiple or alternative universes has been accepted by prominent physicists. It's been affirmed by physicists such as Erwin Schrodinger, Steven Hawking, and Richard Feynman, the first and last being Nobel Prize winners.

"Stuven also explained something called quantum entanglement. This is as strange or stranger than the notion of multiple universes, yet it is even more widely accepted. He told me to record what he was going to say. I guess he didn't think I could explain it. He was right." Gidon hit the play button on his iPhone. Stuven's voice came through clearly.

"So-called quantum entanglement is at once not imaginable, yet we know it is true. What I mean is this: Suppose you split apart an atom into two pieces. You then measure the two pieces after they have flown way apart. It turns out, no matter how far apart the pieces are from each other, if you alter the path or speed of one of the pieces, the other piece instantaneously mimics the movement. They have proven this to be true, both mathematically and in experiments. It is verifiable even if the two pieces are galaxies apart. The results are fundamentally beyond the ability of the human mind to comprehend. So much so that Einstein rejected the theory. He called it 'spooky action at a distance.'

"Religious leaders rarely study physics. We cannot prove God split the Red Sea, but we can prove the two particles are somehow in sync across galaxies. Maybe your case, which involves these inexplicable birthmarks, will create some public interest in these issues. Physicists cannot let go of their need to use jargon. In the books they've written for popular audiences, physicists like Steven Hawking and Richard Feynman could not break away from jargon and failed to make the subject truly readable. As you know, millions bought their books and promptly put them on their bookshelves. My friend calls them 'dusty statues to ostensible erudition.'"

Gidon turned off the recording.

Yael had been sitting quietly, lost in her thoughts and frustrated by her intellect's refusal to assimilate what she was hearing. She stood up and gave vent to her frustration. "Come on, guys! Are we suddenly supposed to believe Daniel was branded in the womb with tattoos from an alternate universe? Or that he's entangled with someone light-years away who has these marks?"

If Yael was hoping to jostle the group into thinking more cynically, she was disappointed.

Daniel shrugged and said, "It's not sudden. One thousand years ago, Maimonides, Judaism's greatest rabbi and philosopher, wrote about creation and God in terms that today's physicists would understand. Maimonides wrote his classic *Guide to the Perplexed* in 1190 CE. He said that one can only describe God in terms of what He is not: He is not corporeal, He does not occupy time or space. The human mind cannot comprehend Him."

"That's interesting," Yael interrupted. "But what of all the anthropomorphic ways the Bible discusses God? The creation story, the splitting of the Red Sea, the Ten Plagues God brought down on Egypt. There are hundreds of passages like this in the Tanakh and Christian bible."

Daniel nodded.

"Maimonides addressed this issue directly with respect to the Tanakh. He held that all the stories were allegorical, not to be taken literally. Even the famous description of man's creation—'And God created man in His own image'—was meant metaphorically.

He maintained that the stories were designed to ease the transition of the Jewish people from idolatry to monotheism."

Daniel pulled out his iPhone and retrieved a document he had saved.

Maimonides went so far as to say, and I'm quoting, 'to assume God is corporeal, has any properties of any kind, or to ascribe to Him any attributes, is a sin bordering on idolatry.'

"And, as you know, for monotheists, there is no greater sin than idol worship."

"I'm reminded," said Gidon, "of Sherlock Holmes's famous axiom: 'When you have eliminated the impossible, whatever remains, however improbable, must be the truth.' I can't believe I'm saying this, but we do seem to be dealing with paranormal events, and we had best adapt our minds to it, until and unless someone comes up with a better explanation. And I dearly hope someone will."

Gidon excused himself to make more phone calls. Daniel said he had a headache and wanted a nap. Yael accompanied him to her bedroom where they lay silently together, holding each other tightly, fighting the awful disorientation of coming face to face with reality's horizon.

24

Putting the Pieces Together

Nick Williams, a postdoctoral fellow at the Binqus Institute, arrived at his desk early one Monday and found an envelope from Laura Victor, marked, "To All Concerned! Urgent! Open Immediately!" Inside was a photograph of what looked like mirror images of a tattoo of a hand, with its fingers spread apart. But Laura's accompanying note explained that the images were actually birthmarks, which might be the keys to a mystery Dr. Binqus was intent on solving. She instructed all the Institute's researchers to put aside whatever they were working on in order to determine whether they could provide some insight into the mystery. Most of the Institute's researchers, however curious they were about the photographs, had nothing to contribute and put them aside.

Nick was about to do the same when he suddenly had a vague memory of something he'd seen while studying the Elephantine Papyri. These were a collection of ancient Jewish manuscripts dating from the fifth to the first century BCE. One of the most famous papyri was an exchange of letters with the religious authorities in Jerusalem, discussing the ritual practices for celebrating Passover. The dry soil of Upper Egypt preserved the documents.

Brown turned on his computer and loaded a page from the papyri. It had no writing but included drawings of various valued objects. He focused on the picture of a small cylinder. He remembered noticing that the word *Hoshen* in Paleo-Hebrew, ﾞﾟﾞﾟﾞﾟ, meaning breastplate, was etched on the cylinder's surface. There were two other marks, which Brown had thought were dents in the metal. Now, magnifying the image of his screen, he was stunned when he saw that the tiny markings appeared to be perfectly drawn representations of the pictures of the birthmarks Laura had circulated.

Dr. Hallie Rachèl, the Addington Roel Professor of Archeology at the University of North Carolina at Chapel Hill, made the next discovery. Recently married, she'd been away on her honeymoon for a month. On her return, she found the urgent letter from Laura Victor, with the picture of Daniel's birthmarks ("They are not tattoos"). Hallie stared at the birthmarks in disbelief. Then she opened a second envelope from Laura, which had just arrived. It contained a blown-up picture of a page from the Elephantine Papyri, which contained the page that Nick Williams had found. Hallie studied the materials and then dialed the Institute and asked for Laura.

"Hi Laura, it's Hallie," she said, when Laura picked up the phone. "I just got back from my honeymoon and saw the materials you sent me. I think you should get Maxwell on this call."

Laura told Hallie she would find Binqus and call back as soon as possible. A half hour later, Binqus and Laura were on speakerphone with her.

"Hi, Hallie," Binqus said. "Congratulations on your marriage. What do you have for us?"

"As Laura knows, I've been studying the so-called Samaria Papyri, found in the Dalia Cave near Mount Gerizim. The Samaritans used the cave as a refuge. Among the materials we found was a partial parchment scroll that describes a chest possessed by the Samaritans, which is said to contain the breastplate used by the high priest in Solomon's Temple. The man who wrote the scroll was named BabRama. We know from other sources that he was the high priest at the Samaritan temple on Mount Gerizim. The Samaritans believed the breastplate used in the Jerusalem temple rightfully belonged to them. When the temple in Jerusalem was destroyed, BabRama somehow managed to acquire the chest. But as I said, we only have fragments of his scroll."

"What's this got to do with the hand configuration?" Binqus asked.

"The scroll contains a warning. The chest can be opened only by a person with birthmarks in the same shape as those that appear on Daniel Ornstein's shoulders. Anyone without the birthmarks who tries to open the chest will die."

"Hallie, how sure are you about this?" Binqus asked.

"Sure enough to share it with you. So that means very sure. I'll be in touch if I come up with any more information."

"Not 'if,' Hallie," Binqus said. "When."

Hallie laughed and hung up.

Binqus and Laura stared silently at each other for a long moment.

"How do we proceed from here?" asked Binqus.

"Well," Laura replied, "we've uncovered several facts that seem related: The inexplicable birthmarks on Daniel Ornstein's shoulders. A story of a magic breastplate in a magic chest that can only be opened by someone with those mysterious marks. That's a lot of magic—too much for my taste, except that I can't explain the events in any other way that makes sense. But while you might call Ornstein's birthmarks a supernatural phenomenon, that just means—as with so many other phenomena we've examined— we don't yet have a rational explanation. The emphasis being on the word 'yet,'" Laura emphasized. "We should focus on the cylinder referred to in the Elephantine Papyri, which Nick Williams described. Is it too implausible to consider that the cylinder contains information about the breastplate, perhaps even a map that shows where it was hidden? I vote that we consider the possibility."

Binqus nodded. "Laura, I want you to make inquiries. Find out who this Daniel Ornstein is."

The Israel Museum, Israel's foremost cultural institution, was situated on a hill in Jerusalem, adjacent to the Gi'vat Ram campus. Every year, the museum was the recipient of hundreds of artifacts and documents of historic value, including several from Maxwell Binqus. Display space was always a problem. Almost all new material went into storage after it had been classified and indexed. The museum allowed accredited Bible scholars to access its research files. William L. Prospur, chair of the archeology department at Cambridge University, had been continuing his review of the Solomon Schechter files for a biography of Schechter. On this, his last day, he spent most of the time examining the strange bronze cylinder Schechter had acquired and the mystifying scroll that it contained, written in a manner that suggested a very sophisticated encryption.

Marla Karr, a graduate student in archeology at Hebrew University, was one of the many beneficiaries of Binqus's largesse. Her primary duty as a grantee was to spot information of potential interest to the Binqus Institute's broad agenda. She worked with the Institute to acquire replicas and facsimiles of items from the museum's collection that could be of interest to the Institute's varied agendas.

Karr had noticed Prospur's fascination with a cylinder and scroll that were indexed together in the Schechter archives. She thought the mysterious items would be of interest to people at the Institute, so he was surprised when Laura Victor declined his offer to obtain professional reproductions. Karr was naturally outgoing and liked to talk to visiting scholars about their work. Prospur was a gregarious Englishman who didn't hide his frustration in trying to determine the nature and meaning of the cylinder and the scroll.

He told Karr, "Schechter found the cylinder when he was unearthing manuscripts and materials from the Cairo Genizah. He removed the scroll but eventually put it aside when he was unable to decipher the writing or symbols. It is my belief that the cylinder was created during the Jewish occupation of a military installation at Elephantine Island, most likely having something to do with the Jewish temple that existed there from around 500 to 200 BCE. We know that several Torah scrolls and other artifacts from the Elephantine Jewish community were sent for safekeeping to the Great Library in Alexandria. Albrecht and other scholars have written that as the library deteriorated, some of that material was transferred to Egypt, Palestine, and Babylonia, which were the major centers of Jewish life around 500 CE. I've sent photographs of the scroll to Bible scholars in the United States and here in Israel. None of them got any further than I have."

Karr didn't know of any new projects at the Institute to which the cylinder and scroll might be germane. Nevertheless, on the off-chance that on a second look, Victor or someone else might find them of interest, she took his own photographs and put them in the mail.

Victor ran to Binqus's office waving the Karr photographs and interrupted an interview Binqus was giving to CNN.

Binqus took one look at the pictures and said to Victor, "Pack your stuff. You're going to Jerusalem."

Prospur left for England the same day Victor arrived. She headed straight to the museum's annex, where Karr had arranged for a private conference room. After exchanging greetings and sharing some sandwiches Karr had ordered, they placed on the large table the cylinder, the glass-enclosed leather scroll, other possibly relevant documents, and a microscope. She brought him up to speed about what the Institute had recently learned about the cylinder from the Elephantine and Samaria Papyri.

Two weeks later, Victor and Karr felt they could advance a speculative but credible hypothesis. Given the etchings on the cylinder, they believed that the encrypted leather scroll concealed the location of the breastplate that the Levite high priest had worn in Solomon's Temple. They developed a picture of events they thought was plausible: Zadok, the last high priest of the temple in Jerusalem, who was mentioned prominently in the Elephantine Papyri, had led a group of exiles to the island. He had taken the breastplate with him, secured in a chest that, they believed, could only be opened safely by a Levite who bore the birthmarks. They speculated further that Zadok buried the chest on the island and created the cylinder and scroll to enable a future Levite to recover the breastplate and bring it to a new temple in Jerusalem.

Unfortunately, they couldn't decipher the scroll any more than Schechter or Prospur and his colleagues could.

Wholly apart from whether Daniel Ornstein's birthmarks related to a biblical mystery, they represented an unquestionably paranormal phenomenon. Binqus wanted to find out whether Ornstein had relatives who also displayed the marks. As he had done in the past, he turned to Dr. Sebastian David Royce, a man of science whom he greatly respected.

Royce was the Stephen M. Chan Professor of Biophysics at New York University Medical School and the school's thirty-eight-year-old wunderkind. Binqus had spotted Royce some years earlier as a scientist with the potential to be an auspicious force in medicine. He appointed Royce a "Binqus Scholar," the most prestigious level awarded to the Binqus Institute's outside researchers. Royce had spent several weeks as a visiting scholar at the Institute, assisted by two research assistants. One of his pet projects was researching medical techniques described in the Old and New Testaments. Both Binqus and Royce were understandably delighted when Royce's article on the subject was published in the prestigious *Journal of Semitic Studies*.

When Royce received the email marked "urgent" from Laura Victor, along with a picture of Daniel Ornstein's birthmarks and the McBride video, he had the same reaction as everyone who'd seen them. A private video could be doctored. But a photograph from a hospital's database was not likely to have been photoshopped.

Royce pulled some strings and submitted the photo to a central NYU office in charge of a vast repository of public and private records. The information included photographs and DNA data from the New York State Medical Examiner's Office.

His request produced two hits. First, they identified pictures of Avi Cohen, an NYU Medical School intern who had been killed in a bus accident years earlier, and whose shoulders were photographed by the attending medical examiner. They were also able to access a tissue sample extracted from the corpse by the examiner. Based on that DNA, they identified a New Yorker by the name of Elenna Cohen. Her plastic surgeon, Dr. N. Brace Dratler, was affiliated with the NYU Medical Center, and his files were in its database. In his Elenna Cohen file, Dratler had noted that her birthmarks were unlike anything he had ever seen or read about in the medical literature. He also noted that he had preserved the patches of the skin he had removed. They were on file in the Medical Center's Organ Tissue Depository.

Within a probability factor of approximately 98 percent, Royce identified Elenna and Avi Cohen as brother and sister, and Avi Cohen as Daniel's biological father.

Royce called Binqus. "Maxwell, the file you sent me strains credulity. And I've seen some really weird stuff."

He summarized for Binqus the close genetic relationship among the three people whose records he'd examined.

"The video could have been doctored, but the marks on Ornstein's and Cohen's shoulders are not likely to have been forged. One picture is from a hospital, the other from the New York Medical Examiner.

"You're telling me these can't possibly be fakes?"

"That's my conclusion, yes, which means we are dealing with a supernatural occurrence."

"I need your help on this," Binqus said. "Could you come up here on Thursday? We'll have dinner at the Red Lion Inn in Stockbridge, and I'll arrange a room for you there."

Stockbridge, Massachusetts, was a lovely, picturesque town. Royce recalled the last time he stayed at the inn. The food was excellent.

Binqus felt a wave of excitement. The pieces were coming together. Royce was brilliant. He would be a significant addition to the team. Binqus placed a call to Michael Harshman of the Dupont Consulting Group. Binqus had often turned to Harshman for help. He was smart, reliable, and thorough.

It was an easy assignment. Within a matter of days, Harshman had located Elenna Cohen and obtained the basic facts of her life. He didn't need to interview anyone. He confined the investigation to public record documents and a little computer hacking Binqus didn't need to know about. Harshman's investigation hadn't uncovered any evidence that Daniel Ornstein and Elenna Cohen knew each other or had any nonbiological connection. He was quite surprised to discover that Cohen was visiting the Samaritan community on Mount Gerizim. All of this he duly reported to Binqus.

Royce was not your traditional physician. For one thing, he smoked cigarettes. He was also substantially overweight. When Binqus ordered the swordfish, Royce ordered the twenty-four-ounce ribeye with a large side order of hash browns. Binqus did not give Royce great odds for living past sixty. Royce claimed he would change his ways in two years, when he turned forty. Despite his smoking and heft, Royce was energetic, a hyperactive doer, exactly the personality type Binqus preferred. Binqus had invested in a number of biotech startups that were based on Royce's research. More of them were successful than not. Both men had earned significant amounts of money from their stock holdings.

Over dinner, Royce confirmed his enthusiasm for the project. As he tucked into his steak, Binqus told him everything the Institute and Harshman had discovered so far, including the fact that Ornstein's biological aunt had been visiting the Samaritans at Mount Gerizim. Binqus gave Royce a folder with all the information they had about the project. Royce looked through it and pulled out an enlarged photograph of the scroll that had been removed from the cylinder.

"My team's theory," said Binqus, "is that this may be an encrypted map leading to the chest and the breastplate somewhere on Elephantine Island."

Royce focused on the scroll's writing. It was an elegant script, using alphabetic-type symbols. Royce was fluent in seven languages, including Arabic, Sanskrit, and Chinese. And he could read Hebrew. He was familiar with the Phoenician alphabet and derivative scripts such as Paleo-Hebrew. He also knew quite a bit about cryptography. But he could not relate any of the markings on the scroll to any language or encryption methods of which he was aware.

"Your reaction is the same as the experts on my staff. They've found nothing remotely similar," Binqus told Royce.

Royce was reminded of the excitement he'd felt when he launched his career by discovering the recessive delta-gene *thetta*. Its mutation was a leading cause of some forms of dementia. Now, he was caught up in a mystery that hinted at truly paranormal forces.

Royce closed the portfolio. He had seen enough. He would put aside all his other projects and devote his full time and intellect to the task of solving the mystery of the scroll. Binqus assured Royce that he would reimburse any grantors whose projects with Royce would be materially disrupted.

"The Samaritans have been trying to reclaim the breastplate for some twenty-five hundred years," Binqus told Royce. "They've finally found Elenna, who was born with the marks. The question is, why is she still at Mount Gerizim? It's possible that she couldn't open the chest, or the chest does not contain the breastplate."

"Maxwell," Royce said, "what if the breastplate isn't in the Samaritans' chest? What if the cylinder scroll you've discovered describes a location somewhere else? And what if you need someone with the birthmarks to decrypt the scroll?"

"What are you suggesting?"

"Well, we have the scroll. And the Samaritans have someone who may be able to decrypt it."

Royce pulled out his iPhone and did a quick internet search.

Just as I thought. As your file indicates, Yehoshaphat Aharoni is a high-level member of the Samaritan community. Harshman reported that Elenna Cohen is visiting the Samaritans. Aharoni and I were residents together at NYU Medical School. He is extremely bright, one of the few Samaritans who has managed successfully to blend into the outside world. He's on the staff at Hadassah Medical Center. I can talk to him, feel him out. We can offer them access to the cylinder and the scroll, and perhaps they can persuade Elenna to try and decrypt it.

"The other possibility is Daniel Ornstein. Have you considered recruiting him to see whether he can decipher the scroll?"

The waiter appeared to clear away their plates. "I'll leave you the dessert menus," he said.

"By all means," said Royce.

Ignoring Royce's interest in the menu, Binqus said, "It's an idea, but I think it could be too risky. We've explored his background. Ornstein is close to the Gileadi family. He might be romantically involved with the Gileadis' daughter, Yael. The father, Gidon, is a linguistics professor at Hebrew University. I'm working with him on another project, one that might coincidentally be related to the mystery of the breastplate. My point is, Gileadi might feel obligated to report this to someone at the university or within the government. In that case, the government will certainly advise the religious authorities that a critical artifact from Solomon's Temple has been found. Relics from the First Temple period are extremely rare and deeply revered. We'll lose all control."

"I understand," Royce said, signaling the waiter. "I'll have the cheesecake with the chocolate sauce," he told him.

"An excellent choice," said the waiter. He turned to Binqus. "And for you, sir?"

"A latte," Binqus said.

"No dessert?"

"Thank you, no."

The two men topped off their dinner with a half-bottle of 1927 Taylor vintage port. They had reached an agreement on a concrete plan going forward. The question was, how would Aharoni and Sanballat react to their proposal?

25

Teyku

W hen Daniel and Yael awoke, they left their fears and anxieties under their "happy sheets," as Yael called them. After a run along one of the many paths in nearby Sacher Park, they joined Ronit and Gidon in the Gileadis' kitchen for lunch.

"I've done more research," Gidon said. "No one knows what happened to the breastplate and its twelve stones after Solomon's Temple was destroyed. I want to check whether somebody in the Orthodox community has information about the breastplate that isn't public knowledge."

"Oh no!" Yael groaned. "I know where this is going. Abba, are you sure you want to get Uncle Azariah involved?"

Ronit's brother, Rabbi Azariah Yerushalmi, was the nasi, or president, of the New Sanhedrin, as well as chairman of the *Boneh Ha'Bayit Hachadash*, the Builders of the New House. One of the critical problems facing the New Temple Project was that any new Jewish temple had to be built on the same spot where the first two temples had stood. Its most important room, the Holy of Holies, had to enclose the *Ehven Shekinah*, the Foundation Stone, the enormous granite rock that was said to be the first piece of matter God had created, and upon which, according to the Book of Genesis, *Yhahveh* had ordered Avraham to offer Isaac as a sacrifice.

Yael liked her Uncle Azariah well enough on a personal level, as did Gidon. But spending time with him was difficult. Even Ronit, Azariah's sister, was vehemently opposed to his messianic zeal for a Jewish theocracy in Israel.

"Sorry," said Gidon to Yael. "I already called him. I told him you're writing a paper for your Bible class on the breastplate's twelve stones, which the Torah refers to as the *Urim* and *Tummim*. He's delighted to talk to you. I don't like to lie to Azariah, but I don't want him to suspect we're investigating the possible whereabouts of the real breastplate."

Ronit said, "If anyone knows something about the whereabouts of the breastplate, it would be Azariah. But his agenda for a third temple is fraught with danger and the likelihood of great violence."

"Understood," said Daniel.

"That's right," Gidon said, "If Azariah and the Haredim have their way, the al-Aksa Mosque and Mosque of Omar will be torn down to make way for a third Jewish temple, where they will make the sacrifices and perform all the other rituals specified in the Torah.

They've already replicated the temple Menorah—the seven-branched candelabra made of solid gold—and many of the other vessels used in the temple. They made everything in strict accordance with the directions recorded in the Torah.

They've tried to fashion a breastplate that met the Biblical specifications. But they haven't been able to reach a consensus on the meaning of the Hebrew words used to identify certain of the twelve stones, the *Urim* and *Tummim*. If they found the true breastplate, it would ignite an intense effort by the Haredim to build the third temple and tear down the two mosques. That could lead to a renewed war with Egypt and the other Muslim states surrounding us—and probably some of the forty-nine other countries with Muslim majorities.

"Israeli society is far from having a consensus on implementing such a policy. But if Azariah and his crazies got their hands on the real breastplate, the momentum to build a third temple could become problematical."

"My brother is very charming and persuasive," Ronit said, placing her hand on Daniel's shoulder. "Young people who meet him often end up studying Talmud in yeshivas for the rest of their lives."

Then, placing her other hand on Yael's arm, she smiled and said, "I have very different hopes for the two of you."

Heichal Shlomo, the former seat of the Chief Rabbinate of Israel, which had been turned into an art museum, was located on King George Street in one of the oldest sections of West Jerusalem. Rabbi Azariah Yerushalmi had his office above the museum.

Azariah appeared truly delighted to see Yael. "Welcome, Baruch Hashem." Azariah used the word Hashem, meaning "the name," as Jewish tradition forbids Jews from saying the name itself except in prayer.

When Yael explained she was doing research on the *Urim* and *Tummim* for a class on religious symbolism, Azariah's eyes lit up. Yael had prepared by reviewing the various passages in the Book of Exodus that described in minute detail how the breastplate, the Hoshen, was to be fashioned: the scarlet, gold, and purple fabrics; the gold settings; and the *Urim* and *Tummim*, the twelve stones that the Bible identified by name.

"How were the Israelites able to find the *Urim* and *Tummim* in the Sinai desert, when many of the stones were not native to the area?" Yael asked.

Azariah smiled. "You're not the first to ask this question. It was debated by the rabbis who wrote the Talmud some fifteen hundred years ago. The answer, or non-answer, they came up with, was 'teyku.'"

From his years at Jewish day school, Daniel was familiar with the concept of *teyku*.

Yael shook her head. Her kibbutz education hadn't included Talmudic study.

"*Teyku*," she said, repeating the strange word. "What does it mean?"

"We believe the Torah was handed down by Hashem, blessed be He, to Moses on Mount Sinai. The Torah provides a Jew with an all-fulfilling existence, an enchanted universe, if you will. But human logic cannot explain some of the laws in the Torah. For example, the Torah prohibits wearing garments that are made from a combination of wool and linen, which we call *shaatnez*. No one, not even our greatest rabbis, has come up with an explanation for this prohibition. And so, what we say is *teyku*, which is an anagram that means the answers to such questions will be provided when the prophet

Elijah returns to herald the coming of the Messiah. There are many rules set forth in the Torah that we cannot explain, either fully or at all. Your question falls into this category. So, the answer is *teyku*." Azariah laughed. "Do you perhaps have a question I might be able to answer?"

Daniel and Yael laughed along with him. The atmosphere in the room was one of warm family feeling: an uncle, his niece, and her boyfriend.

Daniel was impressed. The rabbi's self-effacing nature veiled his obvious erudition and sophistication. His charisma was palpable. Small wonder he was a leading figure in the Haredi community.

After further discussion of the breastplate's characteristics and its disappearance after the destruction of Solomon's Temple, Daniel asked the obvious question. "What do you think happened to it?"

Azariah stroked his beard, sat back in his chair, and said, "Some people believe that the Babylonians took it as booty, along with the holy temple vessels, when they destroyed Solomon's Temple. If this is true, it might be buried somewhere in the ruins of ancient Babylon. In the Book of Nehemiah, it is written that when the Babylonians were conquered by the Persians, Cyrus the Great allowed the Jews to return to Jerusalem and build the second Jewish temple. He returned all the temple vessels taken by the Babylonians. Although there is reason to suppose they could have returned the original breastplate, no record exists of the *Urim* and *Tummim* being used in the Second Temple. Some scholars believe the breastplate was sent to Egypt, where a large community of exiles existed, but we also have no record of that. So again, this is a historical mystery."

"Another teyku?" asked Daniel.

Azariah's face lit up. "Ah, Yael, you have found yourself a budding Talmudic scholar."

Turning to Daniel, he said, "Any chance you might join some of our study groups? You would enjoy the intellectual challenge. And who knows? You might find your faith again."

The comment caught Daniel off balance. Careful to show respect, he said, "What do you know of my faith?"

"*Hashem*, blessed be He, gave me a gift of insight. I can see you have had a great pain in your heart for many years. The Torah provides a path to peace in one's heart and soul. It's why the Jewish people have survived for thousands of years despite all manner of persecution."

Daniel was unsettled by the rabbi's perception. *Do I really carry pain so obviously?* He tried his best to respond diplomatically. "I'm sure we all carry with us the pain of unresolved events in our life. I'm always interested in new ways to achieve insight. I'll consider your offer."

The rabbi sighed and said, "You won't, of course, but I already knew that. Nonetheless, I see you are a very bright man, who truly loves my niece. Having love in your life is, of course, one of Hashem's greatest gifts. I am very happy for both of you. Now, are you sure there's nothing more to your question about the breastplate? We are, of course, very interested in any leads. You never know when the needle in the haystack might stick someone, eh?"

"I'm afraid this is just a school assignment," Yael said, concerned that her uncle had asked the question.

Azariah trusted his instincts. As soon as Yael and Daniel left, he told his assistant to call his son, Yaveni.

"Tell him I want my niece and her boyfriend followed twenty-four-seven. There have long been rumors of a map showing the hidden location of the breastplate and perhaps other artifacts from the First and Second Temples. They may or may not be onto the location of a map. We cannot ignore the possibility."

Yael and Daniel had stopped at a nearby cafe to drink coffee and analyze their meeting. "I think we blew it," said Yael. "*Abba* will be pissed."

Daniel nodded. "I felt as if he could see right through us. Your uncle is scarily clairvoyant."

26

"You're Going to Keep Your Martian, I Hope"

Daniel and Yael told Gidon and Ronit about their visit. They shared their concerns that they had aroused Azariah's suspicions.

"I should have known better," Ronit said glumly.

"Well, I've also got some good news to report," said Yael. "Yehudit called to see how Daniel was doing. She told me that after our meeting, she took out and studied a diary her sister had kept, in which she wrote the details of her exploration of the cave. Yehudit told me about the diary in the strictest confidence. She doesn't want any of it to become public knowledge."

Zahava's diary confirms that the staircase with the etched drawing of the breastplate opens to a corridor that leads to a fork with chambers on each side. The left chamber is a burial area, with several sarcophagi resting on stone outcroppings. In the right chamber, near the rear wall, she found a large opening, like a basin. It was empty. Next to it was a stone slab that Zahava thought might have been used as a cover for the opening. It had an etching of the hand configuration. All around the area she found human bones littering the floor.

"At the point of the fork, Zahava thought there were indications of an entrance from far above. It was blocked with stones."

Daniel had been staring at Yael with a strange expression. He was silent for a few moments after she stopped speaking. Then he said, "There are answers for me, or the beginning of answers, in that cave. I feel certain of that. I need to explore it."

Yael took Daniel's hand. "I'm coming with you," she said.

Gidon frowned. Daniel's plan involved illegal trespass onto territory that was subject to Palestinian control. But he also understood why Daniel felt he had to explore the cave.

"Daniel, if you feel so strongly that the cave may open your box of riddles, I think you have to go. You need to know the truth. As we do."

Ronit nodded in agreement.

He worried about Yael going with Daniel. But it spoke to the bond she and Daniel had developed. In any event, it was a decision she had the right to make.

"Okay," said Yael. She stood up and, as if preparing a military operation, began to articulate a plan. "We have to try to calculate Zahava's sense of where the aboveground entrance might be located. Yehudit believes the entrance would be outside the eastern wall of the surrounding Herodian structure. We'll ask her more about it when we see her."

Daniel and Yael drove to Hevron in Ronit's car. They'd deliberately chosen a moonless night. Before they arrived, Yehudit removed the framed drawing from the front hall of her apartment and hid it under her bed. Daniel's doctors didn't think he would suffer another episode if he saw it again, but Yael didn't want to take the chance. They could bring it out if Daniel wanted to look at it. For now, they wanted to focus on the entries Zahava had made in her diary.

Yehudit opened her sketchpad and drew a picture that corresponded to Zahava's description of the corridor and the caves. According to her notes, she had seen a hint of light bleeding through the rocks high above the spot where the two caves branched off at the fork. After consulting several maps, everyone agreed upon where they should begin their investigation in the field outside the Herodian walls.

They walked the half-mile to the wall. Yael ran her hand along the stones, savoring their texture, thinking of those who may have touched the same spot two thousand years earlier. The blocks of ashlars were identical to those King Herod had used in rebuilding the Second Temple. Determined to experience what her sister had recorded, Yehudit limped along. They approached an area devoid of all light and put on the night-vision glasses Yael had obtained.

After hours of a frustrating and fruitless search, Yehudit stumbled upon a circular grouping of buried stones. Chopping around them with her small shovel, she created an opening. She took out a powerful flashlight and trained it on the hole she'd created. It was still covered with too much dirt, so she called Daniel and Yael to come help her. They dug into the earth and gravel that had held the stones in place for hundreds of years. Sweat drenched their clothing as they continued to dig for what seemed like hours, until they expanded the hole so that it was large enough for a person to climb through. They had discovered the vertical entryway about which Zahava had speculated. Using a flashlight to look down, Daniel estimated it descended around thirty feet.

Dawn was approaching. Daniel placed a GPS locator on the spot. They carefully replaced enough stones to cover the opening and hurried to get back to Yehudit's apartment.

The next night, they returned to the site and removed the stones to uncover the opening. As Daniel was readying the climbing rope, Yehudit asked him to stop. She took out her iPhone and launched the *Mechon Mamre* "app," which offered the text of the Old Testament in Hebrew and English. She turned to the Book of Genesis, Chapter 23, and extended her arm to bring Daniel and Yael close to her. Standing on the site of the first piece of Jewish-owned real estate in the Promised Land, they quietly read the verses together. *"And Avraham hearkened unto Ephron; and Avraham weighed to Ephron the silver, which he had named in the hearing of the children of Heth, four hundred shekels of silver, current money with the merchant. So, the field of Ephron, which was in Machpelah, which was before Mamre, the field, and the cave which was therein, and all the trees that were in the field, that were in all the border thereof round about, were made sure unto Avraham for a possession."*

They switched on their headlamps as Daniel attached waist harnesses and secured the climbing rope. He then positioned himself to belay Yael and Yehudit and lowered each of them down. When they were safely on the ground, Daniel executed a quick rappel and joined them. He wasn't worried about exiting. He could easily use the wall's cracks and crevices to climb to the surface and then secure Yael and Yehudit with the rope to help them ascend.

Standing in a small circle, they took their bearings. They were at a fork at the end of a corridor leading from a clearly visible staircase about twenty feet away. There were chambers to the right and left of the fork. Daniel hung back, while Yael and Zahava walked over to the staircase to see whether Zahava was right about the etched drawing of the breastplate on the wall. She was correct. It was a beautiful piece of work by an obviously gifted artisan. They gave Daniel a thumbs-up sign and took pictures.

"Are you okay?" Yael asked Daniel.

"I'm fine. Let's go check out the chambers."

The walls of the corridor were made of stone, possibly granite. Daniel noticed many cracks from the minor earthquakes that had been occurring in the area for eons. They entered the chamber to the left and saw six sarcophagi where the three Jewish patriarchs and three of their four wives were buried. Before entering the cave, they had decided that they would not touch the graves. If the breastplate was hidden in any of the remains, they would do no more than take pictures and discuss the situation with Gidon and Ronit.

After they photographed the cave area and the sarcophagi, they went into the chamber to the right of the fork. It was empty, except for bones that littered the floor.

Yehudit spent several minutes examining the remains.

"I think these are the skeletal remains of three people," she said. "Two of them appear to have died violently from head wounds."

They saw the opening on a stone shelf near the rear wall, exactly as Zahava had described, as well as the slab of stone, which she said had an etching of the hand configuration.

They had been in the cave for over an hour. The air was thinning. The small area could barely accommodate three adults who were expending so much energy. Daniel was about to call for a retreat when he saw a number of cracks in a section of the wall above the opening. His hands were too large to fit into the narrow spaces. He called Yael over to search the cracks while he aimed the light. After unsuccessfully searching several of the cracks, she scrunched her hand into a fissure high on the wall and was surprised when she touched what felt like metal. Slowly extracting it, she saw that it was a metal cylinder. She brushed off the dust and used a bit of water to clean it.

Daniel began to feel faint. And when Yael handed him the cylinder, he experienced the same kind of electric current as when he'd touched the tablet he'd picked up at Yehudit's home.

Shining his headlight onto the cylinder, Daniel noticed the word for breastplate, etched in Paleo-Hebrew. He could also see a minute etching of the hand configuration. Daniel handed the cylinder back to Yael and sat down. His birthmarks had begun to sting painfully. He did not want to pass out again.

Yael and Yehudit examined the cylinder. Here was likely evidence of the breastplate!

Yehudit noticed the cap that had been soldered onto the cylinder. She said, "These are the kinds of cylinders they used at the time of the First Temple. This one is sealed. More than likely, there's a scroll inside."

But there was no time now to study their discovery. Yehudit placed the cylinder in her backpack. "Daniel, we need to go," she said. "Are you ok?"

Daniel's birthmarks were tingling, but the sharp pain was gone, and his head was clearing.

Yael watched as Daniel effortlessly climbed the thirty-foot vertical stone wall, using only cracks in the wall for support. He instructed Yehudit and Yael to tie themselves to the rope, and he assisted them in climbing up to the surface. Yehudit might have been somewhat lame, but she was very strong and agile. Daniel was amused that she had less of a problem than Yael. Taking great care to stay quiet and unobserved, the three trespassers retreated to Yehudit's apartment.

They had entered and searched the Cave of the Patriarchs without getting caught. And they had found an artifact that not only had etchings of Daniel's birthmarks and the word "breastplate" in Paleo-Hebrew but also might contain a scroll from the time of the First Temple.

Back in Yehudit's apartment, Daniel did not wish to get too close to the cylinder. He sat apart from Yael and Yehudit as they examined their find with Yehudit's powerful halogen lights and her magnifying equipment. Yehudit put on latex gloves and used pliers to pry the cap off the cylinder. Then, using tweezers, she carefully extracted the leather scroll that Zadok had inserted in the cylinder twenty-five hundred years earlier. The leather was surprisingly supple; she was able to unroll it without tearing or marring it in any way. Yehudit had decades of experience working with ancient manuscripts. This one was not a fragile piece of parchment. It was meant to last. Even so, when the scroll was unrolled, Yehudit could not recognize its language or alphabet. It was a very sophisticated encryption. She examined photos she had kept of the tablets and sensed a resemblance in the methodology of the symbols. But her mind could not convert what seemed to be a similarity into a meaningful theory.

Nevertheless, the three of them felt exhilarated. They had achieved an improbable success in retrieving a cylinder and scroll somehow related to the ancient Jewish breastplate, which possibly contained answers to the enigma presented by Daniel's birthmarks, drawings, and visions.

Early the next morning, while Daniel was placing their belongings in the car, Yehudit put her arm around Yael and said, "You're going to keep your Martian, I hope."

Yael kissed Yehudit on the cheek and said, "Are you kidding? He cooks scrambled eggs with his mind. And," she teased, "you'd be amazed at what these Martians can do under the covers."

Yehudit laughed.

"There's real magic between the two of you. I'm so happy you've finally met the right guy. You deserve it."

Daniel came back to say goodbye to Yehudit. They held each other in the kind of embrace reserved for true comrades.

Yael had left a message for her parents the night before, after the group had returned from the cave. She had withheld details, saying only that they had a "good day" and that she would call tomorrow. Now, she phoned her parents from the car.

Her mother answered. "Yael, I was getting worried. Are you okay?

"We're all fine. And very happy."

"So, what happened?" Gidon demanded.

Yael laughed. "Relax, Abba, we'll be home soon. And the story is worth waiting for. Put the coffee on. We have a lot to tell you."

Ronit had a feeling that "the kids" had not eaten very well on their trip. She prepared a huge breakfast—eggs, cheeses, muffins, and Yael's favorite pancakes.

Her instincts were correct. Yael and Daniel ate as if they had been fasting. Between mouthfuls, they reported every detail of their adventure in Hevron. Ronit and Gidon were stunned when Yael showed them the cylinder and the scroll, which Yehudit had placed in an airtight glass container.

"If I heard this story from anyone but you two, I'd think it was made up. We have to ask Michael Stein to examine the cylinder and scroll. If anyone can figure out what the markings mean, it's Michael."

One of the world's most respected experts on ancient Jewish manuscripts, Stein had studied, translated, and catalogued thousands of papyri and scroll fragments that had been found in a multitude of caves in the Judean desert. The Dead Sea Scrolls were the best-known collection of such manuscripts, written in Hebrew, Aramaic, and Greek.

Stein looked forward to invitations for dinner at the Gileadis' home. A gourmet cook himself, he often invited Gidon and Ronit to dinner at his home in Kiryat Anavim, the kibbutz where he'd grown up and still lived, seven miles west of Jerusalem.

Stein arrived in midafternoon, and they gathered on comfortable chairs in the Gileadis' library. Ronit served tea, and Gidon laid out freshly cut fruits and biscuits. Daniel told Stein his entire story: about his birthmarks and all of the visions and events he had experienced. Yael then filled him in on their expedition to the Hevron cave. She brought out the cylinder and scroll.

"May I see them?" Stein asked, referring to Daniel's birthmarks.

Daniel pulled down his collar and removed the Duoderm patch on his left shoulder. He allowed Stein to satisfy himself that it was not a tattoo. Stein sat back down, obviously puzzled and confused.

Gidon stood up and poured Stein a generous amount of his best vodka. The good professor took a long pull.

"My friend," Gidon said, "we are all hoping for some rational explanation for all these events, an explanation that does not require us to accept that we are witnessing paranormal occurrences. So far, we don't have that explanation. According to every source we've consulted, birthmarks like Daniel's are simply not possible."

Stein shook his head, drained his glass of vodka, and began an intense examination of the cylinder and scroll. He looked through a magnifying glass at the word "breastplate" in Paleo-Hebrew, which he could read fluently, and at the indentations in the shape of the hand configuration. He agreed with Yehudit's dating of the cylinder to the time of the First Temple. "We have found pieces of cylinders like this. But I can tell you that no complete cylinder of this kind has ever been found, let alone one with etched writing and symbols or a scroll inside."

He extracted the leather scroll from Yehudit's container. Someone had taken care to use the very best writing template available. The questions were who, when, and why.

After examining the markings with the magnifying glass, he said, "What we have here is a very sophisticated encryption. I have never seen anything like it."

Despite his reaction to the scroll in the cave, Daniel felt drawn to pick the piece of leather off the table. His shoulders immediately began to twinge. He heard the sublime melody he had first heard in his grandmother's apartment. Suddenly, the symbols and markings began to glow. The scroll became warm to his touch, and then too hot to hold. Daniel raised his hands an inch above the leather, which sat on the table. The letters and symbols then shifted and disappeared, replaced by new markings. The event lasted only a few seconds.

Daniel moved away from the table, grabbed a chair, and sat down. His face had turned white. He was sweating profusely. Yael went over and took hold of his shoulders to steady him. Using her shirt sleeve, she wiped his sweaty forehead. Ronit brought over a bottle of cold water, which Daniel immediately drained. He raised his hand to signal that he was okay.

Stein cautiously picked up the leather scroll, which was now at room temperature. He was astonished by what he saw. The writing had been decrypted, revealing a beautiful Paleo-Hebrew script.

"How is this possible?" Stein asked, now confronting the reality that unnatural forces were unmistakably operating before his eyes.

"Michael, this is what we've been dealing with," said Gidon.

"Can you read it?" Yael asked.

"This is utterly fantastic," Stein replied. "Just unbelievable. Yes, I can read it. It purports to be a message from Zadok, the last high priest of Solomon's Temple. It says it was written ten years after the temple's destruction by the Babylonians. That would be 576 BCE."

"According to this manuscript, when Solomon's Temple was destroyed, Zadok led a group of refugees from Judea to Elephantine Island. He brought with him a chest that contained the sacred breastplate used in the temple. It says that *Yhahveh* directed him to hide the chest on the island and to create two cylinders with copies of this message: 'Only someone with birthmarks in the shape of the Kohanim's hands when they give the priestly blessing can open the chest. Be warned that anyone else will immediately die.' It makes sense. At the time Zadok emigrated to Egypt, there had been a significant Judean military base on Elephantine Island for at least one hundred years. An entire community, made up of many families, lived there. Seeking refuge there would have been a logical strategy."

Stein turned back to the manuscript. "There is a map on the reverse side of the scroll. It seems to show that the chest is in a cave on the island. Here are grid lines, arrows, and symbols. Figuring this out will require topographical maps. And don't forget, there have been minor quakes and normal geological movements, so it may not be so easy to find the cave using this map."

Stein was exhausted and visibly distressed. His head bent down, he sat in silence, staring at the floor. He was now a member of a special group, each of them struggling in their own way, to assimilate the possibility of a divine reality.

27

Beware What You Wish For

After a delightful breakfast of cappuccino, buttermilk pancakes with blueberries, and a side of home fries, Royce checked out of the inn and drove the twenty miles to the Binqus Institute. He passed through three security posts and was eventually escorted into a conference room adjacent to Binqus's office. After he and Binqus reviewed their strategy one more time, Royce called Aharoni at his office at Hadassah Hospital.

"Shalom, Dr. Royce!" Aharoni exclaimed. "I still have the dry-cleaning bills from our food fights."

They both laughed, instantly rekindling the connection they'd forged as classmates and good friends in medical school.

After some reminiscing, Aharoni asked, "Sebastian, is this a purely social call, or do you need help with something?"

"I'm sure you've heard of Maxwell Binqus," said Royce.

Aharoni laughed. "The crazy billionaire who's looking for life in outer space?"

"That's not quite how I'd characterize him," Royce said. "I'm actually sitting with him at his institute. I'll get straight to the point. We're involved in the search for the ancient breastplate worn by the high priest at Solomon's Temple."

Aharoni's hand involuntarily squeezed his phone. He somehow managed to keep his tone of voice flat. "That's interesting. It's a subject that's always fascinated me."

"Yoshi, we know you're looking for the breastplate. We also know that Elenna Cohen is visiting with you and your friends in Shechem. If I'm talking nonsense, and this is of no interest to you, I've obviously made a mistake. Should I say shalom and hang up?"

Aharoni was startled by how much Royce knew. *The bastards have been spying on us!* He took a deep breath and forced himself to stay calm. "No, my good doctor. You've got my attention. Keep going. Elenna Cohen is here. So what?"

"We know about Daniel Ornstein's weird birthmarks and that Elenna Cohen is his biological aunt. Your interest in her suggests that she was born with the same marks as Daniel. Apparently, your people have long believed that an ancient chest you possess contains the breastplate, and you thought Ms. Cohen could open it. Based on our research, we think it's quite likely that you've never possessed the real breastplate."

Aharoni didn't say a word.

"Yoshi, are you still there?"

"Yes, of course," said Aharoni. "Go on."

"We've uncovered an ancient scroll that appears to locate the breastplate on Elephantine Island in Egypt. It's heavily encrypted. We think it may possibly be the case that someone with the birthmarks could decrypt it. We think it's worth a shot. And that, my old friend, is why I am calling. We can supply a scroll disclosing the possible location of the breastplate, and you have a visitor who may be able to tell us what it says."

Aharoni did not hesitate. The future of his community was at stake.

"Ah, Royce, you and Binqus have done some extraordinary investigative work. Your suppositions are correct. I hope you are right about this scroll. We will discuss your request with Ms. Cohen. I can't speak for her. In the meantime, please send pictures. You have my personal email address, yes?"

"Yes. I'll send them as soon as I get off the phone. And Dr. Binqus and I look forward to hearing from you very soon."

Sanballat and Aharoni told Elenna about their conversation with Royce. Elenna had no reason to believe that she could decipher the scroll, but she had heard of Binqus and was interested to meet him. And she certainly wouldn't say no to meeting a brilliant New York doctor. Aharoni quickly arranged a conference call with Royce and Binqus, and Elenna shared with them the history of her involvement. She also told them of the deaths of Rayut and Auni.

"We've all handled the scroll," Royce said. "We've seen nothing to make us believe that holding it presents any danger. But it's your decision, of course."

"I'm in," Elenna said immediately. "If I survived the chest, I'm sure I'll be okay with the scroll."

Laura Victor had emailed pictures of the cylinder and the scroll to Aharoni. The archives at Mount Gerizim went back thousands of years, and its books were written in many different languages and alphabets. But nothing resembled the symbols on the scroll. Elenna placed her hands on the pictures, with no effect. If there were any chance of her being able to decipher the scrolls, she would need the originals.

Sanballat invited Binqus and Royce to come to Mount Gerizim as soon as convenient. Binqus countered by offering to send a private jet to bring them to the Institute.

The decision was left up to Elenna.

She'd read about the Binqus Institute and normally would have welcomed the chance to visit. But she was enjoying her Middle Eastern adventure. She promptly said, "I vote for you to come here."

As a Samaritan, Aharoni enjoyed both Israeli and Palestinian citizenship. When Binqus's private plane landed in Amman, Jordan, Aharoni was at the airport to greet them. After escorting them through Jordanian customs, he took the group on the four-hour drive along the west bank of the Jordan River to Mount Gerizim. They passed countless olive groves, grape orchards, and fruit trees, as well as many Bedouin settlements. It was the lush and bountiful land, the "land of milk and honey," that had been fought over for thousands of years.

When they arrived at Mount Gerizim, Sanballat and Elenna warmly greeted Binqus and Royce.

"You are one brave lady," Binqus said.

"Welcome to 500 BCE," Elenna replied, smiling.

Over dinner, Binqus and Royce told Elenna and the Samaritans how they had obtained the video of Daniel Ornstein's elongated arm. They explained that the video had led them to discover pictures of his birthmarks and also how the institute staff had discovered the cylinder and scroll.

Elenna continued to resist a magical interpretation of the events. There had to be a simpler answer. Although Elenna found Sanballat and Aharoni charming, she believed they were delusional. The Samaritans had succumbed for centuries to superstition. Anybody could have opened the chest. The video of Daniel's arm was obviously doctored. As for the birthmarks she had been born with, they were flukes of nature which had caused her many embarrassing moments. She hardly thought of them as special, let alone magical.

One thing was certain. This was an adventure unlike any she could have imagined. Even if it all turned out to be nonsense, as she expected, the Samaritans were willing to pay her a fortune. She had moral reservations about taking four million dollars from them. Maybe she would keep the money if something unpredictable happened. But otherwise, she would decline the money. She would ask instead for one of their hand-embroidered kimono-type robes. And maybe a couple of other items: a guided tour of Israel and Jordan; a first-class ticket for her flight home; and a photo of her overlooking the Jordan valley with Sanballat and Aharoni. And then a visit to the Binqus Institute? But only if Royce was there. They'd stayed up talking the previous night, and Elenna was sure that he was as interested in her as she was in him.

They gathered in the Heichal, around the same table where Elenna had opened the chest. Binqus brought out the cylinder and the two tinted glass plates enclosing the scroll. Sanballat undid the tape holding the two glass plates together. He placed the leather script on the table before Elenna and, his voice shaking, asked her to place her hands on the leather. Elenna had dismissed the idea that she could have any effect on the scroll, but to her surprise, she found herself hoping something magical would transpire.

She closed her eyes and concentrated on the tactile sensations of the fine leather. And then, as if on a dimmer switch, the manuscript began to emit a glow which slowly increased in brightness until the symbols radiated with a brilliant light. The scroll became hot to her touch. Elenna instinctively lifted her hands. Her right and left shoulders began to sting at the precise spots where her birthmarks had been removed, and in her mind, she heard a melody, an exquisite set of notes. She was about to lift her hands away from the scroll to rub her shoulders when the letters and symbols began to shift, then disappear, replaced by new markings. The process took only seconds. The glow then dissolved and disappeared.

Like Stein, Sanballat was fluent in Paleo-Hebrew. Unlike Stein, his facility was a function of the Samaritans' ongoing use of its alphabet. The Jewish Torah had once been written in Paleo-Hebrew; but the version used by the Jews since approximately 200 BCE, the so-called Masoretic text, was written in the Aramaic alphabet. The virtually identical Torah used by the Samaritans was written in Paleo-Hebrew. Sanballat had no trouble reading Zadok's twenty-five-hundred-year-old message, which was identical to the message Stein had translated. It was the map, showing the location of the breastplate on Elephantine Island.

The impact on Binqus was more pronounced than on the others. Never did he think he would actually witness a truly magical event. He had devoted his life and much of his fortune to proving that the paranormal was a very real aspect of human existence. He shook his head. *Maybe I never actually expected to succeed? Or wanted to? Beware of what you wish for, indeed!*

28

An Uninvited Guest

The lifestyles of Azariah's sons, Yaveni and Shimon, had diverged as they had grown from young boys to adulthood. Yaveni was a staunch believer in the Haredi way of life. He served as his father's right-hand man and carried the weighty title of Director, Office of the Chief Rabbi of the *Boneh Ha'Bayit* movement.

Shimon, on the other hand, was something of a rebel. He had embraced a less extreme version of religious practice, exchanging the long black coat, black hat, and curly sidelocks for an open-collared shirt, blue jeans, and a knitted yarmulke. Unlike the Haredim, who were exempt from military service, Shimon served in the army and was admitted to the *Sayeret Matkal*, Israel's elite special services unit. Instead of working for his father, he joined Bitachon P'rati, a major security firm with branches all over the world.

On three occasions, Azariah had hired Shamir to track down husbands who had refused to consent to a divorce, and thereby, under Jewish law, were preventing their wives from remarrying. These were spiteful, greedy men, taking advantage of Jewish marriage laws to hold their wives hostage until they agreed to pay what amounted to hefty ransoms. Shimon had no trouble finding the men. He wouldn't confide his methods to his father, only that he could be very "persuasive." He took pleasure in learning that all three women were happily remarried and doing well.

Now, Yaveni contacted him to help fulfill their father's order that Daniel and Yael be followed "twenty-four-seven." The brothers met in Bitachon P'rati's office in Tel Aviv. Shimon told his brother that a "twenty-four-seven" job would be fairly straightforward, but he warned that the job could cost more money if more people had to be followed. "For example, I presume Abba would want Gidon Gileadi followed as well."

Yaveni agreed.

"To watch three people day and night," Shimon said, "requires at least eight experienced watchers. Each person would cost on average one thousand dollars per day. My sources tell me we also need to keep an eye on Michael Stein. He lives on a kibbutz outside Jerusalem, and that would require an extra team. But let's hold off on him for now."

Shimon's firm would normally require a minimum down payment of 25 percent. But this was Shimon's family, and he knew that money was not a problem. "The Rabbi," as his students and friends called him, always kept his word, and the Haredim had no shortage of contributors. Over several decades, *Boneh Ha'Bayit* had amassed a war chest of more than one hundred million dollars to fund their ambitious plans to establish a Jewish theocracy in Greater Israel.

Two of the eight watchers Shimon hired were ex-Mossad; four were ex-Shin Bet, the Israeli equivalent of the FBI; one was ex-CIA; and one was a former officer in the French General Directorate for External Security. They all spoke fluent Hebrew, Arabic, and English.

Shimon divided his people into two teams and outfitted them with the latest communication devices and night vision equipment. He reviewed what he knew about his targets. His Uncle Gidon was accomplished in many areas, but he had never been trained in intelligence. Neither had his cousin, Yael. Yaveni thought that her friend, Daniel Ornstein, was a bit of a *cholem*, a dreamer, but Shimon had investigated him further and learned that Ornstein had been a mountaineering guide and was also an expert archer. It would be a mistake to underestimate him.

When Shimon received word that Daniel and Yael were traveling to Hevron to meet up with Yehudit Mizrachi, he set himself up in a small RV trailer on the outskirts of the city. Shimon would normally face serious bureaucratic hurdles in establishing a station so close to Hevron, if it were allowed at all. But thanks to Shimon's friends in Israeli law enforcement and the army, as well as his father's political clout, they were given permission, and their confidentiality was assured.

Shimon and his people watched Yael, Daniel, and Yehudit visit and survey the field outside the Herodian complex. They watched as their three subjects dug feverishly at a spot just to the east of the walls.

It was John Koch, the ex-CIA operative, who spotted and reported the group's descent through a hole in the ground. He likewise reported their emergence a little over an hour later. He noted that they looked very excited and were speaking in quiet but animated tones. But none of them was carrying a chest or any other artifact.

Shimon's spies had used their night vision equipment to take measurements of the group's backpacks on their way in. They detected no changes in heft or estimated weight after they exited. Azariah instructed Shimon to have Koch lower himself into the caves through the same hole. Koch reported finding nothing but ancient bones and coffins. He took pictures, but, obeying the rabbi's orders, he did not touch or move any of the objects. The pictures showed areas where the dust had been disturbed. But there was no conclusive evidence the Gileadi team had taken anything.

Shimon discovered that Gileadi was inquiring about visiting Elephantine Island in Egypt. Azariah's intuition was again vindicated. They had found something in the caves, perhaps the long-rumored map that was said to show the breastplate's hidden location. Elephantine Island! It made perfect sense.

Now, Azariah had to convince Gidon to let him join the search. He didn't think it would be a hard sell. Gidon did not have the money for a proper excursion to Elephantine Island. Besides, Gidon and Ronit would know they could do nothing to keep him from following them.

When the doorbell rang, Gidon, Ronit, Yael, and Daniel were in the Gileadis' library, filling out visa applications, poring over brochures, and studying maps. Ronit went to open the door. She was surprised to see her brother standing on her porch.

"Azariah, is everything all right?"

"Does a brother need a reason to see his only sister?"

The siblings embraced. "I need to talk to you and Gidon. Is he home?" he asked.

Ronit was sure that her brother hadn't suddenly been seized with a desire to socialize with his sister and her husband. No doubt Azariah had become suspicious of his niece's sudden interest in the breastplate.

"Give me a moment," Ronit said. "He was on the phone, but I'll check whether he's free."

She sighed as she opened the door to the library. "Azariah is here. He says he needs to speak to both of us."

Gidon came out and said, "Azariah! Shalom, welcome! Would you like something to drink? Tea? A little schnapps, perhaps?"

Azaria shook his head. He got straight to the point.

"We followed your group to the cave, and I know that you're inquiring about a trip to Elephantine Island. I believe you have information about a chest that holds the sacred breastplate. We need the breastplate to rebuild and restore the temple. We will bring all Jews back to Zion, to Greater Israel, and welcome the Messiah. *Hashem* be blessed."

Gidon was not a fan of Azariah's religious extremism. Restraining himself, he said, "Azariah, I don't mean to be disrespectful, but you know my feelings about your sect's political agenda. What is it you want?"

"You know perfectly well what I'm talking about," Azaria said, raising his voice. "You have to appreciate that, at least from our point of view, it's a sacred agenda. We're dealing with momentous events that my people and I cannot and will not ignore."

"Is that a threat?" Ronit asked, her voice cold with anger.

"No, of course not. I didn't mean to sound threatening—for the simple reason that our interests are perfectly aligned. We both want to find the breastplate. No one, myself included, knows what power it holds."

Gidon began to speak, but Azariah waved his hand and continued, "I believe you might have found a map indicating that the breastplate is hidden on Elephantine Island. It makes sense. Judean exiles built a temple on that island after the Babylonians destroyed Jerusalem. But a trip to Elephantine, to find and take possession of what the Egyptians would surely regard as a priceless Egyptian artifact, will cost a fortune.

"So, it's simple. You have the map. We have the money. And, in any event, at this point, you can't get rid of us. If you refuse to include us, we'll follow you. The obvious solution is for us to combine forces to search the island for the chest. If finding the breastplate facilitates the coming of a Messianic era, everyone would welcome such an event, no? And I want to get Yaveni and Shimon involved in this. We can trust them," he added. Another big smile. "It will be a family affair. So, my dear sister and brother-in-law, what do you say?"

"What the hell gives you the right to spy on my family?" Gidon demanded, seething with anger. "I should report you to the police. You really are crazy!"

Gidon stood up and walked out of the room, slamming the door behind him.

Azariah had expected Gidon to be upset, but he hadn't anticipated that he would be so enraged. He hoped Gidon's fury was for show, at least for the most part.

Ronit expressed her anger with sharp sarcasm. Using his boyhood nickname, which she knew he hated, Ronit said, "Azi, maybe you should come back tomorrow evening after Shabbat. You can bring your own food and paper plates."

Ronit kept a kosher home, but not nearly kosher enough for Azariah. Ronit gave "Azi" the most contemptuous scowl she could muster and left the room.

Azariah was taken aback by Gidon's and Ronit's reactions to his surveillance. He was usually so adept at reading people and situations, but he had gravely miscalculated this time. He decided to wait in the foyer. After ten minutes, he rose to leave. As he did so, Yael came out and said, "My parents want to talk to you."

Gidon and Ronit were sitting side by side on the sofa. They looked like a pair of school principals, about to discipline the boy who had thrown spitballs.

"Ronit, Gidon, please," Azariah said. "I love you both. I love your children. Except for my wife and sons, you are my only family. It was a fluke you are involved in this. I am sorry I offended you, but I hope you understand that I feel I have no choice in this situation. Whatever happens, we will find out the truth. Baruch Hashem."

He rose from his chair to put his coat on. Looking at Ronit, he said, with a hint of self-deprecating humor, "We should move on this soon. There is no telling what kind of crazies have found out about your discovery."

The tension in the room melted. Azariah's joke had the wondrous effect of coaxing love back from the shadows. The mood changed; the tense atmosphere dissipated.

Ronit stood up, and the siblings hugged.

"I'm worried that too many people already know about what we're doing," Gidon said.

"Not from my side," Azariah assured him. "That's why I'm using Shimon and his professionals. That's just one example of how we can be useful to you. We have money to help you carry out whatever you have planned."

"Well, we do need money, and if we don't agree, we'll probably never be rid of you and your spies." Gidon said. "For all I know, you and your certifiable crazies have bugged our house."

"No, we haven't, but your sarcasm is fair. Again, I apologize. But I sincerely hope we can join forces. It is the only logical choice."

After Ronit escorted him to the door, Yael and Daniel joined Ronit and Gidon in the study.

"I have an appointment at the university in forty-five minutes," Gidon said. "Tomorrow is Shabbat. I'll invite Michael Stein for breakfast, and we'll discuss the situation."

The next morning, when Daniel and Yael arrived, Stein was already busy helping Gidon in the kitchen. As usual on Shabbat morning, Gidon was preparing an elaborate Israeli breakfast: assorted cheeses, hard-boiled eggs, smoked fish, melon, and a choice of breads. Ronit made coffee and squeezed orange juice from oranges that weren't even two days old. Yael and Daniel set the table and brought the food into the dining room.

After breakfast, the group moved to the living room. "There's no point flogging ourselves," Gidon said. "We've been naive, no question. We can't afford any mistakes when we go to Egypt. It's one thing for us to play cloak and dagger in Hevron, our own backyard. That was risky enough. It's an altogether different matter to conduct espionage in Egypt. We've just discovered and deciphered the scroll. I don't think we've had time to appreciate how dangerous and expensive an expedition to Egypt would be. Azariah has the money to hire professionals and make our trip safer. That's all well and good. But I think the money issue is basically moot. It's clear Azariah and his fanatics will follow us whatever we do, wherever we go."

Stein nodded in agreement. "Azariah knows we can't finance this kind of trip. We're not talking about a bus tour to see Cairo and the pyramids. We're going in order to find ancient artifacts in Egypt, on Elephantine Island. We are probably talking about many thousands of dollars in baksheesh—bribes—to various Egyptian officials."

Ronit and Yael nodded. Daniel too. "It seems like a no-brainer to accept the offer," Stein said. "We can't underestimate the dangers of searching an Egyptian island under the nose of the security services of a police state."

"Then it's agreed." Ronit said. "I'll call Azariah as soon as Shabbat is over."

"We'll need to brief them on everything we know. Are you okay with that, Daniel?" asked Gidon.

"Yes. It's the only way this will work."

Gidon told Stein about the project he was working on for Maxwell Binqus, to decipher the enigmatic tablets found by Leonard Wiley in a cave near the ancient city of Ur. They debated whether to inform Azariah about the tablets, including what had happened to Daniel at Yehudit's apartment.

"In my opinion," Daniel said, "the tablets are extremely relevant to the mysteries we are investigating. I believe they are intended to work in sync with the breastplate, specifically the twelve stones, the *Urim and Tummim*. But I don't know how."

"I vote we hold off discussing the tablets with Azariah," Gidon said.

Daniel disagreed. "What if he knows something about the tablets that we don't? We can't afford to waste time."

Stein concurred, but Ronit and Yael agreed with Gidon. They decided to wait and see how the meeting progressed. Gidon said he would bring the tablets in the event it made sense to show them to Azariah.

That evening, with the Sabbath concluded, Ronit called Azariah at home. He was happy to hear that they had agreed to collaborate. Gidon suggested meeting at a conference room at the university's Trumpeldor Student Center at the Mount Scopus campus. Azariah agreed, and Gidon made the arrangements for eleven o'clock on Monday.

29

Simple Human Kindness

A zariah was accompanied to the meeting by Yaveni, Shimon, and two trusted members of his community. Gidon, Ronit, Stein, Daniel, and Yael were already there, setting out bottles of water and plates of pastry. While the two groups were seating themselves at the table—the Haredim on one side, Gidon and his group on the other—Gidon drew Azariah aside.

"Azariah, what we are going to tell and show you and your group is something you pray for three times a day. I'm talking about actual miracles in the here and now, paranormal events you can touch and experience. I can tell you that the experience can be extremely disquieting. Maybe your beliefs will help you, I don't know."

Azariah frowned, as if to say he doubted very much that nonbelievers might be privy to genuine miracles. Not wanting to sound condescending or dismissive, he said, "Well, I'm anxious to hear."

The Haredim lived in a cloistered world; some of them openly displayed discourtesy and disrespect when encountering outsiders. Azariah, who spent a good deal of time in the outside world, had coached his followers on some basics for interacting with secular Israelis or with Israelis who, like his son Shimon, were merely *dati*—religious, but not ultra-Orthodox.

It was likewise well understood that the Haredim were often confronted by ugly, discriminatory insolence from secular Israelis. This would not be the case with Gidon's group. They dressed modestly as a sign of respect for Haredi sensibilities. Yael wore a long-sleeved shirt and jacket and a skirt that fell below her knees. Ronit wore one of her more conservative suits and, as a married woman, covered her head with one of the hats she wore to synagogue on the High Holidays. Gidon wore a hat, and Daniel wore a beret. Stein put on a yarmulke.

Gidon stood up to introduce Daniel. He pointedly emphasized that Daniel would be sharing extremely personal information with outsiders for the first time in his life.

Hours earlier, as the Haredim were finishing their morning prayers, Azariah had sternly warned his followers that any breach of confidentiality, regarding any aspect of what they would hear, would result in his issuing a cherem. It was a powerful warning. A cherem meant that the person was excommunicated from the community, shunned even by those closest to him. It was equivalent to capital punishment. Indeed, in one case, a cherem was associated with a suicide two days after it was issued.

Daniel had been dreading this moment, but he had agreed to expose his most closely held secrets, if it meant perhaps solving the mysteries that had tormented him for so many years. Yael squeezed his hand as he rose and went to the lectern. A large screen had been hung on the wall. Daniel hit the return key on his computer. The first image appeared: Daniel's shoulders, with circles around his birthmarks, magnified.

"You may think what you're seeing are tattoos. I promise you; they are not. I was born with these marks."

The Haredim immediately recognized the iconic hand configuration used by the Kohanim to bless the congregation. Daniel ignored their whispers and continued. The next image was of the cylinder and scroll they had found in the cave. Daniel zoomed in, magnifying the markings on the cylinder, highlighting the etching of the Kohanic hand configuration. Then he focused on the encrypted symbols on the scroll. He hit the return key again and the computer simulated the transformation of the symbols into neat lines of Paleo-Hebrew.

"Did that really happen? How?" asked Eliyahu Yarkon, one of the astonished Haredim.

Daniel replied, "Professor Stein extracted the scroll and placed it on the table where we were sitting. I picked it up. It grew warm, then hot to the touch, and I had to put it down. Then the symbols lit up brightly. When the light and heat disappeared, we had before us a legible message in Paleo-Hebrew. Stein read it. It was from Zadok, the last high priest of Solomon's Temple, written twenty-five hundred years ago."

Daniel took a step away from the table. He clenched his fists to hide his trembling hands and faced the Haredim, who couldn't hide their skepticism. They muttered to one another about heretics telling crazy stories. What was the rabbi thinking?

Stein handed out three pieces of paper stapled together: a picture of the original encrypted markings; the Paleo-Hebrew words into which they had transmuted; and his translation of the Paleo-Hebrew into modern Hebrew.

"Please follow along while I read the words," he said. After he read Zadok's message aloud, Stein turned to Azariah. "Do you agree with my translation?"

Azariah, who was fluent in Paleo-Hebrew, nodded. "One hundred percent."

The room fell silent. Daniel thought: *The Haredim pray for miracles. Are these the miracles? What if this quest contradicts the core of their belief system, essential to their way of life?*

Dov Alveret, one the rabbi's trusted lieutenants, spoke up, voicing what all the other Haredim were thinking. "Forgive me, Rabbi; I am prepared to do what you ask—to work with these people, to assume that we have a message from Zadok, Ha-Kohen. But first I have to satisfy myself that these really are birthmarks. Everything we've heard about the scroll could have been invented."

When Daniel seemed to hesitate, Gidon gave him a look that said, *We need them to be convinced. A photo won't persuade them that God carved signs on your body.*

Daniel removed his shirt and allowed Alveret to examine him. Alveret gently rubbed his fingers back and forth across the area of Daniel's shoulders where the birthmarks appeared. He shook his head in disbelief.

"Thank you, Mr. Ornstein," he said. "I apologize for the intrusion, for discomforting you."

He turned to his Haredi colleagues and said, "Those are not tattoos. I have no doubt, it's a miracle from Hashem."

Azariah knew that his acolytes were seriously unnerved by what they had just seen and heard. He understood their anguish. It wasn't simply that they were witnessing unfathomable paranormal events. They were also deeply troubled by the fact that *Hashem* would have picked nonbelievers to reveal His plans. *Every day, three times a day, we pray to Hashem; and yet, he chooses an apikores, a nonbeliever, to be His messenger?*

Stein's oversized briefcase contained the tablets from the cave at Ur. Now, Gidon stood up and said, "I've debated whether to disclose what I'm about to show you. But we agreed to share everything relevant, and I've concluded these tablets are related to the other mysteries."

He removed the tablets from Stein's case.

"Professor Stein and other experts have done all kinds of tests on these tablets. They estimate that they are at least eight thousand years old, far older than any other writing that's been discovered. All we have established, apart from their age, is that there are four symbols arrayed in hundreds of thousands of groups of three."

He looked at Daniel, who understood what Gidon was reluctantly asking of him. He nodded and stood up again, as Gidon explained, "It's the tablets' reaction to Daniel and no one else that leads me to show this to you."

Daniel stretched out his hands above the tablets, which began to glow and radiate heat. The symbols seemed to be floating. Then, the light faded, and the tablets again grew cold to the touch. Daniel lifted his hands and rubbed his fingers on his jeans to cool them off.

The Haredim sat in shock. Was this Ornstein a Houdini? Hashem's prophet? The Messiah? But wait! The glow from the tablets had quickly vanished. The markings had not changed into words as they allegedly had on the scroll.

Daniel didn't know that Stein had brought the tablets to the meeting. Now, he turned pale. He was sweating profusely and felt as if he might faint. He tried to grab his chair, missed, and was about to fall when two strong arms reached out and grabbed him. Dov Alveret, who was sitting two chairs away, had leaped to Daniel's aid, wrapping his arms around his body barely in time to catch him. Thrust together by circumstance, it was a poignant moment: two men from different worlds, physically embraced, one giving and the other receiving simple human kindness.

The moment passed; the men disentangled themselves. Daniel thanked Alveret, sat down, and sipped some water. Both of them felt uncomfortable and embarrassed. Finally, Alveret looked at his colleagues and said, "The answer is no, I wouldn't have done the same for one of you."

The entire group laughed. It was a welcome, lighthearted moment.

Azariah asked Gidon to give him a moment alone with his group. They retreated to a room next door. Azariah spoke calmly to his followers. He placed his hand approvingly on Alveret's head. He then explained that *Hashem* does not worry about whether His actions are understood by mankind, even by His most devout believers.

"The truth is that Daniel may be a holy man—not the Messiah—but like the prophets of old, a man selected for a mission by Hashem. It is often the case that such people come from walks of life different from ours, people we would not expect to be called upon by the Most High. The Torah tells us that Moses, our nation's most eminent teacher, fled from Egypt to the land of Midian. He thought that the plight of his brethren in Egypt was not his problem. He was a simple shepherd. He had a new Midianite wife and two children. But *Hashem* appeared to him as 'a burning bush that was not consumed.' Moses was terrified; he wanted to run away. He certainly didn't want to return to Egypt, to lead hundreds of thousands of slaves into the desert. But did he refuse Hashem's calling? Did he say 'Please, I'm not observant enough, I'm content here. Find someone else?' What did he say?"

The Haredim answered in a chorus.

"*Heneini.*"

"That's right," Azariah said. "Moses said, '*Henaini.* I am here. I am ready.'"

The rabbi's lecture—carried by his deep voice, sparkling bright eyes, and nourishing smile—worked a calming effect.

The two groups agreed to meet again in two days. The Haredim were, understandably, especially confused. They needed time to assimilate new realities, which affected their core understanding of God and His purposes.

Despite Daniel's ability to turn the scroll's gibberish into a discernable message from Zadok, they still couldn't pinpoint the location of the chest on Elephantine Island. Not even close. Zadok's map showed two symbols—on the top, the Hebrew letter, צ, probably signifying north, and on the bottom, ד, likely connoting south. The group was able in a very rough way to identify the ancient temple of Khnum as the point of origin for the network of grid lines on the map. Perhaps Zadok had intuited that the pagan temple had a better chance of enduring, even in ruins, than the Jewish temple.

The lines led to an area on the western bank of the Nile. Even with climate change and the passage of centuries, the area was still far above the point where the Nile flooded the land every year. Yael had found an 1898 topographical map of Elephantine, drawn by British cartographers. They had indicated the location of many caves. They were all seemingly integrated in a massive rocky shelf a short distance from the beach. Yael produced photographs of the general area, taken from a skiff on the Nile.

"This is an area we will want to check out carefully. It is an area of monstrous rocks and more caves than you can count. I doubt the one we will be looking for will be so prominently exposed."

Shimon was in charge of arranging the logistics for the trip. He had welcomed Yaveni's invitation to help the Haredim on "a delicate matter." He was happy to be working with his father and brother. He was also pleased that the project would involve "normal" family members: Uncle Gidon, Aunt Ronit, and his cousin, Yael.

He laid out a preliminary protocol for a trip. He was pleased to quickly receive Gidon's and Azariah's agreement, which included his recommendation that the expedition team should consist of Yaveni, Gidon, Stein, Daniel, and Yael. Azariah was unwilling to shave off his long beard and *peot*, but he issued a ruling that allowed Yaveni to shave his beard and *peot* and be groomed in an Egyptian style. Ronit, Azariah, and the others would remain in Israel. Shimon, as chief organizer, would travel separately.

30

Successful Failure

Binqus, Aharoni, Elenna, and Royce were busy making plans to visit Elephantine Island. Sanballat, who had little experience with life outside of Mount Gerizim, would remain behind. Aharoni would update him via satellite phone. The Samaritans lacked the communication and other facilities needed for planning the trip. Binqus paid for two suites at the King David Hotel in Jerusalem as a base while they finalized their arrangements. They would travel by car from Jerusalem to Amman and then fly to Cairo. Laura Victor had booked the *Meroe*, one of the more luxurious floating hotels, or dahabiyas, which transported tourists up and down the Nile. She had reserved the entire boat to serve as a private and secure base of operations. The ship's kitchen staff was given paid leave for a month, and Binqus hired a kosher catering service so that Aharoni could eat with the rest of the group.

The group's Nile voyage would take them to Luxor and then on to Elephantine Island, just to the east of Aswan. They would stop en route at Amarna. Binqus was keen to share his expertise from his previous visit to Amarna when he'd worked there on his PhD thesis about the pharaoh Akhenaten, whom some scholars called the "first monotheist" for his efforts to eradicate the polytheism that had been Egypt's religion for thousands of years.

While he was in Jerusalem, Binqus decided to call Gidon Gileadi and arrange a meeting to discuss the "tablets project" he was funding. Neither of them knew that each possessed one of the two Zadok scrolls or that they each were planning the same trip to Elephantine Island with the same objectives.

Daniel insisted that the tablets be brought to Elephantine Island. Gidon did not disagree, but it presented him with a dilemma, heightened by Binqus's call. He could not ignore the fact that the Binqus Institute retained legal custody of the tablets. He considered himself obligated to ask Binqus's permission to take the priceless artifacts to a foreign country.

Gidon considered the prospect of involving Binqus in the project. It not only meant compromising the secrecy of the operation, but also, given Binqus's money and staff, he might insist on taking command of the project. Then again, Gidon thought, maybe that would be a good development. With his organization and financial resources, Binqus could enhance their efficiency; he could also arrange for assistance if the group's activities triggered an investigation by the Egyptian authorities. Gidon knew that Binqus had donated millions to the new Grand Egyptian Museum being constructed on the Giza plateau. But even if his group voted in favor of working with Binqus, he would still have to persuade Azariah to work with a non-Jewish television preacher. For now, Gidon decided to wait.

When the two groups met at the King David Hotel, Binqus created a story to explain his presence on Mount Gerizim. "I just visited the Samaritans' temple mount. I've been asked to fund a major archeological excavation. This is my first trip to the Holy Land, so we're spending a few days being tourists in Jerusalem."

Gidon took out blow-ups of the tablets and showed Binqus the thousands of rows of tiny characters or symbols. Binqus was well aware that the tablets had been exhaustively studied in prior decades with no results.

Gidon's team was using the most recent technology, but his people still hadn't come up with any theories that made sense. "Maxwell, we still haven't found anything," he reluctantly admitted.

"I know. That's why I'm optimistic. I constantly lecture my staff about the critical importance of failure. I have always lived by Edison's admonition that 'success is one percent inspiration and ninety-nine percent perspiration.' We're facing the same problems with the 'gold' flakes that were found sticking to the tablets. We gave samples to NASA to see if they could make sense of a chemical element not found in the periodic table. They're still studying the material."

"Keep at it, Gidon. If you need more resources, just let me know."

The two parted company after agreeing that Gidon would visit the institute in six months and give a lecture at the University of Massachusetts.

Binqus impressed Gidon. He was smart, competent, and sincere. He felt comfortable about including him in their expedition.

31

Baksheesh and a Prayer

himon arranged to lease a jet to transport the Gileadi group to Egypt. They would
fly from Israel to London and then to Luxor. It was a costly arrangement, but it was
Azariah's money, and he raised no objections. After arriving in Luxor, the group
would drive south to Aswan. It would then be a brief boat ride to the Mövenpick Resort
Aswan Hotel on Elephantine Island.

Egypt's new ambassador to Israel, Shamir al-Azari, was an ambitious man. He had
risen rapidly in the Egyptian diplomatic corps. Tel Aviv was a sensitive posting. His
appointment showed that the Egyptian president respected his loyalty and competence.
When he was informed of an inquiry by Shimon Yerushalmi to convene an "interfaith
symposium" on Elephantine Island, al-Azari saw a golden opportunity to elevate his
reputation. He imagined what his superiors might think: *This fellow al-Azari, he's a
shrewd player. A well-publicized conference, held at the site of an ancient Jewish temple,
hosted by the tolerant Egyptian nation, friendly to Israel and the Jews.* It would enhance
Egypt's international status.

They met at the Cafe Med at the Tel Aviv Hilton, a frequent meeting ground for
diplomats. "The idea has merit," al-Azari said to Shimon. "But if it doesn't play out as
planned, I will be serving camel dung to my family in Sudan—if I'm lucky. I've tested the
waters with my Cairo liaison officer. He passed along the request to one of the president's
top aides. Word came back that the president is interested in such an event taking place.
Cairo will accept my recommendation, but as I said, it will then be on my head."

They both knew how the game was played.

Shimon handed al-Azari a large envelope. "Here are the basic plans for the conference.
I appreciate that you're taking a risk. But I think this can be a major win/win. If we do go
forward, my people will need assurance that there will be no undue interference. You'll
have to get rid of the puffy-chested goons wearing hand-me-down blazers that don't fit
and don't conceal their guns. Clergymen will not come if they're surrounded by men
who look like gangsters."

Al-Azari put up his hands and feigned insult.

"Such stereotyping! But not to worry. Our security forces don't wear sports jackets. I'll
pick out some skinny women. Anything else you want to get off your chest?"

Shimon chuckled. "I know this will work out well for our two countries—and for both
of us. I think you will find the outline of the plan quite reasonable and eminently doable."

When al-Azari returned to his office, he opened the envelope and extracted $10,000 in crisp American bills. His expectations had been more than satisfied. Shimon was a serious person. The money was accompanied by a two-page, double-spaced outline of the group's plan and a tentative program.

Al-Azari called Shimon two days later, a lightning response by Middle East standards. He told Shimon that the visas and other approvals could be ready for pickup by the following day. "But my superiors would appreciate a more detailed outline of the project, better than the one you gave me in the envelope. We all want to avoid any glitches."

"Of course," Shimon replied.

Shimon did not want to risk the plan for a few thousand dollars. At the same time, a bribe that was too large could raise suspicion. Shimon decided that an additional $4,500 would be accepted as reasonable. The entire sum should be more than sufficient to grease the wheels so that the project could proceed with official authorization. Al-Azari could justifiably hope for additional payments as plans for the symposium proceeded.

The next day, Shimon went to the Egyptian Embassy and handed al-Azari's secretary another envelope. Shimon waited. The reception area was an impressive space. It was decorated with the kind of wall-to-wall and ceiling hieroglyphics found in the tombs of the pharaohs.

Shimon reflected on the audacious nature of his group's scheme: Israelis coming to Egypt to steal a priceless relic from 500 BCE. He recited to himself the ancient Jewish prayer for those embarking on a voyage, fitting for a nation that had wandered for centuries among so many countries: "*Lord, save us from every enemy and ambush, from robbers and wild beasts on the trip, and from all kinds of punishments that rage and come to the world.*"

Al-Azari emerged from his office, smiling and holding a thick envelope filled with documents. He handed Shimon all the requested visas. He included any other written permissions that might be necessary.

"I cleared everything with Cairo. Your group has permission to set up a meeting tent on the island, invite scholars and support personnel, and conduct a symposium. You may broadcast it, but, and this is the only serious restriction, any broadcasts must pass through the censor. Our people in Aswan are looking forward to working with you to plan the details: the precise location, lodging, catering, and so on."

Shimon smiled broadly. "Not to worry, my friend," he said. "This will go smoothly. Elephantine Island is the site of ancient Egyptian and Jewish temples, of Coptic churches and mosques. It is the perfect setting."

"I couldn't agree with you more, *habbibi*. We are also excited. *Allah yadhhab maeak.* May Allah go with you."

Ambassador al-Azari's nature was to be suspicious. It was one of the reasons he had survived and advanced in the Egyptian bureaucracy. He wasn't convinced that Shimon was telling him the truth. His office had just processed visas for another group, led by Maxwell Binqus, also going to Elephantine Island. The group included two Americans and a top-level official of the enigmatic Samaritan community.

Two unusual groups planning trips to Elephantine Island at the same time. This could not be a coincidence.

After arranging to deposit his bribes in his Swiss bank account, al-Azari placed a call to Achmed al-Sayid, constable-in-chief of Aswan Province. He advised Achmed about the impending arrival of two groups of foreigners.

"I'm uncomfortable about the synchronous timing of their visits. Stay alert, and make sure to keep me informed."

The more al-Azari thought about it, the more nervous he became. For any number of reasons, one or both of these excursions could collapse on his head. Following the practice of many of his colleagues, al-Azari had some time ago purchased a condominium in Argentina, in San Carlos de Bariloche, where many of Hitler's henchmen had taken refuge after World War II. The area was now home to fugitives from the Shah's Iran, Assad's Syria, Qaddafi's Libya, Putin's Russia, and other regimes that had earned the loathing of the world community. In the large safe he kept in a closet at home, al-Azari had stored a briefcase with the cash and other documents he would need to escape with his family through Sudan, then to Morocco, and on to Argentina.

32

The Crazy Cave

Mawlid al-Nabi al-Sharif, which celebrated the birth of the Islamic prophet, Muhammad, was a national holiday in almost all Muslim countries. It was also the birthday of the fraternal twins, Achmed and Malak al-Sayid. They were born five minutes apart in the Nubian village of Siou in the Egyptian province of Aswan, just across from Elephantine Island. Twin boys were cause for celebration, but the day ended in tragedy when their mother died on the evening of their birth from the strains of labor. Unable to care for both children, the twins' father, Jibril, had placed Malak in the care of his older brother, who lived with his wife in Cairo. They were childless and embraced the opportunity to care for their nephew. When Jibril died five years later, the couple adopted Malak. Achmed was raised in Aswan by his grandparents.

The two brothers saw each other on holidays and family occasions. They developed a strong friendship, but they grew up with very different personalities. Achmed was a calm, thoughtful, and obedient youth. He hated the endemic corruption that was destroying Egypt economically and eroding its traditional culture. Malak, on the other hand, was brash, aggressive, and exceedingly ambitious.

As youngsters, Achmed and his friends frequented Elephantine Island, a short distance away by sailboat or motor skiff. They played games of hide-and-seek and explored the boulders and caves that characterized the area. Achmed and his comrades knew all the caves inside out. All except one.

They called it *al kahf al majnun*, the Crazy Cave. People told stories about it from ancient times: tales of strange winds and demons, of people entering but either never coming out or emerging as lunatics. There was also the legend of an intense, diamond-like point of light at the back end of the cave.

Achmed and his friends knew not to enter the Crazy Cave. It was one rule they all obeyed, until one night when G'niya, Achmed's friend, showed up unnaturally pale and unable to speak.

It was the festival of Ramadan, the month-long holiday, when Muslims prayed and fasted during the day and then took part in *idftar*, the elaborate meal enjoyed with friends and family after the call to the Maghrib prayer at sunset.

On that night, G'niya and his family broke their fast at a restaurant on Elephantine Island overlooking the Nile and the nearby cataracts. Bored by the conversation, and well-fed by a supper of roasted mutton and eggplant, G'niya sneaked away and wandered aimlessly.

Lost in thought about a beautiful, black-eyed girl in his class, he followed a path that, it was later conjectured, led him to the area of the Crazy Cave. Never, in the subsequent years of his brief life, did G'niya talk about his experience. Neither could the doctors or psychiatrists whom his parents consulted ever determine why he had lost the ability to form words. He died in his sleep at age fifteen. The doctors could not identify the cause of death.

Achmed chose to enter the Egyptian military service and was admitted at the age of seventeen to the prestigious Egyptian Military Academy in Cairo. He trained to serve in the Egyptian Legion, Egypt's elite corps of special forces. His intelligence and bravery impressed his superiors; they promoted him to captain of a special forces brigade. On one occasion, as he was leading his men in the Sinai, he discovered a hidden stronghold of ISIS fighters. They outnumbered his unit three to one. Nonetheless, by maneuvering his soldiers to the south and pretending there was an escape route where none existed, his unit wiped out most of the ISIS detachment. They took the prisoners back to Cairo where, in a dank prison basement, they "persuaded" them to disclose key ISIS facilities, which the Egyptian Air Force then destroyed.

Wounded in the encounter, Achmed lost the use of his right arm. He developed an amazing proficiency at shooting a handgun with his left hand. He was remarkably accurate from as far as thirty yards.

Achmed was awarded the Order of Honor Star, one of Egypt's highest military decorations. He also was given the position as constable-in-chief of Aswan Province. It was a choice placement, even if it didn't fulfill Achmed's broader ambitions for a military command. At thirty-five years old, he was happily married with two young children. A heavyset man of medium height, with coppery skin and a moustache, he looked the part of an elite Egyptian soldier turned bureaucrat. It was a look that pleased him.

The principal responsibility of the constable-in-chief was to foil smugglers from Sudan and Ethiopia. Achmed spent weeks traveling from one border town to another. With the tourist season approaching, he was spending more time in the Aswan area. Now, he was staring at a raft of documents from two groups planning visits to Elephantine Island. These didn't strike him as typical tourist visits.

One set of visas included the multi-billionaire Maxwell Binqus; a doctor from New York University; a Jewish woman from New York City; and a high official of the Samaritan sect. The other set of visas was for a group that claimed to be investigating Elephantine Island as the site for an interfaith symposium. The advance party for this group included two distinguished Israeli professors and the chief administrator of an ultra-Orthodox Jewish cult, bent on destroying the holy mosques in Jerusalem and rebuilding the Jewish temple.

Achmed was uneasy. The warning call he had received from the Egyptian ambassador to Israel, Shamir al-Azari, heightened his concerns. The visit of the Gileadi group had been cleared, however, with the presidential palace. Presumably, the palace saw political value in demonstrating that Egypt was not anti-Semitic.

Egypt's large, historic Jewish community had been expelled in the 1940s and 1950s, their belongings confiscated. The Egyptian authorities allowed them a small amount of cash and one suitcase of belongings. This largesse was conditioned on the Jews signing a declaration whereby they "gifted" their houses, cars, clothing, and other possessions to the Egyptian government—a government that saw little reason to distinguish between being anti-Israel and anti-Jewish. But times changed. The Egyptian government had just finished restoring an ancient synagogue in Alexandria, despite there being barely enough Jews to hold services. The event had been showcased to the world media.

Israel and Egypt had engaged in three major wars, and now they were parties to a peace agreement. Achmed had no intention of stirring up trouble. On the other hand, it was equally dangerous to ignore a scheme that could embarrass the government. He decided to have his most trusted deputy thoroughly search the guest rooms where the two groups were staying. Assuming nothing suspicious was found, he would invite the two groups to visit him, and he would endeavor to make them feel at home, safe from interference. He had gone through the routine countless times: "Welcome, my friends. How can we help you get the most from your visit?" Looking them in the eyes, Achmed would be able to discern their sincerity.

33

Traitorous Diplomacy

David Kaplan, the recently appointed U.S. ambassador to Israel, unwittingly brought about the convergence of the Binqus/Samaritan group and the Gileadi/Haredi group. A prominent immigration lawyer who had become a multimillion-dollar real estate developer, Kaplan was a charter member of *Yachad*, a foundation that subsidized Azariah Yerushalmi's *Boneh Ha'Bayit* movement and other Haredi organizations.

Nondescript looks were useful for diplomats. Kaplan was qualified on that account, as he always seemed to be wearing the same suit. But he was not a diplomatic person. A heavyset man with a slick mane of gray hair, he was known for his crude behavior and his open disrespect for those he disagreed with. Various mainstream Jewish organizations had been united against his appointment by the president. Kaplan was a fanatic's fanatic. He did not hide his obsession. He wanted to realize the goals of a greater Israel in years, not decades or centuries. His vocal support for large new settlements on the West Bank and building a third Jewish temple conflicted with decades of American policy. Nonetheless, supported by the ultra-right wing in Israel and by the politically powerful American evangelicals, he was confirmed by an unenthusiastic Senate vote of 52–46.

It has often been said that the State of Israel owed its existence to Lord Arthur Balfour, the British foreign secretary who, in 1917, issued a formal declaration stating, "His Majesty's government view with favour the establishment in Palestine of a national home for the Jewish people, and will use their best endeavours to facilitate the achievement of this object." One scholar, Shalom Goldman, wrote that Balfour was part of the evangelical "Christian Zionist" movement. Balfour's "religious beliefs influenced his political decisions, particularly on the question of a Jewish return to Palestine, which he felt would be the fulfillment of biblical prophecy."

In the United States, beginning in the nineteenth century, evangelical organizations had actively sought to alter the character of the United States from a pluralistic, secular nation to a nation governed by Christians based on biblical law. The current vice president of the United States, George Raines, a die-hard evangelical, committed himself to establishing the groundwork for the ultimate apocalypse, a government based on biblical law, or "Christian Dominionism." The attorney general also flatly rejected the Founders' belief in a secular republic. "Free government," he said, "is only suitable and sustainable for a religious people."

President Hugh Scott Westfall was not himself an evangelical Christian, but he was politically dependent on their movement; it was a critical component of his base. He aggressively implemented major evangelical objectives, such as appointing extreme right-wing Supreme Court justices, recognizing Jerusalem as the capital of Israel, and supporting lawsuits and other efforts to blur the separation of church and state. Like the vice president, Secretary of State Clyde Riggs saw his role in apocalyptic terms, as part of "a never-ending struggle . . . until the Rapture"—the End of Days when Jesus would return and whisk the righteous away to heaven. Leading senators and House members echoed these sentiments, calling for the faithful to "take the Lordship of Christ, that message, into the public realm, and to seek the obedience of the nations. Of our nation!"

Evangelicals vociferously condemned Binqus, whose message focused on the importance of good works during one's lifetime. To his TV audiences, numbering in the millions, his message was clear:

"Faith alone is not enough. To feel Jesus in our hearts, to truly accept Jesus, one must want to follow Jesus's precepts. Loving our neighbor, helping the poor, welcoming the stranger, telling the truth, placing worth over wealth. Just to say we believe in somebody who did all those things—that, my friends, is plainly not what the Father or any loving divine being would want."

Binqus routinely got one question that both amused him and reinforced his belief in his idiosyncratic ministry. "If we focus our lives on good works, and there is no reward of the afterlife, why not, as Saint Paul also said, just"

Binqus was unceremoniously disinvited to a White House state dinner one week before it was held. When President Westfall found out that a billionaire TV preacher with millions of followers had been so rudely treated, he personally called to apologize and invited Binqus and his family to a private dinner at the White House.

Kaplan was on a mission to fulfill the ultimate goal of ultra-Orthodox Judaism, even if that mission conflicted with his oath of office to the people of the United States. In one case, while Kaplan was visiting an ultra-Orthodox village in Israel, he was photographed holding up an image of Jerusalem's Old City with a rebuilt third temple replacing the Mosque of Omar. Several Israeli journalists confronted Kaplan, demanding to know whether he represented or espoused a change in American policy. No American administration had ever suggested or even hinted at a policy whereby the mosques on the Temple Mount would be demolished to make way for a new Jewish temple. Kaplan told the Israeli journalists, reporters from the country where he was representing the United States as its ambassador to "keep your mouths shut." The State Department issued no rebuke.

Kaplan's staff monitored the arrival in Israel of foreign dignitaries and persons with significant political or social standing. When he was informed of Binqus's visit, Kaplan checked with his superiors at the State Department. They reviewed the matter with the White House. During dinner at the White House, President Westfall and Binqus had found they had a number of interests in common, in particular, archeology and philosophy. Afterward, the president occasionally called Binqus, sometimes to discuss a new archeological find or a scholarly article he had recently reviewed. At times, he called because, he said, he wanted to get another opinion on some policy issue. Binqus was flattered, but he was also savvy enough to know that the president was hoping Binqus would make a major contribution to his reelection campaign.

Kaplan was told to give Binqus a warm welcome and to schedule a reception in his honor. When he called Binqus to extend the invitation, he asked, "Are there any people you'd like to join us?"

Binqus mentioned Michael Stein, who, six months earlier, had been a guest lecturer at the Binqus Institute.

"Of course, we will invite the good professor. Anyone else?"

"Thank you, yes. Elenna Cohen, a New Yorker, is a fascinating woman who's become a great friend of mine. The other is Professor Gidon Gileadi. He's running an important project for me at the Hebrew University."

Of course, I've heard of Gileadi," Kaplan said. "Linguistics, right?"

"Yes."

"Where shall we send the invitations?" asked Kaplan.

"Send them to me at the King David Hotel. I'll make sure they're passed along."

"Wonderful! We're looking forward to welcoming you and your guests."

Binqus replied, "I am grateful and honored, Mr. Ambassador."

Kaplan warmly greeted Binqus and his friends when they arrived at the West Jerusalem building that was temporarily serving as the United States Embassy, while a permanent facility was being built.

He toasted Binqus: "I'm delighted to have this opportunity to thank you on behalf of the people of Israel for your support of the Israel Museum, as well as so many other good causes."

Binqus tipped his glass and took a sip of the excellent merlot, grown in the Galilee.

Kaplan introduced Binqus, Gileadi, Stein, and Elenna to Yoram Epstein, the Israeli minister of the interior. Epstein was one of the few secular Jews in the Israeli Cabinet. "Reverend Binqus," he said. "I thought your article about your country's Founding Fathers was brilliant."

Gidon nodded his agreement. "It was fascinating. Imagine, Thomas Jefferson composed his own version of the New Testament that made no mention of miracles."

"Thank you," Binqus said.

Kaplan, who was painfully aware of the evangelical movement's condemnation of the article, winced and walked away.

"While we're together here, I have a question," Epstein said. "My office is notified of all visa applications to Arab countries. Last week, my staff advised me that the three of you, as well as an official of the Samaritan community, the two sons of Rabbi Azariah Yerushalmi, and a famous microbiologist named Sebastian Royce, had submitted visa applications to the Egyptian Embassies in Aman and Tel Aviv. In each case, the stated purpose included a visit to Elephantine Island. I imagine it may have something to do with the ancient Jewish temple that once existed on the island. But if it's not some big secret, I'd love to hear more. Are you going on some kind of joint expedition?"

Epstein took note of Binqus's and Gidon's shocked expressions. It seemed as if they had no idea that they were each planning a trip to Elephantine.

Gidon was not about to tell Epstein he was planning an interfaith symposium on Elephantine Island. Epstein would likely share that information with others in the government. He would naturally assume that the conference was being held with the cooperation of various Israeli government ministries, as well as the Egyptian government. Any inquiries could raise questions that would doom their excursion.

Gidon needed to come up with a story that wouldn't raise any red flags, a story that Epstein would regard as bona fide tourism.

Forcing the most genuine laugh he could muster, and hoping that Binqus would also believe his explanation, Gidon spun the best story he could come up with on the spot. "Maxwell, are you also planning a trip to Elephantine? What a crazy coincidence. We've been planning a family trip to Egypt. The rabbi is my brother-in-law. He couldn't go, but he wanted his sons to pray at the site of the old temple. My daughter Yael and her boyfriend are also joining us. Yael is studying Egyptian history."

Turning to Stein, Gidon said, "Michael is a dear friend of my family and is coming with us to examine manuscripts found in the Cairo Genizah, and currently in the possession of a Coptic monk living on Elephantine Island. It's taken us months of planning to put all this together."

Binqus was sure that Gileadi was lying. But he also needed to keep his agenda a secret from Epstein.

"An interesting coincidence," Binqus said. "But I'm going on business. My primary interest is not Elephantine, but Amarna. I have an ongoing project concerning the reign of Akhenaton. As for the Samaritans, I'm working closely with them on excavations at the base of their temple on Mount Gerizim. When the deputy high priest—a doctor, by the way, who practices at Hadassah—heard we were planning a trip to Egypt, he asked if he could come along. He believes there may be ancient relics on Elephantine Island from the Samaritan temple."

Gidon noticed that Binqus's reason for his trip had changed from the one he'd given at their meeting at the King David Hotel. He thought Binqus was dissembling in the same way he had. He was eager to find out why.

Epstein considered the explanations he had just heard. Elephantine Island was not a prominent destination for tourists, or for scholars for that matter. He was not persuaded that the two trips were unrelated.

"Well, I hope you enjoy yourselves," he said. "I've always wanted to visit Amarna. Please keep in mind that the relationship between Israel and Egypt is of critical importance. I assume you're working with the Egyptians if you're looking for antiquities. They are incredibly strict."

"Of course, Yoram, not to worry," Binqus replied. "I've made hundreds of trips like this. My staff is in constant contact with the Egyptians."

The minister was somewhat reassured by Binqus's response. He knew Binqus had conducted many such expeditions in other countries.

"Best of luck to all of you!" he said as Kaplan rejoined the group.

Kaplan now became the gracious host. "My friends, please," he said, smiling. "Scripture tells us that man does not live by bread alone. You're in the Holy Land. Please, help yourself to the buffet. My chef makes excellent hummus, tahina, and grape leaves. He bakes his own pita, and his baklava is said to be the best in the city."

For appearance's sake, Binqus and Gidon filled their plates. But as soon as they were alone, Binqus said, "Okay, Gidon, we obviously need to talk about what exactly is going on. No way you'll convince me you're taking the rabbi's sons to pray on Elephantine Island, or the rest of the bullshit you just told us."

"I can say the same about you."

Gidon suggested that they meet the next day at his office on Mount Scopus.

Binqus agreed. Just one question for now. Are you planning to bring someone named Daniel Ornstein to the island?

Gidon was astonished by the question. "Yes," he said. "Daniel is involved in our plans. I assume that tomorrow you will tell us how you know him."

He then paused, then said, "Look, Maxwell, I know nothing about any plans you have to visit Elephantine. But the reason we're going has to do with the tablets. I was going to brief you in full, but I needed the rabbi's permission to do that, and I haven't had the chance to raise the issue with him. I still can't believe it's a coincidence that another group is interested in Daniel and Elephantine Island."

Binqus laughed. "My dear professor, look at the bright side. Of all the mysteries we are both interested in exploring, we now have the answer to one of them."

"What is that?"

"There are no coincidences."

As he was preparing to leave the reception, Epstein took Kaplan aside. "David, can I have a word?"

"Of course."

He said, "Binqus and Gileadi claim to be taking separate, unrelated trips to Elephantine Island. I'm not sure I believe their stories. But I thought you'd be interested to know that among those going are the Haredi Rabbi Azariah's two sons, and someone I doubt you're acquainted with, a Dr. Yehoshaphat Aharoni, a top lieutenant to the high priest of the Samaritans. And then there's Binqus, as well as Professors Gileadi and Stein. Something about this strikes me as suspicious. I'm going to keep an eye on them. I suggest you do, too."

Kaplan listened and feigned indifference. "I will. Thank you, Yoram."

Could it be related to the breastplate? Kaplan was convinced it was. He knew a Jewish community had existed on Elephantine Island and that it had built its own temple with the help of Zadok, the high priest who fled Jerusalem. He also knew that the Samaritans claimed the breastplate for their temple on Mount Gerizim. Now, Azariah's two sons and a high Samaritan official were going to Elephantine Island, supported by respected Bible scholars and the billionaire Maxwell Binqus, who was known to be obsessed with finding evidence of paranormal events.

34

A Grand Design

Malak al-Sayid, Achmed's brother, had the handsome, sun-chiseled features of a desert sheik. His adoptive family lived in an upscale neighborhood in Zamalek, in West Cairo. He had been a star student, graduating from Cairo University at the top of his class when he was just seventeen years old. He joined the Egyptian Ministry of Foreign Affairs and held senior posts in Istanbul, Paris, Moscow, Washington, and Tehran. Fluent in the language of every country where he had been stationed, he was a rising star in the Ministry.

But Malak was anything but a typical Egyptian. He was an Islamic extremist. He detested the West for its legacy of colonialism, which had ravaged the Islamic world. The Jews were drunk with military power. They had taken Arab lands in Palestine, inalienable lands under Islamic law, as if the Muslims, who had graciously allowed the Jews to live in their countries for centuries, were responsible for the Holocaust unleashed upon them by the Germans. The Zionists were determined to steal more land on the West Bank and even in Jordan. They lied and schemed incessantly, shamefully violating the laws of their sacred Torah. Worst of all were the Americans. They were craven religious hypocrites, pretending to love Christ, a figure glorified as a great prophet in the Koran, while starving their poor and pitting one group against another. Malak hungered to find a means to utterly humiliate and annihilate these despicable, self-righteous infidels.

While stationed at the Egyptian Embassy in Tehran, Malak came under the influence of a charismatic imam who discerned Malak's talents and fiery hatred of the West. The imam introduced him to Ali-Aliosseini Khamenei, Iran's Supreme Leader, the highest and most powerful office in the Islamic Republic of Iran. During dozens of secret meetings, Khamenei and Malak plotted about how Iran could sow fatal discord within the United States and Israel.

Khamenei was a sayyid, an imam who traced his lineage back to Muhammad. Islam held that in the three hundred years after Muhammad's death, Islam was championed by the so-called Twelve Imams. No successor to the Twelfth Imam, Hujjat Allah ibn al-Hasan al-Mahdi, had come forward, because according to Islamic tradition, Al-Hasan did not die. He entered a period of occultation, alive but "hidden."

After surviving an assassination attack, which badly injured his arm and lungs, Khamenei had the army build a large, impregnable bunker below the Saidabad Palace Complex in Tehran. It was to his private chamber in that bunker, adorned with books, pictures of revered imams, and ancient relics, that Khamenei regularly retreated when he sought to meditate upon his most cherished objective, the creation of a World Caliphate: a world governed by devotion to Allah and His holy word, as interpreted and enforced by himself and his fanatical devotees. Khamenei envisioned that upon achieving his World Caliphate, Hujjat Allah ibn al-Hasan would appear. Before finally claiming his reward in paradise, Al-Hasan would anoint him as the Thirteenth Imam. He would then enter the state of occultation, to be revered for centuries to come.

In Malak, Khamenei found not only a fellow Islamic radical but also a cunning political tactician who had formulated a real-politic strategy for achieving the objectives of Islamic fundamentalists.

They called their plan "the Grand Design." Its essence consisted of aggressive support for the Jews and evangelicals in their quest for a "Greater Israel." That objective entailed Israel's annexation of Palestinian lands; its conquest and annexation of a significant portion of Jordanian territory; and the destruction and replacement of the Al-Aqsa Mosque and Mosque of Omar with a new Jewish temple. The Arab nations surrounding Israel, and other Muslim countries, would never accept such actions. Major warfare would once again break out between Israel and her Arab neighbors. The plan contemplated that the evangelical community would draw the United States into the conflict on behalf of Israel.

It was difficult to predict the precise nature and magnitude of the ensuing conflict. What would Britain and Europe do? What would Russia and China do? But Malak and Khamenei were convinced that the conflagration would cripple, if not destroy, its mortal enemies, America and Israel. It was a truism of history that great countries destroy themselves from within. Here, the two countries would be torn apart by internal conflicts—between the Haredi zealots and secular Israelis, and between the extreme right-wing evangelicals and secular Americans.

Using elite personnel who had sworn to him their absolute allegiance, Khamenei pursued any credible events that might trigger the required firestorm of events. With Malak's help, the Supreme Leader, who controlled billions of dollars in secret accounts, funneled many millions to the Haredim and evangelicals to help them convert more followers and pursue the objective of a Greater Israel, an objective that all three groups temporarily shared.

One of Malak's key relationships in Washington, D.C., and a primary recipient of Iranian funds, was Deputy Director of the National Security Agency K. J. Quinn. As a prominent leader of the evangelical movement, Quinn advocated replacing American secularism with Christian Dominionism. Quinn had urged his many Twitter followers to watch the movie *Left Behind*. He professed to praying daily that he would be "raptured to heaven," like the fervent believers in the movie.

During his posting to Washington, Malak had also developed a good relationship with David Kaplan, who was serving as assistant secretary of state for Middle Eastern Affairs. The Supreme Leader and Malak were delighted when it was announced that the president had appointed Kaplan as the new U.S. ambassador to Israel. Malak was keen to assist Kaplan in his publicly stated intent of helping the Haredim achieve their objectives.

When Malak finished his tour at the Egyptian Embassy in Tehran, Khamenei told him to return to Egypt and stay there. President Yasir Fattah el-Nasser of Egypt, a great fan of Malak's work over the years, personally welcomed him back and appointed him deputy director of the Ministry of Foreign Affairs.

35

Nothing New Is Ever Different

The more Kaplan thought about the Binqus and Gileadi expeditions to Elephantine, the more convinced he became that they were on the trail of the breastplate. He had to find a way to take possession of it. It would help the Haredim, and it would be a feather in the cap of the president. He could announce the accomplishment to the evangelical community, his critical right-wing base. Second only to his desire for a Greater Israel, Kaplan wanted a seat on the Supreme Court. His prospects for an appointment would be enhanced by whatever actions he took that would allow the president to strengthen his standing with the evangelicals. Kaplan's problem was that if the breastplate were found by either or both of the Binqus and Gileadi groups, he lacked the operational resources to "liberate" the holy artifact.

Kaplan called Quinn. "I need to see you tomorrow. There's been a critical development regarding the Greater Israel and third temple issue."

Quinn agreed to set aside time the next morning.

After a ten-hour flight from Tel Aviv, Kaplan was ushered into Quinn's fifteen-hundred-square-foot office in the Harry S. Truman Building. It was hard to believe that the office of the secretary of state was even larger. On the wall behind Quinn's desk was a fifteen-foot framed painting of Jesus on the cross. Such a religious display violated explicit regulations of the General Services Administration, which were based on the constitutionally required separation of church and state. Quinn disregarded the rule. A lawsuit filed by Citizens for the Separation of Church and State was on appeal, after having been summarily dismissed by a new judicial appointee to the federal district court for the District of Columbia. The judge's nomination and Senate confirmation had been forcefully pressed by the evangelical movement. In her opinion, the judge had written, "It is hard to conceive of a more beneficial atmosphere for decision-making on vital American interests than to have the Lord's presence reverently displayed."

Kaplan wore an old-fashion fedora. As always when he took off his hat, he checked that his yarmulke was in place. Kaplan and Quinn chatted about Washington gossip for a few minutes. Then Kaplan told Quinn what he'd learned from Yoram Epstein, Israel's minister of the interior, at the reception for Binqus in Jerusalem.

"I'm convinced it's the breastplate," Kaplan said.

"What makes you think so?"

Kaplan didn't have to explain the significance of the breastplate to Quinn. By virtue of thousands of books, videos, conventions, podcasts, and numerous "Christian Zionist" websites, a great many evangelicals were knowledgeable about Judaism. Many had learned to read the Tanakh in Hebrew, observed Jewish dietary laws, and kept the Sabbath on Saturday. They knew all about the breastplate and the twelve stones the Bible called the *Urim* and *Tummim*.

Kaplan gave Quinn a summary of his thinking. Then he said, "The problem is, we don't have any details on their activities. We need to have them closely followed. If it's the breastplate, we have to get hold of it."

Quinn required no convincing. "David, this is wonderful information. If it's true, I'll do whatever I can to help, but it can't be an official government operation. I'll talk to the secretary of state and Vice President Raines. There are very experienced people, including ex-Special Forces, whom we use in situations like this. I'll go to Cairo myself with two of the men. If we can get the breastplate, we can ratchet up the momentum for Israel to tear down the mosques and annex the West Bank."

Quinn liked Kaplan. He hoped that he would accept Christ and be saved. Otherwise, he and all other nonbelievers would go to hell. Quinn realized that many people couldn't understand why honorable, ethical men and women should go to Hell if they did not accept Jesus Christ. It was a difficult truth. But it wasn't for him to question why. It was the way God had planned it, according to the evangelicals' widely disputed interpretation of John 14:6: "I am the way, the truth, and the life: no man cometh unto the Father, but by me."

Kaplan returned to Israel with Quinn's assurance that he would be kept in the loop. Quinn gave him a satellite ("sat") phone with a special frequency, so that they could stay in close contact. Quinn was prepared to do whatever was necessary to get the breastplate. He notified Tony Powers and Tim Norton, another war-hardened NSA agent. Quinn had used them before on especially sensitive missions. Both had done "wet work," NSA-speak for assassinations. Both were devout evangelicals and were fluent in Arabic.

Although this was not a government-authorized operation, Quinn and his two aides flew to Cairo in the U.S. Air Force jet reserved for the secretary of state. When the jet landed in Cairo, Quinn was driven to an NSA safe house. Norton and Powers stayed on board and flew to Aswan.

Quinn summoned a trusted member of the U.S. Embassy in Cairo and gave him a letter from President Westfall, to be hand-delivered to President el-Nasser. The letter stated that Quinn was in Egypt on a private matter of great importance to the president and that he and his two assistants would be traveling to Aswan and Elephantine Island. The letter requested that President Yosef Fattah el-Nasser assign the local constable, Achmed el-Sayid, to assist Quinn. President Westfall personally signed the letter and added in his own handwriting, "Yosef, I won't forget your help."

El-Nasser smiled when he read the letter. He sent word that he would, of course, help in whatever way possible, as long as Egyptian interests were not prejudiced. To be owed a favor by the president of the United States was an invaluable diplomatic asset.

Within the hour, Achmed received a directive from his superiors, informing him of Quinn's visit and forwarding files with pictures of Norton and Powers, as well as their background information. Achmed was to place himself at the service of these very special guests, as per the orders of the Egyptian president himself. Secrecy was paramount. If all went well, he would likely receive a sizable bonus. He didn't need to be told what would happen if he did anything to negatively affect the trip.

Quinn had received an NSA file on Achmed. He was surprised to learn that Malak al-Sayid was Achmed's brother. The coincidences were starting to pile up. Quinn thought it was a positive sign, a divine signal.

He called Achmed to make sure there would be no local interference.

"I've heard very good things about you," Quinn said. "You have an impressive file. I greatly appreciate your confidential help on this personal mission I've been handed by President Westfall. I'll be coming down tomorrow."

"We will help in all ways possible, Your Excellency, whatever you need," Achmed replied. "I was informed just a little while ago that you wish us to keep an eye on two groups of tourists. One is staying on the party boat *Meroe*, the other in the Mövenpick Resort Hotel on Elephantine Island. I have already placed them under routine surveillance."

"Excellent. Thank you, Achmed. I look forward to meeting and working with you."

Quinn was glad that Achmed had initiated surveillance of the two groups. But Norton and Powers would take over as soon as they got settled. The three of them would take care of business on their own. They would follow the Israelis and Americans and take possession of the breastplate. Norton and Powers would then kill all of them and dispose of the bodies. It was a regrettable but necessary decision. This mission could represent an inflection point in the arc of world history.

36

Declination West Is Best

Binqus, Royce, Aharoni, and Elenna had left for Egypt a week before Gidon's team, to allow time for a leisurely trip up the Nile on the *Meroe*. They stopped twice along the way—at Amarna and Luxor. In Amarna, they reviewed the remains of the great temples and statues Pharaoh Akhenaten had built. Sitting around the ruins of an ancient sculpture, drinking strong Turkish coffee and biscuits, Binqus recounted how Sigmund Freud, in his book *Moses and Monotheism*, had theorized that Moses, whose name is Egyptian, was a priest in Akhenaten's monotheistic cult. When the pharaoh died, Moses infused a monotheistic belief in a tribe of slaves, the Habiru, which he brought out of Egypt, promising them a homeland in the lush valleys to the east and west of the Jordan River. Whether these were the Hebrew slaves of the Bible was a question that had fascinated Binqus from the time he studied the Bible as a boy in his hayloft.

The group also briefly stopped at Luxor. Known in ancient times as Thebes, it was known in modern times as "the world's greatest open-air museum" because of its magnificent tombs, temples, and hieroglyphic writings.

Going up the Nile from Luxor, the *Meroe* docked at the Elephantine Island marina, adjacent to the Mövenpick Resort Hotel, where the Gileadi group had checked in the previous day. Shimon was staying nearby at a nondescript hotel. He had smuggled into Egypt two sat phones that would allow scrambled, encoded conversations and text messaging. Playing their role as the advance scouts for their "interfaith symposium," Gidon, Yaveni, and Stein met with various religious leaders: Muslim imams, Coptic and Roman Catholic priests, and even a Zoroastrian cleric. They also met with representatives of hotel and catering services from Aswan, Luxor, and Cairo. They asked for proposals for the assembly and maintenance of a large tent, which could be wired to handle sophisticated computers and audio/visual equipment. They scheduled meetings with the mayor of Aswan and with dignitaries from surrounding communities. Shimon, working with Laura Victor, was able to schedule enough appointments to fill a two-week visit.

Gidon and Binqus remained concerned that the Egyptian authorities would become suspicious. Gidon's proposed interfaith symposium did not explain the presence of Binqus's group. Gidon and Binqus expected questions: *Did your two groups just happen to coordinate your trips to Egypt? Whom did you speak to in Amman, Tel Aviv, Cairo? Why is the Samaritan here? Are you here, Reverend Binqus, for pleasure or business? Is this an archeological expedition?*

Elephantine Island encompassed a small area. Prominent visitors were easily noticed. Binqus and Gidon decided that members of their groups should make a point of bumping into one another when they visited restaurants in and around Aswan. The strategy worked. After a few days of these chance meetings, several of these "new friends" started dining together. Then came a joint trip of intermingled members of the groups to visit the temple of Philae, dedicated to the ancient Egyptian goddess, Isis. Two days later, they toured the stone quarries of Aswan. In ancient times, over ten thousand tons of rock had been hewn with great precision and hauled hundreds of miles to Luxor, Amarna, Heliopolis, and other ancient cities. During the days that followed, the groups frequently went sightseeing and ate their meals together. They soon came to be seen as just another bunch of undifferentiated tourists.

After five days of joining in the activities, Daniel and Yael split off to search for the cave described on Zadok's map. Consulting modern topographical charts as well as a dusty survey from colonial times, they plotted a variety of routes along the crest on the west side of the island. They climbed over and around the enormous boulders that characterized the area. Although Daniel's mountaineering experience wasn't of much value, he had studied how to navigate territory using a map and compass. Daniel knew he had to make "declination" adjustments to account for the ever-changing differences between geographic north, which is portrayed on a map, and magnetic north, portrayed on the compass. Now he concluded they needed to move farther west. They traveled only a short distance before coming to a spot where Daniel's shoulders began to twinge.

37

"Brother, What Are You Up To?"

Yehoshaphat Aharoni and Michael Stein carefully guarded the two original leather scrolls that Elenna and Daniel had decrypted. They kept them on their persons at all times. No one else had a copy—no one, that is, except Elenna. Disobeying the group's agreement, she had held onto the map and a facsimile of the scroll's message. Decrypting the scroll was an experience beyond anything she could have imagined. She often took out the manuscript to see whether something magical might happen again if she concentrated on it, but the magic was presumably embedded in the original scroll. Frustrated because she couldn't replicate the phenomenon, she kept her copy tightly folded and hidden in her mascara case.

Achmed directed Madi Bin Yofge, one of his senior officers, to search the visitors' rooms. In Elenna's room, Madi found documents concerning her vintage clothing business, letters from her brother, and a brand-new diary. Madi was fluent in English. Elenna's entries about Royce brought a smile to his face. He was not so jaded that he couldn't enjoy reading of a woman's hopes for new love.

He continued to conduct the kind of thorough search he had performed countless times before. When he found the manuscript in Elenna's mascara case, he unfolded it and took pictures. He knew what Hebrew looked like. This was not Hebrew, and certainly not Arabic. He assumed it must be a significant document because she had purposely hidden the scroll. He hurriedly sent the pictures to Achmed and reported that his searches had otherwise turned up nothing suspicious.

Achmed agreed that the writing on the document was neither Hebrew nor Arabic. "Maintain surveillance on the two groups," he ordered Madi. "I'm going to Cairo to show this manuscript to an expert who may be able to translate its meaning. I'm leaving right now, and I'll be back before noon tomorrow."

By "expert," Achmed was referring to Malak. Achmed did not begrudge his brother's prominence in the Egyptian Foreign Service or his close ties with the Egyptian president. Quite the opposite—he was proud of his brother's accomplishments. But he knew little about Malak's actual work. Malak was a devoted family man, or so it appeared when the two families came together. Achmed was a practicing Muslim, but he was not particularly religious or political. He didn't care whether the Jews continued to control Palestine. It was really the Arabs' fault for agreeing to let Jordan annex all the territory that the United Nations had allocated for a Palestinian state. Now, it was a land riddled with illegal Israeli settlements, but good luck kicking out the Israelis. For Achmed, of greatest importance in the sordid history of the Israeli/Arab conflict was the 1973 war, which the Israelis called the Yom Kippur War. It had shown the strength of the Egyptian Army and redeemed its reputation after the disastrously humiliating 1967 Six-Day War.

And Egypt could not afford another war. Achmed believed that his country could benefit tremendously if it entered into broad trade and investment agreements with Israel and Israeli companies. Egypt would help counter Iran's continued attacks on Israel's legitimacy, while Israel would provide Egypt with innovative technology to improve its economic future.

Malak was delighted to hear from Achmed that he was coming to Cairo the next day. He arrived in time for a delicious dinner prepared by Malak's wife, Yava, an excellent cook. The mood was festive.

After dinner and the customary chatting and playing with Malak's two children, Achmed said, "Yava, can I borrow your husband for a few minutes?"

"Of course, go," Yava said. "I don't mind if he smokes one less cigarette in the house."

The two brothers walked in silence along the narrow, tree-lined streets of Malak's neighborhood. A chain-smoker, Malak immediately lit up one of the harsh but aromatic Cleopatra Kings he preferred. Achmed, who rarely smoked except when he was with Malak, took the cigarette Malak handed him.

They strolled in silence for a few minutes. Then Achmed handed Malak pictures of the scroll Elenna had hidden in her mascara case.

Malak studied the map and the message Zadok had written. He couldn't read it, but he was intrigued. "Where did you get this?" he asked.

Achmed told him about the two unusual delegations simultaneously visiting Elephantine Island and the circumstances under which he'd obtained the picture of the document.

"I came to you because I think this document might hold a key to why these groups are here, and why the American president personally asked for el-Nasser's help. Before I go to my superiors and make a fool of myself, I thought you might have some insights into the origins of the writing, that you might even be able to read the script."

Malak stared at the writing. "This is written in the Phoenician alphabet, also known as Paleo-Hebrew. It's most unusual. Very few intact documents exist from Zadok's time.

"Can you read it?"

"No, but I can use a computer program to transcribe the letters into modern Hebrew, which I'll be able to read."

The brothers returned home and retreated to Malak's office.

"This will take some time, several hours at least." Malak said. "I'm going to scan this to my computer." He pointed to the sofa in the corner of the room. "Why don't you take a nap? You look as if you could use some sleep. I'll wake you when I'm done."

Achmed was delighted that Malak was able to help him. He hated the idea of involving his superiors before he understood the situation as fully as possible. He lay down on

Malak's sofa and was fast asleep within minutes.

When he awoke, it was 5:00 a.m. Achmed washed and prayed and then padded into the kitchen. The house was asleep except for Malak, who was baking fresh pita, a family tradition. Before Ahmed could say anything, Malak wearily greeted him.

"Brother, I have done my best. I can transpose the letters to modern Hebrew, but what comes out is nonsense. If it is a message, it's been carefully encrypted. If not, perhaps it's the scribbles of a schoolboy practicing to be a scribe. They've found thousands of such writings, a kind of penmanship lesson. In any event, I'm sorry, but I couldn't read it."

He gave Achmed a printout of the document.

"It was worth a try," Achmed said, trying to hide his disappointment.

The truth, however, was that Malak had been able to transcribe and read Zadok's scroll. He was dumbfounded by what the ancient high priest had written and by the map that showed where the all-important breastplate was hidden. While Achmed was asleep, Malak launched his Photoshop application and deleted various of the proto-Hebrew characters and words. He printed out the bogus version on a clean sheet of paper.

"The original you gave me got a bit chewed up when I scanned it. Damn machine is twenty years old. But my computer got the scan, so I was able to print a clean copy.

Achmed folded the document and placed it in his back pocket. "It was worth a try. I am very grateful for your effort."

"It's nothing. Now, please, have some breakfast. It's Mama's pita recipe."

On his flight home, Achmed felt thoroughly depressed. It wasn't just that Malak could not help him. Achmed hated Cairo. On the elevated roads winding in and around the city, with a population exceeding nine million, he saw thousands of empty apartments in brand-new buildings, thousands of window frames without glass. Corrupt officials had authorized the construction without adequate planning, bilking the state of billions of dollars in public funds, enriching their swollen Swiss bank accounts. Piles of garbage lined the roads to the adjacent towns. The area looked like a bombed-out war zone.

This is what Western tourists saw when their buses wound their way to the Giza Plateau to see the pyramids, which were among the greatest marvels in the world. *Small wonder they consider us backwards. This is why Western society prefers the educated, sophisticated Israelis.*

His depression lifted almost immediately on his return to Aswan. He felt the beauty of Egyptian culture and the warmth of its people. Surely, a means would be found to integrate traditional Egyptian culture into the modern era. *Inshallah!* With Allah's help!

He had taken an early plane home. It was a short two-hour flight. The meeting with Quinn was scheduled for 3:00 p.m. It was now 10:00 a.m. Achmed climbed a hill next to his office and lit his hookah. Cannabis was technically forbidden to Muslims. It was haram, but, unlike alcohol, the prohibition was not explicitly mentioned in the Koran. Achmed hoped Allah would forgive him a periodic indulgence. He inhaled deeply and instantly began to unwind. On an impulse, he reached into his back pocket and took out the sheet of paper Malak had given him. He studied it casually and then more carefully. Although he could not read the words, he had carefully examined the original message, and he realized now that many words were missing. Leaving his hookah on the ground, he rose and ran to his office. He confirmed his suspicions by checking the copy he had made of the original before he had left Aswan. Malak had changed the content. Worse, he had taken his brother for a fool, thinking he would not notice.

Brother, who are you? What are you up to?

Whereas Achmed left his brother's home in a dejected mood, Malak could not have been more elated. Allah had unquestionably presented Malak with an opportunity to begin the process of disruption and conflict outlined in the Grand Design.

He didn't want to call attention to the search for the cave and holy relics described in Zadok's scroll by declaring it an official Egyptian operation. If Egyptian authorities got hold of the chest and the breastplate, the artifacts would become part of the public relations campaign for the new Egyptian Museum. El-Nasser would never give the breastplate to the Jews, who would certainly use it as a sign from God to tear down the holy mosques in Jerusalem and build a third temple.

No, the Egyptians had to be kept out of this. Malak would work behind the scenes. He would leave it to Quinn to find the cave, take the chest, and dispose of the foreigners. Quinn and Kaplan would then ensure that the artifact was passed along to the most radical right-wing extremists and Haredim in Israel and also make certain that the news of its recovery was broadcast to the evangelical community. He would present the issue to Quinn on a purely transactional basis: the stereotypic greedy Arab looking for a payday.

Quinn would pay dearly for the document Achmed had discovered. The money was unimportant to Malak. He would make sure that most of it found its way to Achmed, his family, and his adoptive grandparents' poverty-stricken tribe. Yasir Sadit, a cousin and close friend of the twins from youth, occupied a high position within the tribe. He and his eight sons knew every inch of Elephantine Island. Malak called Yasir to enlist his help monitoring the foreigners' moves in and around the island.

Yasir assured Malak that he and his sons would track the movements of both foreign groups. He called back two hours later and reported that they had assembled in a conference room on the Meroe and were being watched by agents from Achmed's constabulary office.

Malak didn't know that Quinn was already in Egypt. Satisfied that the Gileadi and Binqus groups were properly covered, by Achmed as well as Yasir, Malak called Quinn's private cell number on a secure line. He told Quinn that he had information vital to his evangelical agenda.

"Events are moving quickly. People are on Elephantine Island searching for the breastplate from Solomon's Temple. Representatives of the Haredi are involved, as well as a Samaritan priest and Maxwell Binqus. I have a document written by Zadok, which explains why these people are here—and where Zadok hid the breastplate. That's as much as I'll say over the phone. You need to come to Cairo as soon as possible."

"Malak, I know about the groups on Elephantine," Quinn said. "I'm actually already in Cairo to find out what they're up to. I'm leaving for Aswan tomorrow. I want to see the document you have. I'll text you my address. Come as quickly as you can."

When Malak arrived, Quinn was drinking expensive bourbon and smoking a seventy-five-dollar Cuban cigar. Quinn knew enough not to offer Malak an alcoholic drink. Instead, he handed Malak a forty-dollar bottle of "Minus 181" water from an artesian well in Germany.

Malak thought, *The Americans certainly know how to waste money while millions of their people live in poverty. The new caliphate will ensure justice and equality for the entire world. Inshallah.*

He put down the bottle of water. He wasn't thirsty.

"Look, K. J.," he said. "I'll give you this document, but I want to be compensated if you agree, as I think you will, that it contains information fundamental to your cause. I can get you more information from the same source. The information is of no religious interest to me, nor does it affect Egypt's national interests. But given what I understand of your convictions and agenda, you should find this information priceless. I am not happy here in Egypt. I would like to take my family to Argentina. I believe a payment of five million dollars would be a bargain for you."

Malak had translated the message into English. He had also printed out a computerized depiction of Zadok's map. He gave the translation to Quinn but kept the map in his briefcase.

Quinn poured himself another drink and studied the message for several long minutes.

"Malak, how do I know this isn't a fake?"

"It's genuine. This document was found hidden in the Jewish woman's mascara case in her room on the Meroe. I can vouch with my life for the person who found this."

Obviously excited, Quinn said, "Okay, Malak, you've got yourself five million dollars. What additional information can you provide?"

"The message I gave you was on one side of the scroll. There was a map on the other side."

Malak removed the map from his briefcase. "Here are Zadok's directions for finding the cave. You know I was born in Aswan, and my brother still lives there. There's a cave on Elephantine Island called *al kahf al ajnun*, the Crazy Cave. As boys, we were forbidden from entering it. One boy disobeyed and was rendered mute for the rest of his brief life. He died when he was fifteen. I think that is the cave."

"I'll give you the map for an additional five million. As we speak, our American and Israeli visitors are no doubt looking for the cave. You must proceed quickly but cautiously. If my government finds out what's going on, it will have no choice but to take over the search. At that point, only Allah, blessed be He, will know when anything useful to your cause is found or will be shared. You also need to be aware that over the centuries, the topography of the island has changed. During my lifetime, an earthquake caused some ground movement in the area where I remember the Crazy Cave was located."

Quinn agreed to the additional payment.

Malak gave him a copy of the map and his bank account information.

"Call me if you need help. If I can do anything, I will," he said. "I trust you will wire an appropriate additional payment for any new and useful intelligence. Above all else, it's crucial that my involvement be kept totally secret. I am trusting you with my life."

Quinn agreed that if Malak provided additional relevant information, he would wire him additional compensation. He also told Malak that his brother Achmed was involved. He played down the coincidence.

"El-Sisi assigned him the task of shepherding the groups around Aswan and providing whatever assistance they might request. It's Achmed's territory, so it's understandable.

But I can assure you that your brother will know nothing of your involvement or even that I'm acquainted with you."

After Malak left, Quinn called Secretary of State Raines and Vice President Riggs. Both were excited by Zadok's message and the map, and they agreed to the payments Quinn had promised Malak. They also assured Quinn of their full, continued support. For now, Quinn decided against calling Kaplan. He would be essential for the endgame, after Quinn had secured the breastplate. To involve him now would risk losing control of the operation.

Quinn made the arrangements for wiring the money to the accounts Malak had given him Then he packed his bags and left for Aswan.

38

Kissing Cousins

The Zadok scroll didn't mention anything that connected it with the eight-thousand-year-old tablets discovered in the cave near Ur. But Daniel insisted that they be brought to Egypt. He was certain that the tablets, the breastplate, and the stones were all related. After everything that had transpired, the team was not about to second-guess his intuition.

Binqus, who had donated over a million dollars to the Israel Museum, had no problem arranging to have the tablets sent on loan to the Nubian Museum in Aswan. Museums regularly shipped artifacts all over the world. The director of the Nubian Museum was only too happy to accept the tablets on a temporary basis. After examining them, he saw that they displayed symbols he could not decipher. He put them in the museum's safe. The assistant director was coming back from vacation the following week. They would discuss how and when to display the tablets.

After the two groups had spent six days on the island, Shimon invited everyone to a meeting that evening on the Meroe. He had arranged for the caterer to provide a kosher Middle Eastern smorgasbord and encouraged everyone to enjoy the many different dishes. After the caterers had cleared the dishes, and they had the room to themselves, Shimon said to Daniel and Yael, "The floor is yours."

"Yael and I found the cave," Daniel announced. "I had a very strong physical reaction to a specific spot we had identified as a possible location. We had to dig out a lot of rocks to create a small opening, so we could crawl in."

"And?" Yaveni said, unable to control himself.

"And we found the chest. The chest opened only when I put my hands on the etched configuration. Inside it were the breastplate and the other garments of the high priest. The stones shimmered and glistened. They were beyond beautiful. Pick a word: magical, breathtaking, spectacular! I'm excited for all of you to see them soon. Obviously, we need to get the chest and leave the island as soon as possible. But first, we have a problem to solve," Daniel said.

He turned to Elenna, who stood up next to him. Since embarking on her improbable adventure, Elenna had read everything she could about the Samaritans. She knew more than everyone present, save Aharoni.

Daniel and I have agreed that neither of us will open the chest before we settle a fundamental issue. And to do that, Azariah and Sanballat need to join us.

"As most of you know," she continued, the relationship between the Jews and Samaritans was poisoned over two thousand years ago, maybe three thousand, if we go back to Avraham and Baasha. Both the Jews and the Samaritans have been desperate to locate the breastplate. But now that we are poised to recover the sacred object, the question is who will take possession of it? We don't want to ignite an ugly confrontation between two groups who revere the same Torah and share an identical faith and belief in *Yhahveh* and His ethical monotheism.

"What we are saying—what we are insisting upon—is an end to the conflict between these two communities. The Samaritans must be welcomed back into the fold of the Jewish people. Their place of worship on Mount Gerizim must be recognized, and the different traditions and customs they have adopted over the centuries must be respected as authentic. They, in turn, must recognize Jerusalem as the center of worship by the Jewish people. The chest will be retrieved and opened, its mysteries revealed, by a people reunited or not at all. We do not have time for debates among the various religious groups or votes in the Knesset. An agreement between the two leaders will be enough. Azariah and Sanballat need to take a solemn oath before God."

"I don't know why Daniel and I were chosen to bear these birthmarks," she added. "But Daniel and I have been given the power to access the breastplate. We think this opportunity is one aspect of the mysteries we are confronting. It's not some coincidence that brought together just the right group of people—people who happen to be high officials of the Haredim and Samaritans."

Gidon could barely suppress his admiration. Binqus was also pleased. Finally, two people had been given the leverage needed to resolve an historically intractable dispute.

Shimon suppressed his smile. He would enjoy watching this play out. *Finally, someone has put my father in a box. He won't like it, but I don't see how he can turn down the proposal.*

Yaveni was of a very different mind.

"This is absurd!" he shouted. "My father will never agree. Nor can he speak for all the other Haredim, let alone all Jews!"

Aharoni was stunned by the proposal, which presented a potential solution to his people's survival. "Daniel, Elenna," he said, "we would like nothing more than to achieve harmony with the Jews. According to Baasha's prophecy, our hope lies in the breastplate. He may well have foreseen that our salvation will come, as the Bible says, only when our people are but a 'remnant.'"

Daniel had been consumed with his ghosts since he was a boy. Now he believed that he was on the verge of solving at least some of the mysteries that had plagued him. He had found the chest. He had touched the breastplate and the stones. But even before he and Elenna arrived on the island, they had discussed the problem of who would possess it. It would be an ironic blasphemy to recover the breastplate, only to inflame the age-old conflict between the descendants of Baasha and Avraham.

"We expected your reactions," Daniel said. "To be blunt, they are irrelevant. The only relevant fact is that, for whatever reason, some power, call it whatever name you like—*Yhahveh* , Hashem, God, Allah—chose Elenna and me, two secular Jews, to unlock these mysteries."

"We will have limited time at the cave, so we need to get this issue resolved now. We know there will be many dissenters. And as prominent as Azariah is in the Haredi community, he does not, as Yoshi points out, speak for all of them, let alone all Jews. But if Sanballat and Azariah make this agreement, I think other segments of Jewish society will join them—if not now, then in the future."

Yaveni shook his head. "What you're asking for is wonderful but naive. Peace and love among the Jews and the Samaritans! It's simply not possible. You are wasting precious time. Our mission will be exposed while you are making decisions no one has given you the right to make. Your only job is to open the chest. Our leaders will take it from there."

Aharoni said, "I don't share your view, Yaveni. I believe *Yhahveh* chose Daniel, and Elenna as well, for a momentous mission. I believe Sanballat would be amenable to an agreement. We have always considered ourselves to be part of the same faith. You should call your father, Yaveni."

Yaveni rose to make the call but shook a finger at Aharoni. "Your ancestors copied our Torah. Over two thousand years ago, the rabbis established that the Samaritans are not Jews."

Stein suddenly lost his patience. "Why are we even having this debate?" he shouted at Yaveni. "There are fewer than one thousand Samaritans alive today! My suggestion, Yaveni, is that we inform the rabbi and see whether he believes, as you apparently do, that the Jewish people's overriding concern is to persecute nine hundred and fifty Torah-observant worshipers of God until they die out."

Yaveni held up a hand. "*Kvar maspeek.* Enough already." He took the sat phone and left the room to call his father.

Yaveni's face was pale when he returned fifteen minutes later to report his father's decision. "The rabbi agrees to the proposal," he said. "I have written down the points of the covenant."

Daniel, Elenna and Yael reviewed the piece of paper.

"This is correct," Elenna said.

Aharoni picked up the paper and left the room to speak to Sanballat. He returned fifteen minutes later.

"We also agree."

There was applause, smiles, and head shaking. The most common refrain in the first few seconds was, "Who would have thought?"

39

Kadosh L'Yhahveh

Quinn had described Norton and Powers to Malak as NSA veterans, ex-Navy Seals, as the best of the best. Malak was relieved to hear this. He needed people who could read the map and secure the chest and then efficiently dispose of the Gileadi and Binqus groups. The Grand Design would be kick-started into high gear.

Quinn joined Norton and Powers in a conference room in Aswan's Shepherd Hotel. They discussed Achmed's latest report: the Americans and Israelis were closeted in a conference room on the *Meroe*. Quinn decided it was time to terminate Achmed's involvement. He called and ordered him to immediately withdraw his people who were watching the *Meroe*. Norton and Powers would take over their positions.

Thirty minutes later, Norton and Powers had crossed the Nile from Aswan and reached the positions abandoned by Achmed's men. By the time they arrived, the room on the *Meroe* was empty, and nobody had any idea where the group had gone. It was the first of several costly errors in tradecraft that Quinn would make. He had many talents, but running a surveillance operation was not one of them.

Malak kept in close contact with his cousin, Yasir, who had deployed his sons to follow the foreigners. He reported that Achmed's agents had inexplicably left their positions just as the people on the *Meroe* were preparing to depart.

Malak heaped curses on Quinn's head. If Quinn and his two "best of the best" Navy Seals couldn't handle the job, Malak would have to take over the operation himself.

He told Yasir, "I need you and your sons to keep track of the foreigners. And maybe more when the time comes. Quinn is an idiot."

"It's not a problem, my brother."

Before they left the *Meroe*, Daniel explained how Zadok's directions led to the cave.

"Zadok's chart shows directions in terms similar to modern maps. It has lines pointing north and south. The spot on the map for the cave is here. Zadok used a magnetic compass to draw his map. Most people think you can use a magnetic compass to find places on any map by following the needle. But, as many lost hikers will tell you, you can't get to that location today unless you account for how magnetic north has changed since the map was drawn."

"Stein believes Zadok drew his map about seven years after he joined the community at Elephantine, approximately 579 BCE. Since then, magnetic north has moved twenty-two degrees west. Yael and I adjusted our compass by that number, and it led us to the spot where my shoulders began to hurt. As I said, we removed enough rocks to crawl inside. When we came out, we replaced the rocks and hid a GPS locator. No one looking at the site would see the entrance to the cave."

Shimon had decided that the groups would be divided in two. One would be on Elephantine Island, finding the tunnel that led to the chest. The other would be coming from Aswan, after retrieving the tablets from the Nubian Museum. Then he had to reunite the groups and get the entire team out of Egypt and back to Israel. He wondered again whether bringing the tablets to Egypt had been necessary. Adding a stop at the Nubian Museum was a major security risk.

"Stein, Yaveni, and Royce will go with Daniel and Yael to the cave. Elenna, Aharoni, Gidon, and I will go with Maxwell to retrieve the tablets," said Shimon.

"The *Meroe* is a hotel boat. We will leave it here. I've rented the *Hermes*, which is much smaller, faster, and quieter than the *Meroe*, and it has two small dinghies. It's tied up on the dock two boats down from us. We'll go around the island to a beach that's below the bluff where Daniel and Yael located the cave. We'll tie up at a mooring about thirty yards from the beach. Daniel and his group will board a dinghy and row to shore. After they secure the boat, they'll take the dirt path leading up to the area of the boulders and the cave."

Turning to Binqus and the group going with him to retrieve the tablets, Shimon said, "After they're off, you'll take the *Hermes* to the museum. It's only a thirty-minute boat ride. Maxwell will retrieve the tablets, reboard the *Hermes*, and you'll return to the beach where we will have dropped off Daniel and the others."

"I will stay here and keep an eye out for any trouble. If all goes well, Daniel and his group should come down to the beach with the chest and the breastplate soon after you return with the tablets. We'll then drive the boat to a deserted location to the south, where, thanks to Maxwell, a helicopter will be waiting to take us to a landing strip in Saudi Arabia. Maxwell has also arranged for a private jet to take us directly to Jerusalem. We have to move right now—and quickly. For some reason, the three Egyptian goons who have been watching us have disappeared. No one's surveilling the *Meroe*. I was planning to . . . how shall I say it . . . disable, the Egyptian spies. But it turns out Egyptian security is pathetic."

Yaveni stood up and said the prayer for safe travel, to which all present said, "Amen."

Quinn's original plan was to follow the foreigners to the cave. Norton and Powers were heavily armed with handguns and Heckler & Koch machine pistols. Quinn was incensed when he was informed that the group from the *Meroe* had left before Norton and Powers arrived. Following the group to the cave was no longer possible.

Quinn told Norton and Powers to wait for him on the pier at the Elephantine marina while he looked to his backup plan. He had transmitted the map on the back of Zadok's note to cartographers who worked for the NSA. Finding the cave amid the boulders would require precise GPS coordinates. The NSA cartographers were, of course, aware of the difference between magnetic and geographic north. But based on Quinn's instructions, they had used 586 BCE, the year Solomon's Temple was destroyed, and Zadok had fled to Elephantine Island.

Unfortunately for Quinn, it was the wrong date. Zadok had created his map at least seven years after he reached Elephantine Island. The NSA's declination was off by a small but significant degree: a full kilometer to the east of the cave. When Quinn, Norton, and Powers arrived, they found nothing to suggest any caves in the immediate vicinity. They saw huge rocks and likely areas for caves to the west and south. Heading in a southerly direction, they soon got lost among the boulders, some of which were forty feet high.

Quinn decided they should split up. Norton and Powers would go farther south. Quinn headed west.

The midday heat was oppressive. Quinn, who meant to exercise but never found the time, soon felt exhausted by having to negotiate the craggy terrain. He rested frequently and quickly drained his canteen. Suddenly, he heard what sounded like people whispering. Peeking around the rocks, he saw people working hard to expand the opening of a cave.

Quinn reached for his sat phone and then realized that he didn't have one. Norton! Goddamned big-shot Navy Seal. He was in charge of the equipment.

But this was no time to fantasize about how he would deal with Norton, who at least had given him a handgun and an extra clip. A veteran of the war in Afghanistan, Quinn had killed in combat and was prepared to do so again. He recognized the people he was watching from pictures taken by Achmed's spies. After about fifteen minutes, they had cleared a large enough space to squeeze into the cave without having to crawl.

Quinn figured he would enter the cave, point his gun at the group, and order them to back away from the chest. Maybe he would shoot one of them to show he was serious. He would grab the chest and order two of the men to come outside and replace the rocks and stones in order to seal off the cave. When they were finished, he would kill them. The others, who would be entombed in the cave, would eventually die of starvation, thirst, or asphyxiation.

Quinn would have plenty of time to get away.

Daniel led the group to the spot inside the cave where the chest was hidden. His birthmarks were pricking him again, and once again he experienced the profoundly beautiful melody. He placed the chest on a bench and placed his hands on the etchings. The chest clicked open. Royce had set up a bright halogen lamp that illuminated the entire area. Yaveni handed Daniel a yarmulke. Daniel nodded and put it on. The group gathered around the chest, eager to see what they had worked so hard to secure.

As Daniel was about to reach into the chest to remove the garments, his birthmarks stopped stinging. The melody, too, had disappeared. Turning his head, Daniel was confronted with the images of Nathan and a beautiful woman, just as he'd seen them at his grandmother's apartment and on Mount Rainier. But now, the woman was facing him, and he immediately recognized his mother. She looked exactly the same as she had when he was ten years old, before the tragedy. Although he was able to move freely, everyone who had come with him to the cave seemed to be standing absolutely still, as if frozen in place.

His mother came forward and placed her open palm on Daniel's face. Her hand was soft and warm against his cheek. He couldn't hold back his tears.

"I have so much to tell you, my son," she said, her voice just above a whisper. Daniel's heart hurt when he realized how much he'd missed seeing her adoring gaze.

Standing there, face to face, she confessed to him that she had lied about his conception because she'd so badly wanted another child. "I realized too late that I shouldn't have lied to your father, but we both adored you. Once you were born, and he held you in his arms, I don't think he would have cared that you weren't his biological son. He loved you so much."

"Aside from you, do I have any relatives who are related to me by blood?" Daniel asked.

Miriam smiled. "You've always felt very comfortable with Elenna, haven't you? There's a good reason for that. She's your aunt."

Daniel shook his head. It was too much to take in all at once.

"I know this is overwhelming, but I have more I need to tell you," Miriam said.

"Please don't tell me that Yael is my sister," Daniel replied, half joking.

"No, my darling," she replied.

Miriam's face had been transformed. It was now the face of an old and wrinkled woman. Tears were streaming down her aged, lined cheeks.

"Daniel, my darling Daniel," she cried. "You did not start the fire. I left a candle burning in our bedroom. I was responsible for the fire."

Sitting down, she put her head in her hands. And then, from the depths of her unfathomable pathos and shame, she began to scream with incalculable anguish. The screams continued, interrupted only by more inhaling to fuel the next wave. Daniel thought his ears would burst.

Miriam finally raised her head and pleaded with him. "Can you ever forgive me? Will you give me your blessing, son?"

Daniel felt an intense pain well up in his core. He tried to imagine forgiving her. He could, of course, utter the words, 'I forgive you.' But he'd spent so many painful years blaming himself, feeling unloved and rejected by her. And she had allowed herself to succumb to cowardice. How could he find the strength to forgive the pain she'd caused him? And yet, she was his mother. How could he shut her out of his heart?

He looked again at his mother. He struggled to find the right answer to her plea. Finally, he said, "I am obligated to forgive you. It pains me to think of the torment you must have suffered seeing me blame myself. What you did was wrong. But I will always love you. As for having my blessing, yes, of course you have it. God bless you, Mommy."

Nathan stepped forward and reached out to Daniel. The brothers wrapped their arms around each other in a fierce embrace.

"I love you, Daniel," Nathan whispered.

"I love you, too, Nathan," Daniel said. "I've never stopped missing you."

The figures of Miriam and Nathan shimmered. And then they were gone.

Daniel was thrust back to reality. He saw his colleagues gathered around, whispering, as if in a place of worship, waiting for him to take the breastplate out of the chest.

Did I have a waking dream? he wondered. *Did I always sense the truth about the fire? Have I been protecting my mother all these years?*

Daniel turned and focused on the chest. But he stopped short again when he noticed a square piece of satin cloth on the ground: It prominently displayed a picture of two black hands in the Kohanic hand configuration. It was an exact reproduction of the hands he had drawn as a boy, based on his mother story about the magic handkerchief. He had only recently shown the drawing to Yael.

As he bent down to pick it up, Yael said, "Damn it, that was supposed to be a present. I had it made from the drawing in your notebook."

Daniel examined the beautiful cloth. It was exactly how he had drawn it, except for one detail. In the upper left corner, the cloth had a small image of his face when he was ten years old.

"Yael, where did you get this picture of me?" He looked as surprised as he sounded.

Yael took the cloth and examined it. She checked her bag. The handkerchief she had made was still there. She had no idea how a copy came to be sitting on the floor, an exact duplicate with the addition of ten-year-old Daniel.

"Daniel," she whispered. "I know the fear of battle, of facing death and the prospect of painful, crippling wounds. This is different. For the first time in my life, I am terrified."

Daniel took off his jacket. The Torah and many other texts described the arrangement of the vestments. In his wallet, Daniel kept a picture of how a prominent scholar had drawn the high priest dressed in his garments. He took it out and handed it to Yaveni, who had been instructed by Azariah to help Daniel in whatever he might need.

Daniel reached into the chest and removed the vestments. They felt and smelled remarkably fresh, without the slightest odor of mold. Yaveni helped him get dressed in the white robe with long sleeves and the blue gown with embroidered replicas of pomegranates hanging at the bottom. Yaveni then arranged the ephod, or apron, which was woven with gold and blue threads, and placed the sash around Daniel's midsection. Yaveni placed the breastplate over the ephod, attached by gold chains and blue linen ribbons.

The group was awestruck as they contemplated the beauty and magnificence of the vestments and breastplate, the sparkling stones in their gold settings. Daniel looked as if he had been transported back to a time twenty-five hundred years earlier.

Yaveni was shaking too violently to help Daniel with the miter. When Stein stepped up, Yaveni placed his trembling hand on Stein's shoulder, smiled, and nodded his permission for Stein to place the holy object on Daniel's head. It was white with blue stripes, and it had a gold plate saying *Kadosh L'Yhahveh* (Holy to *Yhahveh*).

Binqus had no trouble retrieving the tablets from the deferential director of the Nubian Museum. They drove the *Hermes* back to the mooring off Elephantine Island, from where they could see the Zodiac that had carried Daniel's team. It was tied to a tree ten yards from the water's edge. Now they would wait. According to Shimon's timetable, if all went well, Daniel and his group, along with the chest, would arrive within the hour.

Binqus brought the satchel containing the eighteen tablets into the yacht's stateroom. The mood was tense. Would Elenna have any reaction to the tablets? Would they respond to her touch?

Elenna opened the satchel and took out the tablets. She had the same reaction Daniel had experienced at Yehudit's apartment and at the demonstration to the Haredim on Mount Scopus. The tablets grew warm and then hot to the touch. As Elenna put the tablets on the table, the symbols rose and danced in the air for the briefest moment. Then the glow vanished, and the tablets became cool.

"Perhaps they will react more significantly in the presence of the breastplate. Let's hope Daniel shows up soon," Gidon said.

40

Fools Following the Foolish

Shimon's plan hit a snag when Daniel was unable to take off the vestments, neither by himself nor with the help of Yaveni or anyone else. Daniel attempted to walk to the cave's entrance, but with each step, the priestly habit felt heavier and heavier. After five steps, he could not move any farther. He sat down, with his bewildered friends gathered around him.

"This has to do with the tablets," Daniel said. "We need them here."

Royce took out the sat phone and typed a terse message to Shimon. "Cannot leave C. D says to bring items."

Shimon would know that "C" stood for "cave" and "D" stood for "Daniel." The items, of course, were the tablets. He had rehearsed dozens of scenarios with the group, including one in which, for whatever reason, they couldn't remove the breastplate from the cave. Shimon texted back that his group was on the way with the tablets.

Shimon led them onboard the second Zodiac and quietly rowed to the beach. They then climbed quickly and silently up the steep path to the top of the cliff. When they reached level ground, Shimon was there to lead them to the entrance of the cave. Shimon would continue to watch out for intruders and would be the last to take the trail back down to the beach. He assumed that anyone outside the cave was an enemy. He hid behind one of the boulders, laid the Uzi on his lap, and waited.

Peering at the landscape from his secluded spot, Quinn wondered where Binqus's group had come from. He saw Shimon take out his Uzi and hide behind one of the boulders. Once again, he cursed the absent Norton and Powers.

Yasir and his sons had been following Quinn, Norton, and Powers, as well as the Gileadi and Binqus teams. There were now three groups on the ridge, and only Yasir knew about the others. He called Malak to brief him on the latest developments.

"Everyone left the *Meroe* and boarded the Hermes, a smaller, faster boat. One group was dropped off at the beach below the bluff and proceeded to the cave. The other group took the boat to the Nubian Museum. Binqus went inside and returned about twenty minutes later, carrying a satchel. They drove the boat back to the beach, moored the boat, and took the second dinghy to shore."

Yasir then reported that he had seen the other foreigners enter the cave, except for the one with the Uzi.

One of my sons spoke to the director of the museum, who said that the satchel contained eighteen thin stone tablets with tens of thousands of symbols. They had been found in ancient Mesopotamia at a dig in 1924. The director said the tablets had been sent to him as an unsolicited loan by the Israel Museum. Normally, a loan would be for months or years. The director did not expect anyone to come to claim them so soon.

"As to the Quinn team, they arrived at the *Meroe* after the *Hermes* left. They set out on foot to search for the cave. After a while, they split up. Quinn's two associates have been floundering around south of the cave like a couple of clowns. Quinn saw the Gileadi group at the cave and has been watching it ever since. It looked as if he were searching for a phone to call his associates, but he apparently doesn't have one. He keeps fiddling with his Beretta. Tell me what you want me to do. You have certainly gotten yourself into some very weird *alqarf.*"

"Quinn promised to give me a sat phone and a number to call, but he either forgot or changed his mind," Malak said. "We didn't know about the tablets until just now. The Gileadi and Binqus groups have gone to extraordinary lengths to bring these tablets to Egypt and then to the cave. I need to move now. I'm inclined to abandon Quinn and go to my backup plan."

Malak had felt a great momentum building for the Grand Design; now he saw it slipping away. He had planned to use Quinn to get the breastplate to Kaplan and on to the Haredim. Malak had never fully trusted Quinn, whose irregular behavior was validating his concerns.

Norton and Powers decided to turn west. A half an hour later, they found Quinn squatting on the ground. He urgently motioned for them to get down; then he briefed them in whispers on what he'd seen. The two groups they were tailing were inside the cave.

"I'm happy you decided to show up. You have the phones and most of the weapons," he said.

Quinn called Malak on Powers' sat phone.

"I've been trying to reach you," Malak said. "I have more information I'm sure you'll agree to pay for."

"Oh, yeah? What's your information?" Quinn said, sounding as if he needed to be convinced.

Malak summarized the comings and goings of the foreign trespassers. "The director of the museum told my people that the stone tablets had thousands of symbols in an unknown script. But Zadok's message doesn't mention any tablets."

Quinn knew nothing about any artifacts beyond the chest containing the breastplate and vestments. He said, "Okay, Malak, you'll get your money. Another two million dollars. I agree, it's good intelligence."

"This is the first time I've heard about ancient tablets," Quinn told Norton and Powers. "If they went to all the trouble of getting them to Egypt and then retrieving them, they must be important. We need to get our hands on them as well as the chest."

Despite this new mystery, Quinn was feeling more optimistic. He now had up-to-date knowledge of what Gileadi and Binqus were doing. He felt reassured to have been reunited with Norton and Powers. And the Israelis and Americans were all together, in a cave with just one entrance. It would be a simple matter for Norton and Powers to complete the mission as originally devised.

After his call to Quinn, Malak decided that he could no longer entrust the fate of the Grand Design to someone so obviously incompetent. He initiated a backup plan he had worked out with the Iranian Supreme Leader. All he needed to do now was motivate President el-Nasser.

Malak called the president on his private line and told him he had discovered a highly irregular visit to Elephantine Island by K. J. Quinn, deputy director of the NSA. "He's a crazy evangelical. He's trying to help the Haredi Jews with their plan to tear down our mosques and build a third Jewish temple. He's trying to steal Jewish artifacts from Solomon's Temple, which he believes are buried in a cave on Elephantine Island."

El-Nasser was outraged. He told Malak about the note he had received from the American president. "Letting the Americans steal our archeological treasures is hardly what I would call a personal favor. Westfall's doing it to galvanize his evangelical electoral base."

El-Nasser could not afford publicly to condemn the president of the United States as a liar and a thief. The matter had to be discreetly resolved. But his most immediate concern was the situation at the cave on Elephantine Island.

Malak suggested an aggressive strategy. El-Nasser liked it. Recovery of the chest would be an Egyptian operation. They would deploy a complement of elite commandos from an Egyptian frigate stationed at the Aswan High Dam, just ten miles south of the island. El-Nasser put Malak in charge of the operation.

"Try not to kill too many Americans. That would undermine my bargaining position with Westfall. To get me to agree to cover up this outrage, he will have to approve the arms sale we've been pushing, notwithstanding the Israeli objections."

Malak was working from his office at the Foreign Ministry in Cairo. He immediately ordered the captain of the frigate to deposit seven of his thirty soldiers on the beach at Elephantine Island. They would be on station in thirty minutes. Within thirty minutes after following the path to the cave, the commandos would take possession of the artifacts, arrest the foreigners, and bring them to the frigate.

El-Nasser loved the image of President Westfall squirming on the phone when he told him that his spies had been caught. But Malak had no intention of allowing Egyptian officials to take possession of the breastplate and tablets. The plan he had sold to el-Nasser was a ruse.

Yasir and his tribe hated the Egyptian government. They were being starved out of existence, forced to move to filthy urban areas that offered them an existence far inferior to their current way of life. Yasir had always considered Malak an evil genius. His deadly scheme for getting the chest was proof of that. His plan was for Yasir and his sons, assisted by several other trustworthy tribal relatives, to surprise and kill the seven Egyptian soldiers and all of the foreign trespassers. They would then enter the cave and take possession of the breastplate and tablets. Yasir's oldest son was an expert bomb maker. He would bring an explosive device that would obliterate the cave and everyone in it. He would leave behind American-made bomb components, to be found by the Egyptian soldiers who would hear the explosion and rush up to the cave from the beach. The traces from the explosion would point to American foul play on Egyptian territory.

If the press covered the explosion or related events, Malak would keep the breastplate and tablets secure until the stories were old news. As soon as feasible, he would give them to Kaplan or whoever was best positioned to use them for the Grand Design.

Yasir and his team had moved into position. They were invisible among the giant boulders. Lacking sophisticated equipment, they communicated in their traditional manner, tapping stones against rocks in short and longer patterns, much like the Morse Code.

Malak called Quinn. "El-Nasser found out about the Gileadi and Binqus groups. He went berserk. Egyptian commandos will be here within half an hour. You need to leave! Now! This is the most valuable piece of information I've given you. And it's for free. Goodbye and good luck."

Quinn cursed Malak. *This may be Egypt, but I'm working for the president of the United States. I need to make sure that we take possession of the artifacts. Malak has committed treason; he's in no position to give orders. Neither does he have an interest in the outcome, assuming he's been truthful. In any event, his involvement is no longer needed or wanted.*

Malak assumed Quinn would stay. It didn't matter. If Quinn and his two thugs were still there when the soldiers arrived, Yasir and his tribal warriors would kill them, too.

Achmed's phone rang before dawn. Soldiers were invading Elephantine Island. Achmed woke up his lieutenants and rushed to the police station. He called the duty stations in the surrounding areas, as far as Luxor. They knew nothing about such a mission, not even whether they were Egyptian troops. Achmed then raised the alarm with the Cairo office. The officer who answered the phone knew nothing about the mission.

"Stand by," the officer said.

A few minutes later, he received a call from a higher-ranking officer. "The president says this is a top-secret maneuver. You and your officers are to leave immediately."

41

Hitting the Wall

Shimon watched in horror as he saw seven heavily armed Egyptian commandos working their way up the trail to the cave. He didn't know what had gone wrong, but he could think of no other option except to surrender. He sneaked into the cave before the soldiers got close enough to see him.

Daniel was about to open the satchel holding the tablets when Shimon rushed in to advise them of their predicament. It was over. Their great adventure was finished. The question was whether they would survive.

Daniel was seated, clothed in the habit of Israel's ancient high priests, effectively imprisoned in the cave. He had tried to move forward, but he hadn't tried to go backward. He stood up, took a deep breath, and, to his relief, discovered that he could move backward to the recesses of the cave. Royce grabbed the satchel that contained the tablets and followed Daniel. Elenna looked for the empty chest, but it had vanished. The entire group then hurriedly walked to the back of the cave until their way was blocked by a boulder. An intense light shown from within the rock. The light was being emitted by a gemstone, a jasper, identical to the one embedded in the breastplate Daniel was wearing. It seemed to twinkle in harmony with the twelve stones.

The group was huddled together against the large rock when they heard the soldiers entering the cave. Within seconds, they could see them looking through their rifle scopes with powerful white lights and red laser beams. The lights crisscrossed the room. It seemed as if dozens of lights shone on each of them. Gidon ordered everyone to raise their hands in surrender. They did so, as the light and laser beams continued to hit every surface and corner of the cave. But the soldiers were no longer making any forward progress. It was as if they had bumped up against a wall.

A few of the soldiers came within two feet of some of the group and shone their rifle lights right in their faces. The soldiers turned to their commander to receive their orders. The group had apparently become invisible or was somehow shielded from sight. The soldiers were ordered to carefully inspect the part of the cave that they could see and feel. They did so and confirmed that the cave was empty.

The commander, a native of Luxor, had heard legends of a "crazy cave" on Elephantine Island. Certain that this was where he and his men now found themselves, he ordered his men to exit as quickly as possible. He reported to Malak, who began cursing nonstop, invoking every obscene phrase he'd ever heard. What the hell was happening? When the commander reported to him that the *Hermes* was still moored and empty, Malak ordered another fifteen commandos to join the seven returning from the cave. They scoured the area, in some cases passing Yasir's people by just a couple of feet. They saw and found nothing suspicious.

Daniel and the rest of the group didn't pause to wonder at their salvation. They cautiously returned to the front part of the cave. The soldiers had disappeared. Shimon went outside to keep watch.

The halogen lamp was still burning. Stein set the satchel down and took out the tablets. It was time to see whether they reacted in some way with the breastplate.

The first thing that happened was that the robes and breastplate that Daniel was wearing glowed and then vanished. The twelve stones, freed from the breastplate, hung in the air. They were joined by the stone that had been embedded in the large rock at the back of the cave. As if choreographed to do so, the thirteen stones circled around the group, gathered above the tablets, and irradiated them with an intense beam of white light. Then, blinking on and off as if in farewell, they sailed away through the roof of the cave.

The group was stunned to see that the tablets had been dramatically altered. The eighteen thin stone panels now exhibited modern Hebrew letters.

Shimon ran in, saying the soldiers had gone back to the beach. They were safe for now, but they would have to stay in the cave until the Egyptian naval forces left.

42

A Coded Challenge

Yasir had created a hole in the sidewall of the cave. It was too small for him to see people moving about, but he saw the table where Binqus had placed the satchel with the tablets. He watched as the breastplate—the exact artifact that Malak was so desperately trying to acquire—disappeared. And he saw the stones illuminate and transform the tablets and then fly off.

Yasir was a tough man, hardened by forty years of tribal life in the desert. His parents had both been tortured and killed by former President Mubarak's security police. He had been drafted into the army when he was seventeen and had spent several years in the army's substandard barracks. The highlight of his army career, the highlight of his life, was that he'd been one of the first soldiers to cross the Suez Canal when Egypt swept through Israel's supposedly invincible Bar Lev line during the first days of the Yom Kippur War.

When he was a child, Yasir had played with Achmed and other friends on Elephantine Island, exploring the boulders and caves. They found quite a few ancient coins and other artifacts which their parents sold. He knew all about the Crazy Cave. He remembered what had happened to G'niya.

Yasir was an observant Muslim; he prayed five times every day. But he never worried about philosophical questions. Allah would provide. Allah was just. Now, he was seeing things that were way beyond his understanding. He loved Malak, but here was magic or sorcery at work. He was not meant to be involved with such things.

He called Malak and told him he could not continue. "My dear cousin, Allah is in the cave. The breastplate vanished, the stones flew around, and they shot lightning into the tablets. Then they flew away. I can't stay here."

"Yasir, calm down. What exactly did you see?"

"I told you. The garments dissolved. The breastplate is gone. Vanished."

Malak tuned out the rest of what Yasir described, including how the stones had flown through the roof. He was shocked, not so much by the "magic" as by the fact the breastplate and stones had disappeared. In his office overlooking central Cairo, Malak fell to his knees. *Allah, have you abandoned me? Do you not wish for a caliphate to proclaim your grandeur to the entire world?*

Malak's world, the Grand Design, was no more. He was alone, his dreams crushed.

He struggled to find the energy to say goodbye to his cousin.

"Yasir," he finally said, "go, take your family home. These people are fooling around with stuff that is haram. I agree you should leave. You've done everything I needed. I'll visit you soon and give you a great deal of money. The Americans were very generous. May Allah bless you."

Yasir welcomed Malak's response as well as the promise of money. "Inshallah."

Malak slumped to the floor. He opened the drawer of his desk and took out his prized Russian Makarov pistol. Before he pulled the trigger, he said, "I testify that there is no God but Allah, and Muhammad is the messenger of Allah."

When Supreme Leader Khamenei could not get in touch with Malak, he had the Iranian Embassy in Cairo make inquiries. The answer came back to him that Malak had committed suicide. Khamenei was devastated by the news. The World Caliphate had once again been delayed, and his hope to become the Thirteenth Imam had almost certainly suffered a permanent blow.

Quinn, Norton, and Powers saw the soldiers enter the cave and soon thereafter emerge alone and empty-handed. The Americans and Israelis hadn't left the cave before the soldiers arrived. How had they avoided detection?

Quinn debated with Norton and Powers about whether they should enter the cave. Then Quinn saw Shimon, followed by the rest of the Americans and Israelis, exit the cave. Binqus was carrying a satchel, but they saw nothing that resembled a chest or the breastplate. Quinn was growing more frantic. Here he was, the U.S. deputy director of the NSA, on an Egyptian island, deep into an illegal operation. If he didn't act immediately, he could forfeit a prize—the Rapture and Second Coming—that he cared about more than his own life.

Quinn told Norton and Powers to make sure to kill every member of the group. Expert shots, they moved into their positions. As they lifted their guns, they were both hit from behind by fatal shots to their heads.

Quinn saw and heard his comrades' heads explode, their brains splattering all over his fifteen-hundred-dollar safari jacket. As he raised his revolver and frantically looked around, his hand was blown apart by another bullet from the rear. Writhing in pain, Quinn heard someone direct an order at Shimon.

"Drop your weapon!"

Shimon did not know the person who gave the order, but he obeyed the man. He didn't want to be the next victim.

"Go! All of you. Now!" the man shouted. "The soldiers are on the beach. You can't go back that way. You must hike across the island to the *Meroe*. Go now!"

Daniel and Yael led the group to the marina. They boarded the *Meroe* and drove it to the spot where Binqus had his helicopter waiting.

Achmed checked each body. Norton and Powers were dead. He removed all their identification. Quinn, moaning in pain, watched as Achmed took one of Powers' shoes, spit on it, and then stuffed it in Powers' mouth. Quinn recalled that such actions by Arab tribesmen were signs of utter contempt. But why? Did Achmed somehow know Powers?

Achmed handcuffed Quinn and then dragged the bodies of Norton and Powers into the cave. Achmed called for a chopper to bring Quinn and him to the old Ottoman-era jail in Aswan.

The cold jail cell stank of urine and death. One of the guards perfunctorily bandaged what was left of Quinn's hand. He had lost three fingers and was whimpering in pain. But his captors paid no attention to his pleas for painkillers or water to quench his all-consuming thirst.

Quinn was ready to die. The object he thought would serve to bring the End of Days had vanished, unless it was in the satchel that Binqus had carried—and he had no way of getting that. Neither could he look to official American channels to rescue him. He was on a rogue mission that conflicted with a long list of Egyptian and American laws. He was, in two words, royally screwed.

A police officer entered the cell, grabbed Quinn by his wounded arm, and marched him to a building across the street. He pushed Quinn into a freshly scrubbed room that smelled of disinfectant. There were a couple of tables and three chairs. Achmed and his deputy, Madi, walked in.

"Would you like some aspirin and something to drink?" Achmed asked.

Quinn nodded frantically, but Achmed simply sat down across from Quinn and lit a cigarette.

Madi placed some pills and a bottle of water on the table where he was observing. He left and returned with a hot pita and cheese sandwich and placed it next to the water and pills. He left again and then returned moments later with a neatly folded blanket, which he placed next to the water, food, and medication.

"My friend," said Achmed, "I have a tape recording of you ordering your friends Norton and Powers to shoot the Americans and Israelis. Those two men are dead, as you well know. The forensics and other circumstantial evidence will point directly to you. You will almost certainly be executed. If I were you, I wouldn't be sad about that. In my opinion, death is far more preferable than spending your life in an Egyptian jail. They are not as modern and clean as the one across the street. However, since I was the one who killed your friends, I would consider foregoing murder charges, but only if you give me a taped, video confession that explains why the American deputy director of the NSA is sitting here with three fingers missing."

He smiled and continued, "If you are candid, I will consider shipping you back to America. They may not kill you; indeed, they may send you to one of their jails with ping pong, card games, running in place, and such."

"Of course, we do not want you to be uncomfortable for your video confession. Before we start, I can have your hand numbed and professionally bandaged, give you a change of clothes, hot food, water, and coffee before we start. You will be checked by a doctor to ensure you are giving your statement voluntarily and in good medical condition. After your recital, you can have some codeine and, if you like, one of the very excellent cigars we found in your hotel room. The choice is yours. I need your answer now because we are past closing time here. If you decline or can't make up your mind, we will have to return you to your cell. We'll keep the blanket, food, water, and pills here. You can have another chance to decide in the morning."

Quinn was in too much pain to think straight. He signaled his agreement. Four hours later, the food, coffee, blanket, and codeine had temporarily dulled his pain and relieved his despondency.

Achmed was sure that if made public or placed in the hands of President Westfall's enemies, Quinn's confession would bring down the Westfall administration. Even aside from the confession, Achmed had found among Quinn's possessions a copy of Westfall's letter to el-Sisi asking for a "favor." Egyptian security forces also had transcripts of Quinn's calls to the secretary of state and the vice president. It was a ridiculously amateurish plot hatched by incompetent conspirators.

The group endured the three-hour chopper ride to the landing strip in Saudi Arabia. Laura once again proved her worth and arranged for the trip to Jerusalem on Binqus's plane to be recorded as a private tourist flight. She also arranged to have Yaveni, Aharoni, and Yael brief Ronit, Sanballat, and Azariah on a secure phone connection from the plane and to have them meet the group at a private airfield at Ben Gurion Airport.

A van met them at the airport and brought them to the conference room on the Scopus campus. Roni, Sanballat, and Azariah were waiting. After Shimon gave a detailed history of what had transpired on Elephantine Island, an animated discussion took place about the possible meaning of the tablets—the four Hebrew letters endlessly repeated in groups of three.

Azariah and Sanballat sat in silence, as if in mourning. The breastplate, the essential purpose of the trip, the reason they had all taken so many risks was gone. The stones were gone. They had no idea what message the tablets were meant to convey. The two men, tortured by the uncertainty of their communities' future, were light years out of their comfort zones.

Binqus had set up a computer, video camera, and projection screen to display the tablets. They could see blowups of the tablets, but the seemingly endless groupings of Hebrew letters seemed as meaningless as the encrypted symbols had been. There were just four letters: ג, צ, ת, א. Aleph, taph, tsadi, gimmel.

Stein stood up and pondered the tablet projected on the wall. After several long minutes of silence, he said, "If you read them right to left, as one reads Hebrew, they translate in English to A, T, C, and G. They are in groupings of three: אצת, then גצא, and so on."

Royce and Aharoni were visibly startled and excited. They simultaneously jumped up from their chairs and shouted, "It's DNA!"

"My friends, what we have here is a very sophisticated and complex DNA chart," Royce said.

"Sebastian," interrupted Stein, "I'm a Biblical scholar, and you're the award-winning microbiologist. Can you explain what you mean to those of us who aren't scientists and skipped biology at university?"

Royce went to the computer and found one of many DNA websites. "This is it," he said. "This is the famous double helix. DNA is made up of these four molecules. A, T, C, and G. In groupings of three, they code for every cell in every living thing on the planet."

Royce was about to expound further, but Gidon interrupted him. "Sebastian, it's fascinating. But can you please get to the point? You know, DNA for dummies."

"Sorry, but I'm feeling overwhelmed by the magnitude of what we're seeing. If these DNA sequences have meaning, it would be the greatest discovery in history." He fell silent for a moment and then said, "To put it as succinctly as possible, I think we have been invited to modify the human genome."

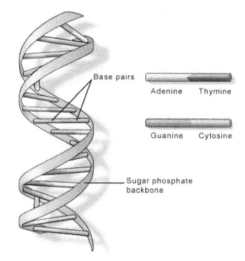

Royce fell silent to give the group time to contemplate what he was saying.

Elenna placed her hands on the eighteenth tablet. Suddenly, the computer-projected image on the wall shimmered, and the image of thousands of symbols was replaced by Hebrew letters arranged as five sentences. Elenna felt her shoulders sting where her birthmarks had been removed.

Suddenly, the symbols flamed and burned themselves into the wall.

We do not exist in your time or place.
When we came here, we sought to create an exemplar of a moral and ethical society.
The ten commandments reflect this objective.
But the most important of the commandments—thou shalt not covet—has proven impossible for your species to obey.
We have returned to make possible your observance of that commandment and achievement of the kind of world we intended.

The group sat silently for many minutes, no one wishing to break the majesty and uniqueness of humanity's first pubic, unambiguous communication from an alien race.

Finally, Gidon said, "I suggest we take a break. I'm sure we all need to talk in private or perhaps just be alone."

Daniel and Yael went off together. A new world was unfolding. Daniel finally had a framework for interpreting the events that had haunted him for most of his life.

43

A Revenge Well Taken

The White House receives thousands of telephone calls every day. Many are crank calls; most are expressions of political views. Only a tiny percentage of callers ever got past the experienced switchboard operators.

Madi Bin Natan called the White House switchboard as soon as Quinn finished giving his lengthy confession. By prearrangement, Achmed went home and left Quinn in Madi's care. Madi didn't know how much of Quinn's tale to believe, but he was sure of one thing: Quinn hadn't recognized him.

Madi had been part of an Egyptian army unit that had been sent to Afghanistan as a show of support for the United States after 9/11. It was meant to emphasize Egypt's innocence in the infamous act of terrorism. Most of Madi's unit had been wiped out in the Battle of Tora Bora; Madi had barely survived after being hit by a bullet in his right leg. The bullet was lodged in his knee, just at the point where the femur attached to the tibia. When American troops picked him up, he thought he was being rescued, so he was shocked when they threw him into a black room, tied him up, and accused him of being a top al-Qaeda lieutenant.

Two NSA agents interrogated and tortured him for ten days before his true identity was confirmed. He was released without so much as an apology. By then, the wound in his leg had become so seriously infected that it had to be removed above the knee. Even if he hadn't lost his leg, he would always remember his tormentors' faces.

When Quinn notified Egyptian authorities that he and his associates would be visiting Aswan, he forwarded files with pictures of himself, Norton, and Powers. Madi was shocked when he recognized Powers and Quinn. Achmed and Madi were best friends. Achmed knew what Madi had suffered in Afghanistan at the hands of these Americans. Madi was filled with gratitude when Achmed told him that he had desecrated Powers' body in the tribal manner by shoving the enemy's shoe into his mouth.

In the police station, Madi sat down next to Quinn, took his injured hand, which was throbbing with pain, and squeezed it until Quinn fainted. Madi waited. He was in no rush. When Quinn came to, he was moaning in agony, and his hand was dripping blood.

Madi showed Quinn a photograph of an Egyptian soldier in his army fatigues. It had been taken when Madi first arrived in Afghanistan. When Quinn didn't recognize him, Madi cut through his left pant leg to reveal the spot where his prosthetic leg was attached. Quinn suddenly understood who Madi was. He remembered the gaping wound on the leg of the man he and Powers had tortured.

The phone in the old barracks room was an ancient rotary dial device. Madi said nothing as he dialed the number listed on the internet for the White House. Quinn heard Madi tell the switchboard operator that he had a message for the president. Knowing the call would be recorded, Madi said, "Please tell President Westfall that K. J. Quinn, the deputy director of the National Security Agency, is sitting with me in a tent outside the city of Aswan in Egypt. Please tell the president that Mr. Quinn suffered a gunshot wound to his hand and is missing three fingers. Also, please tell the president that as soon as I hang up, Mr. Quinn will be executed."

Quinn stared at Madi as he put down the receiver. Before Quinn could beg for mercy, Madi fired a full clip of bullets into his chest. Madi sat back and enjoyed the deep satisfaction of what his father would call a "revenge well taken." As previously arranged, two of Yasir's sons arrived ten minutes later. They took the body and threw it into a tent some miles away.

The next call Madi made was to Al Jazeera. He gave them the GPS coordinates of the tent and told them to expect an email attachment containing Quinn's full videotaped confession. Madi then went home, made love to his wife, and looked forward to watching the news on the seventy-inch Samsung TV that Achmed had dropped off.

Two days later, he watched with satisfaction as FBI agents arrested the vice president and the secretary of state for treason, among other offenses, and escorted them in handcuffs from their homes. Both gentlemen were unapologetic in admitting their supreme fealty to a religious cause, which superseded their oath to uphold the Constitution—an oath "take[en] . . . freely . . . without any mental reservation or purpose of evasion . . . so help me God." Two months later, rather than face an impeachment trial, President Westfall resigned.

44

The Tablets of Destiny

The scientists figured out the DNA puzzle. A gene-splicing procedure was developed to implement the modified genome. But the question that couldn't be answered—not by neuroscientists, psychologists, or ethicists—was what the world would be like if the human race lost its capacity to covet, to feel envy and greed.

Some argued that this primordial emotion lay at the heart of humankind's creativity and that it was, in any event, an essential trait of the human species.

Few were eager to unleash a mechanism that could change the essence of being human. The United Nations unanimously passed a resolution requiring all member states to enact legislation banning the procedure until its nature and effects could be thoroughly studied. But despite the ban, an underground movement caught the imagination of a growing number of people.

They called it the Repletion Movement, referring to the ability to fulfill all of the Ten Commandments. Members called themselves Repletes. They formed Repletion communities, made up of men and women who had the procedure performed on their children within the required time window—no more than one week after birth. The technology to perform the gene-splicing process was expensive, and few scientists had the requisite training. Very few procedures were done in the first years after the Tablets of Destiny came to light on Elephantine Island.

Believers in Jesus, Yhahveh, Allah, and other deities fought the notion that the technology had been brought by entities from another reality. It was understandable. Billions of people could not easily give up the beliefs that had sustained them and their ancestors for millennia. They rationalized, interpreted, misinterpreted, distinguished, advanced innumerable conspiracy theories, and wrote many books explaining why the Tablets of Destiny, as the story came to be known, was a hoax.

Credible and incredible so-called influencers and thinkers insisted that Daniel's freakish birthmarks were simply that: freakish, no more unbelievable than the person born with one body and two functioning heads. Magicians had no difficulty transforming scripts to different languages simply by touching them. The Egyptian soldiers told many variations of the strange wall that allegedly blocked their way at the end of the cave. Their stories were dismissed as Egyptian propaganda aimed at promoting tourism to Elephantine Island, southern Egypt, and the new museum. The deniers insisted that every alleged paranormal event could be scientifically explained or exposed as so much nonsense. And yet, an increasing number of people were coming to understand that something unique and profound had been revealed that would alter the course of human existence.

Epilogue

The Israeli government, and the dozens of Jewish organizations and religious sects around the world, did not know what to make of Azariah's announcement. Suddenly, the leader of the most important bloc of Haredi Jews was recognizing the Samaritans as ethnic and religious brethren. There were many political and religious differences among the various Haredi sects, but they were differences of nuance rather than of fundamental substance. Azariah's stature as a scholar and rabbi was unmatched, as was the respect he commanded across religious and secular segments of Jewish society in Israel and abroad. There were, to be sure, the usual denunciations by the "crazies," as Azariah called them. But by and large, the initiative was a massive success. The ancient past was just that: ancient and past. The rapprochement was a celebratory event covered by secular and religious television stations all over the world. Here was Rabbi Azariah Yerushalmi, a prominent Jewish advocate of Greater Israel, praying at the temple on Mount Gerizim. And the next day, there was Sanballat and a delegation of Samaritans praying at the Western Wall in Jerusalem. There would be years of intense debates about the details of the so-called "merger." But, as the minister of religious affairs jested, the seemingly endless arguments "should be taken as proof of the merger's Jewish authenticity."

After "the Events," as the entire episode came to be known, Sanballat worked feverishly to integrate his community into the Jewish mainstream. Rabbi Azariah was writing a book on the religious implications of the Tablets. He was also holding seminars and meetings with troubled members of Haredi communities. Did *Hashem* appear? Where do we go from here?

Binqus had created a new organization, the Foundation for a New World. His mission was to work with the United Nations to establish a responsible pathway for understanding the DNA sequence, its nature, and the long-term ramifications. He appointed Daniel and Yael as co-chairpersons. The organization was not often in agreement with the fanatical leaders of the Repletion Movement.

Everyone understood that although it would take decades, if not centuries, for the human genome to be permanently altered, the process could not be stopped. Other traits of the human species were not being altered—human curiosity and an urge to enhance enjoyment of a finite lifespan.

The entire group reunited every year at the conference room on Mount Scopus. The building had been taken over by the Israel Museum. Many artifacts of the group's adventures were displayed, the largest being giant blowups of the tablets, the smallest being Elenna's mascara case. The group's annual get-together celebrated the anniversary of the day when they were given to understand what the eighteen tablets meant and when they first saw and read the message on the on the wall. The group looked up at the wall where an exquisitely embroidered copy of the message occupied the space where Stein had initially projected the tablet's image.

Sanballat led Azariah and the others in the Shehecheyanu prayer, giving thanks they were "granted life, sustained, and enabled to reach this occasion." It didn't much matter that the Hebrew prayer was technically addressed to the traditional Jewish God. It was the customary, time-honored prayer, and everyone present agreed it was a good way to begin their reunion.

Daniel thought that whoever or whatever had created the tablets, they came from an alternate universe. Everyone had an opinion. Some of the oldest questions—where do we come from? and are we alone?—could be better understood. But now there were equally confounding new questions. What would the future look like? And would the strange beings that seemed to be orchestrating mankind's destiny return? And to what end? And still the oldest question had not been addressed—why are we given consciousness, why are we constrained to perceive, to feel, to celebrate the gifts of life, only to die?

Alo'el said to Q'aphael, "Your belief in the power of free will and reason was a failure, just as I predicted it would be. Humans were candid in recognizing their addiction to evildoing. Consider the Bible they wrote about the creation of the world. One of the first stories is about Cain murdering Abel, his younger brother, because Cain coveted the attention and approval that their God—the divinity they conceived in their own image—had given to Abel."

"The next story their Bible relates is about how God found all of mankind so despicable that he drowned everyone in a huge flood, sparing only the righteous Noah and his family. 'The inclination of man is evil from his youth,' are the words of their God as recorded in the Book of Genesis."

"Humans wrote these truths down early on. They understood that their nature doomed them to repeat Cain's behavior. And they have done so on ever-greater scales, killing hundreds of millions in wars and letting tens of billions suffer and die from starvation. For hundreds of years, their greed led them to capture and drag tens of millions of human beings from their homes in Africa, their greed for free labor and money leading their religious leaders to champion these efforts as the will of God. By their very nature, they have always been incapable of obeying the Tenth Commandment."

Q'aphael 's response was measured. "I still think the experiment was worthwhile, even if it failed. We have learned a great deal."

"At the core of the human beings we created, there exists an intense dissonance between, on one side, their inclination to envy and their greed for personal wealth and pleasure, and, on the other side, their desire to control these instincts because of the horrific evil they cause. The same species created a Jesus, preaching love of one's neighbor, and a Hitler, insisting that some humans were inferior and did not deserve the gift of life."

"There is another lesson—a surprise, actually. The dissonance generated masterpieces of art and music and literature found nowhere else in any dimension, and the art directly reflects the species' inherent inability to bring about the kind of civilization we wanted for them."

"I look at Michelangelo's painting on the ceiling of the Sistine Chapel." Adam is lying down, looking exhausted, almost disinterested. He extends his arm limply, unable or unwilling to grab onto a god's earnestly extended hand.

"Humans could not bring themselves to grasp that hand—our hand. Having given them reason and free will, I thought they could. I was wrong."

Alo'el said, "*Yhahveh* seems enamored of this race and has petitioned to stay."

Q'aphael replied, "The petition has been granted. He will continue to observe, assist, and report."

Glossary of People and Place

Abba—Hebrew word for father.

Shamir al-Azari—Egyptian ambassador to Israel.

Achmed al-Sayid—Constable-in-chief of the Aswan Province in Egypt; fraternal twin brother of Malak al-Sayid.

Malak al-Sayid—Achmed's fraternal twin brother; develops Grand Design with Iranian Supreme Leader.

Al-Aqsa Mosque—Third holiest site for Muslims, marking location where Muhammad ascended to heaven.

Aliyah—Hebrew word meaning to "go up" and referring to emigration to Israel.

Alo'el—the divine entity who crafted the eighteen tablets initially rejected for inclusion in the design of human beings.

Yehoshaphat *"Yoshi" Aharoni*—Devout Samaritan; doctor working at Hadassah Hospital in Jerusalem.

Amarna—City on the Nile in southwest Egypt built in 1346 BCE by monotheistic Pharaoh Akhenaten.

Ancient Mesopotamia, Canaan, and Egypt

PATH OF THE ANCIENT HEBREWS

Varda Artzi—Daniel's first cousin; lives on an Orthodox kibbutz in Israel.

Tzionah Avineri—Friend of Yael who accompanies Yale and Daniel to Hevron to investigate meaning of tablets.

Palestinian Authority—The interim self-government body that exercises partial civil control over the Gaza Strip and the West Bank.

Moshe Ayans—The Israeli ambassador to the United States.

Jefferson Bible—*The Life and Morals of Jesus of Nazareth*, completed by Jefferson in 1820.

Baasha—Avraham's nephew (his brother Haran's son), progenitor of Samaritans.

BabRama—Samaritan high priest when Solomon's Temple was destroyed in 586 BCE.

Maxwell Binqus—Billionaire preacher; CEO of the Binqus Institute for the Study of the Unknown.

Nick Williams—Scholar at Binqus Institute; expert on Elephantine Papyri.

Crazy Cave—*Al kahf al majnun*. Cave on Elephantine Island where Zadok buried the chest and breastplate.

Dalia Cave—Cave where Samaria Papyri were discovered. Located in the large area known as the Wadi Dalia.

Cave of the Patriarchs—*Ma'arat Hamachpelah*, a "double cave" bought by Avraham from Ephron the Hittite; burial place of Avraham, Isaac, Jacob, and three of their four wives.

Charan (Haran)—Mesopotamian city where Terah takes his family after exile from Ur. See map.

Avi Cohen—Daniel's deceased biological father; Elenna Cohen's brother; had birthmarks in Kohanic hand configuration.

Elenna Cohen—Avi Cohen's sister; Daniel's biological aunt; born with birthmarks in Kohanic hand configuration.

N. Brace Dratler—Plastic surgeon who removed Elena Cohen's birthmarks at age sixteen.

Yosef Fattah el-Nasser—President of Egypt.

Elephantine Island—Island on the Upper Nile at the first cataracts; location of Crazy Cave.

Eradu—Mesopotamian home city of Ivri, destroyed by cataclysmic meteor.

Yoram Epstein—Israeli minister of the interior.

Cairo Genizah—Collection of hundreds of thousands of ancient Jewish manuscripts stored in a small room above ben Ezra Synagogue in Fustad, old Cairo.

Mount Gerizim—Location of Samaritan temple to Yhahveh.

Gidon Gileadi—Professor of Linguistics and Epigraphy at Hebrew University of Jerusalem. Father of Yael Gileadi.

Ronit (née Yerushalmi) Gileadi—Gidon Gileadi's wife, Yael's mother. Brother of Haredi Rabbi Azariah Yerushalmi.

Yael Gileadi—daughter of Ronit and Gidon Gileadi.

Gusma—Miriam Ornstein's mother.

Habibi—Hebrew word for "friend."

Boneh Ha'Bayit Hachadash—The "Builders of the New House." A group dedicated to building a third Jewish temple on the Temple Mount in Jerusalem, replacing Al-Aksa Mosque and Dome of the Rock.

Hebrew University of Jerusalem—Established in 1918 on Mount Scopus. After Jordanian army took control of the Old City in 1948, a new campus was built at Gi'vat Ram in West Jerusalem.

Haran—Youngest son of Terah, father of Baasha.

Haredi/Haredim—Ultra-Orthodox Jews who seek to establish a Greater Israel, including a third Jewish temple in Jerusalem and all the areas, west and east of the Jordan River, specified as the Promised Land in the Bible.

Hashem—Meaning "the name" in Hebrew, this word is used by religious Jews to refer to God.

Proto-Hebrew—Alphabet based on Phoenician alphabet, used in Palestine from approximately 1000 BCE to around 300 BCE. Replaced by Aramaic alphabet still in use today.

Herodian Complex—The area and walls constructed by Herod the Great, *circa* 5 BCE, to enclose the Cave of the Patriarchs. It is the oldest worship complex of its kind in the world.

Hilkiah—Chief Levite assistant of High Priest Zadok.

Ichtar—Terah's wife, mother of Avraham.

Pierce Incident—Daniel saves billionaire Raymond Pierce on Mount Rainier.

Isaac—Son of Avraham, father of Jacob.

Ivri—Survivor of Eradu, obeys divine order to create chest and breastplate; his story becomes the basis for the Ivri Legends.

Jacob—Grandson of Avraham, son of Isaac, progenitor of twelve tribes of Israel.

Jeda—Servant of Samaritan High Priest BabRama.

Jericho Conference—A conference in December 1948 that ratified Jordan's annexation of the lands on the west bank of the Jordan River, which had been designated by the United Nations for an independent Palestinian state.

Hallie Rachèl—Addington Roel Professor of Archeology at the University of North Carolina at Chapel Hill. Identifies manuscripts about chest and breastplate among Samaria Papyri.

David Kaplan—United States ambassador to Israel.

Ali-Aliosseini Khamenei—Iran's Supreme Leader, conspires with Malak al-Sayid to conceive of Grand Design.

Kibbutz—A collective farming system implemented by immigrants to Palestine in the early twentieth century.

Tony Powers—NSA operative working with K. J. Quinn.

Marla Karr—Grantee of Binqus Institute; works at Israel Museum and sends picture of second Zadok cylinder to Binqus and Laura Victor.

Kohanim—Members of the tribe of Levi who were the priests at the Jewish temples and whose descendants continue to perform the divine blessing in Orthodox synagogues.

Dr. Fern Kreinen—Librarian at Daniel's Jewish day school.

Temple of Khnum (ram god)—On Elephantine Island, near the old Jewish temple.

Levites—Members of the Israelite tribe of Levi, custodians and stewards of the temples in Jerusalem, including preparation of sacrifices, performance of prayers (Psalms), and music.

Maimonides—Revered Jewish rabbi and philosopher of the twelfth century.

Elizabeth (née Binqus) McBride—Binqus's sister, married to Lloyd McBride.

Lloyd McBride—Binqus's brother-in-law, member of Rainier expedition during Pierce Incident.

Marduk—Chief Mesopotamian god, defeats evil Tiamet.

Meshech—High priest of Ur when Ivri arrives.

Yehudit Mizrachi—Zahava's sister; epigraphic expert.

Zahava Mizrachi—Yehudit's sister; illegally enters Cave of the Patriarchs, writes narrative, and draws pictures.

NSA—United States National Security Agency.

Nanna—Goddess beloved of Marduk, worshipped at Ur temple.

Tim Norton—NSA operative working with K. J. Quinn.

Mosque of Omar (Dome of the Rock)—occupies place on Temple Mount in Jerusalem where two Jewish temples stood. Encloses the "Foundation Stone" upon which Avraham was told to sacrifice Isaac.

Daniel Ornstein—Biological offspring of Avi Cohen; son of Miriam and Michael Ornstein, born with birthmarks in the shape of the Kohanic hand configuration.

Miriam Ornstein—Mother of Daniel, Nathan, and Leah.

Michael Ornstein—Father of Daniel, Nathan, and Leah.

Nathan Ornstein—Daniel's fifteen-year-old brother, dies in a fire at home while babysitting ten-year-old Daniel.

Elephantine Papyri—Dated from the fifth century BCE and discovered on Elephantine Island; one manuscript references cylinder Zadok hid in the temple he built on the island.

Samaria Papyri—Group of papyri from c. 350 BCE found in the Dalia Cave near Mount Gerizim.

Laura Victor—Director of Binqus Institute, former chancellor of the University of Georgia.

Raymond Pierce—Billionaire whom Daniel rescues on Mount Rainier.

Q'aphael—Leader of divine entities who created humanity.

K. J. Quinn—Deputy Director of NSA.

Rayut—Third member of modern-day Samaritan Trio (with Sanballat and Aharoni).

George Raines—Vice president of the United States.

Amos Rivlin—Daniel's friend; Daniel takes him on a climb of Mount Rainier.

Dome of the Rock (Mosque of Omar)—occupies place where the two Jewish temples stood, enclosing the "Foundation Stone" upon which Avraham was told to sacrifice Isaac.

Samaritans—A group of Yhahveh-believers, descended from Abraham's nephew, Baasha.

Sebastian David Royce—Stephen M. Cahn Professor of Biophysics at New York University.

Selebs—The three priests allowed access to the chest and breastplate in the temple of Nanna in Ur.

Sengrel—Mystical survivor of Eradu's destruction, shows up to speak to Baasha and Daniel.

Silash—Slave trader who becomes a follower of Avraham.

Solomon Schechter—Jewish scholar at the turn of nineteenth and twentieth centuries, catalogued the Cairo Genizah.

Michael Stein—Renowned professor of Bible studies at Hebrew University.

Anika Taloosah—Deputy foreign minister of the Republic of Ghana.

First temple—Solomon's temple, 940–586 BCE. The breastplate made by Ivri was used throughout this period as a divine oracle and occasional weapon.

Second Temple—Built around 515 BCE and renovated and rebuilt around 20 BCE by King Herod the Great. A replica of the Ivri breastplate with no magical qualities was used after original breastplate, dating from the time of Ivri, was taken by Zadok to Elephantine Island in 586 BCE upon the destruction of the First Temple built by King Solomon in 940 BCE.

Tenth Commandment—*"Thou shalt not covet your neighbor's house; thou shalt not covet your neighbor's wife, nor his male servant, nor his female servant, nor his ox, nor his donkey, nor anything that is your neighbor's."* (Exodus 20:17)

Terah—Father of Avraham and Haran, grandfather of Baasha (Haran's son).

Tiamet—Evil primordial god in Mesopotamian mythology.

Torah—The Pentateuch: the first five books of the Old Testament: Genesis; Exodus; Leviticus; Numbers; and Deuteronomy.

Trio—Samaritan high priest and his two chief assistants.

Tzionah—Army friend of Yael, accompanies Yael and Daniel to visit Yehudit Mizrachi (expert on encryption) in Hevron.

Yasir Sadit—Leader of Bedouin tribe near Aswan, cousin of Malak and Achmed al-Sayid.

Azariah Yerushalmi—Head of *Boneh Ha'Bayit* organization, most prominent leader of ultra-Orthodox Haredi Jews; brother of Ronit Gileadi.

Madi bin Yofge—Chief deputy of Aswan Constable Achmed al-Sayid.

Urim and Tummim—Twelve magical stones in gold settings on the Jewish high priest's breastplate used in the First Temple. One stone for each of the Twelve Tribes of Israel: carnelian, topaz, smaragdite, carbuncle, sapphire, emerald, jacinth, agate, amethyst, beryl, onyx, and jasper.

Ur—Birthplace of Avraham and site of Nanna's temple.

Hugh Scott Westfall—President of the United States.

Leonard Wiley—Archeologist who excavated ancient city of Ur in 1924.

Yaveni Yerushalmi—Haredi son of Rabbi Azariah.

Shimon Yerushalmi—Religious but non-Haredi son of Rabbi Azariah.

Yom Kippur War—1973 war between Israel and neighboring Arab countries Egypt, Jordan, and Syria.

Zadok—Last high priest at Solomon's Temple (destroyed 586 BCE).

Zedekiah—reigned as King of Judea from 597 to 586 BCE; last of the line of Judean kings tracing their lineage directly from King David.

Acknowledgements

I wish to acknowledge the invaluable help of my wife, Robin Phillips, who supported my decision to leave my law practice and to abide the advice of my favorite mythologist, Joseph Campbell, "to follow your bliss." This book could not have been completed without the steadfast help of my editor, Deborah Chiel, who was patient and exacting in her work, supplying critical advice on the various plots and subplots and the many characters. I also wish to thank my daughter Dr. Halley Katsh-Williams Brown, and my sister Shelley Katsh, as well as Mary Somoza Lorraine Williams, Alison Lew Bloomer, Larry Fox, Robert Cerillo, Jane Malmo, Suzan Lipson, Paul Victor, Steven G. Schulman Nella Hahn, and David Yohai for reading and providing comments on various drafts. Many others read portions and also gave invaluable advice. I thank them all. A special, heartfelt thanks to my son-in-law Nick Brown, who provided constant, loving support to our entire family during my son Emmet's fatal illness and helped me honor him by finishing this endeavor.

All errors large and small are solely the responsibility of the author.

About the Author

Salem Michael Katsh is a scion of a famous Jewish family that traces its lineage through generations of chief rabbis and Hebrew scholars. After attending a Jewish day school in Manhattan, he studied at the Hebrew University in Israel, graduated with a B.A. from New York University, and a J.D. from New York University School of Law. He practiced law as a partner at Weil, Gotshal & Manges, and Shearman & Sterling. Katsh co-authored *The Limits of Corporate Power* (Macmillan 1981) and wrote more than forty articles for legal journals. He has been recognized in various *Who's Who* publications and *Best Lawyers in America*. He retired from the practice of law in 2017 to work full-time on writing novels.

He lives with his wife Robin Phillips, and their ebullient Labrador retriever, Bo, in Orient Point, NY.